ALEC MERCER

DEAD UNDERGROUND

ALEC MERCER

DEAD UNDERGROUND

Jaideep Bhoosreddy

Ocean Paperbacks

A Division of Ocean Books Pvt. Ltd.

ISO 9001:2008 Publishers

The views expressed in this publication are those of the author, inspired by real world events but not directly related to them.

The moral rights of the author have been asserted.

All characters, events and entities in this publication, other than those clearly in the public domain, are fictitious and any resemblance to real persons, living or dead, is purely coincidental.

This publication contains strong language and mature suggestive themes like conspiracy, torture and murder. Not recommended for small children. Recommended for adolescents and adults. Parental discretion advised.

Published by
Ocean Paperbacks
A Division of Ocean Books Pvt. Ltd.
4/19 Asaf Ali Road,
New Delhi-110 002 (INDIA)
e-mail: info@oceanbooks.in

ISBN 978-81-8430-240-0
Alec Mercer: Dead Underground
by Jaideep Bhoosreddy

Edition
First, 2013

Price
Rs. 200.00 (Rs. Two Hundred only)

Printed at
Bhanu Printers, Delhi

To My Supportive Mother

Acknowledgement

I would like to thank everyone involved with my novel. I would like to express my deepest gratitude to everyone, who at various stages had been an integral part of bringing my wild imaginations into black and white.

Heartfelt thanks to my mother, for staying by my side during high and low. She listened to my crazy ideas and was not quick to reject them.

Deepest thanks to my father for taking the time out of his immensely hectic schedule, and dedicate it to editing and critiquing my novel. I admit it was hard, but once I got him to start, the rest was easy.

Special thanks to my little brother for his countless but crucial help. He conjured up most of the names and details, which gave the story the beautiful flavour it now has.

I would like to thank the people at CERN. They showed me the highest degree of professionalism. Their quick responses and answers have been very useful and deeply appreciated.

Sincere thanks to my publisher. Their decades of expertise are what I came to trust. Their ocean of knowledge actively works beyond my expectations. The novel is everything I had envisioned and even better.

Lastly, sincere thanks to all my friends, taking on a project like this can be extremely daunting. I am happy to receive their support and unconditional faith. I am completely indebted with gratitude to all the wonderful people who came together to help me accomplish my goal.

Jaideep Bhoosreddy

La Monde
Sunday, November 12, 2012
FRONT PAGE

Revealed:- Stable anti-deuterium particle isolated by CERN scientists. Next stop Fusion Energy.

In 1965, scientist working at CERN isolated a sub-atomic particle known as anti-deuteron at the Proton Synchrotron. A type of antiparticle of the nucleus of deuterium, consisting of an antiproton and an antineutron—only they were unable to synthesize a whole atom. After the launch of NASA Space shuttle Endeavour to the international space station fitted with CERN's AMS module pioneered by Samuel Ting and six hundred other scientists, they received information about pockets of antimatter located throughout space even in our solar system. Yesterday, Nobel Laureate Giuseppe Beauvais and his team have announced in front of the world media that after an extensive study of these particles they have synthesized the first stable anti-deuterium particle. They believe that this discovery would be a base which would provide a far more effective and sustainable source of energy at extremely low cost of production. According to Dr. Giuseppe Beauvais, "This is the discovery we have been waiting for! Antiparticles, we have observed from as far as the space and as close as the atoms; but never were we able to work with them, to properly experiment with them, but the cache of data and samples provided by the AMS have proved extremely helpful. After carefully observing the material brought to us by NASA, we were able to replicate them in laboratory conditions and the results appear to be um, *comment vous dire...moins de fructueuses*."[1] His partner Gaulle Carlisle also stated, "If we are correct then our research will provide a new type of fusion energy which is cleaner, far cheaper, and commercially applicable than the current model at ITER. *Donc nous souhaiter bonne chance*."[2] Whether they succeed or not only time will tell but we hope they do so before we run out of oil to run our engines.

1. How you say…more than fruitful.
2. So wish us luck.

Prologue

"How old is she? Sixteen I presume?" Gaulle estimated, sharing the excitement of the man who was reclining on the chair across the round table, with the exuberance of a little child.

"Seventeen actually..." Giuseppe corrected with partial smile which simultaneously crept up his time-riddled face. Of the two highly knowledgeable men, he was younger, but when it came to his intellect, there was none other to compare. The smile on his face widened across his jaws as he reminisced the innocent petite little face of his only child. "See how fast they grow!—As if it was only yesterday when I held her delicate little body in my arms; almost an adult, now!" Giuseppe admired with pride.

"And if I know her even a little bit, then she is awake even now—just waiting for daddy to come home." Gaulle expressed his admiration for the little girl in his sharp Manchester-bred accent which he had perfected over the years. "Look at the time! It's four in the morning! You should go home—try to spend some quality time with your daughter." He encouraged.

Giuseppe turned back, his eyes searching keenly for the wall clock hanging overhead the door behind him. The one at which his colleague Dr. Gaulle Carlisle was staring. The hour's needle was past three and the longer minute's needle was reaching fifty and 'AM' was written in small capital but distinct letters.

"Ten to four!" he stated. "Is it this late?"

"Yes, it is! Go home, get some rest—for once. What you are doing is not good for your condition at all."

"—but we're so close! I couldn't possibly..." Giuseppe murmured.

"Oh, don't be a fool!" Gaulle revolted, "Everybody's here! I'm here! I think we can manage a day over here without you for once!"

"Okay! Okay! I'll go!" Giuseppe accepted. "But inform me of anything that happens!"

"Say, if the filters melt down...I will inform—" Gaulle's words cut off under the pressure of a deafening sound.

He rose up in response to the majestic red light on the leeward side of the room which came to life as the whole room reverberated by the shrieking noise of the emergency alarm. *Holy Terror!* The mood of the vacant room shifted quickly. The dark scarlet light made the room seem small, as if all of a sudden the entire break room shrunk. "What in the world?" Dr. Carlisle continued, with much concern. It was not a common sight to have the emergency alarm buzz up the place. Though the LHC itself covered a vast twenty-seven kilometer circumference, it was closely monitored with such scrutiny that not even a flicker could start without prior information and a written consent allowing it. So, if the emergency evacuation alarm had been sounded in the LHC, then the underlying cause was most definitely an issue of serious concern.

Not a second later, the pager hanging on Giuseppe's belt case vibrated. As he lifted it up with utmost urgency, his eyes became hollow with shock as he read the two-line message displayed on it.

"I can see how well they are doing!" Giuseppe retorted angrily at his colleague, almost scared, as he began hurrying out of the vacant break-room and down the neon lit corridors, signaling Gaulle to follow him immediately. Even through the dark, Gaulle would see the terror in Giuseppe's eyes piercing into him.

Dr. Carlisle, puzzled as he was, began chasing Giuseppe as best as he could. Star marathon runner that he was, running came to him naturally. But in all the years, there was not one time when Giuseppe could outrun him. Today, he did. A sign of how grave the situation they were in.

A similar buzz aroused in the front pocket of his lab coat. He pulled out a similar device from his pocket and began examining the same message which was displayed on it.

Code F2A:

Radiation Leak Detected

"Mercy! What's happening?" Dr. Carlisle's jaws dropped.

Seconds later, they reached the ATLAS EXPERIMENT OBSERVATION ROOM, which was already brimming with panic and chaos. They flooded into the expanse of the room which was their state-of-the-art command center. Instead of the extremely pleasant and appealing golden yellow color, the chrome panels, the luminous terminals, all they could see was the dull mechanical red which diffused through the numerous emergency lights.

Giuseppe ran straight to the one workstation at the center of the room. As he reached the terminal, he sat down on his chair, pulled up his glasses and gazed at his console screen.

WARNING: FILTER MELTDOWN IMMINENT

LHC LOCKDOWN IN **00:02:17** Hrs.

"Holy hell!" Gaulle gasped in fear as he shifted his stance. "How the hell did this happen?"

"People! Evacuate the LHC immediately!" A voice commanded across the room. There was raw fear in the voice. *A peculiar sight!*

"Move in an orderly fashion towards the Exit 8. Follow the LED lighting on the floor towards the nearest exit." The emergency recording started playing.

But the two scientists knew better. The LHC was a massive labyrinth, a colossal maze of underground tunnels, equipment, filters, chambers and the best equipment money could afford. They knew that they were too far off from the containment seal to make it in less than three minutes.

Almost instantaneously, Giuseppe picked up his mobile phone and desperately began pounding on the tiny buttons as fast as he could.

To: **Élénoré Beauvais**

Au revoir, Mon Amour.

He knew that the radiation which was leaking could be interfering with the communication channels. He knew the hard lines were truncated as part of the emergency protocol. Most likely the last of the containment seal had already been closed. Emergency methods at CERN were drastic but necessary. Nobody wants another Chernobyl to happen. When radiation leak is detected by the HAZMAT sensors, it is not like the doors close. The entire wall of the LHC, the same twenty-seven kilometer circumference of it, is covered by radiation proof panels, every inch of the LHC's exterior. Absolutely no part is missed. The systems follow emergency protocol automatically. It is as if a new skin grows over the entire ring of the structure almost instantaneously and as a result external power lines, communication lines, LHC Computing Grid cables, network lines, everything is truncated. He knew better than to waste his time by picking up the landline placed a meter away from him on his desk. No way to send the message outside the vicinity of the ATLAS module. But he had hope, hope was all he had left.

It did not make sense. Nothing which was happening was remotely making any sense at all.

Reactor meltdown? With scores of trained technicians constantly monitoring, reporting the core temperature, pressure, heavy proton generation, carbon sink saturation and almost every tiny detail, how could there be a reactor meltdown! But there was and Giuseppe, so caught up with other things was ignorant of this small paradox. Things happened so quickly, he did not have any time to think on such matters.

With tears rolling down his face, he pressed the send button. *Goodbye, Éllén.*

The Guardian
Friday, January 13, 2014
FRONT PAGE

Massive gamma explosion at CERN LHC kills 283 scientists. World renowned scientists Dr. Giuseppe Beauvais and Dr. Gaulle Carlisle reported dead.

At 3:50 AM local time, a massive amount of gamma radiation was detected by the scanners in CERN which tripped the HAZMAT alarm in the complex. As no communication was successfully established, officials have assumed the worst. The radiation is contained in the LHC underground complex below the radiation lock present in the facility and although word of a leak is not heard, they are sweeping the whole twenty-seven kilometer circumference of the LHC to be on the safe side. Presently, the focus is to contain the situation and prevent any spill that might occur and do more damage. Experts comment that someone surviving the blast would be nothing short of a miracle. The scientific community mourns for the loss of their colleagues and prays that God provide strength to the families of the victims.

Among the victims are global icons in quantum physics, Nobel Prize winners Dr. Giuseppe Beauvais and Dr. Gaulle Carlisle who were recently awarded the Nobel Prize in Physics "for their pioneering work in the discovery of a heavy elementary particle of a new kind." Along with their team, they were currently conducting experiments in the field of Fusion Energy Development. *For more, turn to Page 8.*

1

Dealt With

12:33 PM
Bearing Tower
101st "Executive" floor
Office of CEO and Chairman; Bearing Oil & PetroTech Intl.

"You have a call waiting on your Tele Presence, Mr. Meyers", crackled over the intercom. "It's a blocked number—should I take the message? Maybe it is a glitch from that new feature you've got installed over the company's network. I'll have I.T. look into it."

The secretary's assertion was an understatement to the hidden technology at work. It was a complex multi-tier DSG network encryption software designed and fabricated to the CEO'S needs by the International Logistics and Support Agency, a sister corporation to Bearing Oil & PetroTech. The engineers who wrote it, called it 'The Trace', an engineering marvel no less. It prevented eavesdroppers from hearing the most confidential conversations. It worked in such a unique fashion that even Cisco could not realize about their monitoring leaks. The exact conversation was obviously encrypted, so to prevent the servers at Cisco and ECHELON from figuring out the mischief played by them, it dumped a carrier signal on their network and the real conversation was hidden intermittently in the form of metadata, which to the server appears as something equivalent to comments compared to the program and because of the massive amounts of data they manage, the systems just pass up these "comments" through their server. This program, though not patented, was one of its kind as it was quite difficult to replicate. It was something he was really proud to have and though he could not show it off, a self-satisfying smile would always crawl up on his face.

But not today. Not now.

"That won't be necessary, Pam", replied the CEO with superhuman effort to preserve his rich British accent in his usual calm, soothing voice. His mind was in a different state. That anonymous call was not strange to him. His brain turned into a neurological cocktail of anxiety and anger.

"No direct contact I specifically instructed him!" His orders relayed in his head, his face red with anger. "Which part was he unable to comprehend?"

Turning his mind to his immediate surroundings, to his eager secretary waiting for his orders, "Pamela, could you bring over the cash flow statement—in say, half an hour?" Turning his attention to his overly zealous secretary. "And I'm not to be disturbed before then." He replied in his assuring voice which echoed in the office next to his.

"Sure sir." Pamela replied as she jotted it down in her digital tab.

Burning under the scorching heat of the summer afternoon sun, the driver of a black Genesis cried with agony. His spine was cramped; his tired buttocks were hurting and sweat was running its course under the fiery celestial orb. "Worst assignment ever! I'm going to call in sick tomorrow." He gave out a deep yawn, stretching his arms apart.

"God keeps track of our sins, dude." His partner chuckled. "Think about it!"

"Shut the hell up!" He yelled, pointing an agitated eye at his partner.

The black Hyundai parked at the corner of Wacker St. and Jackson Blvd had two Federal Bureau of Investigation surveillance agents. Eating cold and soggy deviled-ham sandwiches while gulping pop soda were trying to monitor and 'surveil' the building. Right up to that moment, their efforts had proved most futile.

The FBI and the Securities and Exchange Commission were suspicious of the company's insider trading and other illegal activities but they could never quite put their finger on it. Bearing PetroTech was a master of the art. Money laundering was the one thing in which the bureau had a lucky streak, something which does not happen every now and then. Only if the Federal Bureau of Investigation knew what the company really does and how high its Chairman's powers reached, would they realize that sometimes, things that happen in this world are in no one's control. Or at least not in theirs'—not for a long time.

The building was formerly known by a different name, Willis Tower. Located at 233 South Wacker Drive, Chicago, it was the tallest building in America. After the 2013 renovations, the controlling firm was bought by PetroTech in a hostile market takeover which after acquiring its naming rights named the building PetroTech Tower; and after the high profile merger of Bearing Oil and PetroTech along with few smaller companies, the building finally, for some reason, came to be known as Bearing Tower became the worldwide headquarters of Bearing Oil & PetroTech International Ltd.

The glorious tower stood as a beacon of light for modern corporate America. Gladly notorious for being the most energy efficient building in the world, the building had passed every benchmark for corporate energy efficiency and resource management. It was even reported in *The New York Times* that

"The green wave starts from Bearing Tower. The pioneers in modern energy development."

This massive silver silhouette had one hundred and eight floors, though the one hundredth floor to the top floor was actually the office of the Bearing Oil and the rest are leased out to other corporations.

The room was totally white and that too with the brightest shade. The office was on the east side of the building. To allow maximum sunlight and to obtain high energy efficiency, the east façade of the building was made of special glass panels. It had layers in between them through which special liquid crystals are made to pass. Due to difference in light spectrum absorption, the color and intensity of light entering the room was controlled. It was not very hard for every newcomer there to subconsciously relate the suite to one of the old matrix movies. Most of the articles in the room were white. The white table, book shelf, and the expensive, top-of-the-line ergonomic arm chair, also white, faced perpendicularly to the glass wall. Right behind the boss's chair hung a huge portrait of a shepherd leading his sheep through the green pastures, symbolic of an idea; the driving force behind him.

The atmosphere in the room was still tense. He was the kind of person who even in the worst of situations would face them with grace and a sound mind. He remembered about the surveillance team outside the building, trying to get the one important scoop so that they could bring the company to its knees. "Dream on!" He thought. He would always publicly preach one fact that there should always be some healthy competition in men. It keeps us sharp and our minds agile; failure to follow this, according to him, made us dull and weak.

A holographic panel materialized from the high density projectors situated inside his desk. The green screen came to life, as it displayed the incoming caller. BLOCKED was written in bold letters. He motioned his hand to accept the incoming call. No sooner than he entered the encryption key in the holographic keypad, the lights in the room dimmed, the floor in front of the desk caved in, giving way to the projection platform which rose up to the floor with a mechanical hitch tone. The glass window became opaque and suddenly the bright room turned dark. The holographic projector turned on emitting a large array of light beams from three corners of its circular base, creating a virtual screen.

"Cisco TelePresence: Connecting via Trace", chanted the machine in a hollow soul-less voice along with the text floating over the three-dimensional screen.

"Decrypting"

"Locating Connection Point…Found"

"IP Address…137.138.144.169"

The satellite view of Earth appeared on the screen as the machine resolved the location of the incoming caller.

"46°14233N 6°32193E… Resolving: Geneva, Switzerland"

"Connection Established"

The immaterial screen gaping in the center of Richard's office materialized into a convincing window through a computer screen thousands of miles apart and into the office of the aged scientist who occupied most of the screen. There were cupboards filled with scientific journals, many of which had his name on the cover, Reuben Sloane. It was as if Reuben was actually leaning on the opposite edge of the pristine white table. Reuben's temple had ridges deeper than the Grand Canyon and his raised eyebrows were disappearing into his hairline. His whole demeanor signaled to Richard Meyers that the news was definitely not going to be pleasant at all. The anger at the incoming caller was turned into anxiety by the ominous trouble which was rushing towards him.

"What is it then?" Meyers enquired of him.

"The reports, sir, are true. I've even seen it with my own eyes. They will meet their deadline within the next week!" The old scientist with a slouching belly reported. "Not only have they recreated a stable specimen of the T7 Anti-Deuterium ion, they've gone as far as creating an almost perfect perpetual fusion reactor. There still are some clinks here and there, but they are making rapid development. We're too late. What should we do, sir?"

"Do what you did back in 2014. The radiation will destroy all the evidence…and the witnesses."

"I'm afraid, sir, we are past that point." Sloane informed. "They developed something remarkable, sir. They devised a process of converting the gamma radiation into antimatter by reverse polarized colorization, which not only completely negates pollution and energy loss gradient but also gives back some reduction in the raw material cost. Let me tell you sir; their discoveries are of the level of Einstein himself. This woman, Élénoré Bassét, is truly God gifted. She gave the paper on 'Advanced Theory of Relativistics—her postulates reach the domain where others stopped. The project is based on it. The things she says are beyond my understanding! Sir, she has perfected the process! It is the world's first perpetual source of energy. It can destroy us!"

"Damn it Sloane, how could you let them get so far", he shouted along with a bang on the desk which resonated in the whole room, but not a sound was heard outside.

"I don't know, sir. Things aren't what they seem over here. No one even knows what they are doing. God knows where they are getting their funds from. If it wasn't for the anomalies in their energy consumption, we would have never known until it'd be too late," Reuben briefed.

"It's already too late; a perpetual energy source is bad for business. Their research needs to be destroyed and the researchers must be *dealt with*", Richard said with a tone of deliberation.

A sudden knock on the door diverted his attention away from the screen and towards the door. "May I come in?" The singsong voice of his secretary came from the other side of the door.

"Just a minute", replied the boss to her secretary. "You do nothing from now on, just observe and report. I'll set-up a channel for us to communicate. And don't ever contact me on this line!" He commanded Sloane as his fingers reached for the end call button.

"Of course sir." Sloane replied, soon after which his hazy apparition blurred into oblivion.

The New York Times
Thursday, March 12, 2025
BOSTON

Drug lord Christophe Alejandro killed in a strenuous police bust in broad daylight. 15 local criminals arrested. Hometown girl rises to glory.

Sources reveal a year-long covert operation conducted by the Boston Police Department to break the backbone of Boston's back alley drug scene. The longstanding duel would have continued were it not for the heroic efforts of one courageous detective, whose name is revealed to be Detective Aisha Summers. An undercover officer for more than a year, Detective Summers provided crucial information which led to the end of a very powerful and merciless drug lord, and also led the police raid and shot Alejandro in the course of the operation.

Christophe Alejandro had a mighty influence on the city's politics. Sources also reveal that Alejandro was a major lobbyist and an influential back-door politician and also one of the richest men in the city. He ran many illicit operations besides drugs, with the city's corrupt administration in his pocket.

Due to the brave efforts of Miss Summers, the streets of Boston, if not cleared, are still going to be cleaner than before. Department's Press Liaison Mathew Ford stated that the young Detective Summers will receive a medal from the mayor for the heroic bravery which she had portrayed.

2
Welcome Aboard

10:30 AM
Federal Bureau of Investigation
Illinois Field Office

"Aisha Summers reporting for duty, sir." The sharp young woman reported. She was distinctly in her late twenties, with an even more distinct sparkle in her eyes. The spark to excel. Ambitious.

The room was like any other average-sized room. It projected expanse, despite its size in the extra-ordinary building. She stood just behind an array of exactly five black leather seats placed with exact precision, as were the rest of the objects in the room whose walls were covered with framed certificates, pictures and medallions. A nice contrast over the light pink polymerized paint—its shade so light that its pigment would be best described as sepia-brown. The heavy office desk carved from a prime piece of a hard fragrant mahogany trunk shared the majesty of its occupant who sat on the chair behind it with a somewhat curious smile on his face.

The woman standing in front at first glimpse seemed feminine enough. A thin but robust tall girl with long luscious blonde hair. She had an extremely light tan on her body which was revealed by slightly revealing bra line and at the edges of her sleeves. She was not in her normal office clothing. Instead of her crème white shirt under the pressed black two-piece office jacket and plaited pantaloons, she was wearing a light gray half-sleeved sweat shirt with BOSTON written in bright red flowing letters accompanied with a tight body hugging dark blue denim jeans, which perfectly complimented her figure. Her hair let loose, were almost sensual but her face annoyed, almost as if she was shocked at the curses hurled by a pathological drunk and insulted. The reason for her revolting apparel soon became apparent to the silent observer, but he decided not to make an issue of it.

At the first glimpse, she did not seem the strong type, not by a longshot. Her feminine essence overpowered everything else. But she was strong, determined. Jonathan had received first hand eye witness reports supporting the idea which was hard to grasp. A decorated detective in the Boston's State Police's organized crime division, 12th Precinct, Aisha had won many laurels.

Those laurels were the reason why she stood there right in the office of Jonathan Valerie, Director of Federal Bureau of Investigation's Illinois field office.

Much unlike the normal procedure, she was not recruited into the FBI from college, or through any interview from where she would have received her training at Quantico. She was selectively called for the job. And she decisively accepted it, ambitious as she was.

"Ah...Special Agent Summers! Congratulations on your new promotion. I think you will find the Chicago weather very welcoming. How was the Orientation seminar?"

"Boring!" Aisha gave a sharp and unhindered reply.

"Bold and to-the-point!" Jonathan admired. "I know you... I know all about you, Agent Summers. Know this...there is a fine line between pride and arrogance and its best you know where it is."

"Understood." She replied, unconstrained as she was.

"Good." Valerie replied. "I assume you have been briefed about your case?"

"Sir. I think that I'm a bit overqualified for a baby-sitting assignment! This was not the reason why I came here. I came for something bigger than this." She argued.

"Well, what did you expect agent?" Valerie smiled. "The fact of the matter is that we've got many overqualified agents working menial cases. Why should you be any different? Besides I am not going to waste my breathe convincing my subordinate."

Aisha frowned. "Listen..." Valerie leaned forward. "Prove yourself here, just as you did back in Boston. And then we will talk. Now, close the door on your way out." He ordered, pointing courteously towards the door.

"Fine." Aisha grunted as she stomped out of the office with the rage of her towering impatience.

3
Ce qu'il lui

7:59 PM
Organisation Européenne pour la Recherche Nucléaire[1]
Super Large Hadron Collider (SLHC)
Outside the underground complex: Main Entrance

A woman was running frantically through the campus grounds towards her remote destination. She had big, blue eyes which were glistening like the foaming ocean gyrating in a violent yet eternally calm vortex. Her deeper platinum blonde hair with the bright golden radiance of the setting sun, though long was not very luscious. They went a few inches below the shoulders which were waving along with the cold evening breeze. A good 5'10" in height, she had a slender built. A few years off forty, she was a senior scientist and researcher at CERN, working on a project about which only a handful of trusted people really knew about.

Ce qu'il lui![2] *Finally, all that you had envisioned will come true. Today is the judgment day.*

"Excusez-moi!"[3] She repeated as she nearly missed bumping into scientists and students on her way. Clumsily, she would collect herself as she dashed into the empty void canvassed by perfectly trimmed meadows, perfectly clean streets, marred by interludes of street lights which provided the only semblance of a faint illumination. Her thin body, bobbing from side to side, as her feathery light straight flaxen hair floated by the buoyant caressing touch of the cool wind, ran straight and fast. Her swift and nimble feet moved with urgency. Her hands, giving its best effort, was proving inadequate to provide support to her purse, her files, her folders and many of the crucially important artifacts one might find on a woman's person.

She had a rough day. Throughout the last month all that they were doing was streamlining their process, experimenting to improve optimization and efficiency. It was extremely tedious and meticulous work. Though the success rate was ever increasing and after every experiment they would be miles ahead, yet the road ahead was longer

---

1. European Organization for Nuclear Research.
2. This is it!
3. Excuse me.

and it did not run straight down but it had twists and turns like a river which meanders in the plains after it reaches a certain stage and each turn had different paths to choose from.

Vingt-quatre heures à partir de maintenant, tout sera fini. Je vais enfin retourner à Marseille, comme je l'ai toujours voulu.[4]

Ever since her teens, she had always been a nerd. Growing up, listening to his father's crazy scientific gibberish, hearing him and his British friend sit in the courtyard, brainstorming for clues, for puzzles, for answers and staring at their excited, amazed faces as they worked, she had, at a very young age, chosen a very bold career path for herself. There was but one goal in her mind, which was to work as a scientist at the LHC at CERN just as her father did.

She had all those faint memories about the time she used to live in the residential quarters near the campus.

All the times spent here, all those memories some good, some bad. But the nightmares never stopped.

But when she was about seventeen, she moved back to France to live with her mom, step-father, and their two twins. And although she was adored by her parents, she had never felt that she was truly accepted. In her heart, she always was a third wheel, a burden, even though her parents never thought of her in that way. They knew how much hardships she had been through. They would take special care of her, do too much pampering, stay overly protective and see that she did not get hurt. They just didn't realize how she felt and what she was going through. They would act weird around her. Extra cautious and ever so careful. Amanda and Jeremy, her young cousins, felt jealous of the way their parents were treating her and not them, the sudden importance which their new step-sister had apparently stolen from them. After a while, when it became clear to her that her own cousins did not want her to be there, she knew she had to go. It was as if her fate in its own curious manner was tempting her to go back. She was travelling on a road leading her nowhere but the beginning. And back she went, at the first chance she got and paved her own road, looking back not once. She was on a mission, a mission she took upon herself to accomplish.

Ce qu'il lui.[5] She pondered. Now she hoped that she would be able to live happily. And that her past torments would not matter anymore and she'd be *free. Libre.*

---

4. Twenty-four hours from now, it'll all be over. I'll finally get to go back to Marseilles like I always wanted.
5. This is it.

On the eve of her self-proclaimed freedom, even an introvert, reclusive, withdrawn woman like her had gone out with her friends to a restaurant nearby. Admittedly, it was a bit high-class for her taste but she was willing to make an exception for the special occasion. Sitting in the dimly lit, oxygen rich dining area of an extremely fancy and eloquent booth, only one thought was repeating in her mind.

Soon I can leave all this behind me.

She sat there, as the meatball lasagna with cherry tomato and the duck breast cooked in Pan Jus arrived, sipping a glass of what seemed to be a very quaffable bottle of Crémant d'Alsace as a toast for their imminent success. It was all good for a while. She almost started enjoying it as she began piercing the cold blunt prongs of her fork into the succulent piece of duck meat, until her acquaintance from the LHC Computing Grid suddenly popped into the picture. It seemed that her *"friends"* had invited him over to dinner. Seeing the man made her edgy, though her friends assured her that nothing sinister was going on.

"...nothing to worry about." She thought.

She knew what her friends were doing. Most likely, they planned this all along.

"Adele?" Pulling her aside. "What's going on?" She asked.

"Rien!"[6] She replied back in the most non-chalant fashion. "Tomorrow is a very big day. Today...just enjoy, relax, have fun—for once."

Soon, one by one everybody went home. Adele was the last one to go. As she rose up, she bid him and Élénoré goodbye and started cat walking towards the exit in the most feminine manner, she turned back with a devilish wink and a playful smile on her face, and then sent her a secret signal with her hands as she walked away.

Staring at her in anger, suddenly her cheeks turned deep red. Her ocean blue eyes could not believe what she had seen. What that little minx had left for her. She just sat there for a while. Not one single word from her mouth. Just pondering, contemplating, scheming, and planning.

Finally, she could not take it anymore. There was still many a morsels of that succulent duck breast on her plate, but at the time it seemed that she was not destined to have any more. In one voluptuous gulp, she finished her sparkling wine, patted down her lips with the table napkin and said, "It was a lovely evening, but I've to go."

6. Nothing!

"You do?" The IT guy replied, confused as any of Shakespeare's protagonists.

It was not that the sudden blind date was not her type. He was big, strong, and highly knowledgeable in a very specialized field much distant from hers. The fact of the matter was that she did not have any type at all. Although she did not mind spending time with him, the notion of flirting with someone or making small-talk was pure terror for her and connecting with her peer group just was not her forté.

As she rose up, Mr. IT mimicked her blindly only to find himself walking her to her car watch her drive away and finding himself standing there alone, contemplating over what exactly had happened.

She just hurried back to her apartment, flustered. She uncorked another bottle of Vouvray,[7] poured it into a glass till it brimmed over the edges and spent the rest of the night watching her childhood videos, crying. The sweet but dry flavor of the Pine au de la Loire ironically mirrored her feelings. Her life was as dry as firewood feasted upon by the termites.

"Enfin!"[8] She spoke. Panting, breathless as she reached the grand entrance to her destination back at CERN as she breezed back to herself.

Just a few paces before the entrance leading to the SLHC, a solitary guard post was located. The light emitting from the fluorescent tube lights came out of the window along with a crackling voice of the commentary of the UEFA Super Cup, indicative of the fact that the guard on the roster had already reported for duty.

Inside, reclining on the plastic chair with a half-broken leg, his legs crossed over one another resting nicely over the desk, with his iPhone resting over his broad chest and his 'I love New York' cap positioned perfectly over his face, covering it almost completely, so that on the off-chance that somebody came in there to look, the ignorant stranger would simply presume him to be asleep and not bother. The iPhone was tuned into the BBC repeat broadcasts of the UEFA Super Cup in Britain. He had heard it a dozen times, but he was listening to it again simply because it was the only form of entertainment which was left with him, since his PS VITA broke. Covered beneath the iconic cap, the lustrous metallic black eyes, as intimidating as a giant black whole, were ever so vigilant of their

7. A particular type of wine which is sweet but dry in taste.
8. Finally.

near and distant environment. He was wearing a plain black round neck T-shirt with a simple Gucchi logo on the chest, which closely hugged his broad shoulders and chiseled body, trademark traits for a soldier who had served the better part of a decade for the United States Navy Seals. His military haircut along with the range of tattoos on his body, all revealed of the kind of past he had. The T-shirt was covered with a black hooded soft leather jacket with its sleeves folded just above the elbow which oddly mixed well with his dark blue crushed denim jeans. His body of 6 feet was proving too big for the tiny security post. Mercer had witnessed quite a few sunsets in that tiny guard post over the years, he had forgotten all about the inconvenience the small working space caused him. The end of his contract though had brought all that inconvenience back.

"Finally, the job is done!" He thought. "Maybe after getting my paycheck I could fly over to the city and watch the game live from the stadium."

It is said time is the perfect medicine when it came to the injuries of the heart. Time had proved its worth in Mercer's condition. Seven years ago, he was angry, hostile, irritated, aggressive, anti-social, and anti-life. His condition had led him to prison and worse but it was when he had accepted this job, things changed. It was as if his anger, like a cancer, went into remission. After seven years, his dull mind had let go and forgotten the horrid happenings of his past. Maybe a change in scenery was needed, but a major part was played by his only friend at CERN, Dr. Élénoré Bassét. As if she answered his broken hearts cry for help, it was her who led his transformation and brought him to the boring life leaving him like any other average human, nothing special, just as it was supposed to be.

Alec Mercer was one big fan of the Manchester United Club. Watching soccer matches on his cellphone, or listening to the commentary over radio and tracking the teams' scores was a hobby which he picked up during his posting in CERN, when it was suggested to him by Dr. Élénoré Bassét, the lead researcher of the group of scientists whom he had to protect. When the half-time was announced, feeling a bit tired from yet another day's boring work of doing absolutely nothing, he yawned vigorously and stretched his muscular arms sideways, only to the result that the leg of the armchair gave in to his weight and he fell through on the ground. Getting up he realized that he should utilize his time to pack up his stuff from his office for the last time. Seeing that nobody was around, he thought it would be best if he used the time to de-assemble some of his surreptitious equipment. So he picked up his phone from the ground, gave a keen glance over the body hoping that it was not scratched, turning off the radio app, he dialed the number of the Cointrin International Airport to book a ticket to Heathrow so that he could catch the UEFA Super Cup Finals.

Though not many were now visible, people were still strolling through the beautiful fields of the campus, some were going back to their residential quarters, after spending the evening reading some technical journals, some were going towards the mess hall. He stuck his head out of the window giving a quick scan of the surrounding, searching for the signs.

"Air france Cointrin International helpdesk, how may I help you?" a voice emerged from the speaker of the mobile phone.

"Yeah, listen, I need to reach the Manchester to catch the finals, so I'd like to book the last plane which can meet my deadline", he replied.

"Of course, just a second", the speaker replied courteously with a smile and an obvious chuckle which could be heard at the end of the receiver.

Unable to catch anything suspicious or out of the ordinary, he pulled back his head from the window. While he was talking, with his other hand he pulled out his modified black diesel carry bag with a red stripe. He unzipped one of the pouches in the bag and threw in random stuff inside, like his iPod, novels which he still kept in pristine condition between his snacks, and the PS Vita which Dr. Élénoré had presented him so that he wouldn't get bored sitting on his back all day long. He then closed the zip, flipped the bag over so that the bottom got on top and opened the zipper which when unzipped increases the volume of the bag. Under it there was a cleverly concealed zipper which opened a pocket present between the inner cloth linings of the bag. It was internally lined with a cloth-like carbon-aluminum mesh fiber which did not allow external scanners to be able to see what was stored inside and can also act as an impromptu bomb disposal container because of its capacity to withstand many tons of pressure and extreme heat; at least the hidden pouch can, the bag probably won't survive. Turning back, he bent down to access the state-of-the-art storage locker, which because of its appearance camouflages into its surrounding, blending in and hiding in plain sight.

"We have flight which departs in...."

He tapped it to activate its unlocking mechanism causing a green holographic security panel to emerge from it.

"Actually, could you hold on for a moment", he interrupted her and put his thumb over the receiver.

The securer panel simultaneously performed the usual identification tests like retina scanning, capacitive fingerprint scanning and voice comparison to authorize usage.

"Alec Mercer..." Appeared on the security console. The name of the owner. It also began playing a prerecorded loop stating the credentials of the user.

"Mute, you!" he instructed the machine, which then became inaudible, although the text ran for a few seconds and Voilà, the locker folded open with a hissing noise.

"You were saying?" he replied back to the female in the phone.

No sooner than the safe opened, he felt that he saw some figure in his peripheral view, dashing towards the compound. Recognizing the familiar slender built coupled with her light blond hair and the slightly less height of the woman, he signaled her to come near the post.

The safe contained many bundles of cash; kept in different currencies and denominations mainly in francs, euros, and dollars for use in case of emergency. One thing was common; they all were unmarked, non-sequential bills. On the inner wall, an array of weapons ranging from rifles to personal defense weapons. A Heckler & Kosh MP7, a Belgium VBR PDW, a SIG P229R, a Beretta 92FS or M9 as the military calls it's civilian counterpart, and a M16A4 assault carbine was hanging on the wall in their pre-carved outslots, along with their attachments. Below them was a large cache of ammunition, pre-loaded magazines, a swede brown leather holster, a light, thin Kevlar bullet proof vest and a few grenades and bricks of C4.

He emptied his storage locker, stripping it of its armaments and ammunitions, and dumping those which his diesel bag could carry, with just enough time to welcome his new guest at the security window in front of him.

"Yeah, that'll do, but make that two." He replied to the receptionist on the phone as he waved towards the sole entrant piercing through the glass separation between them. Alec pressed the button camouflaged beneath the cheap guard table. A bland mechanical hum marked the opening of that same Plexiglas window.

"Hey Élle, I'm going to London to catch the finale. Would you like to join me? I know that you don't want to stay here. So, what say? It'll be fun."

The expression on the face of the woman changed; her cheeks

blushed to bright pink.

"Je ne peux pas", she replied not realizing that she started speaking French, her native tongue.

"Sorry?" Mercer pretended as if he did not understand. Over the course of his career, he had picked up many languages and was quite fluent in most of them; even if he did not, it was quite clear what she meant. The reply was in denial.

Perhaps she is just not ready for a connection like that with someone. From what little he knew about her, and whatever more he deduced about her, one thing was predominant. She was fragile; as delicate as the recipe for a perfect soufflé.

"Oh sorry, I forgot that you do not know French", she apologized. "I'm sorry, but I can't travel with you or anybody for that matter. You'd be better off alone or with somebody else."

She thought of leaving him the same instant, but could not. There was a sort of dark magnetism about him which made her want to be with him, spend time with him.

At the same time the airport receptionist asked, "How would you like to pay, monsieur".

Knowing Élle far too well he instructed her, "At least don't run, this won't take more than a minute."

She could not do anything now. He had already told her to stay. There was something about him that always made her happy, unfortunately, due to her own lack of self-confidence in social life, she'd distanced herself away from him.

Into the phone he said, "I'll pay from my Master Card but book just one, my companion canceled." He quoted his credit card number to her.

"Sorry monsieur, this account seems inaccessible." With a sigh, the perky airport attendant replied after a small interval.

"Inaccessible, huh? Could you please check it again?" Alec stressed with apparent surprise.

"I did sir, this card won't work. Do you have anything else?"

"Yeah I've a visa yeah, the number is 9703 4566 3456 9011…ok, I'll hold."

"So, rough night, huh?" he spoke, trying to make idle conversation with her. "How did the date go?"

"Yea, you could say that…wait, you knew?!" she asked him, flushed with anger and with a hint of curiosity. Curious, because apart from a chance friendship with Élenoré, his interaction with the team was almost none.

"I hear rumors. As you know…grapevine spreads fast and wide." Mercer smiled.

"I hate Adele for doing that to me!" She scorned from her heart's deepest pit.

"Sorry monsieur, the machine is giving the same message. I've checked it thoroughly, your accounts are inaccessible; do you have any other?" The receptionist's voice sieved through the iPhone.

He knew the fact that his accounts were working just fine. He instantaneously began wondering why. "I don't believe that any of my other cards will pull through when my main ones won't work." He said turning away from Dr. Élénoré but signaling her to stay. His trained mind on the other hand began working possible causes and scenarios.

"I'm sorry sir, but we won't be able to hold the seat unless a payment is made. Is there anything else I can do for you?" The receptionist stated.

"No, that's quite all right. Thank you." Mercer replied.

"Wait, don't hang up! You can use my card?" shouted Élénoré who had been listening to his conversation.

The call got disconnected. "That's odd", he wondered. "Do you have any signal on your phone?" he questioned her.

"Let me check", she said and as she did she opened up her purse and rummaged through her stuff until she found her cell.

"Hmm, strange!" she scorned, "No bar. How can it be? We have our own reception tower!"

"This is not good." He brooded. "Last time this happened…"

Is it really happening now! After all these years!

"Cards not working! No signals in the phone!" He said to himself.

He was willing to bet the salary he got at CERN that her card will also not work. "Hopefully, you are wrong, Alec; otherwise—" he thought, "Nevertheless I need to get access to the underground facilities."

He remembered the day he was given the assignment.

"You were to be left in this prison to rot. At the least you should show some respect to the man who is getting you out!" this old acquaintance from the CIA grunted. He was a man who went by the name General. A man of high power and repute but nothing more than a self absorbed bureaucrat or at least that was what he thought of him.

"And why is that?" Mercer enquired.

"Uncle Sam needs you, son." He replied.

"You must be joking!" Mercer scoffed.

"...you will be provided with a new identity—Alec Mercer. You will have no ties with the US or any of its agencies. Till you complete the assignment, your official status would be as it was." Announced his old boss with a serious tone. The General was nothing more than a call-sign for the man. He was a man who came with higher powers and knew how to get work done, even with all the bureaucracy and red-tape, but now the signs of worry and tension were as clear as sky on his experienced face.

"No tac-support?" Mercer enquired.

"No!" was the strict and firm reply, "Upon your deployment we will provide you with a weapons package through one of our front organizations in France. And that's all the help you will get."

"What makes you think I'll accept another assignment, after what you guys did to me?" Mercer roared with his deep-seated anger, all of which was directed to his captor-of-sorts. "You once were also a soldier, *General*. What would you have done? We were being used!—As somebody else's personal hit squad! To them a soldier is useful only when he completes the mission! No questions asked! But if you ask them, raise flags, they hang you out to dry!" He wanted to bang the weak ply board desk hard to prove his point, but the strong metallic handcuffs attached to his wrist and his chair prevented him from doing so.

"Listen to me son", said the General with a hint of empathy for him. "What you're talking about, I know it all too well. But what would be better than living the life of a retiree while getting paid for it".

"I can probably make a hundred times more if I work paramilitary." Mercer scoffed.

"You're better than that, son. Listen, I know the trouble doesn't bother you...money buy you. And it's hard to turn you around once you have made up your mind. But please...listen to me. This assignment is a breeze. Plus you'll be on a payroll way more than your basic pay—Way more than what the CIA would care to give!"

"Screw those animals! And I hope you know your math because seven hundred bucks a day is much more than what you can ever get in this job and they don't leave you to dry." Mercer stated. "It's no use sir, I made up my mind, as it is you don't have any leverage over here, might as well save your breathe."

Mercer was right. Though back then he was not Mercer. Still he was as resolute as they come. General knew that. Closing the blinds of the see-through window of that detention cell, he whispered with a deep sigh. "I did not want to use this card on you." He scoffed. He moved forward towards the camera placed opposite the desk and with a gentle touch, switched it off.

"You are going to accept this assignment", the General replied, smiling.

"Oh yeah? What makes you so sure?" Mercer smiled back.

"You are annoyed at the army, son; rather you should be angry at the people responsible for such orders. What happened with you was wrong, but if you remember, this is US Military son, and over here we still have to follow orders. I'm not saying that what you did was wrong but everybody's hands are tied. Those orders came from the highest levels. What *could've we done? You...."*

"Yeah right, what could have you all do than save your own sorry asses, huh? If it's all the same to you, please spare me from this morality crap lecture!"

"Son, I'm giving you a chance to retaliate back at what was done to you, accept this assignment and finish it, and it will cause them insufferable pain."

"Is that so?" he pondered. "What is the assignment?"

"A team of scientists are doing some top-secret classified experiment in CERN it is being secretly funded by our government. Although we have no intel on what they do is under tight wraps, we have indications that there might be an attempt to shut the project down."

"Indications?"

"This project was conducted back in the 2000, that is until an incident; a gamma blast in 2014 shut it down. Although officially they reported nothing, signs of tampering were found at the site."

"Yeah...I remember that. It was worldwide news...created a lot of panic. You don't mean?"

"They were murdered—to stop the research. We assumed that all the data was lost but some chatter picked up by ECHELON suggests that the data was copied before the incident. Pieces of intel suggest foul play and if the perpetrators get wind of the research being reopened they'll do anything in their power to never let the findings see the light of the day. Plug every leak."

"You mean kill them…just as they did before?"

"Yes."

"This all is good, but how does it relate to me? To the death of my team? To the men responsible for all this mess? My family?"

"The men responsible for all this and much more are connected to you more than you realize, son. You have known me long enough to trust me. I hope. When time comes, you will know 'the who', 'the when', 'the why'. You will know everything you want right now. But when you do, you will regret it. So…just leave it be."

"Ok, so my job is to protect the scientists?"

"No."

"No?"

"Your mission is to protect the research, nothing else; if you can protect them without compromising your mission then do so otherwise save the data and bring it back stateside."

"But the people?—the scientists?" Mercer scoffed as he leaned back. Objectives. Priorities. The men in their holes in Langley detach themselves so much that collaterals and damages is nothing more than the statistics and data they are able to present. Nothing more than a well-played game of chess, no matter how many pawns they sacrifice. Mercer knew that all too well.

"They knew the risks when they entered the project." The General lied.

"Okay I'll do it." Alec said, without giving it another minutes thought. "Anything to stick to those sorry sons-of-bitches who screwed me!"

"Another thing, we have reason to believe that this organization has contacts and sources everywhere, so minimum contact with the locals at all times. Is that clear?"

"Clear sir."

"And I don't suppose that this mission you are offering me will ever make the books?" Mercer enquired.

"No. You suppose correct."

"And my status?" Mercer asked again.

"Same as before. No ties. Nothing. We have arranged for you to be released from this correctional facility. You are no longer a prisoner.

Mercer came back to his senses. Élénoré stood beside him. The mission objectives relayed at the back of his mind.

Save the data… Just save the data.

4

On the Move

"You do not need me." Élénoré stated. "I can front you the cash. Travelling so far? I've never been anywhere except France and Switzerland." She said unaware that he wasn't listening to her.

She turned to leave when he stopped her. "Wait, take this. It's your friend Sasha's. She left it in the control room below. The janitorial staff brought it back, it'll cover the...wine spill", he said handing her over her colleague's lab coat.

"Listen, today is my last day of work." Mercer paced. "I've been asking you for years now about what you guys do down there, you never told me—At least show me today."

"But it is confidential; I can't possibly tell anyone who is not authorized!"

"Hey, I know I am not a scientist, but I know that after you guys complete your little experiments you publish the results in articles and get Nobel Prizes and what not.... It is going to be public sooner or later but I won't be here later."

I can't allow him inside, he doesn't have clearance, she thought. *The data is not even given to the Computing Grid, I can't allow him! Although it is just Alec, what will he do, he won't even understand what we do. So I guess there would be aucun mal, aucune faute.*[1] *Besides, how can I say no to him? He's so nice.*

"OK", she replied after an exceptionally long and awkward pause.

"Cool, why don't you call up the elevator meanwhile I'll just grab my stuff."

"OK then", she replied and started walking. Her mind is restless continuously thinking whether she did the right thing by saying yes; compromising the research by inviting him down; that too on the last day.

She reached the massive gates of the complex.

A holographic scanner scanned her identification card and retina. After being validated, the massive door started opening slowly with a creaking noise. She moved in and called the elevator. Alec exited his post positioning his backpack on his back and with long striding steps, pulled up his sleeves.

---

1. No harm, no foul.

"I've never got the chance to see what's inside." He exclaimed with outward joy.

"—Because you don't have enough security clearance." She winked at him.

A good few miles away from that tiny security post, dwarfed by the mere presence of the mammoth entrance of the ATLAS module, two men, lying on their chest, looking through the Jaguar-10 night vision tactical scope, were staring directly at Élénoré.

"Last High Value Target has arrived. Heading towards entrance. The security guard is following her." He reported. "Should we intercept?"

"Non-essential. Just stick to the plan." A firm voice commanded.

5

Special Assignment

Outside the CERN facility. Twenty minutes ago.

"OK boys, today is the biggest pay day of our entire lives; given we do things right and carry our mission well, that means no jumping the gun Hunter...yeah I'm talking to you! When the mission is live, we will have three main objectives; first smoke, second collect and destroy, third eliminate. Hunter...you are on a special assignment".

"What's that?" Hunter inquired.

"I need you to go to the Director's Office and run this tracer through her computer. An agency team has intercepted her en-route; made it appear as if she died in a freak accident a few minutes ago. So don't expect any trouble, but be cautious nonetheless. Do it with utmost discretion—meaning NO SHOOTING."

"Aw man!" Hunter groaned.

"Alpha team!" Commander Blake ordered.

"Sir." A select few from the group shouted in one single reverberating voice.

"Your main objective is to breach these underground tunnels which run through the complex at the co-ordinates provided to us. You will provide us the ingress to those underground tunnels. On entry, you have to access this air shaft–over here, leading to the air-conditioning plant and release the Trebetalin drug into the system which will disrupt their mental status. But you will kill the lights first, here, the master control panel. Kill anyone in the way. Bravo and Charlie teams!"

"Sir!" Another group yelled in a single roar.

"Bravo will clone and obliterate all data and evidence from the server room down in the LHC complex and Charlie will eradicate all backups in the name of project SORCE at IT department. Be careful that you do not make any human contact. Delta team will be on me. Our client has provided us with a list of scientists down there who actually understand about what they are doing. The rest are only responsible for different parts of this complex. He wishes that the people on this list do not remain privy to that information. So we have to find each and every one of them and kill them. We have their probable location so this should not be a problem. Bear in mind, there is one person we are not to harm. The particulars are in the file. Sasha Zubrensky, Female, Russian, Blonde hair, 5'11" in height. She would be the only person who'd be wearing a mask. In case of any emergency switch to backup channel nine. After completing your assignments, reach extraction LZ at Geneva International Airport; a cargo ship will stay there in hanger seven. So keep your masks on, communications line clear and feed live, and we won't have any problem. Check your PDA for mission specifics. Is everyone clear?"

"Clear."

"Let's move out. Alpha one-six. You do recon."

Big League

"You paged me?" Special Agent Aisha Summers enquired from her frustrated Deputy Director.

"Yes... Come in...and close the door", Deputy Director Valerie replied. His tone was grim.

He motioned her to the chair, "Sit down."

"First of all...what I'm about to tell you should not leave this room. At all." He put his fingertips against each other in front of his face, his elbows resting on his mahogany desk as he stared at the employees of the office on the opposite side of the translucent glass wall; anguish was printed on his forehead.

"Okay", she replied.

"Now that this is cleared." He explained. "The Bureau is compromised. I've just received a conformation of this fact from the

Department of Homeland Security. Our liaison with Homeland tells me that every government enforcement agency has been infiltrated, possibly to the highest level."

"What?! By whom?"

"The sleepers are reporting to Bearing Oil."

"Okey, but why tell me?"

"I've read your file; you've made quite a few headlines in Boston...although your methods were...interesting. Maybe that is what is required. Anyway you are new here and not quite settled in to be in their payroll. I need you to investigate them. Find me something to pin them down. I want them brought down on their knees!"

"You got it!"

"Keep things only between us. I don't want the other agents poking where they are not supposed to. You report to me directly!"

7

Project SORCE

9:16 PM

"What is it that you guys do?" Mercer leaned forward.

"We break quarks." She answered with a devilish smile.

"You break what?!" Alec was puzzled.

"You see, in the times of Dalton, we believed that an atom is the smallest particle there is." She explained with the pride of a true scientist. "Obviously, we were proved wrong, when one by one we discovered electron, then proton and then neutron. Once again we were able to split them into something called quarks. People thought that was the end, but that was just the beginning."

"So...you break quarks?" Alec reiterated, puzzled as he was.

"Oui.[1]" Élénoré replied back with the same enthusiasm.

"That sums about it." He remarked with a chuckle. "I guess we're in the same line of work—breaking stuff."

Ellen's head panned towards him almost too briskly. She seemed to be offended by Mercer's casual remark which he had made

1. Yes

thoughtlessly. "It's not that simple and absolutely not as plain as you so casually put it! It is a science—very precise, very exact, and very accurate. We make ground breaking discoveries here!" She protested, defending her field. Were she not wearing that old and loose scientist's lab coat, it would have become very difficult for some bystander to believe that a pretty woman like her could be so knowledgeable.

"Why're you getting so upset?" Alec asked baffled about his mistake. Although he wanted to emphasize on the 'ground breaking' part of it, he was smart enough to suppress it.

"—Because you are downgrading our work!" Élénoré protested back, harder. "What is it that you do, anyway?"

"I'm sorry. It was just a joke!" Mercer apologized. He knew that there was nothing terrible than the wrath of a woman. "What is it that you do?" He asked, carefully heeding to his every word.

"Glad that you asked!" Élénoré replied with the joy gushing back to her. "Essentially, the only workable reactants we have is still—a proton. For years, scientists and researchers like us had been accelerating high energy beams of protons, striking them at one another. They would break into countless particles—neutrinos, bosons are just some of them. But after all the advancements in nanotechnology and cybernetics we were able to run experiments based on the Superstring theory... and like uncle Stephen used to say—"

Mercer listened closely, keenly. He did not understand most of it. Information left his brain as soon as it entered.

To him it all seemed as one of those Discovery Science episodes, although very interesting from a scientific point of view, his mind was unable to completely grasp it. Still, he gazed at her with deep thoughtful eyes. Besides, "Any intel is good intel"; this was what his handler used to say. And something was about to happen. He could feel it in his gut. The blocked cards... the jammed signals. Textbook guidelines for asymetric warfare. And if his feeling was right which usually was, they were in for one hell of a night.

"And –this is the control room, where comment vous dire?[1] the magic happens."

ATLAS Module

PROJECT SORCE

Experiment Observation Control Room

They entered a massive light yellow shaded, almost cuboid room. There are many rows of workstations throughout the room. Most of them were occupied by the scientists, who were already present in the room, working on their desktop holographic panels. Graphs, charts, statistics, data and such were flashing on the GCD displays which hung on the walls. A lot of chatter could be heard coming outside. The atmosphere stressed; much more than it usually used to be.

"Today is the day, guys!! Where the hell is she?" One of the researchers, dominating the scientists' cacophony, shrieked.

"Don't know, Reuben, I've got no signal on my cell. You try calling her." Adele replied in a non-chalant manner. "No wait a minute, there she is. Who the hell is this?" Pointing across the large room towards the door behind Reuben Sloane. All the heads in the room turned towards the same direction. Everybody gazed with blank ghastly eyes. The sight was practically shock personified.

An untagged Man walking about inside the SLHC Complex? Preposterous!

Reuben was already skidding on thin ice. He wanted to pull off the last remnants of white hair which were left on his bald scalp. The loose saggy skin on his body was scarred, not with wounds but wrinkles. His belly pushing harder at the light blue shirt but it was kept at bay by the strong buttons of his pristine white lab coat. Seeing Élénoré his little face smiled but as he noticed her partner his smiled eroded.

His mind could not comprehend the fact that after the next few hours the project would be officially over. Unofficially, it already was. All the work was done. The readings were checked and double checked. The project had already proved itself viable and commercially successful.

The horrid events of that fateful night looped in his mind. It was a night decades ago but what he did then had scarred his soul for eternity. He remembered that he sent his peer away from his terminal. The man was responsible for maintaining the gamma absorption ratio in the reactor core. He remembered as he sat on his terminal and disabled all the warning systems of the LHC. Using the same terminal he uploaded a virus, which completely crumpled the famous LHC safeguard mechanisms. Then he left the experiment observation room and entered the ATLAS module where he manually override the absorption panels causing the CAB sheets to purge itself out of the LHC. This led to the destruction killing 283 scientists, as those sheets no longer neutralized the gamma radiation.

The radiation killed the scientists but he had a bigger part in it. Now he stood with another collection of intellectuals, of a younger era, doing the same work he damned his soul to prevent from happening. All that death, that blood soiled his hands for nothing. He merely delayed an outcome. Reaching a time in his life, he started looking at life beyond the worldly matters, and he was not at peace with his actions in the past.

"We won't stand this! We've reached phase seven." He cried, pulling himself together. "Firstly, despite all my protests, you ignored my warnings. We need more time to prep this. Do you want another gamma blast to send us to the other side?"

"How much more time do you want?" replied Élénoré, crossly "Ever since you have joined this group you've been wanting more time! More time for the particle collision experiment? More time for the PS/SPS accelerator tests? Huh? Did we blow to bits then? Or in the injector experiment? Or in the T7 deuterium synthesis. It seems as if you just want to slow us down, Sloane. We've done far dangerous experiments in the past, nothing bad happened then; nothing is going to happen now! Besides, our contributors are getting agitated. They are waiting for results; I can't keep them in the wind much longer. The stats already prove our theory; there's no reason to be afraid. I'm going to tell them the project is a success."

"These contributors don't know about half the things that we deal with over here. They just look for the end result. Things in our field are not like that. Just tell me who they are? The Liaison officer may be some company spook. I'll talk to him. Make him understand why we cannot rush the process. Ok?"

"See, there is no need for that because I am convinced that we are ready to take this to the last phase. And rush the process, you say?" she said with a hint of undercurrent sarcasm. "It's been seven years since the start of the project and you still believe we are rushing. You...."

"Hey, who is he right behind you", Sasha pointed towards Alec, trying to suppress the situation and to know about this man, who is at a place, where he should have never been."

"Oh, this is Alec. He is one of the security officers of our project."

"Then how come we've never heard of him", she stated, digging deeper.

"Well you know the little white post near the ATLAS module entrance...."

"Yeah...."

"He spends most of his time sleeping there!" Élénoré joked.

There was a sudden burst of laughter in the room.

"It is true." Alec concurred, awkwardly.

But Sasha was not amused. She pulled Éllén aside and began interrogating her. "What is he doing here? Is he cleared to be here?"

"I brought him to show what we do here." Élénoré explained in a very casual fashion. "Don't worry! He will leave here clueless...."

"But why?" Sasha leaned.

"Because he asked me to show this place as it is his last day of job." Élénoré explained.

"So you let him in? Just like that!" Sasha chuckled sarcastically. "If the Director comes to know about this, she would definitely flip you out. How could you...? You have to send him back to his place; where he came from."

He could be a problem!

"Of course not; you must have forgotten but, I am still the head in this operation, and I say—he stays. Now get back to your posts. We've got a lot of work left to complete. Deadline's today and if we loiter around, we'll miss it!"

Turning towards Alec, who in the meantime, became quite the crowd's favorite in the room. "I have to oversee the implementation of the last phase of the project, so if you don't mind...."

"Oh yeah, don't mind me, I'll just stand over here..." moving to the spot behind the last terminal where he was pointing. "And out of anybody's way. Okay."

"Merci." Élénoré thanked.

On one wall of the observation room, there was a big transparent glass panel, which acted for the dual purpose, as a window to the predetermined part of the LHC where the particles are supposed to collide and also as a monitor where the latest stats of the project are displayed in real-time. Unlike before, due to the advantages of the development in nanotechnology in the field of computer applications, they do not have to conduct one experiment and spend months analyzing the data obtained by it. Now the processers analyze the data and create graphs, charts and simulations from all the data gathered by various modules installed in the collider like the ATLAS, CMS, B71, and B72, so on and so on, greatly reducing much of the pressure off the researchers, giving them more development to analysis-time than before.

Éllén always thought of the CGD panel as her own terminal. Rarely would she utilize the workstation assigned to her, rather she would stand before the CGD, saying that standing over there gives her a sense of perspective. Moreover, it is the feeling she gets, that her terminal is bigger than others for the simple fact that she is their boss.

"People, this is it", she said to her subordinates with a hint of pride over the achievements they had accomplished. A pep-talk to boost the morale of her crew, but nothing more came to her than those four words which she had already spoken. She was never much of a people person. Deducing; there would be a sense of awkwardness, she moved on to questioning about the position of the experiment; about the preparations. "Hey Adele, are the LHC magnets in position?"

"Forget the magnet, who is your friend back there?"

"I told you all, he is the securi—", her speech was interrupted.

"Yeah, yeah, you told us THAT. But is he your boyfriend?" Adele poked for information. After a little pause she exclaimed. "Now I get it!"

"Get what?"

"He is the reason why you didn't want to go out with Sam? Didn't you? You just didn't want us to know about him. Right?"

"No! Of course not he's just a friend; nothing else", Élénoré screamed, her cheeks began blushing.

"Girl, don't even try. I know you are into him. I can tell! You didn't even deny that he isn't your boyfriend."

"But he isn't!"

"I know, dear, he isn't." Adele smiled. "Little Éllée has a crush on the security officer. Doesn't she? And he is extremely good looking too! What would be the size of that thing?!"

"Of what?!"

"Don't act so innocent!" Adele remarked. "Okay then, you don't want him. So can I have him?"

Élénoré's face reddened. Her heart beat increased, chest started pounding. Her arteries swelled with the excessive blood.

"See?!" Adele remarked with pride. "Got you?"

Élénoré flustered. "Wh— What? That is so not true. Why don't you spend some more of your ample time at your terminal?"

"Chill darling, my work is already done; we are just waiting for the heavy ion guys to do their job before we can proceed."

"So the magnet is in place?"

"The magnet is in place and charging."

"We've just got confirmation; the particles are loaded in the accelerator."

"Initiate the sequence, now."

'The CAB filters operational?" She asked.

"Yes." The straight forward reply.

"What about the coolant flow?"

"Steady 100 PSI at 277 Kelvin." Denise answered.

"Okay then" Élénoré finally concluded.

"Operation SORCE, Phase 7 is online—now. Class one personnel evacuate underground facility.... Non-essential personnel please evacuate the facilities...ATLAS vault is now a restricted area...."

"Alpha one-six, in position", resounded in a military intelligence grade high frequency long range transceivers miles away from the Experiment Observation Room.

"Intrusion team prepped and ready", a voice reported in.

"Target in sight", another broad voice confirmed.

"This is Alpha one-actual; give me a Sit-Rep!" A voice commanded.

8

The Signs

"Are magnets charged?" Élénoré questioned her subordinate.

"Magnets are charged to full strength." She replied.

"Is evacuation procedure complete?"

"Complete." Somebody else replied again.

"What about Safety Checklist?" Élénoré enquired with caution. She did not want to repeat the same dreadful mistake again.

"It is checked about an hour ago. Can we just do it?!" The woman replied, agitated. Everybody in the room had given up their night's sleep and mind's peace for the completion of this project. Naturally, everyone was agitated. Everyone wanted it to be over soon.

"Okay! Activate the magnets!" Élénoré ordered.

A scientist began typing something on his computer. CERN used an operating system called Scientific Linux, developed inside CERN itself; today it is the only renowned operating system in the scientific community. On the screen, the words 'Magnetic Field Strength' began displaying, along with a percentage, which kept on increasing as the magnetic field inside the PS/SPS accelerator was increasing. Soon, it reached from zero to hundred percent.

"Activating...magnetic field strength...magnetic field at full capacity; 14 Terra electron-Volt." He reported.

There was a moment of silence, everybody's eyebrows raised

and all eyes were on Élénoré.

"Introduce particles into the accelerator." She commanded. It was the order everyone was waiting for. Again, somebody pressed some buttons and reported.

"T7 Deuterium ion successfully introduced into the PS/SPS accelerator." He reported. A ring of applauding cheered the tense environment. "The negative atom inserted."

"Run it to one hundred thousand oscillations!" Éllén commanded. Alec stood there, behind her. Nothing of it made any sense, but if the scientists clapped, he clapped with them.

After a short moment, another voice announced. "Particles at 99.99% speed of light. Ready for insertion." Somebody announced. "Note the time...8:26 PM. Introducing particles inside the SLHC collider in three...two...one.... Particles successfully inserted into the SLHC collider."

"Magnetic field stable. Beams Converging. 250,000 oscillations and counting!"

"Increase temperature to 1,000 Kelvin." Élénoré directed.

"Yes ma'am." Somebody responded.

"200,000 oscillations...250,000 oscillations. Beams converged within operational limits."

Ce qu'il lui. This is it!

"Open the intake valve." Élénoré commanded. "Increase pressure to fifty thousand PSI."

Everybody stood up, watching in awe at the largest CGD panel in the room, which was tracking the two beams inserted into the collider. Soon, they would collide, in a massive exothermic reaction, giving out heat up to 1,000,000 Kelvin, which should be used to heat up the water cooling supply installed specially for this project. Rest was basic physics. The coolant would be converted to steam which would do the basic work of rotating the turbine which in turn would rotate the shaft leading to the generator, which would transform the heat energy via mechanical energy to electrical energy. The output would be clean, cheap energy at a time when a common man is unable to afford electricity.

"Watch the CGD, people! We have events!" A manly voice shouted, alerting those who were still working on their terminals.

On the same CGD, the two particle beams could be seen as they finally collided with other. The reaction was violent, and caused a bang, which could be heard inside the ATLAS Experiment Observation Room, the opposite particles annihialating each other producing enormous amounts of heat and gamma radiation energy.

"Temperature rising! Current temperature – 400,000...600,000...800,000...1 000,000 Kelvin."

Every person in the room filled with cheer and joy. It was their hard work which was finally paying off. Their work was almost done. All that was left was the formalities. One million Kelvin hot temperatures are enough to convert water to steam for considerable amount of time, providing more energy than any operational nuclear power-plant can provide. But one final phase was left, conversion of Gamma radiation into basic anti-quarks, which later synthesized into anti-matter which would provide as raw material later in the reaction.

"It's not over...not just yet!" somebody remarked.

True.

Conversion of energy into matter is something people have tried to play with ever since Einstein's theory of Relativity. The process though achieved once successfully, did not leave a single doubt in their minds when it came to its safety. The procedure was as extremely delicate as it was important for the improved efficiency they had achieved.

"Activate the RDE!" Élénoré ordered. "Insert the CAB filters."

"Oui, Mademoiselle." One scientist replied.

All the while, Mercer just stood there in the corner, his eyes panning through the room, scanning for suspicious activities. Soon, he did find what he was looking for. He saw the frame of a frail woman, with almost same physical attributes as Élénoré but she had the whole demeanor of a Russian. She was acting nervous, almost paranoid, flustered, looking here and there. Even the mere clapping and applauding threw her into a mental fit. A second later, she glanced at the console window at her terminal, peeked at her watch, collected her stuff from her desk and started walking unobtrusively towards the other exit of the room; the door from which Mercer and Élénoré entered.

Mercer knew something was off. He was counting on it. Luckily, he was able to spot the odd thing out. Decisively, he walked up to the front end of the room, towards Élénoré. Pulling her aside by her arms he told her to follow him.

Élénoré was completely baffled, taken by surprise, for a minute she was not even sure what exactly was going on. She started resisting, asking him to stop.

"Do you trust me?!" He asked in a brief moment. There was

not much time to waste.

"Well...I guess!" She replied back, hesitantly.

"Then trust me—and follow me!" He ordered her. "Bad things are about to happen and you are not safe here!"

"What?!!"

"You'll see!" he delayed her. Back inside the ATLAS Experiment Observation Room, the particle physicists and scientists were truly amazed as to what was going on. The stranger had almost dragged their supervisor by her hand out of the room.

What's going on!

"What are we doing?" She asked, frantically.

"We are following a lead!" Alec replied.

"I don't understand! What the hell are you talking about?" Élénoré cried. " I have work back there!"

"You'll see!" He returned a firm reply.

Élénoré wanted to back out, but she did not see a choice. Seeing no other option, she just followed him blankly.

Moments later they heard distant words being uttered ahead of them.

"The project is successful. It produced the desired output. I have all the data I need. You can proceed as planned." They heard the distant words being articulated in à hushed feeble tone, in distinctly slight Russian dialect.

Élénoré recognized the voice instantly. She knew who she was, and the context of her dialogue with the anonymous caller.

Alec loosened his grip of Élénoré's hands. He knew she had realized the situation, and now she probably would not hesitate. Much as he anticipated, Éllén followed him quietly.

They followed the blurred and hazy figure in the dim lighting of the sparsely separated florescent lights and the guide lightings on the floor. All the while Mercer was watching and listening to her every move and every word. The woman, Sasha, finally entered a brightly lit locker room, much similar to the ATLAS Observation Room behind them. Noiselessly, Alec, along with Élénoré, not more than a few steps behind him, followed the woman as she slowly opened up her locker revealing a Military Grade Air Mask, but the second she realized that someone was watching her from behind, she quickly disconnected the call as she tried to conceal the mask from the intruder and slowly turned around to face them.

"Oh! It's you! You nearly scared me to death!" She remarked with a clear sigh of relief. "What are you doing over here?!" She asked Mercer, with slight disgust in her voice as she panned her eyes towards Élénoré who was following him timidly, whose face looked red with a cocktail of shock and anger. Mercer reached forward and grabbed Sasha's hands and the mask which she was trying to conceal.

"So it is a gas attack?" He questioned her with all his wrath, each word articulated clearly in the hollow room.

"Wh—what? What the hell are you talking about?" She retorted in an apparently surprised tone.

Behind him, Élénoré had had enough of following Alec blindly, not knowing what was going on. "Who is your buyer?" She demanded. Sasha scoffed at her question. "What are you talking about?" She replied with a smile.

Seeing that Sasha was not going to break down, he pulled out the gun holstered neatly inside his bag, and aimed it firmly at Sasha.

"Your cover's blown! Don't play with me!" Mercer yelled so hard that the whole room reverberated. "Answer the question!"

Seeing the shiny metal pointed at her, she panicked. Her eyes widened at the brilliant gray circular rim of the suppressor inches from her face. Sweat drops broke off from under her right ear pinnate which ran down to her neck, tickling her soft hairless skin. "you are gonna let him talk to me like that?"

"How many?" Mercer pressed hard.

"How many what?!" She jumped. "Keep that thing away from me!!"

"How many men?" Mercer repeated with a raised tone.

"I don't know! What are you talking about!!?" She cried. "Vy s uma soshli?!"[1]

Mercer cocked his gun, still pointing his piece at her.

"How many?"

"I don't know!!"

He reached for her other hand, and grabbed her wrist even before she could realize what happened. He raised her hand by the same

1. Are you crazy?!

wrist, displaying the carbon black air filtering mask, she had been concealing in her hand. "Don't play coy? Just tell me what I want, and maybe…I'll let you live!" He cried.

"I don't understand! What do you want from me?!" She bellowed.

Mercer slowly brought his forefinger towards the trigger, squeezing it even slowly, keeping the gun horizontally at her temple.

"Okay…okay!! I'll tell you everything I know! Just please don't kill me!!" She requested with tears running down her cheeks.

Mercer pulled back his gun. "How many?" He repeated the same question.

"I don't know…dozens at least!" She explained.

"Men?" Mercer inferred.

"No—Teams." Sasha replied with the fear for her life clear in her whimpering voice.

"Point of entry?"

"Somewhere from the other side of ATLAS Observation Room."

"They'll extract you?" He asked quickly. She nodded saying yes. "How'll they ID you?"

"The mask and my physical description. I have to wait here for them—till I get instructions."

"Éllén…you don't want to see this! Turn around!" He instructed Élénoré, with a gentle, understanding tone. Calm.

"No!" Élénoré denied strongly. She did not turn around.

"Okay then…." Mercer gave out a deep sigh as he holstered his gun smoothly into its belt. His hands then quickly grabbed Sasha, one hand at gripping her thin neck and the other placed over the neck and almost instantaneously his hands pressed with a crushing surgical blow to her neck, crushing her spine, killing her instantaneously and painlessly.

Élénoré screamed. "What did you do?"

"What had to be done!" he explained plainly, without any sign of remorse.

"You murderer!" Élénoré could not believe her eyes. Her wish of wanting to know the buyer faded. She just could not believe what she saw. The man she trusted was a murderer and she was with him, alone. But it was not fear or horror that she felt, it was the profound pain which had made her heart much heavier to bear, the pain of betrayal; betrayal from Sasha, the traitor and from Alec, the murderer. Quickly, Alec stuffed the corpse in the empty locker behind them.

"Listen…no one is buying anything! They will steal it, and they will steal it now, neutralizing anything that comes in their way."

Mercer explained as best as he could, and fast. "That means us. They will kill us!"

The traces of the fluorescent lights all around them closed down, abruptly. The red sirens hung around the edges of the wall began humming an almost lyrical jingle but at the same time, spreading fear even in Mercer's heart.

"It has begun!" He stated with urgency.

"What?!" She shouted. "Explain!"

"Listen! I don't work for CERN! I work for the US…for the same people who fund your experiments. When time comes, my objective was to secure your data. That time—is now!" Mercer explained.

Élénoré took a step back in shock.

"Maintenant, certaines personnes très mauvaise ne voulez pas que votre travail à terminer. Et ils sont sur leur façon de s'assurer à ce sujet![2]" Alec spoke in perfect french. "These…people—are trained killers. And they will kill you and all your closest friends!" Alec explained. Éllén was speechless, as if someone jolted her with a stun gun, found herself struggling for breath.

"In few minutes…some terrifying, horrifying people will come, and they will kill both of us if you don't do exactly what I say? Okay?" He asked.

"Okay." was the feeble reply.

"Wear this mask. When those people challenge you, ask you for verification, I want you to reply like a Russian, just like Sasha. I'll be behind you, hiding in one of these lockers, with my gun ready. Our chances of escaping are extremely thin. If anything goes wrong, I'll open fire but that's not what I'd like to do. Tell them that you are Sasha Zubrensky. Tell them that these lockers are empty, and they don't have to check them. Everything—our very lives depend on whether your acting is good and if you can pull through!"

That was certainly a lot of pressure which was stacked on her shoulders a bit too suddenly, but she did not have any choice. In order to be able to live, she had to do things she had found beyond her caliber.

Sooner than the both of them expected, they soon began hearing gunshots and yelling and crying and groaning from both sides around them.

"Ready yourself! They will be here any minute! Wear the mask tightly...it would be a gas attack!" Alec ordered. Saying this Mercer

2. Now, some very bad people do not want your work to finish. And they are on their way to make sure about that!

crammed into the locker closing the locker door behind him. Élénoré had never seen him this way. It was like there were many pages of his personality and she had read from one of them.

With a gas attack imminent, one thought alarmed his mind. The one mask he had he gave it to Élénoré. With no intel on the unknown chemical he not only put the assignment at risk but also risked his own life. But he know he would have it no other way. His intensive training left him with a very high threshold, something which Élénoré did not possess. He knew if the gas would contaminate his quadrant, he would be in big trouble.

Élénoré followed his instructions to the letter and wore the mask just like he said, trying to conceal her face as much as she could. Mercer was hiding behind her, inside the small locker, his gun trained outside, past her.

For an awkward moment, she stood there silently, with fear gripping her heart as she heard the strings of gunshots and the cries of people yelling for their lives. Soon, she heard the distinct footsteps of a multitude of legs, reverberating in perfect harmony, approaching her ever so steadily.

"Sasha Zubrensky?" Commander Blake asked her with a serious tone. All his men were clad in heavy Kevlar armor and in their completely black paramilitary uniform, their mere walking shook the ground beneath them and their M4 automatic assault rifles induced terror inside her heart.

"Da." She replied in an outwardly calm and collected tone, in a non-chalant Russian tone.

Her face was very unclear and undistinguishable under the dominating red light of emergency alarm. "Follow that path, ma'am! Our man is guarding the entrance; he'll take you to the LZ." He told her politely, and as he did, he along with his men made their way forward, leaving her behind, alone.

"Da." She replied but Blake didn't pay much attention to her. He and his men kept marching forward.

After those armed mercenaries were finally gone and the path was clear, Mercer exited from the locker, and as he did he grabbed her right hand and quickly began running towards the other side, with long winding steps.

9

The Escape

The Tunnels
Super Large Hadron Collider

It was a perfect example of hurried commotion and suspense. People were getting killed. Blood spill everywhere. In order to survive the eminent firefight, they escaped into the tunnels. Though Mercer was a hardened war-vet, yet he had bitten more than he could chew. Although he did not directly encounter the assailants, he could easily identify that there must be more than ten of them killing all those scientists using high caliber ammo.

There was a series of intermittently placed yellow LED bulbs and fire extinguishers which ran through the tunnel on their left along with two shielded cables which carried electricity throughout the tunnel, an array of white fluorescent lights ran over the ceiling transversely, overhead ran many grey pipes welded to the aluminum panels on top, a big, bright blue pipe at the center ran throughout the tunnel along with the rest of the equipment, the top-right arc of the tunnel, bolted to those panels were many devices and equipments setup there for detection and data collection. The big blue pipe was the continuation of the SPS accelerator where the particles were accelerated to 99.999997% to the speed of light before being injected into the main Super Large Hadron Collider tunnel; it appeared as if they were giant oil barrels bolted end-to-end together in a circular form, the circle being twenty-seven in diameter spanning between two countries, France and Switzerland.

The air filtration in the sector stopped with a short signal. Not only the air oxygen level decreased, the poison levels were increasing at an alarming level. Without an air mask, Mercer knew he had to escape the sector as fast as he could from the mercenaries and the poison.

"What do we do?" said Élénoré, excited not with happiness but with fear and sorrow, "They are going to kill us!"

"Not on my watch." Said he trying to keep his calm, "Nevertheless, before anything else I need to protect the data!"

"Where are the underground servers?" he questioned her with a sense of emergency.

"Servers?" She replied hesitantly.

"I know!" he squealed, "Don't pretend! You've just got to trust me."

"Trust me." If he'd said that at any other time, she would probably have done so. But things were different now. She saw her friends life squeeze out of her. Sasha murdered right in front of her, killed by Alec. Though it was already established that she was the mole, their inside man; the cause of all her current misery, yet she was not cruel enough to celebrate her death. But the screams of the massacre in the ATLAS experiment room changed her attitude towards her. Left her in shock.

"Trust you? The only reason I'm with you is because they are spitting lead back there. And it seems you did nothing but lie to me, and now you ask me to trust you?" she cried angrily. "Tell me...is Alec even your real name?"

"No."

"Oh my god." The shock left her mouth wide open; her starry blue eyes were in denial. She distanced herself away from him the same instant.

"What is it, then?" She fumed at him, furious.

"That is not relevant—not at the moment!" Mercer replied. "Listen, we have two minutes—tops, before they realize you have gone. From what I understand, their whole mission now hangs on their ability to kill you, because only you know the bigger picture; because it is you who knows everything! Now, They are going to KILL you, and I am trying to SAVE you, understand?" He said emphasizing on each syllable, "Is this reason good enough to trust me?"

"Je suppose."[1]

"Trust me; I'm on your side. Just do as I say, and maybe you'll get out of this alive." Élénoré gave a hesitant nod.

"Okay." Mercer let out a sigh of relief, collecting himself, calibrating his senses. "Where are those underground servers?"

"They're in sector UW 25, near ALICE module."

"Direction?"

"That way." Élénoré pointed with her thin arm stretched straight towards the door from which they came in.

"You mean we've to go through the...ATLAS module?"

"But they have already captured that quadrant!" Mercer exclaimed. "Is there a way by which we can flank them?"

"We can cut through the SPS accelerator", suggested Élénoré.

---

1. I guess.

"Then hurry up, but stay behind me AT ALL TIMES", he instructed, "Understood?"

"Understood" Élénoré replied.

Saying this they started running towards the Accelerator chamber, though not for long. They realized something.

"It's taking too bloody long!", he remarked.

"There must be some scooters in that sector." Élénoré said, letting out a desperate smile.

"Scooters?" Mercer ridiculed.

"Yeah, maintenance uses them for transport, down here." Élénoré tried to explain.

"Hope we get there in time. Everything depends on it." Mercer exclaimed.

9:00 PM
Detachment Server Room
Sector UW 25
Super Large Hadron Collider

"Come on Jordon, they are finishing up over there", said Leo, urging his partner to hurry up, "Why the hell are you taking so damn long?"

The miniature of a room was occupied by the two mercenaries. The room itself, a makeshift server room was riddled with countless multicolored wires which relayed in from all direction exposed in the plaster ceiling above. The room was small. Much of the room was occupied by the industrial scale mainframe servers.

"Shut the hell up man", Jordan replied, agitated, "It is not hundred or two hundred GBs, its twenty bloody thousand GBs. It's bound to take time."

"But they're having all the fun!" Leo exclaimed with the agony of a little grounded kid peeping at the friends playing in the park.

"Stop acting like Hunter, he's psycho!", warned Jordan, "—and close to getting pounded. Just do what you're supposed to do, that is, if you don't want to get screwed up."

"Yeah man, good point." Leo came around.

"Back to work.... Upload the encryption SERT." Jordon commanded.

"Upload complete. Routing data through SERT; port 5676." Leo replied just as he hovered through many windows of research data which he routed to Jordan.

"Connection Link established. Connecting; Data Courier. Encrypting and dumping. Transport Stream established." Jordan stated. "It's gonna take some time."

"Yeah, but in the meantime, you can go on our next objective. I'll plant the C4 on these servers and you pack it over there." Leo said with an eerie smile.

Minutes later the room resounded again by the sound of a distinctive electronic beep which marked the completion of the task at hand. "Done. Encrypted and transferred." Jordan reported as he hastily began stowing away all his equipment and storing the Data Courier inside the magnetically sealed tamperproof lock case.

All the data, safely inside that protective case, away from temptations reach. People were dying for the contents of that case. Somewhere in there lay the secrets to the millennia old feud in the scientific community and the power to dominate the world.

"And still we've got a little time to spare, there must be a few left in second quadrant." Leonard chuckled.

"Sometimes you scare me, man!" Jordan said.

"Wait, did you hear that?" Leo marked. A very distant sound of muffled footsteps could be heard in that empty chamber.

"I did. I thought this section was clear."

"Ready your weapon!" He commanded in his cautious voice.

But then a voice crackled over the high frequency radio transmitters, "I'm approaching your sector, Leo, do not shoot me!"

"Copy that. You were a pound of finger pressure from losing yours, man!" Leo replied in the transceiver.

"Are you done here?" Jordan enquired.

"Yeah…just…about…yeah done." Leo replied back with a smile as he fastened the C4 on the last of the consoles in the server room.

"Then let's get to a safe distance before lighting this baby up." Jordan exclaimed.

Over the transceiver, a distinct commanding voice emerged. "Panther secure?" It asked.

"Panther is secure. Delta-one-actual. Ready for extraction." Jordan reported.

Hardly did he say this, than they heard a metallic rolling sound approaching them. They turned back to investigate, but even before they could, the rolling device activated. A new type of an Electro-

Magnetic Pulse Grenade recently developed in DARPA; it emitted a sonic blast along with the electromagnetic pulse. First, it discharged the pulse, frying all the equipment, including their transmitters and earpieces. They screeched in their ears like feedback in a radio.

"CONTACT!" He screamed instinctively, pointing to the obvious, knowing that backup won't arrive.

The bright white room went dark as all the lights and the electrical circuiting short-circuited. The backup systems activated, as the dual lines are shielded because of its proximity to the reactor core and the magnetic coils. In case of any mishaps, the other is supposed to kick in, which came to the advantage of their assailant, who was hiding in the dark, like a lion hides in the bushes in the Savanna before approaching its prey.

And then a sonic blast radiated and hit them with a deafening squeal. Their ears were ringing, and they felt dizzy and unable to stand balanced as the blast damaged their occipital lobe. They were like sitting ducks and there was nothing they could do to prevent their impending doom. Fortunately for them, their death came swift in the form of two well-aimed suppressed gun shots. The faint sound is all they heard before their lifeless bodies fell to the ground.

"Stay here, no matter what. Come in when I say so", Mercer instructed Élénoré before moving forward to confirm his kill.

He moved towards the dead bodies he had just killed, and as he stood over them, he inspected their bodies. He frisked both their bodies and salvaged all that he could; aware of the trouble he was in, he knew better than to let the stuff go to waste, besides it could give him a better knowledge about the attackers. To his luck, there were spare air masks on the dead mercenaries. Mercer grabed the mask hastily as his eyes scanned the area keenly while applying the mask on his face. After perfectly securing the mask on his face he finally took a deep breath of air.

In his business, knowledge is power, and priceless. He had been hearing, what they had been saying, and decided to use the opportunity. He did not have enough support to neutralize all the attackers. They were too many of them. About a dozen in ATLAS module itself, the two of them in the server room and as he had heard many of them were active in the whole sector. They were killing all the witnesses, erasing all the evidence. He had killed these two, but sooner or later somebody was bound to come here to investigate. He would be a sitting duck, and just like those two and in all probability, would meet the same fate. So he could not stay here to protect the research, but he could not just leave the research, because whatever it was, it would definitely fall into the wrong hands. After all, the ones who had sent those PMC soldiers were not rooting for world peace. He did not have anything which could carry all the data in the servers. He needed something tremendously huge to carry all the data. Seeing no other option, he bagged the Data Courier case in which they had already transferred the data, although it could possibly have some risks, yet he was sidetracked by what was caught his eye. He noticed that instead of disarming the C4 circuitry, the EMP blast triggered the count down, way down to zero.

"Shit!" he shouted. Things are never easy for him. Sprinting down the end of the room, he sealed the door and ran to the end of the corridor. "Run!" He shouted at the empty expanse at top of his lungs.

"What?" replied Élénoré, waiting eagerly for him. Standing alone in that eerie tunnel, she was lonely in the tunnels, lonely and scared to death. Not a streak of light to comfort her scared soul.

"RUN! RUN, RUN, RUN! RUN!" He shouted again and again. There was no time to waste. The size of the C4 was not much, maybe a few pounds, but his experience told him that in such constricted spaces and with no route for the blast to channel through, it would plummet directly into the tunnels and bake them alive, like in a furnace.

10

The Squelch

The feedback sound echoed in the ATLAS experiment observation room, from where the two had escaped under the noses of the assassins.

"What the hell was that?" cried Commander Blake, "Give me a Sit-Rep", he demanded in the transceiver.

"Alpha team, clear."

"Bravo team, clear."

There was a static silence for a moment.

"Charlie team?" he shouted, "Where the hell is Charlie team? Jordan, Leo? Respond!"

There was no response. No one replied to give the 'all clear'. Silence was bad, really bad; he knew it. Not sparing a single moment, he dispatched his men to look into the matter.

"David, Dúncan, Snake. Leave that one alive he might be useful. Sector UW 25, Server Room. Move out!" he cried at the top of his lungs. And as he said that he moved to the remaining scientist, picked him up with his collar and shouting at the top of his lungs, "Unlock the console for me! I need you to access the cameras. Right now this is the only choice you've got to survive."

"Anything, I'll do anything! Please, just don't kill me!" replied the petrified scientist.

Minutes later, the bricks C4 in the server room exploded. And like a woman scorned, it lashed fire spurting out of the server room and it started flowing through the tunnel, looking for an outlet to escape, not that a double-wall protected EMP secured facility would have many. The fire must have jolted 15-16 kilometers with its oppressing heat, anything that came in contact with it perished like a pitiful sand dune in front of the mighty desert storm. Blake felt the chills in his spine when he heard the blast several miles away, realizing that he had just sent his bravest men to a fate worse than slaughter, "Men! Find cover!" shouted knowing that he could do nothing; maybe just to ease his own conscience. Even so, he did all that he could do.

He stood, unknowingly at the same spot where Élénore once stood in the ATLAS Module Observation Room. The CGD was offline at the moment and seemed no different from any other ordinary glass window. He lifted his head up to gaze out into the tunnels. At the moment it was all so serene, just like a man-made wonder. He could see the air conditioning shafts going down, the yellow, blue, green pipes running through the facility. He could see it all. The big silvery aluminum tone equipment which served for different purposes, although alien to him, was quite attractive. He felt the blast rushing towards him, the heat pumping towards him. He imagined it all racing towards him. Sooner than he thought, the looming fate reached him. The deep orange flames of the plastic bomb jolted through the tunnel. The sheer force of the hot air pushed all the soldiers which were sent in the tunnels back the way through which they came. Commander

Blake saw the lifeless bodies flowing in the air through the corridor, the other side of the window and then the strong polymer-glass window gave in to the oppressing pressure, killing him instantly, like his soul yanked out of him.

God!

Mercer had quite a unique talent amongst various other unique ones from his special skillset, which his singular job had been honing in him for years and even years after he had retired, it still came in hand.

Sixty seconds.

He could count down by the clock accurately to the second.

"Hurry up, there's no time left!" he shouted in a coarse voice at the top of his voice when he started hearing footsteps from the other side of the tunnel.

"We'll never make it!" Élénoré replied. She was worried, more than she was scared.

"Faster!"

"This is as fast as I can run!" she replied. Mercer had taken quite a lead by now. Time was of essence here and he could not just leave her behind, to die. So he backed a few paces, held her hand as tight as he could and both of them just sprinted blindly, hoping to outrun the eminent blast.

Forty seconds.

Footsteps were becoming louder. He could guess that the assassins had entered the tunnel. "Shh! Shhh!" He signaled her to get behind his back while they were still running. "They're coming from the front. There is no escape route in this tunnel. We are stuck up." It was a perfect place for cover. The faint illumination, narrow alley. He could take every enemy combatant out single handedly. Though he could not claim his stronghold there. Not there. Because a few chambers back the rack of C4 detonator was actively nearing zero.

"But we can't just stay here!" she cried.

Right then something quite familiar was caught by her eyes.

This might help us out.

The bullets started flying. Élénoré hid herself at a shallow depression at the side of the wall of the tunnel. Mercer on the other hand took cover behind a thick metallic wedge which housed the maintenance panel for the staff. As Élénoré protected herself from the tiny rockets which hurled at her, Mercer pulled out his Belgium VBR from his bag pack, pressed it tight to his chest, his eyes trained through the brilliant Red-Dot tactical scope mounted on the weapon, decisively he picked his targets and took them out. Élénoré was shocked once again as she saw Alec fight. She did not recognize him. He was not her friend. But her mind reminded her that there was no time. The blast was imminent. They turned towards a queer metallic door. Élénoré swiped her access card in the security console and the door buzzed open. As it did they were invited by a thrust of extremely bone-chilling cold breeze, but at the moment she was too preoccupied to care. She signaled him to follow her. "Quickly!" She bellowed as she signaled with her hand to hurry.

Twenty seconds.

Mercer took out just one more target as he left his position and dived into the hole in the tunnel wall as the door hissed to a close behind him.

"Behind those containers!" she yelled. There was a very, very slight chance of survival, but it was something which they can depend upon at least in this situation where their chance of survival is minimal.

They were in the 'Cryogenic Containment Room'. It was a special room designed to maintain the temperatures well below freezing point to store different unstable or delicate but potentially disastrous particles. Should the temperature increase over a certain level in this room, the amount of energy which will be dissipated would be so great that the C4 crisis would appear like a speck of dirt. In reality, in order to escape from a plastic explosion they had bunkered inside a nuclear bomb, literally.

Their chances were slim to none and she knew that.

"Wait! We have to decrease the temperature as low as possible. The console is over there", she said pointing out towards a white touch screen panel completely covered with frost.

"If the blast doesn't kill us, the cold will freeze us to death."

"But if it goes above minus hundred degrees inside those canisters, all of Switzerland will be blown off the map."

"Then I'll do it."

Five... Four... Three...

Mercer scooted over to the other side of the room and wiped the icing off the console then swiped his finger down the virtual thermometer displayed on the screen to as low as it went, to minus 253 degrees Celsius. Obviously, that was the core temperature on the storage containers; still the cold they were facing was colder than anything both of them had seen. The room was not even designed for physical access. The door was mainly for the maintenance staff during inspections. It was humanly impossible to survive that much cold but they only need to last for a couple of seconds.

Two… One.

Running back to her Mercer had already felt the tremendous blast which the C4 gave out. He could imagine the heat and fire galloping outside the double insulated titanium reinforced doors. They sat on the ground, with their backs to the farthest wall, waiting. And then it happened. First, the door just convexed towards them with its bulge widening, then they heard the shrill noise of the metal tearing from the inside like a lonely cat crying in the jungle. They then realized that they had made a mistake. Although they were a bit far from the door, they were directly in front of it. Hearing the metal screeching as it did, Mercer knew that it would come at them with all its force, and speed. Instinctively, he threw Éllén to his right and seeing that there was no more space on her side, he threw himself the other way.

The door, with a final shrill cry as its epitaph, left the final hinges of the wall to which it was hanging on and bulleted towards them with the force provided by the blazing red hot fire behind it, and wedged on the wall behind them just a few inches from Mercer's head. It came at him just as he had jumped out of its trajectory. But things weren't over just yet. The blazing fire which fueled the door towards them, still searching for an exit, came at them with all its force. The red streaks of flame reacted with the ice white mist already dominant in the room to form steam which gave them a bit of relief from the oppressing cold. It came right up to their faces, not more than a few inches apart, and would have gone way ahead were it not for the air conditioning vent, half a meter ahead, which threw ice cold winds which acted as a curtain, a final blow to the raging inferno preventing it from coming any further.

A few minutes later the episode passed. Now realizing that they were freezing inside, they collected themselves and slowly walked out of the enormous room. Luckily, the cylinder containing the unstable particles like the T7 anti-deuterium species was secure and would not explode. If they did, they along with all of Switzerland and most of France would have blown of the map, just as she predicted.

The cold had made them sluggish. Even after they exited out of the big void where once there used to be an entrance and stepped out in the charred corridor. Though it was still burning hot, they were still shivering, rubbing their palms together.

Breathing a sigh of relief, "At last it's all over!"

"Not over yet."

"Why, they're all dead. No one can survive that blast."

"There can be more assassins. It's not safe here, not now. We need to go?"

"Where?" she asked rhetorically.

"Away."

"Bien.[1]"

11

Work Unfinished

5:31 PM
CEO, Office of Bearing-PetroTech
101st Floor

An unassuming call came to the office of Bearing-PetroTech Corporation. The call was made directly from the branch of the International Logistics and Support Agency, located in Milwaukee, Wisconsin, Iowa.

"Bearing-PetroTech, how may I help you?"

"This is Harry Torres, Regional Vice President, ILSA, Iowa. Sir Richard Meyers is expecting my call."

"Please hold." There was a momentous pause.

"Sir, there is a call for you from a Mister Torres, Line one." Crackled over the intercom.

The atmosphere in the room thickened with an air of tension, again. It seemed that whenever anything of that matter was spoken of, it only gave Richard an excess of anxiety and tension.

"What is the meaning of this, Harry?" He shouted on the receiver.

"Don't worry sir; this is a secure line." Torres ensured, relaxed.

"Do I take the operation to be a success?" Meyers dived straight to the point.

---

1. Okay.

"Well sir, not entirely." Torres informed sheepishly.

"Meaning?" Richard pounded.

"We were able to retrieve the backup disks on Project SORCE but a scientist Élénoré Bassét with the help of a security guard, a Mercer escaped the facility along with the copy of the data. Dr. Sasha was also found dead and many of our men were killed."

"Unacceptable! How could you let this happen? Mr. Torres, you must realize that not only the Jami initiative but all our present and future endeavors' success relies solely on this. Now tell your men to retrieve the data from the backup disks on the project and failure isn't an option! You hear me! Failure Not An Option."

"Yes sir. I understand completely. Our men are doing their best to locate Mercer and the scientist too."

"Once you do, eliminate him, but save the scientist, she might prove useful."

12

Running Interference

"Excusez-moi, mademoiselle?" Mercer communicated in perfect French accent.

"Oui?" The familiar female voice transpired from the speakerphone.

"We talked earlier on the phone. My card wasn't working, remember?"

"Oui monsieur." She greeted him as if he were an old acquaintance of her.

"I'd like to try another one." He requested.

"Bien."

"Yeah, it is a Master Card. 9745 8357 3347 5683." He stated.

"Please hold, monsieur." There was a minute of silence.

"Okay I'll hold."

"Yeah Sir, this one seems to be working…and the authorization pin?"

"It's four-eight-six-five."

"Okay, so what would be the name of the passenger?"

"Greener, Jeremy Greener."

"Okay… Mister Jeremy, your flight departs in two hours. The

details are being messaged to you. Thank you for using our mobile booking services. Happy journey!"

"Who's Jeremy?" Élénoré questioned him inquisitively.

"It appears, I am.", he replied in a cold voice. "Picked it off one of the Merc's pocket." He pointed to the bluish ocean green master card.

"Uh…okay. But, this is the tenth plane ticket that you've bought. Will you at least tell me what you're planning on doing?" Élénoré revolted.

"Those men, who were after us, were heavily armed. They had live feed, transceivers, gadgets, everything. Operations this big require some serious tactical support. Whoever is after us is a serious player. We need to tread carefully. The second they check those CCTV's, we'll be on the run for our lives."

"So what do we do?" Élénoré was getting tensed with the feeling of impending doom on her.

"We're going off the grid!"

"What?" Élénoré cried, baffled.

13

Inquisition

10:52 AM
233 South Wacker Drive

"Miss…you have an appointment?" The erotic brunette receptionist asked of the new arrival. "Wait… Wait…you can't go in there!"

But the newcomer was like an express train, nothing could stop her.

"Carl…we have a situation in the Lobby, tell Jimmy to check it out." Crackled over the transceiver hung over the belt of the security guard.

He was just outside the building located in 233 South Wacker Drive, eating his doughnut. A familiar voice buzzed in his earpiece. "Jimmy… We have a possible breach in security…there's a woman in the lobby heading towards the elevator banks, without checking in with the reception. See, what it is all about!"

No sooner did he hear the word 'situation', he rushed back to the building entrance. The doors were massive dark-tan translucent glass door with huge cut-glass door knobs. He pulled it towards him with his usual force and ran towards the bank of elevators.

"Jimmy here…I'm looking into it", his voice echoed back in the main security room of the building.

"Roger that", was the stern reply.

James aka Jimmy prided over the fact that there was not one security breach or theft under his watch. Save for his supervisor, he was highest in command, but he prefered working the grounds, and not sitting in the tiny surveillance control room.

"Target located…making contact."

"Ma'am, this is a private property, you can't be in here without an appointment."

The woman didn't so much as raise a finger.

"You wanna see my appointment…this is my appointment", she revealed the FBI badge clipped in her inside jacket pocket as she scrolled through the building's office directories.

101th Floor

As she located her target, she walked up to the elevators and pressed the call button. The elevator door opened with a familiar ring and she streamed inside. Turning towards the baffled security personnel who was now beginning to follow her, "hmm, your…um…*services* are no longer required."

"What?"

"You can go now." She replied with a sarcastic tone.

Who does she think she is? He wondered. Jimmy ran down back to the building directory, which she was just browsing to see where she was going.

Oh Crap!

"Control…this is James. The woman is heading to the 101th floor. She says she's FBI", he reported through his transceiver.

"What? You serious? You checked her credentials?" The stern but now agitated voice of his superior echoed through all the earpieces in the building.

"No…" Jimmy replied silently in a dull voice.

"James…could you be more dumb?" the superior deliberately berated him over radio to make him look bad.

"All points", the voice shouted giving orders to the rest of the units. "Converge on floor one-o-one…elevator three. Suspect is white female, Caucasian, blonde, wearing grey dress."

The door opened up on the coveted floor where the woman

received a well-anticipated response.

There was one man, waiting for backup, with his sidearm pointed at her.

"Identify yourself!"

The woman raised the badge.

"Identify yourself!" He retorted even more sternly.

She started making face as if she was disappointed by his response.

"Hodges here...I have her...waiting for backup." And as he reported it to his superiors, he moved towards her, pulling out the plastic handcuffs which he intended to strap her hands with, before dropping off to the police. But she was FBI. He wondered if he could do that.

Before he knew it, he found himself chocking for breath on the ground until she left her grip which she had tightly held around his neck. "I know you are doing your job and I even admire it", she said. "But it's for your own good that you stay clear of my way. Are we clear?"

There was no response.

"Are...we...clear?", she asked as she pressed harder.

"Clear... Clear", he replied, chocking, wanting to break free of the dead-lock.

"Good boy."

Then she dismantled the gun in front of him, to prove her authority over him. She pressed the button on the grip which ejected out the magazine and fell near her feet, pulled back the metal jacket over the gun, throwing out the sole bullet in the chamber, and then slid it off the top off the gun and threw both parts to different areas in the corridor and then walked off towards her destination.

"Sir...", a hoarse male voice crackled over the intercom in the CEO's office. The man cleared his throat. "We have a situation over here...there's a woman barging through the building heading towards the office. She's waving an FBI badge. We're running her CCTV footage through facial. She's already put down one man...we're out of position. We'll reach in three minute."

"Stand down your men, Steve", Sir Meyers ordered. "I'll handle it."

She walked down the L-shaped path in the corridor with long confident strides till she reached her destination.

Sir Richard Meyers, CBE

Chairman and CEO, Bearing Oil & PetroTech

She pulled the large tan wooden door away from her and stepped inside.

"Good day, Miss Summers", Sir Meyers greeted her, while reading a multi-page manuscript still printing in the printer next to him.

"Your office works fast, I see", she commented. "But not fast enough to stop me."

"Okay, Miss Summers. You've got my attention. What is it that you want from me?"

"Straight to the point", she remarked in impressive voice. "No small talk?"

"I don't prefer indulging in the normal pleasantries, unless required."

"You know it's only been weeks since my posting here till I hear your name. You're quite the notorious man, *Sir* Meyers."

"I try to live up to my reputation." Meyers chuckled.

"As you must already know they've launched another investigation against you." She informed him with a cunning smile.

"So..." he shrugged his shoulders. "They launch a dozen every year."

"And I'm running it."

"What is this then?" he laughed. "A courtesy call."

"Somethin' like that..."

"OK... I'll bite. What do you want, Miss Summers?"

"I think you know", she smiled playfully as she inspected his room carefully ...and its Special Agent!"

"I don't think I can trust you?"

"You can't...but here's the deal." She stretched out her arms as she peered out of the glass wall to her right. She noticed the black GenX with the FBI surveillance detail inside. "I've been cleaning the scum of the Earth long enough to understand that if you remove something, something else will take place. It's bound to get dirty; you can't keep the streets clean forever."

"So?"

"Now I think I'll take my piece of the pie."

"I don't think that *pie* is for you."

"Money is...."

"What is your offer?"

"You pay me ten times what you pay your usual FBI mole and I'll steer this investigation in your favor."

"This investigation, like many that started before it, will pass. Why should I pay for an FBI agent?"

"The reason is in your hands?" pointing to the manuscript which Richard held in his hands.

Richard already knew that she was too big a threat to act out there in the open. An unknown variable in the equation. A balance too delicate as it is. Snooping around she could discover something she is not supposed to. It was a risk he just couldn't take.

"Okay Miss Summers...." He began leaning forward.

"Aisha..." Summers interrupted.

"Miss Summers, you have yourself a deal. But next time make an appointment" pointing her to the door.

She strode off the room with her boots clanking on the ground while Meyers smiled knowing full well what just happened.

14

An Escape in Progress

"So? What's the plan?" Élénoré asked frantically as she followed Alec, a few paces behind him on the smooth concrete road outside the Geneva Airport.

"We're going to board a plane." He smiled playfully and his eyes glimmered.

"Which plane? You didn't book a single flight for me but a dozen for yourself!" Her legs were hurting. The soles of her heels were poking at her feet. The inch-step of her shoes was intermittently getting stuck in the pavement. She was getting frustrated. Mercer had his own plans and was not telling her much about it.

"Those are not for me", he replied. His eyes were searching keenly for something through the darkness. "Trust me!"

Trust me.

The words were enough for her to follow him to the end.

"This is it!" He yelled as anyone would do after getting a prize.

"What is it?" She yelled even harder. "Il n'ya rien de plus ici, sauf la poussière!"[1]

Indeed, there was nothing in that direction as far as she could see, at least nothing that could be seen by the naked eyes. All that she could see was pitch black darkness. Purple snowcapped mountain ranges shimmering at a distance. Even the heaven closed down its curtain, the clouds no longer able to bear the tragic events which

1. There is nothing over here, except dust!

were happening down there. Because of the dense cloud cover, they didn't even have the luxury of seeing through the moon light. The only light available was the light streaming brilliantly out of the airport ATC tower, but it was too far away to be of any help. But Mercer saw what he was searching for so vigorously. His eyes got accustomed to the darkness.

Élénoré noticed that Alec had left the concrete road and started walking on the dirt track defined by the black soil path, maybe two meters wide in between the field of lush green mountain grass.

"Look to your left", he remarked.

"What?" She shouted. "Can't you just tell me?"

"Look closely; you'll see it." Mercer smiled.

As she was walking, she leaned a bit forward and squinted hard trying to focus in the direction in which he had pointed out. She then was able to spot something, but was still unclear about what it was and how it was relevant to them. As they moved forward, she realized what exactly she was blindly gazing at. It was a metal gate, very old at that. It had a little bit of rust on it and matched perfectly with the fencing on both sides.

"Wow!" she exclaimed in amazement. "You could see that from way back there!"

"I have my ways." He explained with a smile. "Come on, follow me."

They ran briskly towards the same metallic door. Already, Élénoré had reached the top of her capacity. Both her legs were paining with a throbbing, shooting, impelling sting. Her lungs crying for rest. The extremely cold mountain temperatures were an added discomfort to her already restless state of mind. Her breathe was already irregular, tired, wheezing.

"I don't think I can climb that." She cried.

"Don't worry! Just stay back!" Mercer ordered.

"What are you going to do?" Élénoré asked inquisitively.

"Wait and watch." He smiled.

He pulled off the bag from his back, opened the zip and rummaged through the stuff.

"Where's the binary?" He asked himself.

"The what?" Élénoré was puzzled.

"Here it is!" Alec expressed with pride.

He pulled out a black colored tube and applied the green colored jelly on the lock which secured the chains and the gate together.

"This is CIA special issue. It can melt tough metals like re-enforced steel. This is made for cracking safes and stealing intel. It also comes in handy for melting locks because now I do not have to shoot it. It leaves no trail at all. It evaporates without leaving a single trace. Cool huh?" He said as the lock dissolved and its liquid remains fell on the ground, still reacting.

"Yeah it is." Élénoré was a scientist; so she had an inbuilt curiosity for such things. "You know I made something like this in my senior years but mine wasn't untraceable as I was never working for it to evaporate."

"Yeah.... yeah, you're a great nerd. I get that. Let's go! Now!" Alec urged with haste and satire.

They had been walking for quite some time when Éllén asked the question she'd been waiting to ask Alec for quite some time now. "Hey, you'd gone earlier to get something but you never told me what it was."

"You'll know soon enough." Mercer ensured.

Pulling out a five-seven fully automatic pistol from his carry bag he handed it to her saying; "Take it!" His tone was as serious as it could be.

"Are you serious?" She jerked.

"Don't worry, the safety's on." Alec assured.

"I need you to point it at people so that they get intimated by us."

"But why?"

"Because we have to, if we are to escape." He explained. "You'll see that...soon enough."

"Okay then."

"I hope you understand the gravity of the situation we're in. Everything depends on your performance out there." He told her, with both his arms comforting her shoulders.

She took the gun but with some hesitation in her mind.

The dirt track had already transformed into a brick road composed with gray colored crescent shaped bricks. Her heals again started getting jammed between the bricks, so she took them off and was about to throw them off but Mercer did not allow her to throw.

"Now you're getting paranoid", she ridiculed about his behavior.

"Hey!" he stopped, turned back, grabbing her arms tightly with both his war-chiseled hands and yelled. "Wake up! All your friends were murdered; they are all dead; each and every one of them. In CERN, of all places. How would you grade their security after what you saw back there? We...are the only ones alive. You saw them;

you know what they can do and you still say that I'm paranoid. They have enough technology to track your DNA to the ends of the Earth."

Éllén pushed him off of her, "Get off me! Of course, I know that. They *were* my friends, you crétin[2]...ugh..." she groaned. "Merde!"[3]

Alec wanted to apologize to her but he did not. He could not; not because he couldn't muster up courage to say the words to her, but because of the pre-eminent fact that they had absolutely no time at all. All the tension and stress was starting to get to him. Unlike anything before, this time he was not alone. He had to save her no matter what. Unable to say a single word he just moved on.

They reached the much smaller runway made especially for those new age personal transport carriers. Next to the runway, there was a single fueling station where a handful of people were filling up one such aircraft with the ridiculously expensive ATF Air Turbine Fuel.

This one will be perfect!

Reaching closer to the destination, Alec pulled out his favorite automatic weapon from his bag for himself, the dreaded Belgium VBR. Under the Personal Defense Weapon category, the weapon was both lethal and deadly; it's mere sight terrifying but nothing defensive about it, only aggression.

He then started attaching the long black suppressor to the end of the barrel of the PDW, changed the ammo clip and switched it from automatic towards safety but stopped at single shot mode.

"Stay behind me, okay." He warned her.

Moving closer to the bunch of workers, pointing the VBR at them he shouted.

"All of you...get the fuck on the ground!" He bellowed.

"What is happening?" the worker asked ignorantly.

"You're just being plane-jacked." He replied. "Fool!"

The short guy, who was filling by the ATF into the aircraft, began stepping down the ladder but Mercer stopped him midway. "You fill up the tank!" He commanded with outward anger.

"Oui, oui...monsieur." But kept stepping down the ladder.

"Didn't you fucking hear me?" he yelled in agitation.

"Oui, oui...no shoot!" He replied in a feeble voice. But he continued stepping down the ladder.

Mercer had had enough. Not able to take it anymore, he raised his weapon, pressing it close to his chest, peeping through the red-dot reticule.

---

2. Idiot
3. Shit!

"Three...two...one...you had your chance." He pressed the trigger; the bullet sprang out in a muffled scream. The projectile went ahead and got wedged in the ladder just beneath the worker's feet. "Next one will be much higher."

Seeing that Mercer might just kill the poor fellow, she stepped forward to intervene. Raising the pistol, she aimed it at him she shouted, "Foutez le camp de sauvegarder et de remplir le reservoir!"[4]

"Oui...no shoot!" He replied in fear for his life. He re-initiated the oil flow and the one next to the tanker opened up the valve.

"Can't you see that they don't understand English?" Éllén was much closer to those workers than Mercer was, so she heard what the man was saying, while he could not.

In the meantime, Mercer had been lining up the three ground crew workers behind the oil tanker. He had already put the plastic cuffs on their hands and ankles and now he was frisking them for their phones and employee walkie-talkies as he made them lie on the concrete tarmac on their bellies. He took their network cards from them and kept them with him, perhaps planning something for the future. After the tank was full, the short guy also came back along with Élénoré behind him; she pointed her pistol at him.

"Obtenez votre cul sur le terrain!"[5] She yelled at him and Mercer did the same with him as he did with the other crew.

"Now that this is done..." Mercer exhaled with a sigh. "Les gens qui sont derrière nous...."[6] He explained with the highest sense of urgency, explaining them the mess he had inadvertently put them in. "Peut apparaître comme si elles étaient par le gouvernement...."[7] He paused for breathe. "Ils ne sont pas du gouvernement et ils ne sont pas des gens sympas[8]...Ils sont des tueurs et ils vont tuer...vous le second, ils obtiennent ce qu'ils veulent![9] Le meilleur plan d'action pour vous est tout de rester loin de ce gâchis tous ensemble"[10]

Since he had brought them into this situation, he had given them a fair chance, a shot at their survival, which had a better prospect against their own if they just did as he told them. And even if they did not, collateral damage was bound to happen in such situations.

4. Get the fuck back up and fill up the tank!
5. Get your ass on the ground!
6. People who are behind us.
7. May appear as if they were government.
8. They are not the government and they are not nice people.
9. They are killers and they will kill...you the second they get what they want!
10. The best course of action for you is to stay away from this mess together.

Admittedly, he was not that cynical, at least not for a very long time. But in situations like these being cynical is all that keeps you alive.

"Come on…let's go, we have no time as it is." They ran towards the plane, leaving the ground crew behind.

"You did good back there." He said as he securely closed the folding door of the aircraft. "I know." She smiled back.

Just as Alec pivoted the lock on the door, the neon fluorescent lighting came to life. The interiors were plush and pristine. Alec quickly paced towards the cockpit, sat on the captain's seat and just as quickly began tinkering with the vast array of buttons, switches, and toggles as he flipped through the pages of the flight manual for the Solar Impulse aircraft.

At first Élénoré stood by the thin door which separated the cockpit from the rest of the aircraft, but slowly, hesitantly, she came inside and stood behind the co-pilot's seat but then went ahead and sat in it.

Mercer pulled up the aircraft's two-way headset and positioned it properly on his head.

"Cointrin Air Traffic Control." Mercer said. "This is Private Charter Hotel-Bravo-Sierra-India-Golf. Requesting permission for taxiing to private runway seven."

"Solar Impulse charter HB-SIG you are cleared to start, when ready taxi to private runway seven." The voice crackled into the radio headsets. "Roger." Mercer responded.

Mercer could see the ground crew from his window. There was a moment of hesitation in him. He realized that if he would leave them there, incapacitated, they face a grave danger to their life but if he would set them free, remove their shackles, they would, in all likelihood, report to the authorities. He thought it best to leave things as it were. His mission priorities remained.

Slowly, he pushed the lever on his right forward. Simultaneously, the small aircraft began moving forward. The CGD screen which was in front of him told him exactly where runway seven was and even marked the path with a light green light.

Luckily for him, the detailed flight plan which is to be submitted to the Air Traffic Control was already filed in the aircraft's pre-flight log. So, the detailed itinerary of the charter was displayed boldly on the CGD screen. Had that not been the case, he would have had a lot of difficulty influencing the ATC[11] to allow him to access international

11. Air Traffic Control

airspace.

Many private charters from France and Switzerland usually travel the English Channel to United Kingdom. Mercer saw that as the best opportunity. The tiny expanse of international airspace between the two countries was all that was needed for his tiny carrier to make its escape. If he tried to fly in any other country without prior permission, he would, no doubt, be considered as a terrorist threat.

Therefore, he picked out an aircraft that was already being fueled. He deduced that the plan must be prepared for departure, most likely for international travel, and also likely, crossing the English Channel. Luckily, his hunch was right.

Now, the aircraft had reached the start of the runway.

"This is HB-SIG. This is a Priority-One International flight scheduled from Cointrin to Heathrow. Requesting departure instructions." He read out the flight manifest from the CGD screen. "And access for international airspace."

"Acknowledged." The Air Traffic Controller responded. "You are cleared to proceed for take-off. Fly heading Zero-Three-Zero and climb and maintain 9000 feet on QNH."

"Roger that."

Élénoré's heart started pumping heavily. She quickly began buckling every safety strap on her seat as she nervously began fiddling with her fingers. Mercer turned his head towards her and with another playful wink pushed the lever to her right to full-throttle. The engine's mechanical hum increased to a deafening noise.

BBC News World Wide Broadcast

Breaking News. Good Evening, I'm Sarah Caster and Welcome to World Watch. This just in. The officials at Cointrin International Airport confirmed that the two prime suspects of the CERN bombing did in fact escape from Airport, through a separate runway set aside for private charters. In the investigation, it has been revealed that the suspects did provide all the necessary documents for their departure. It was only after the bombing was being investigated and the Airport Security footage analyzed when they realized what had happened. This incident puts a serious question at the level of security international airports present. For starters, who watches those tapes, who scrutinizes the passengers, of even private aircraft? Even if we secure the airports home, how are we to determine the security abroad? What are we letting inside our house, everyday? We have with us Zack Butler, security consultant and expert in the field. Zack, in your mind what is the…

15

Bottom of the Sky

"We're here." Alec told Éllén with the same playful smile.

"What is here? There is nothing but ocean; only ocean all around us."

"No…we are here." Pointing at the analog sensors aboard the aircraft and then reaching out for something.

"Hey! What are you doing?" She freaked out at him. "Did you not say that they can track us through that?"

Before taking off on the runway, Mercer had ripped off the digital sensors on the aircraft along with the communications panel. They were flying blind; invisible to any Air Traffic Controller and invisible to all aircraft near them. Therefore, all the warning systems were unreliable. Other pilots would not even know about their presence in the sky; that is why he flew the plane well below the normal altitude below cloud cover and far from heavy settlements but most importantly away from other planes. Otherwise while descending other aircraft may reach the same altitude and possibly end up in an imminent collision trajectory. But now he was re-connecting those same digital signal systems back.

"What could be the reason", she wondered.

"I'm charting a course just some nautical miles off the coast of Good Hope." He explained to her.

"Okay then."

"But we are bailing out here." He informed.

"What?" it was like she was hit with a splash of burning hot coffee on her face. *Brazilian coffee.*

"Wh—Here?" she asked him in a high pitched voice. "Have you completely lost it?"

But Mercer was quite serious. "Listen…the best course of action for us right now is to make them think that this is a failed escape and that we are dead."

"Sooner or later, they are gonna catch our drift; then what?" Although she did not have the fear of heights, yet jumping off a plane, naturally, was a crazy prospect for her.

"Okay. I'm ready" She reassured herself.

"In about ten minutes." He assured.

Saying that, Mercer rose up from his extremely uncomfortable dull gray captain's seat of the not-so-majestic but extremely advanced HB-SIG and caustiously ambled back to the tail section of the plane. A successor of the longstanding time tested series of Solar Impulse aircrafts which did not even need any fuel as its advanced aeronautical monolithic design and cutting edge solar technology made it quite adept in making infinite circles around the Earth provided the Sun was above it. And when flying in dark, it had an endurance of seventy hours due to its comparatively small fuel tank but highly efficient engine. Riddled with high end features like Auto-Nav, Intelligent Input, and advanced VI interface, the bird was one of the best models that money could buy. Mercer walked slowly through the dimly lit aisle of the private chartered aircraft. He had left the plane in the slightly capable hands of his co-pilot who had, just minutes ago, taken a crash course in piloting a plane.

"Hold her steady!" He instructed her as he made his way out the cockpit chamber, opening the doubly bolted re-enforced door.

Walking back, he reached the washroom located just above the cargo bay of the plane. Tracing the circumference of the space around it he reached the dock where the earlier stewardess had stored the drinks and refreshments. He stooped down, staring fiercely below the dock at a rectangular plank of upholstery covered panel which jumped at him more than its immediate environment.

He pulled out his grey ceramic knife and wedged it behind the cover. Applying all his brute force, slowly but steadily, he was able to tear open and rip out the panel from the wall revealing a dark and empty void behind it which in all probability would lead him into the tail section of the cargo bay.

The tail section, where all the wiring of any passenger or private or military aircraft coalesces, was the target of his journey. The high end aircraft had a pressurized cabin, like any other plane. And such pressurized airplanes have a safety mechanism which prevented the doors, emergency or otherwise, to be opened from above fifteen thousand feet. The plane always has to touch down before, for the doors to open. This was a luxury which Mercer could not afford. The bird which Élénoré was currently flying had, already been reported stolen, highjacked. And only one inference is always taken out from a plane highjacking—a terrorist attack. No country in their right mind would allow such a plane to fly or land in their territory. Most likely, they would simply prefer shooting it out of the sky. He had to bail out. It was the only way. But the plane would not allow it. Although Mercer had disabled the digital control, he still had to override the old-school backup security measures before he could ditch his magnificent escape carrier.

Holding the rails of the serving platform above, Mercer heaved his body and threw himself into that same empty void which he had been gazing for half a second. There was no time to waste. He quickly explored for the Central Control System which was located in the tail section along with other crucial pieces of equipment like the orange Black Box and Communications Relay. Reaching the small console window behind the blind side of the dark chamber, which was the only semblance of a light source in that dark compartment, he muscled his way through the jam packed bay.

Now, inches from the terminal, he began gazing at a complex and ridiculously intricate electronic system, which was ensuring that atleast the plane maintained its altitude in air. One mistake could mean the plane bulleting through the sky like a burning fiery meteorite. Mistake was not an option. He began running his hand from wire to wire, from one end to the other, trying to understand the genius behind it, and its working. What he needed to do was somehow depressurize the cabin, which would fool the electronic systems onboard that the plane had landed and allow the doors to be opened, which would not have happened given that they were flying at twenty-five thousand feet above mean sea level.

After careful examination and scrutiny, he stripped off a wire from its socket in console, only to the effect that the whole bird began reverberating like a screeching crow with resounding echoes of sirens and alarms which resonated all through the plane. The plane started shaking heavily like a mad bull in a ranch. He even felt the drops of sweat on his face slide up instead of down. Quickly, realizing the gravity of his mistake, he pushed the wire back in and secured it tightly. The plane regained its vector and altitude and almost immediately all the sirens stopped.

Mercer had once taken a course in Aviation Engineering which was required for him to complete one assignment in his past. But times had changed, the technology had changed. He tried his best, to cope up, to relate. Another wire at the other end of the panel caught his attention. Without giving a minutes thought, he ripped it out of its holder as he thought of handling the repercussions of his actions later. As he did, he soon began to feel, the slight draft of air around him and slow but steady decrease in pressure.

Completing his objective, he retraced his steps back the way he came, pulled himself up the hole beneath the serving dock and re-entered the cabin, which was now in the process of depressurization. Turning towards the aisle which led back towards the cockpit, he noticed the yellow plastic oxygen masks which hung from the translucent pipes connected to the board overhead. Their window had decreased. Not a minute's time to waste.

He ran towards the cockpit with a hurried gait and decisively opened the door. As he stepped inside he observed the frail, restless image of his co-pilot who seemed bewildered and perplexed as if she had seen hell. Then he realized what she had to undergo moments earlier when Mercer had pulled the wrong wire, but there was no time for apologies.

Élénoré tried to convey what she had been through but found herself stumped and at a loss of words to say.

"Don't worry! It was on Auto-Nav!" He tried to console her. That whatever happened was not her fault. Not specifically pointing to what his role was in all the commotion. "Come on! We...have to go!" He instructed urgently. Slowly, even he was finding it hard to breathe and so did Élénoré, only she found it a little bit harder. He reached the knob near the door and opened what appeared to be a closet, which was filled with parachutes and oxygen tanks for emergency escape. Mercer pulled out one out of the five present there and two of the oxygen tanks along with their strap and holder. Hastily, he moved towards Élénoré, still shocked and stunned, pulled her out of the captain's seat and motioned one of the oxygen mask and tank towards her and asked her to wear it, tightly. Then he also did the same.

Completely clad in uniform, both Alec and Élénoré walked down the same familiar aisle as they reached the center of the corridor, where Alec came to a stop. Next to the luxurious ergonomic chairs with leather upholstery, tables covered with bone china cutlery and gold-plated silverware, there was an emergency window, quite bigger in comparison, compared to the rest, with a brilliant red bar on it.

"USE IN CASE OF EMERGENCY" was written on it.

Nearing the exit, Mercer spaced his legs wide apart to get a supportive stance for leverage, and then with all his might and force, began thrusting the lever downwards. With a frictional hum, the lever opened.

The emergency exit in the middle of the plane was the perfect exodus point for the specific carrier. Clear from the tail wings and the turbine engine, it provided the perfect staging for their exit.

By the time, Mercer had also strapped himself and Élénoré into the parachute satchel which he had pulled out along with the oxygen tanks.

Reaching the door as best as he could, in his extremely uncomfortable attire, he pushed open the emergency door which after opening established a tremendously strong draft. Élénoré standing, in front of Mercer, felt as if she was being pulled towards the exit and soon as she caught a glimpse of the blue world beneath her, froze in fear.

"No! No! No! No!!" She yelled with a deafening shriek, full of terror, but Mercer had dived forward and out of the aircraft and took her down with him.

12:10 PM
Location Unknown
Grid Co-ordinates. 23°39'21.0456" South, 43°7'31.6488" West
Somewhere off the coast of Rio de Janeiro

Éllén found herself plummeting towards Earth. Alec was right behind her as both of them were strapped tight to the same parachute, strong harsh winds hitting her from all directions. Plumeting down aiming at nothing but the bluish-green oceans was definitely far scarier.

The strong wind was constantly lashing down on her. "What are you waiting for?" She squealed pointing at the plastic handle as best as she could. The wind was freezing cold. She could feel her face turn to stone.

"We have to reach the correct altitude." Alec expressed.

Her head was spinning, the wind did nothing but increase her dizziness. She had lost track of which direction was up and which direction was down. It was blue everywhere and the fine line dividing the horizon had blurred into obscurity.

"I'm scared", Élénoré cried.

"Hey! Look at me. I'm not going to let anything happen to you...Okay?" Mercer assured.

She raised her head and looked keenly at his bright radiant black eyes. And suddenly she felt secure. No fear. There was something about him, his face, his lips, especially his crystal clear black eyes which resembled a black tourmaline pendant. She locked her eyes to his and stopped looming about these petty things. One thing she learned for sure was that Mercer had a plan; he always had a plan and he would not let her be in harm's way. She only gazed thoughtlessly in his eyes so much so that she did not even realize that Mercer had deployed the parachute and only came to know about that when he asked her, "Could you hold this for a minute?" handing over the yellow colored hand bag with black and red stripes which he had brought from his brief trip. He had still not told her what was in that bag which had had been carrying all the way from Switzerland.

She tightly grasped the strap of the bag with her left hand and with her right hand she tightly grabbed her arm around Mercer's waist. Mercer tried to maneuver the parachute as best as he could but in vain; he had lost his touch and apart from the most recent injuries, he was also wounded a bit while deploying the parachute due to the jerk he got on his shoulders due to the sudden and drastic, decrease in the acceleration and velocity. It was nothing serious but it did hinder his capability to maneuver the parachute. After becoming a bit comfortable with their descent he took the bag back from Éllén. It had a plastic handle, a black-red plastic handle which he ripped off with full force then he loosened the grip which held the strap so tightly and let the bag fall towards the ocean. Then turning his attention back to the two black straps which hung close above his head which he had been using to control the movement of their parachute. Using them once again, he worked really hard to try and stay just above where he had first dropped his yellow carry bag. Even experienced professionals found it hard sometimes and so did he.

Successfully, he was able to stay just atop what now appeared to be a floatable raft. The black and red stripes clearly marked the edges of boat. A sudden updraft threw them off their course, by just maybe a few meters causing them to land into the chillingly cold waters.

Cold again…they thought.

They paddled through the icy waters making their way to the boat.

Every muscle in her body, shivering with hypothermia, begged to simply tear Mercer's head off. "Trust me! Trust me you say?" she remarked sarcastically. "You didn't do one thing to earn my trust. Always trust me, trust me, and trust me. Don't you ever say 'trust me' to me ever again!!"

Éllén was truly irritated. She had gone way past her patience barrier. Her hair soaking wet, went haywire. Perfectly confused about everything that was happening around her she was unable to get aboard the floatable. Mercer, on the other hand, was quite adept when it came to his skill set. Quickly he heaved through his huge arms and pulled himself; he then turned back, grabbing her hand, he pulled her on the boat.

Phew!

"I'm never going to do that ever again…in my life!" She remarked as she took her spot on the raft. Mercer laid back for a while but realizing that it was time, he went back to the motor jet in-built in the raft. He glanced at his ChromeX watch.

Perfect.

That was the word which echoed in his head as he looked up at the sky, with his palm to shield his eyes, he gazed at the lonely sun which glistened brightly in the hemisphere.

Just perfect!

He wanted to say it out loud.

The motor was a solar operated one, with those new-age carbon alloy infused silicon wafers which can operate even in dim sunlight, not that he had to worry about it as the Sun was shining brightly overhead. He commanded the motor as he began steering the boat and they steadily began skidding in speed on the same cold icy waters.

A lot needs to be done, for sure. Mercer thought.

16

Motel in Brazil

Vida Nocturna Motel
Favela do Muquiço

The past few days' events had taken their toll on Élénoré. She did not even know if her step family was safe or not. At least if she knew what happened to them and then she could chalk it off to fate and try to accept that what had happened, just happened. Whether it was good or bad! Or at least that was what she thought; not realizing that after all that had happened to her, something like this would be like the last wave which was certain to break the dam. People, unable to gauge their capacity, take things too far, leave them depressed and turned down. But not her, as long as Alec was with her, she would still have a glimmer of hope that this storm would subside for her.

It was the time for the carnivale. The streets were packed full with people dressed in strange costumes, wearing masks some with feathers and some with face paint.

Cloaked within the crowd was a single couple who were walking in just the opposite direction of the crowd, struggling to get past. The man had a diesel carry bag on his shoulders and the woman had blonde hair. They paned left from the crowd inside a small, partially demolished, two-storey motel. There was a sly looking man standing behind the counter, he had a small stature, and a slight hunched back which had developed over the years. Seeing that he had new guests, he was filled with ecstasy.

"Mr. Hunt, it's been a long time since I last saw you. Ten years, I believe", he said greeting his new found guests with a sense of familiarity.

"Hello Pietro! I see you haven't changed a bit or the motel." Mercer greeted. "Yeah, it's just as I last saw it; although I would have condemned the building on the first chance I got." He answered bluntly.

"Never mind that, sir", he squawked, trying to change the subject. "I believe you are going to book a room or two of my humble abode."

"Maybe...."

"What? Why?" Pietro cried.

"As I recall, there was a certain someone who informed on me to the police about my whereabouts, during my last visit. Were I not in much trouble, I would have burned down your tiny little motel, right off the map of Rio." Mercer scorned.

"Nothing gets by you, sir. But in my defense, the reward offered was pretty bulky though I was unable to collect. I tell you, corruption in this country—People would do anything to make money, even if their actions would hurt someone else." He announced, unaware of the irony in his own words.

"Uhha!" Mercer chuckled.

"Still, you have my word that you may rely on me. I promise."

"That is the case then, I brought something to sweeten the deal; you still prefer coke to meth?" He smiled with a smug look producing a packet containing five grams of coke which he handed out to Pietro.

"Oh sir, you know me all too well", he said joyfully and as he did he ran out to the back of the counter and after careful consideration, selected a pair of keys from the bunch which were hanging on the wall. Then he brought it back to his tenants and handed them over to the woman saying, "The lift has been out of commission for a while, so you will have to take the stairs. Room 9. It is the best we have; it has a double bed, even has a sofa and a TV. Water is not coming yet, but I'll get it fixed by the morning. I see that you do not have any luggage; good as I do not have a bell boy." He chuckled.

They took the key and followed the path pointed to them by the receptionist.

Room no. 9 was a suite compared to the other rooms in the building. Save for the fact that the paint was starting to come off in some spots, and the faucets were not working, the room was decent enough. There were no pest infestation like in the other rooms and there were clean sheets on the bed, fresh pillows. Staying in such a place was a small price to pay for the luxury of not needing to show their credentials during check-in. Élénoré, who used to marvel at the lifestyle Alec had, despite being a security guard, found the room below his standard, but then…when in Brazil.

"Trust me, I'd rather sleep in a morgue than a place like this but I cannot take you with me to a morgue?"

"Yes, you cannot…." She replied emphatically.

"Now you rest over here for a while. I'll go out and check for exit points, just to be safe. Close the door after me and don't open the door unless it is me and I say 'Quarks'."

He winked as he stepped out of the room saying this. Élénoré followed him to the door and closed all the latches on the door. Until this moment, her brain was functioning on autopilot. She did everything as Alec asked her to do. She started circling about the room in a fast pace, clenching her teeth as she did when she was under stress. Maybe if I had just called the police, then and there, all this would have been over. "What should I do now? I am stuck thousands of miles away from my home, my family and my friends. At least I'm not here alone, Alec is here with me. He will save me no matter what. Maybe I should just lie down it has been hell of a day…." Thinking that she decided to take a nap. She stopped her restless walking, sat down on the edge of the bed and swung back, slowly closing her eyes to rest.

17

Set & Match

"Here!" Aisha remarked with a sense of pride.

"What the devil *is* this?" James asked staring at the flash drive which he picked up in his hands.

"All the proof you need." She smiled closing the blinds of the window.

Valerie was quite impressed. It had hardly been twenty-four hours when he gave her the assignment.

"I knew I chose the right man...uh woman for the job."

He twisted the cover and wedged the miniscule drive into the jack placed on his desk. The machine hummed in a rhythmic tone, two slating chrome-textured rods emerged from the desk. After they raised to their full height, a green desktop appeared in between them which blurred into the familiar blue log-in screen.

There was the iconic FBI logo in the backdrop alongside the words

FEDERAL BUREAU OF INVESTIGATION

Logging in, the computer did its routine start-up scan of the computer.

Norton Internet Security

[F:] NEW DRIVE DETECTED

NO THREATS FOUND

He scrolled the cursor to the drive icon in the sidebar. There was but one file. '000000001.mov'.

What could it be?

He double clicked the singular video file. It opened and as it played out the spark in his dimmed eyes grew ever more readily. In the past as an agent, he would always get the work done...whatever the objective. But the field agents these days as he so eloquently put it "They can talk the walk, but they can't walk the talk." But Aisha... he had high hopes for her.

Guess I was wrong.

"Aisha...Aisha...Aisha." Valerie leaned back on his chair. "You still don't get it, do you?"

"Get what? This is all you need."

"Normally, it'd have been more than enough, but not in this case."

"Wh-What? Why?"

"Many people think they are above the law; that we can't touch them."

"So? We now have probable cause to subpoena their books!"

"This guy's literally untouchable by us. He has serious political coverage not only in our country but also from many others. He has enough power to stone-wall the President."

"But this is video proof that he is bribing an FBI agent and admitting the fact that he has moles in the agency."

Valerie slammed his fist on his mahogany desk. "Aren't you listening to me? I can't have the OPR conducting their Bureau wide inspection! I need those agents even if they are compromised. Secondly, your evidence is weak. He will provide fake documents proving your video is doctored. He can claim that you put him in that situation where he had to accept into giving the bribe. I mean, let's face it. He's not offering the bribe, is he? *You* are giving him the offer. He can go on to say that you were pressuring him to accept your offer, otherwise you'd put false evidence against him...like this. In fact, due to your recklessness, he can also provide the same conversation, in video keeping you as the protagonist where you ask him for bribe and claim that you are a renegade agent. But you don't need to worry about that, I'll vouch for your insane actions."

"You are saying that I can't even put this into evidence?"

"Listen to my words...carefully...If you bring this to the investigation, he'd skate on it, and when all's said and done he'll come down on you like 'Hell Hath No Fury.'"

"You've got to be fucking kidding me. If this case is so booby-trapped then why the fuck did you give it to me?"

"Because you remind me of me when I was a field agent, and also because you are the only one I can trust."

Aisha was lost. She did not know what she could do.

"Have you ever played chess?"

"What?"

"The question is quite simple. Do...you...play...chess."

"Yeah."

"Are you good at it?"

"Better than anyone here, I bet." But as she paused to think she realized something. "But you already know that. You have seen me play, which begs the question why'd you ask me such a strange question in the first place."

"There's one thing that you've got to understand. You are no longer in South Boston. And no longer against niggers and gangbangers. Now you're against a bigger league so you have to act like such. Your aggressive methods won't work here. You've got to plan your steps carefully. Sit down."

"Now that I can completely trust you, let me give you something."

He turned back to an array of cabinets behind him, and opened the safe tucked away underneath them, entering the access pin. The door hissed open. There were many files tucked inside, many from various agencies. Aisha could spot the CIA Confidential Letterhead on one of them. But the prized file was hidden way under them. He pulled out the bulky collection of documents and handed it over to her.

As she briskly glanced over the contents of the package she realized what she was against.

"Read it. Study it. Analyze it. You have no idea what kind of a man he is...and what he is capable of. I asked you about chess. Anything relevant he does is like a chess move, and he already has the advantage. But eventually something will fall out, a wrong move. Then you strike with the finisher. Understand?"

"Yes sir."

"Good. Now it's obvious that he's playing you right now, but eventually he'll give you tasks to check to see if you're really on board. Do as he says, but when the chance comes, strike back at him with all you've got. What I need is something monumental. Something which will send everyone who is covering for him, running...to save their own skin. Then all his political coverage will come for nothing."

"I'll get right on it."

"As you should. Remember, it's a game you've never played!"

18

The ol' Days

Barra de Francesco
Favela do Muquiço

There were intermittent waves of chattering, applause and commotion. On the far corner, there was a fairly big television set, and on that Copa América match between Argentina and Uruguay was playing out and the fans drinking in the bar cheering mercilessly for either one of the two teams playing. A few minutes ago, as he was about to step into the bar, four local cops were dragging out two drunk fans for starting a bar brawl. The argument obviously was about which of the two teams was better than the other. As the cops berated those guys out of bar, Mercer tipped down his head instinctively hoping that the cops wouldn't recognize him from the mug shots which were sent out to all the departments when he last visited Brazil. The bus stations, markets, and police stations had his face all over the place but that was very long ago and things were very different now.

One of the cops on his side glanced at his face but did not pay any attention to him thinking that he's some foreigner who has come here to score some cheap weed so he ignored him.

"El Cóctel del Diablo."[1] He asked the local bartender as he sat down comfortably on one of the stools in front of him.

The bartender, quite famous all around for his mad multitasking skills, was busy watching the match while his hands were busy cleaning the cocktail shaker. Many people including Mercer were witness to the fact that there had not been a time where he was doing at least two to three things at a time. It was his habit, his tendency; something he could not control. There was not much action around him as it used to be in the early days; the days when Killer used to be around.

"El diablo azul? La última vez que me enteré de que la bebida...."[2] Then it hit him.

Could it be? The bartender wondered.

"My man! I always thought if I would ever see one of you guys again. How's rest of your team? Did they make it?"

"Yeah...they did at that time. But you know how it is in our lives. You can't even be sure if you are gonna be able to wake up the next day. Anyway, some of 'em survived, some didn't. But now I've gotten used to deaths."

The bartender realized that he had hit a wrong note. "Sorry I asked that. I heard about that...and...about Christina." He apologized.

"Never mind that...tell me, did my drink take off?" Mercer asked inquisitively. The Blue Devil cocktail was a product of his creative genius. But he left so fast, and never looked back, he never got the opportunity to see its success.

1. The Devil Cocktail.
2. The Blue Devil? The last time I heard that drink.

"It did but with a different name—Marina." The bartender chuckled.

"How have things changed since I left?" he asked him in a prickly dim tone.

"Things are definitely different. Winston Churchill once said, History...is written by the victors. But history is full of shit!" He replied in the same dim tone. "They should probably erect a statue in your name; after all...it's because of you that they gained power. They make all the promises but they don't do squat. America got a more reliable government...a more controllable...weak government. I tell you man, I thought that we did the right thing but I'm not so sure anymore."

"What we did was good for America." He asserted.

"Yeah...I know. God bless America and all that shit!" He remarked sarcastically. "Look...around, don't these people deserve something good for once in their lives. The Capitán was at least doin' something."

"The Capitán was going to spark another world war." He replied sternly.

"Maybe...maybe...we will never know." He was somewhat angry with himself; for what he had done in the past. "All I'm saying is I've seen the rest of the world and I don't think that they deserve more than these people do."

Christopher Marquez, Ex-Navy SEAL had been posted in Rio for as long he could remember. He was a part of remote operatives commissioned to infiltrate different countries... mixing up with the locals. He was posted in Brazil for the obvious reason; his ethnicity, Spanish-Colombian descent. After the assassination contract of Capitán Javier Del Mundo, he returned back to the States, and then went abroad to various places on various missions. But he took a shine for Brazil that he returned back permanently and took up the same job as a bartender which he worked on as a cover. He missed Brazil... he missed the dirt...the people...the girls...everything was almost like calling him back.

"Past is dead...future is overrated. Live in the present; that's what's good for you." Mercer clarified.

"I know man...I know." Marquez complied.

"How are things looking?" Mercer asked, jumping straight to the point.

"Bad...very bad for you. Every Three-letter agency is searching for your trail which supposedly gets cold in South Atlantic. With you, it's always either MIA or KIA. Tell me, how many times have you died since I last saw you?" he chuckled. "I've lost count."

"Off course…tell me, how it feels to be on the run…again. Not that easy, huh. You are getting older, technology is getting smarter…street cams, thermal signatures and all that tech. It'll really be something if you get out of this one alive. With that girl of yours…survival is virtually impossible."

"What do you mean?" He looked surprised.

"Come on Mercer, you know the trouble you're in. That's the reason you came to Rio and not to Langley, that's the reason you think all your aliases are burnt. You…my dear friend are not telling me everything 'cause you think I'll shake off my hands from your sordid affairs. I had expected little bit of trust from you Killer…but then again…you don't trust anyone…do you?"

"So, what do you know?" Mercer quizzed.

"What I know? All I heard is back-alley rumors. After all… I don't get the 'Agency Periodical'…but you will be interested in what I've heard."

"Out with it, man" Mercer replied with a sense of urgency.

"The Agency has issued a Burn Notice. All ties with Langley discredited and all your missions, transcripts redacted. Word on the street is that you are in possession of a bomb or something very advanced which you supposedly stole after you allegedly *single-handedly* murdered the scientists in the CERN bombing. So…you tell me Killer or should I say 'Alec Mercer'…what should I believe?" He asked Killer after the long synopsis of Mercer's predicament.

"They can't pin it all on me…people will never buy it!"

"Whoever is behind this cover up is more than connected." He stressed 'cover up' with a visual hand quote. "They are feeding the stories like crazy and the media is eating it up. According to the CIA, this is the first time that you've emerged after you had gone MIA two years ago in Nepal. They have no idea that you were in Geneva, as if! On top of all that…the bomb scare is causing panic and frenzy all across the world. UN is currently in DEFCON 2. All agencies, everybody are on high alert. No way in hell you are going to enter the States through an airport. The only person who could vouch for your actions…your beloved General…he's gone AWOL. Nowhere to be seen."

"Bomb? I have no bomb!" Mercer specified.

"So that's what you say, but whom to believe?" He asked rhetorically.

"I need your help man. These people cornered me over here. It won't take them long before they're able to zero in on my exact location and storm in. Now...I need two passports for these pictures; stolen identities, nothing fresh. The people who are chasing are smart and connected. They sniff faster than a bloodhound."

"No problem...easily obtainable. Would you like some cash to go with it?"

"Cash...I have. But all my cards are frozen. I've been using the attackers' plastic, but I'm pretty sure that it's burnt by now."

"You didn't change one bit...still salvaging whatever you can get...guess it's what keeps you alive." He smiled. "Okay...it's gonna take some time but I'll get you the plastic, linked to the same alias."

"It's what kept me going." He laughed. "I also need plane tickets to Rome."

"I heard Marvin's stationed there. Hope you are not planning to meet Marvin," he asked clenching his teeth. "Damn it...Killer, that's the first place they'll check. Use your brain and stay clear of that place."

"It's a risk I have to take. You book connecting flights through different accounts. From Rio to anywhere...but then to Rome." Mercer specified.

"At least tell me that you've got a plan." He asked with concern.

"I'm working on it." Mercer stressed.

"You want my advice?" Marquez ejaculated carefully.

"Sure." Mercer said in a non-chalant fashion.

"When traveling in troubled waters..." he quoted.

"Sail towards the eye of the storm..." Mercer finished the quotation. An old sailor's saying popular among the Navy and the SEAL's but appropriate for all situations.

"Find the eye of the storm and you shall find your answers."

"Now go. I'll need some time to prepare this. I'll contact you when it's done."

"And watch your back...there's collateral damage wherever I go."

"Don't worry. I ain't planning to stay here for long. Now that I've made contact with you, I'm gonna get off the grid."

"Good."

"Now pay up before you go." Christopher pointed towards the empty tumbler.

19

Global Collateral

UK Security Service (MI5) Headquarters
Thames House
Millbank, London

"Priority package Intercepted." A monotonous feminine voice stated.

"Acknowledged. Informing the office of the Director General." The station's chief analyst responded.

"What it is?" Hewitt growled on the receiver. "I was not to be disturbed!" He yelled at his incompetent secretary, for he had been interrupted during an important and confidential debrief with the Home Secretary and the gunslingers at MI6.

"It's the chief analyst sir. He requests your immediate presence." His secretary replied cautiously.

"What is it about?" Sir Charles enquired, trying to gauge the direness of the situation.

"He says it is about Operation Flagstaff." His secretary replied.

There was a moment of silence. Hewitt disconnected his phone call. "Excuse me gentlemen...." He addressed the occupants of majestic suite inside the Home Office. "It appears I will have to take your leave." Hewitt announced as he rose up sharply from his grand mahogany chair. For a moment, he was lost in the old Victorian style decoration of the suite in a fairly modern building, in the crimson red paint, and the collection of Gustav Klimt wrapped around in golden frames, in the centuries old room freshener which radiated an essence of wax diluted with natural herbs like cinnamon and rose. The man on the left of him was not particularly pleased with the intrusion during his debrief. The Home Secretary had been keenly observing Sir Charles Hewitt's behaviour especially after he had received that phone call. Sir Charles demeanour indicated that the matter was serious.

"Off course...Sir Hewitt." The Home Secretary replied, seated as he was, "Though I expect to know the emergency which forces you leave our presence."

"Certainly sir." Charles replied.

With long striding steps, he marched out of that room. As he left, his words still resonated in the room. "Patch me through...I'm on my way."

20

Élénoré

Beauvais Residence
Residential Quarters
Organisation européenne pour la recherche nucléaire, Genève

"Don't worry dear; I will be home even before you will take the chicken out of the brochette. And one day I'll teach you the real French cuisine." These were the last words which her father spoke to her. Ever since her parents got divorced, she used to take care of her father in ways which she could like arranging dishes in the dishwasher, keeping track of his appointments, etc. When her father was at work; sometimes she'd go to her friend's house to spend time with them. After coming back home, she always liked waiting for her father even when he was late; as they could not spend much time together. Normally, her father would cook the food in the house; he was a great cook apart from being a great scientist. But when he would come back home late, she would serve him food which she managed to cook. Both of them would sit on the dining table, say their prayers, and spend some time together. Even when he'd already eaten his dinner in the mess and her cooking was not very good, he would eat it all up with a smile on his face to make her happy. "Tomorrow, my dear, I will teach you how to cook real French cuisine" he would say every time he'd eat her food and she'd be hopeful that the day will come soon enough.

But the day never came.

That night, her father never returned. The next day, out of nowhere, her mother came to the house. She packed all her stuff, and brought her back to France, to their house in Marseille. Although nobody talked about it, she knew and she was never the same again.

21

Exposition

The Motel

Suddenly, there was a knocking on the door. “Quarks!” called out a familiar voice.

She went ahead and opened the door. Alec was standing there. His brows were raised. There was a frown on his face. As he came in, he noticed that the windows were opened. He marched straight to them closed them and then closed the blinds. Then he turned back towards her.

“I was just informed by my contact; a standing kill order has been issued on our heads. Now, is there something that you aren’t telling me?”

“I don’t know.” Élénoré replied calmly.

“There is something about your work, which you are not telling me. What is it?”

“Nothing, I told you everything there is.”

“Damn it”, he shouted. “I don’t think you believe the gravity of the situation we’re in” saying this he went up to the television and turned it on, he selected the CNN news channel.

“…and from our European News desk, we have reports coming to us from Geneva about a terrorist attack which has happened at the LHC complex at CERN, the European Organization for Nuclear Research. Ranking at the top in the achievements made here in the field of particle physics, the facility is now under complete lockdown. As of now the only information we are able to get hold of is that among the crew working there at that time, there are two people who are unaccounted for Dr. Élénoré Bassét, Lead Researcher in one of the projects and a security officer Alec Mercer, who according to the sources was in a restricted area even when he was not cleared to be there. At the moment, the officials only have this lead to go on.” The news reader paused for a minute to clear his throat as she smartly camouflaged the new piece of information which streamed to her through her ear-piece. “A DCRI-DGSE special task force is giving a press conference right now; we’ll take you live to the event!”

“…. We’ve tracked payment records of both the suspects from Pakistan and Afghanistan; tying them to the defunct foreign terrorist cell Al-Qaeda. It appears that of the two people who were aware of what the project was; one is suffering from some kind of amnesia and the other person was killed in supposedly a freak accident. Since we are unable to assess the nature of the project done by the team, we are issuing a DEFCON 2 level warning to all the federal departments. We advise other countries to do the same. In the meantime, we will start a fresh investigation in the death of Dr. Rachel Bauer to see if it leads us somewhere. All public and private institutions are to be closed down until further information."

"Mute!" He instructed the innate device. "So what aren't you telling me?"

"I told you everything." Élénoré stressed harder than ever.

"What didn't you get? We've somehow managed to get our names in terrorist lists in almost every country in the world. We might even have to live in the caves of Afghanistan until we are shot in the head like Laden; at least Osama had enough pull to get himself a mansion in Pakistan, we can't even afford that. Éllén, I can call in favors for a little while, not my whole life!!"

Élénoré gave a deep sigh and in a deeper stroke, she inhaled the air as deep as she could, mustering all her courage, and collecting all her thoughts. There was so much she never told him, it was difficult to choose from. Earlier, she was feeling that Mercer did not deserve her trust but now, it seemed that she did not deserve Mercer's trust.

"Shoot! If you want to resume your normal life, that is." Mercer demanded.

"We were experimenting on alternative processes for energy generation." Élénoré explained patiently.

"Okay?"

"When we started out earlier, we weren't able to make much progress, until I found my father's notes and his journal. Before he died, he had already made significant progress in this field. He wrote about concepts and theories on how to produce an atom with a negative nucleus, much like the first anti-deuterium which he had synthesized at CERN."

"All I want to know right now is why they would stop your research every time it is being opened."

"Many people have many reasons…take your pick. But if I were to guess I'd say because we created a perpetual fusion reactor. Free energy…as it were!" She exclaimed with joy which soon, after remembering the recent events turned to sorrow. Her data was lost.

"Could you save it? The data?" Élénoré enquired. "That data in the wrong hands...."

"I have it!" Mercer cut her off. "Something like that would rub a lot of people the wrong way!"

"Perhaps. So what do we do now?" Élénoré asked.

"Now...we wait." Mercer informed. "My man is working on it!"

22

Strange Request

Federal Bureau of Investigation Chicago Field Office
Illinois

"Hello, Miss Summers. I see you've been busy."

"Have you been checking up on me?"

"Just doing my due diligence!"

"Oh...I see. So, what is this all about", she asked him as she pressed the record button on the phone.

"Now, miss Summers. Chivalry will take you only so far, you know." Hinting her not to play any games with him.

"Okay...okay." She stopped the recording.

"I'll get straight to the point."

"There's a man out in the open I want stopped. I'm sending the details over to you...now. Ex-military, ex-CIA; he's trained, volatile and extremely dangerous. His last known alias is Alec Mercer."

"Can't you just send the CIA after him? They have much more resources than we do."

"That's none of your business. I just want law enforcement agencies to be on the look-out for him."

"I'll see what I can do."

"Good!"

The phone line disconnects.

"You still believe she'll pull through? Even after all the evidence I've brought." The man was concerned. "How can you possibly trust her?"

"Victor..." Richard sighed, "You have not been creating assets as long as I have. They all start the same. Righteous, moral, *working for good.* But in the end they all come around. She will too. You wait and see."

"If you say so."

"Now make the call!" Richard said with a sense of urgency. "We have no time to waste."

Back in the Illinois branch of the Federal Bureau of Investigation. Special Agent Summers rushed hastily towards her bosses office.

"Wanna know who just called me?" Aisha was ecstatic.

"Why don't you just tell me?" Valerie frowned.

"Gosh sir, you are such a buzz kill! Anyway, the CEO of Bearing Oil just called. He wants us to track down a man for him. His name…um alias is Alec Mercer."

"Alias?" he chuckled.

"Yeah, the guy used to work for the CIA. And check this out. I did some digging…and guess what I found out?"

"Enough of these guessing", he yelled but not that loud. "Just tell me what you know."

"Okay…okay, remember the explosion and the killings that took place in Switzerland?"

"Because of that mess all federal agencies were ordered to go to DEFCON 2!"

She neatly placed a document on the table and slid it towards him. "Check the list of suspects."

Oh my god!

"Alec Mercer."

"And he's here…in the states?"

"I guess so."

"Then you've got to do as he says." But his tone had changed as he was no longer agitated. Instead, he was worried.

"What's the matter?" Aisha asked with concern. She noticed his uneasiness, his worry. "Something wrong?"

"Go on." Pointing at the door. "Do as he says. Now, leave me alone."

"You know something that I don't."

"Whatever."

Aisha Strode off.

As the door banged shut Valerie picked up the phone and dialed the number he had memorized by heart.

"The number you've dialed does not exist, please check the code or try again later", the female mechanical voice recording iterated.

"Code Bravo Gulf Sierra Charlie. Id: Six-three-two-seven."

"The number you've dia—", the recording stopped.

"Is the line secure?"

"I rather doubt it."

"If the intel is crucial, be discrete!" The remote voice instructed.

"He's here." Valerie informed.

"I'll look into it; anything else?" The unhindered voice responded.

"Not at the moment." The Director replied.

"I expect to be kept in the loop." Was the almost mechanical command.

"I'll keep it in mind." Valerie concurred.

"Until next time." The speaker bid adieu.

"Yeah, until next time." The Director did the same.

23

Source Code

5:47 PM
Tuesday, June 9, 2026
Lockheed-Martin Ammunitions Incorporated
56th Floor, IT Department
Rome. Italy

The intern was wearing his light blue stripped shirt and grey pantaloons as he made his periodical rounds across the floor pushing his mail cart along with him.

"Questo è per te"[1], said he handing him his rectangular package covered with a pistachio yellow packing material.

"E…qui si va,[2] Arianna!" handing her over the white envelope bearing her name. "Non preoccuparti, ha bisogno di tempo da solo, lui tornerà!"[3]

"e per me?"[4], cried Frank popping his head out of his tiny cubicle.

"Non quello che vi aspettavate. E 'solo una scheda con il tuo nome ... e questo è scritto sul retro di esso.[5] See. Significa Qualcosa per te?"[6], handing over the card to the addressee.

It read:

1. This is for you.
2. and... Here you go.
3. Do not worry, he needs time alone, he will return!
4. And for me?
5. Not what you expected. It 'just a card with your name...and this is written on the back of it'.
6. It means something to you?

Frank Millers
"Beijing, China"

The card was dated two weeks earlier. May 26, 2026. His eyes bulged out, face lost its color, turning into a sickly white as if the life drained out of him, the hair on his body stood up in fear and shock. Though the card was addressed to his current alias, the message referred to something else entirely. Like an encrypted message where the passkey was a person's memory, the message unfolded on him, leaving him in shock, flustered. *Seems like a ghost from the past has come back to haunt me,* he thought. He realized that his cover was probably blown, the operation compromised. Turning over the thick white card telegraph, he saw some writings on the other side in a language he was all too familiar with.

符合我在酒店大堂。现在。[7]

Meet me in the lobby, now.

He read the Mandorin text written on the card. He sent the card two weeks ago, and it was written to go down now. His senses got heightened to almost a hypervigilant state, he perceived every little thing around his, nothing got past him.

Is it a trap? An Ambush? Or is it a dead-drop?

Whatever it was, he was willing to take the risk, to neutralize the threat and maintain its operational integrity.

24

The Meet

The Lobby
Lockheed-Martin Ammunitions Incorporated

Marvin stepped out of the elevator into a slightly busy corridor of the Lockheed-Martin Ammunition. The corridor was full of people as it was time for shift change He walked through the corridor which opened into a giant circular room which resembled somewhat a giant Aztec sundial. His head panned from left to right examining the room, looking for the man or package which was supposed to meet him there. By now Marvin had regained his control, the color of his cheeks returned to their original pinkish red. His neatly combed hair was

7. Meet me in the Lobby. Now.

drawn back in, unlike his previous military cropped hair. A chrome blue biker sunglass dominated his face. His rectangular face had chiseled cuts near the jaw line. His bright red shirt was covered by a tan brown office jacket with a loose denim jean lower, which did not make strike out of the crowd but instead made it easier for him the blend him.

Unable to find anything, he approached the receptionist at the center of the lobby. "Hey Lucy; has anyone over here asked for me?"

"No Marvin, sorry. By the way, the dinner is still on for tonight, right?"

"Sì, naturalmente."[1]

"Mi Scusi, signore, mi puoi dire ilmodo di Beijing?"[2] said a man standing right next to him, in a soft voice such that only Marvin could hear what he had just said. The man was a good six feet tall, blonde hair and wore glasses and had a beard, appeared to be some sort of a college exchange student. He had been standing at the reception for quite a while, chatting with Lucy, but his unassuming appearance made it hard for people to notice him, even for Marvin who was standing right next to him.

"What?" he said in a cool tone, though inside he wanted to shriek. "KILLER; is that you?" he said aside to him but with a gasp of amazement.

"Yeah", said he, "I'm never tired of watching you like that."

"I see you have met Mr. Jean Marke", said the receptionist introducing him to Martin, unaware of their pre-existing acquaintance. "You know Mr. Davis has *suddenly* become all so interested in the city's cultural heritage. Could he be more subtle Ah anyway, he asked Mr. Marke to write a book about Rome's untold history, which he would publish with his publication company. I was just telling him about my...", clearing her throat, "never mind."

"Si signore.[3] You must come with me. I know everything there is to know about this city. I reckon you must be living here for a while. Still, I know things you wouldn't find, even in the guide books."

"Well, if you insist. Aprire la strada."[4] Marvin smiled as they walked out of the building.

---

1. Yes, of course.
2. Excuse me, sir, can you tell me how to go to Beijing?
3. Yes sir.
4. Lead the way.

25

Christina

"Honey, I'm home!" The war-hardened veteran announced as he returned home from yet another tour abroad. "Christina!" He yelled.

"Shh...quiet!" Christina came running. The complex expression on her face was hard to understand. There were slight signs of relief, anger and compassion but on the whole there was indifference. "Tyler and Emily are sleeping...you'll wake them up!" She yelled in a hushed fury.

He understood the reason behind her anger and became quiet. He had been carrying many bags on him, each of the same green and khaki colour and the Navy SEAL insignia.

As Christina drew nearer to him, he let go of his burden which came down on the floor crashing.

Christina had grown indifferent, mainly because of her husband's indifferent and callous attitude towards her and her children. It was not that he did not love his family. She knew that he loved them immensely. But after years of marriage, she had grown tired of his loyalty to his service. Many a women who marry a soldier eventually get tired of their husbands unjust devotion to their country, and so did she. Still, she realized that he came home from yet another hell and she should be courteous enough to bring him inside with love, not coldness.

He opened up his arms and Christina walked right in between them. For a moment, both of them stood still as he held her close to his chest and hugged her. Months had passed since he had last felt this way. The feeling of being whole, complete and most importantly, safe. He wanted to get lost in the same feeling and never be found. He gave Christina soft kiss on her lips and she responded back, but there was something missing. She had not put her heart into it, though she was the most passionate kisser he knew.

"What's wrong?" He asked.

Christina did not respond to the question. Instead she asked, "How long will you be staying with us?"

"What?" He was genuinely puzzled.

"You want some coffee?" She countered as she took a few steps back, deflecting the question. She did not want to raise any issues.

"I'd like that." He answered with a smile.

Christina turned around and started walking into the kitchen, while he followed her blindly.

As she entered inside the kitchen, she walked up to the coffee maker and turned it on. The coffee maker was preparing the coffee but she stood in front of it, not turning back towards her husband.

"I don't know when I have to return. I have to await orders." He spoke. "My unit...it got killed in an ambush. I am the only one who survived." Listening to her husband, Christina's heart pounded so hard that she could hear it beating. She bit her lips trying to conceal her agonizing concern. She did feel sorry for him, but stopped when she realised that it was his repeated bloodlust that put him in that situation. She wanted to be a loving caring wife, but just could not pretend anymore to be strong enough to be able to bear the news of some tragedy that could happen with him.

"That's sad." She replied, carelessly. "I mean...sad that your unit got killed. I'm glad you made it home safe."

"Yeah, I know." He replied. "But...things do not add up. Something is fishy. I've decided to stay…check out what is happening."

Christina's heart lit up. "Really!" She smiled vibrantly.

"Yeah." She ran back towards him and hugged him tightly, pressing him close to her bosom. Another kiss followed. One more fierce. More passionate.

26

Olympus Falls

Villa Borghese
Piazza di Siena, 00197 Roma, Italy

"It's nice to see you too." Marvin greeted back. "But why are you here, KILLER?" He asked with a suspicious curiosity.

They walked on the less populated track built from the collection of exotic multi-face bricks as dull as gray but excellent for cardio exercises. The backdrop was concealed with multitudes of green and light green deciduous trees which stood proud of the heritage it presented. After centuries of culture and scandal, long forgotten, the park now represented an afternoon of peace and tranquil, for family and friends.

"I need your help?" Mercer replied. "Right now…the world is

after me! And you are the one person I really trust!" Alec explained as he stepped across the rugged terrain of the exotic local garden.

"What do you want?" Marvin jumped straight to the point.

"I need new aliases! Cash and plastic! And passports and visa! Anything that can get me…and the girl stateside! I have to clear my name", Mercer stated.

"I can get it done…." Marvin replied in a serious tone. "But what do you intend to do once you reach there." He said. "It's gonna be a turf war and that…girl is going to get caught in the crossfire!" Marvin continued.

"I'm still working on it!" Mercer retorted. "I borrowed these from the mercs sent to kill us…" Mercer stated with a smile as he passed the cards and passports to Marvin. "What can you find about them? Who sent them?" He asked.

Marvin raised his iPad which he had been carrying in his hand and kept it steady, horizontal at chest level while his other hand reached for the cards which Mercer aimed at him.

"Same old…same old!" Marvin chuckled. "Bloody scavenger!"

"Scavengers are on top of the food chain, my friend!" Mercer stated with a flamboyant laugh.

Marvin selectively picked up one of the cards, the ocean blue one which caught his fancy and placed it faced down on his iPad. His iPad was directly connected to his ghost server in Venice. He ran optical recognition on the piece of plastic and the server brought him all the information he wanted on the person.

"Macintyre, Jason. He was a gun for hire, ex-pat, paramilitary. Works in ILSA…International Logistics & Support Agency. ILSA is serious business, even for spooks. KILLER, people just do not get rich managing parties and handling logistics. Don't know how long you have been off the grid man, but you ought to know them."

Mercer gave a light minded shrug, as if the term meant nothing to him.

"Think of it like this, when the CIA wants to kill someone off the books, they go to ILSA. That's how deep their power reaches. They have diplomatic immunity in many countries and their properties are nothing short of forts. They do contract killings for their high-end clients; nothing can be proved of course!" Marvin explained. "They employ highly trained professionals, soldiers and mercs all alike, even criminals. Those who work for them are known to have worked for the CIA, the SIS, Mossads, and Spetz-naz…the list goes on!".

"But what's it got to do with me?" Mercer asked, tired.

"KILLER, if you are searching for intel, I'm not the best man... trust me!" Marvin exhaled. "I've been out of the business for a long time now. Echelon took its toll on me. Now I work for the CIA, could you imagine...working assignments like you do—I mean...you did."

"You are the one I trust!" Mercer said. "Trust trumps everything else!"

"Alright then. It's obvious that their primary target is that girl. She is the key. So, that gives us a point to start." He informed as he soon indulged into his razor sharp iPad, working on it meticulously.

"Élénoré Bassét." He stated. "Female. Thirty seven. Single?" Marvin paused for a moment. "Doctorate in...something. Currently employed by CERN."

"That's general knowledge!" Mercer exclaimed. "I could have told you all that!"

Marvin pointed a finger at him, signaling him not to disturb him while his genius was at work. "Project Manager. Project SORCE..." Marvin continued. "Now where have I heard that before?" Marvin pondered.

"Find something?" Mercer asked hastily.

"Perhaps...I remember this case." Marvin stated. "It came in my probationary years in Echelon. The gamma blast in CERN, remember."

"Yeah, I was briefed about that." Mercer concurred.

"Project SORCE! Yes! Whatever those guys did was extremely confidential! The goddamn President was running point on our investigation. Telling us to clean the mess quick! Find the cause!" Marvin continued.

"And did you?" Mercer leaned forward.

"We found enough!" Marvin revealed. "A name...bearing PetroTech! But as you know, our work was borderline illegal. Non-actionable. We could not pursue the case in any court of law."

Mercer had heard the name many times before. Bearing Oil was a lubricant which he always preferred for his Dodge Challenger, Bearing Diesel for the engine; or atleast till he could afford a car. A well-known company in the field of automobile and energy. Hearing its name in relation to this gave him quite a shock.

"It's a company whose growth rate has the Wall Street incumbents puzzled." Marvin informed. "The things we found about this company are baffling really. There's not a crime that those bastards did not commit!"

"One more thing..." Mercer said. "I intercepted a package from them. A copy of Project SORCE of which Élénoré was working on with her team. They were extracting it from the facility before burying us with C4." Mercer continued. "Take it for a spin and tell me what you gather from it, okay!"

27

Requiem Relapse

A Safe House
Venice, Italy

Alec Mercer, call-sign KILLER, had already been through a lot and perhaps no one in the world knew it better than Marvin. He knew things KILLER did not because if he did it'd probably change him from the core; make him more negative, cynical. The intel got to him two days too late. The damage was done. Caught in his mind, in his own internal strife, he delayed himself from informing his friend about the underlying cause which destroyed his life—but now, the damage was done. KILLER had regressed. Even for a man like him, even with his iron will, strong and atypical mind, and rock-hard, unhindered and staunch conviction, the shock would have been too much to handle. Knowing that, he thought it best to keep it to him, at least until the time was right.

The safe house, like any other of its kind, appeared less than ordinary compared to any other of its neighboring buildings which, in this case, hailed from the age-old Italian civilizations. The buildings were old and crumbly-looking, as if they would fall any second, but their foundations, as strong as they could be when they were made, and the architecture was like none other and although time took its toll on these masterful and elegant designs, these remnants of the powerful and probably the most corrupt royal families once strong are still very much intact. The building had a kind of off-brown color, the leaded-coat of paint was crumbling and at countless places, the thin yellow-brown slabs of bricks were exposed. Unlike any other Italian State from that great era which had flurried in an age of knowledge and development, Venice was built completely on sea. Another astonishing technological feat as it was. There was the obvious fact that there is not much room for expansion, but it did expand and modern technological advancements pulled it through. Even so, many of the over the sea structures were frankly, structurally unsound.

Venice is a large city. And this safe house belonged to one of the oldest parts of the city, which contained these last remains. The city of Venice was historically renowned for its smelly waterways, it had more waterways than streets, and the building overlooked one.

Marvin entered from the entrance he had once fabricated in the side alley, just as a precaution, to prevent the city-cams from detecting him. He had already hacked into their systems and its feeds got displayed on his monitor's screen. He could probably loop the video and stop the cameras from recording, but KILLER was an active threat, and Marvin was no doubt at the top in his 'List of Known Associates'. That means they were watching him, tapping his phone, recording his conversations, even if their desperate attempts were nothing but futile. One thing which they did not realize was that he had conducted scores of black-book operations, both foreign and stateside, and both as tactical support and a highly trained field operative. He knew their playbook, all too well. Still, even if they couldn't get him incriminating himself talking to KILLER, even if they were not able to record any actual conversation, Marvin could not just stroll into any random building in Venice. They look for any change in pattern, change in behavior, marked increase in suspicious activities, like, say…strolling into some random, abandoned building in Venice, when he should have been working behind a desk in Rome, thousands of miles apart, let alone the fact that the building was registered to one of Marvin's aliases. If they knew that the building belonged to Marvin, they would definitely be keeping a careful watch on it. Their servers could detect it if the video was being played in a loop, by cataloguing each object in the video and its behavior, so if a set of frames are repeating, they would know.

It smells like shit! Thought he as he climbed up the stairs. As it was located over the sea, the building reeked of the foul and putrefying smell of stale ocean water and dead fish.

He reached the re-enforced concrete secured entrance. He had to pass a series of identification tests in order to establish that he actually was the Marvin Calloway, one and only and not any mediocre imposter. It would disable the security measures to give him access to the actual safe house, boot up the systems, and load his personal configurations. He had been away for years now, due to his new assignment.

The fluorescent white light gleamed.

"Good Morning, Mr. Marvin", greeted a female computer generated voice, "Welcome to Venice. Fifteen seconds till systems operational. Satellite DataStream Uplink Established. Signals strength: 94 Percent."

"Nothing like the good old days, huh?" he smiled with a reminiscent smile which dominated his heart and mind.

The room was small but brightly illuminated; there were at least five other rooms apart from the one which he currently occupied. The structure was surely magnificent and a possible eye-candy for tourists, only if they had the access code and his DNA. Quite grand considering that all of it was underwater. The main room was the server room, and there was an armory, a refectory, and bedroom and a toilet. One could get an aquarium style view sitting right in there. The scenery was elegant, but there was no time to waste admiring and reminiscing. He got right on it, not wasting a single moment. He logged in into his singular terminal, hooked up the DataCourier and did the obvious. Went to Hardware, selected Disk Drives and then the drive 'Data Courier 01 (G)'.

"Just one file?" he smirked as he saw the file but it was of an unknown file type, "All this for just this?! It must contain a hell of sensitive material to boil up a storm, that big!"

He glanced down the screen; saw the size of the particular file. *148 petabytes? What the hell is in there? Must be an encryption container. It's going take a while trying to decrypt this monster.* The problem was not finding the right access key, cause even after finding it, the whole colossal file had to be decoded, bit-by-bit, piece-by-piece.

"Warning!! Unauthorized Data Transmission Detected!" echoed through the machine's recorded voice.

"Warning!!" popped up on the holographic screen of the BackTrack.

"Warning!"

"Warning!"

Instinctively realizing the meaning of the words, he immediately disabled the network connection. "This is bad."

"Oh hell!" Marvin fumed.

Maybe it's not too late to salvage the situation, he thought. He started checking the data transmission server, "Shit, shit! Shit! It's a Pinger. I need to get the hell out of here!"

Understanding the predicament of the situation he was in, he started flurrying all he had in secure cases. He started acting berserk. He had too much stuff to account for. Data had to be extracted, computers and servers had to be destroyed; equipment was to be hauled out. He had a lot of work at hand and time was a luxury which he no longer had.

The safe house was compromised.

28
Wry Smile

Central Intelligence Agency
Headquarters at Langley, Virginia
Signals Intelligence Division (SID)

"What is this?" asked the director as he peered at the large 300 inch GCD panel overhead, in front of him.

"I don't know, sir!" the analyst replied in a dull voice, "Yet." she added.

"You ought to!" he drilled with urgency.

"The transmission was for not more than a few seconds, it closed down abruptly."

"Well, whatever it was, was sensitive enough to make it to my screen, and as I recall, it's your job to find out what!" he argued over her apparent incompetence.

They stared at the screen for a few moments while the analyst pounded down hard on the keyboard, trying to get results done, unless her boss would bellow at her, yet again. There were things he did not understand. The transmissions were gibberish. Only if the end didn't make sense it could have been more logical, because it was broken, but the entire DataStream was nothing but was nonsensical.

"Maybe it's an audio container, or perhaps video." She brooded systematically as she broke the last bytes off and tried to run it, but to no avail.

The transmission which now dominated Jenifer's console terminal did not reach them purposely. Nothing was tagged, no keywords, nothing. If it were, the contents would've been obvious. The transmission was actually meant for ILSA. But ILSA was being covertly under criminal investigation, under constant and extremely scrutinous surveillance. CIA knew the work ILSA did, as some of the high profile jobs were surreptitiously outsourced to the same company. But it was a rogue mercenary operation, they couldn't be trusted. The agency was not leaving any stone unturned to absolve that active threat against the country. They had to be stopped. There was only one mammoth issue of how to expose the true nature of the organization without exposing the agency itself. They were preparing for the worst.

The transmission was for ILSA. The header of the transmission made that amply clear. But the intel they had been gathering did not only make them a threat only against the Agency but more like a national threat against the country. Ergo, whatever was on that DataStream, there was not a flicker of doubt on the director's mind that it was crucial to national security. His frustration therefore was genuine but underlying it was fear. Something the rookie analyst could never understand.

"Got it!" Jenifer exclaimed hysterically, just as she saw a window pop up on the screen. 'Access key found' which replaced itself with another message. 'Touch to open' it read.

The analyst shifted her body as she leaned into an alternate posture. "It has co-ordinates and location. Venice—" She read.

The director's bald head panned from the analysts terminal to the screen overhead, "Maybe you're not so bad after all, Jenifer!" he said with a brief impromptu feeling of elation.

The map on the screen zoomed. From Europe to Italy to Venice. Right down to the building where Marvin had bunkered in. It was the live three dimensional feed from the satellite imagery.

"Building's registered in the name of Henry Bale. I'm running him right now." Jenifer stated with pride as she dragged Henry Bale's credentials through the IFR software.

"I don't get it!" The director pondered, "This is a big break we caught in the last few months. They've gotten sophisticated, more skilled, and smarter, somehow. They've managed to dodge our radar for so long somehow. Wha—"

"Sir?" Jenifer hollered.

"Yes?"

"We've got a hit on the name, but from the classified archives." She informed.

"What did you get?" The director pounced.

"Not exactly. My terminal doesn't have high enough security clearance."

"Run it through my credentials!" He ordered, hastily.

There was a brief moment of silence, while the analyst was working. Admittedly, the incompetent one had been able to provide far better results than even the most skilled analysts. But it was not

CENTRAL INTELLIGENCE AGENCY

Washington D.C. 20505

<u>CLASSIFIED PERSONNEL ARCHIVE</u>

CONFIDENTIAL

Name: Henry Bale

Known Alias: ████████, Frank Millers, ██████████

Military Call-sign: ██

Age: 38

Sex: Male

Spouse: Single

Qualifications: BS for Computer Science Engineering (Suma cum laude) and MS in Heuristic AI Derivatives

PhD. for 'Security Algorithm for Network Intrusion Prevention'

Mental Description: Trained, Lethal and dangerous.

High value asset.

Classified potential risk.

Background:

- 1998 - Joined Massachusetts Institute of Technology
- 2003 - Joined ECHELON after clearing background check. Employed due To extreme notoriety in the field of network security. Designated to the Department of Signals Intelligence.
- 2013 - Transferred to European Branch in Britain. Oversaw intelligence gathering operations related to Project SORCE. . Used illegal methods to obtain the █████ Intel suggest ████████

the illicit terrorist operation bombing in CERN.

Employee History:

- 2016 - Joined the Central Intelligence Agency. Recruited in National Clandestine Services in the Special Activities Division.
- 2023 - Last known alias lethal force permitted..
- 2024 -
- 2024 - . Specialist special task force undercover in
- 2025 - Last known alias . Worked undercover in uncover illegal backdoor arms trade by high level internal security consultants.
- 2026 -

their fault, and neither was it her apparent newfound skill. It was something more than a suspicion of his, that there was a security leak in the agency. No matter how hard he tried he could not find it. All the assets were constantly vetted and re-vetted countless times.

Maybe now I got him. The feeling of success pumped deep through his veins on the thought. "This…this Bale guy. He could be connected to this somehow."

"Sir?" Jenifer motioned him to type in his clearance PIN, and as he placed the last stroke on the Enter key dozens of classified documents flurried through the screens. 'EYES ONLY' was written across the pages with bright red ink and most of the text was redacted. Jenifer's gaze widened along with her boss who stared at those scores of documents with no outward expression on his bald face.

"Okay, so Henry Bale alias Frank Millers alias Marvin Calloway alias Sergei Romani." She read. "He is actually one of ours. He's currently stationed in Rome in some covert operation, no intel on the work he's in. The op is classified but his handler's details are in the file. Here you go…."

"He's supposed to be in Rome, why is he in Venice? Whatever it is…", he wondered, "Time to patch the leak!"

"Honey, pull up the traffic cam feed around that building!" He ordered, a bit gently than his usual self.

"Just a second." Jenifer replied back.

"Anything?" He asked a minute later.

"I've matched anyone and everyone who's come near this building since last week with facial recognition. Not a single hit. Hey, are you sure one week?"

"Trust me. I had a chat with his handler. Six days ago he deserted his operation and went AWOL and off the map. He got this card and got spooked, no one has seen him since. They are sending full briefing of his mission. Pull it up on the big screen…. Alright then…. He works at Lockheed Martin. Pull up all the cameras. Fifty sixth floor…. Roll through them…. There!"

"I see him. He's spooked alright."

"Yeah… Roll back a few frames…. Freeze!… Punch in on that, will you. I wanna get what he's reading."

"Beijing…hmm…China. And I think that's Mandorin. Zoom in a bit and make it clearer."

"You speak Mandorin?"

"Two tours to China in the UN peace keeping force!" He smiled. "So, it says…. Meet me in the Lobby…. Now."

He was onto something and he knew it.

"Follow him, as best as you can." He urged.

The analyst tracked him through the week old video footage, meanwhile the director was busy on his phone, "...I'm not sure, sir, but it is something." As the call disconnects, he dialed another number. "This is Jameson Theroux, Director of Operations, SID. I'm raising Operational Protocol to level two. I want Brian and Chelsea on their terminals this instant!" His tone commanding and demanding.

"I'm at the Lobby. He's exiting the bank of elevators and... now into the uh...you should call it a gallery...so many paintings!" Jenifer exclaimed.

"There he is! Looks like he's searching...searching for someone", he peered patiently as he studied his every move, "Who's that guy? With the...um...hat and glasses...."

"Sorry sir, not enough profile to run it through facial."

"It's alright, sadly we can only be so lucky for so long", he was sad indeed but not put down completely. They had made ginormous progress, maybe not against ILSA directly "It's quite alright, Jenifer, follow them as far as you can. And make this douche-y looking guy your priority. He's smart. I sense it. If your luck continues, then maybe you could get him on satellite surveillance, they for sure would be able to scan what's under—all that disguise. One other thing. Activate any local assets, wet agents we have over there, I want audio and video surveillance teams scouting that building in Venice. And when your idiot friends return, tell them to report to me in my office" said he, stern and firm.

I've got to put my head around this.

29

Screw Ups

Washington D.C.
Capitol Hill
11:02 AM

A black stretch-limousine rolled out the east front of the capitol building. Inside it the infamous Sir Richard Meyers was attending to a call.

"Hello!", said he in his royal grandeur into his earpiece, "Before you speak, might I warn you that if you have called me to inform me of another one of your screw-ups, you can kiss your position, goodbye!"

"Sir, you do not have the power!" Torres retorted.

"Let me remind you that I have controlling interests in your tiny operation. Just an incentive for you that if you don't provide results, I'll make you pay!" Meyers reminded.

"Luckily, for both of us, we've got a lead. The DataCourier which we had lost in the Operation has been connected to a machine somewhere in Venice, our specialists have got the co-ordinates of the device and...you'll be happy to know that our extraction team is already en-route. You'll have that drive in your hands in no time and Alec Mercer will be dead."

30

Bite Me

"Bite me!" Marvin replied with a loud shriek. There was a cynical, condescending smile on his face.

The safe house came under attack in a matter of minutes. In two more minutes, he found himself strapped and tied to the chair. He wriggled his hands constantly trying to leverage his way out of the grip but the knot was unbreakable, a distinctive style of a man who underwent the training of the Green Beret.

His captivators came in with terribly swift and decisive moves, moving like perfectly aligned cogs of a clock.

"The safe house is secure, sir." The mercenary who tied his knot relayed on the radio. Marvin could count six unwanted guests standing inside his safe house and from the looks of it, more were on the way.

One man in particular, a tall stallion of a man, was too keen on working on Marvin's face like a punching bag. He kept throwing repeated punches on Marvin. It was not late until Marvin's face turned red with blood, broken capillaries and pierced skin.

"Enough!" Hunter bellowed. His walk inside the room was swift as the rest of his team. He entered through the door and walked straight up to Marvin.

"Good evening." Hunter greeted with his boasting pride. "Having a nice day, it seems."

"Piss off!" Marvin retorted. Seeing Marvin's unyielding attitude, Hunter signaled his man with a nod of his head.

The mercenary brute, along with two sets of hands, flipped his chair back, drowning him in a sky-blue pool of water. A long wait before revealing him of his oxygen deprivation and pulling him out. Marvin was gasping for every breath. An unsuspecting blow brought him back to his senses. Marvin spat the excess water and saliva from his mouth.

Marvin knew his cards. He would be alive as long as the information was with him, albeit the pain was inevitable. There was nothing he could do about it.

"Where is he?" were the slowly articulated words. Hunter leaned so close to him that he could feel Marvin's shallow breath on his face. He pulled out his standard issue black ceramic knife and began caressing the bruised skin on Marvin's face.

"Who?" Marvin smiled coyly.

"Sir? A minute." One of Hunter's lieutenants pulled him aside. "You should have a look at this!" He pointed his vision to the tablet he held in his hand. There was a minute-long conversation between them after which Hunter came back to Marvin, squatted down in front of him.

"The Legendary Henry Bale! What an honor!" He greeted with a momentous blow of the ceramic knife to his right hand, wedge to the chair through his metacarpal bone in his wrist. He shouted hesitantly in vain attempts to subvert the pain. "Fuck!" He groaned deeply, the hot white pain radiated. The pain, though, did not end as Hunter continued to twist it to increase his pain.

"How much does the Agency know, Mr. Bale?" Hunter asked curiously with much visible concern.

Marvin answered back with a smile.

"Try to understand Henry." Hunter said. "I am a charismatic sadistic psychopath. You will answer all my questions and more or else you will meet your most certain death, and trust me when I say this, it would be excruciatingly painful."

National Geographic Channel

Water

Finally, it has happened. A liter of packaged drinking water costs hundred bucks. Non-potable water costs fifty. With increasing difficulties in water processing thanks to the startling water salinization across the globe, the planet is now facing an acute shortage of drinking water. What would be next, we wonder? We do not have enough food, water, fuel, land, nothing. Times are so hard that middle class lives like paupers and the ones poorer now seize to exist. United Nations' World Health Organization has issued a warning to the situation. This is one of "the biggest man made health calamities" the population is facing. The Earth might remain covered four-fifth with water, but the fresh water reserves have shrunk to 0.25 per cent. A startling new low, according to latest projections by the scientific community. Unless a miracle technique of desalinizing is researched, the scientists believe that the present graph of fresh water availability will not sustain the ever-increasing population.

31

Remote Observer

Central Intelligence Agency
Headquarters at Langley, Virginia
Signals Intelligence Division (SID)

"Report!" Director Jameson Theroux's voice resounded in the heavily occupied chamber. "Give me a Sit-Rep!" He commanded as he pressed the matt black distinctive knob which activated the military grade transceiver with multi-key encryption.

His bald visage revolved around as he observed the hurry and flurry which had come to dominate the entire floor of the Signals Intelligence Division of the CIA, thanks to the meticulous efforts of his rookie analyst, who was now running point on the entire operation, the Agency had got a major breakthrough, setting things into the momentum in which they needed to be. The room could be generalized into navy blue, with the wall perpendicular to the array of terminals bearing the seals of the majestic agency and its partner in crime, the seal of the United States of America. Unlike earlier, almost all the terminals were now occupied by their respective hosts, who were literally dragged back from their coffee breaks and night shifts on the order of Director Theroux.

"WET teams in position!" Jenifer stated as she peered into her console.

"Just observe and report!" Jameson articulated. "No contact whatsoever! Maintain a low profile!"

"Yes sir!" A voice crackled from the terminal.

"Where's my visual?" The director bellowed, strict as he always was. "I want eyes on that building! Yesterday!" Stressing on the urgency of situation.

"Pulling feed now." Chelsea reported. "Coming up on the big screen…now."

Instinctively, Jameson's head gazed a few rows across the room, at the dominating 300 inch CGD panel on far wall, directly in front of him.

Patiently, Jameson stared at the extremely sharp and clear image which presented an exact description of the happenings half way around the world. The multiform dirty yellow building, half towards its way to extinction, dominated the display panel which dominated the majority of the east facing wall. With a deep seated sigh he retorted, "The man we are chasing is a CIA trained black ops operative!" He breathed. "If I can spot my people from the crowd, then so can he! He knows our playbook all too well!"

But what else can we do!

"Inform me the second anything happens!" The director ordered. "I'll be in my office."

32

Requiem Relapse II

Marvin's Safe house

The elevator ran at its peak velocity; it had a long way down. When it reached its destination, the doors creaked as they opened. Mercer walked down the dark corridor. Between the blinking dull red lights and dark black walls, there was not much to see. But it was quite creepy. Anybody lesser than Mercer would have been scared to death; but Mercer did not. He could not. Peoples' lives depended on him, Éllén depended on him. He compartmentalized his fear and kept it aside. His senses were heightened, as always in such situations. He knew things were wrong. He stretched his right arm into the bag he was carrying on his back, and instinctively pulled out a flashlight and his left hands went round his back pulling out the sidearm he had holstered in his denim jeans. His arms stretched straight in front of him, muscles flexed, his eyes following the iron-sight on the metal jacket of the gun, his right hand carrying the light underneath the gun, to provide light to the target, and to provide support for recoil. He was slowly approaching an even darker room. Pitch dark and nothing in sight. He was just at the mouth of the door in front of him, when suddenly his eyes caught something in his peripheral view. It was a massive dark object which flew right past him on the other side of the dark tinted wall and as it did Mercer instinctively turned towards it pointing his gun at it. "*What* the...", he wondered. The light from the flash light was majorly getting reflecting off the wall, as it should, but Mercer realized, that the walls weren't opaque, they were made of glass or polymer, so he horizontally pressed the torch directly against the wall so that all of the light would pass through it instead of reflecting off of it, and so that he could get glimpses of where he was at. The trick worked. Light passed through the wall and reflected off of things beyond it. He could make out figures of massively large poles which ran all the way from top to bottom, and on the top he could also see some shimmering on the top gleaming from behind a large object, and then yet again, he saw what had swam past him. It was a dolphin and he understood that just as he saw the shiny, beady eyes of the magnificent beast and he then knew that he was underwater.

"Classic Marvin..." he thought, "just when you think you've seen it all." But something was bugging him which was increasing his already active suspicion that something was wrong, terribly wrong. An abandoned building was common, for a safe house at least, but blinking emergency, the pitch darkness, everything, was not as it should be. "Marvin seemed to be excited about something, so he'd be all over me by now. So where is he?"

Thinking of Marvin, his mind focused on the task at hand, and on the door which was present in front of him. He turned towards the door; he could see something bright blinking at a distance, everything else was pitch dark. There was an option in his flashlight to choose the level of intensity and angle of illumination. He turned both dials to Max and threw the torch into the room. The torch gyrated about itself and lightly illuminated most of the room. Mercer was shocked at the image that he saw. Stunned for a moment, he quickly groped himself back to his senses. The massive room was round and dark. There were an array of now-distorted computers and machinery, motherboards, hard drives, RAM all ripped out as if in a hurry. Something else was missing; it was the DataCourier. Gone. But Alec did not notice it. All he could see was the bloodied face of his specialist, as the light of the rotating torch faced him, even if for a second, he could see the motionless and tortured façade. Then the light moved on, leaving behind the pain and agony. He realized what had happened. He had seen people getting tortured; he had been tortured for years by the FSB, and even tortured many in Guantanamo and during operations, without breaking a sweat. Occupational hazard. But seeing Marvin's tied hands, the knife hinged in his palm, his bruised face and body, all wet, his eyes were as red as fire and blood was oozing out instead of tears, his mouth gagged. His head hanging down forward but the body was upright as his chest was also tied to the chair. Suddenly, he lost his reason to keep fighting for. Were he not a soldier, he would have wept for his friend, but as he was taught by his sergeant, "A soldier never fears, a soldier never cries nor does he weep for a fellow soldier for he is strong and brave and courageous, and also because doing so tarnishes the name of the dead. Instead he moves on, he fights, fights for what his fellow died so that his death doesn't go in vain and his life had a cause."

This can't be!

33

Day Dreaming

The New York Diner
Downtown New York

"Sir?" The eccentric waitress enquired as she prodded the arm of one of the regulars at the deli. "Are you all right?"

"Huh? What the—", Marvin was startled as he woke up from his alcoholic slumber, "How did I get here?"

Recognizing her voice, soft like snow falling, it was his favorite waitress who took special care of him.

"Mystique? What are you doing here?", he pondered.

"I would ask you the same question but sadly I already know the answer", she replied.

"Wait, what? The CourierDrive? Where is it? How did I get here?" Marvin rambled hysterically, "I don't get it?"

"Look around, you will in a minute." Mystique gave a pitiful smile.

He glanced around, looking out of the window. He saw the bustling streets of New York, from cars to bicycles all revving on the majestic crossroads until the signal went red and all of them came to a halt. He turned his attention to the inside. The brown upholstery of the cushioned seats, the linen, and the shiny chrome objects all hanging around and the counter, he realized he was sitting in the New York Diner.

"How did I get here?"

"I dunno, maybe with the morning crowd, but I didn't see you until right now. What I don't get it is that even when you've drunken all your kidneys out, how you end up over here. Don't you have a place to go…you know…like the ones we call home." The sarcasm in her voice was clear but it was mixed with concern, none of which was visible to Marvin. He had a splitting migraine—a major hangover and nothing was clear.

"Maybe I wanted to see you."

"Very funny."

"Aren't you gonna take my order?"

"I know what you always take, dear. So I already did."

"How 'bout some Irish coffee with that, honey?"

"Don't honey me! You'll not get anything with alcohol over here. Not even that much! Not under my watch!"

"Okay. At least gimme some aspirin. My head is killing me right now."

"Sure. I'll see if we've still got some."

There was a bit of banter between them, she cared for him, maybe like a brother. She loved him nonetheless. She cat walked back towards the kitchen but stopped as one of the other customers called out for her. He was facing away from the door and away from Marvin, but he turned back as if to stare at something behind him.

What the—?

The man was faceless, but his apparent brow line was raised. There were depressions where the eyes were supposed to be, and his mouth was nowhere to be seen.

The image was horrifying, even for a war-hardened vet; he was startled, pulled backed his chair and jumped on his feet. More heads turned, but all of them were same, faceless.

"No, no, no, no, NO!" he shouted, "this can't be happening."

Misty, rushed back towards him. "Marvin, what happened?" She put her hand over his shoulder trying to console him, bringing down his agitation.

Marvin looked at her, hoping for some sort of *something*...but then not to his surprise even her face was…faceless. Seeing her from so close, but unable to see her pearl like eyes, it freaked him. He threw her out of his way and ran out of the diner. He pushed through the door and sprinted, away from the ghostly place. *What is happening?* He couldn't understand. I've been here a thousand times. *I must be dreaming!* He wondered. And like the popular saying he pinched himself to check. But he didn't wake, but he only felt the pain pulsing through his forearm. There were many pedestrians walking on the sidewalk, all of them staring at the singular man. Marvin leaned forward, supporting his weight through his arms on his knees. He was panting, breathing heavily. Tiny drops of sweat coalesced together and reaching critical level started running down his cheeks, until they broke off and fell on the solid hard concrete pavement. All he could see was the faceless faces of the crowd. He felt them hovering over him. He stood upright, mustering all his confidence and then he found himself pushing himself through the crowd; there was one drinking coffee without his mouth, another eating a hot-dog, one carrying a leather briefcase, all of them stumbling in amazement. He pushed them away with all of his power, applying the zenith of his force. They all tumbled over each other. As he crossed the human wall, he stepped on the road, and prepared for another sprint across the road. Abruptly, he heard the screeching noise of tires reaching strongly towards him. His head panned left. A Chevrolet Impala, grinding its brakes, was skidding towards him.

Oh shit!

The metal grating car, hit him with a high impact velocity. He felt a strong sharp sting in both his knees and then there was numbness. His head was also hurting as it smashed through the now-tattered windshield. There was a broken shard of glass that went completely through his right palm, which pained him like hell. His eyes were blood red as all the shards sliced the hardened skin on his face. He felt the ribs in his abdomen protruding out of his stomach.

He looked up to take a glimpse of the driver and another shock hit him, so shocked that no words came from his mouth.

"KILLER?! What are yo—?" He wondered but the shock overwhelmed him, his eyelids grew heavy, still full of pain, the image in front of him faded slowly away into the darkness, the pain vanished completely, if only for a miniscule moment.

Slowly regaining his consciousness, he slowly opened up his eyes to the bright shining light he could see flickering behind the veil of his eyelids, so bright that he even felt the heat comforting him, providing a wee bit of relief. He opened his eyes and even though it burned and he felt all his power and strength was drained right down to the last joule, he mustered together all his strength just to do such a minor task that the human body does it involuntary, and even then the pain hit him harshly when it did, he just had to open his eyes. To see whether he was dead or alive, alive to live his wretched life again, to see if he was in heaven, or in hell for all the sins he had committed, and all the lives he had taken in the innumerable wars. Even when he was put down, he was a determined man, never gives up hope.

Never say never.

He opened up his eyes and the hazy image cleared gradually and as it did he could see a man holding a torch a bit too close to his eyes and shouting, at the top of his voice.

"Marvin? Marvin? Can you hear me?" Mercer yelled, "Marvin?!"

"Huh?"

"Can you hear me?", he repeated with a sigh of relief.

"Yeah, sure. But I won't be unless you stop shouting", he chuckled to lighten the mood.

"Can you move?" Marvin tried to readjust but the pain was simply too much to bear. His mood changed and the expression on his face became serious, "I lost it. You trusted me with it, and I bloody lost it. I'm sorry."

"Don't worry about it", Mercer consoled.

"They tortured me just for fun. They knew things. Knew everything, but they still... Oh no! I remember, get the hell out of here, it's a trap!", he shouted as loud as he could but his voice was still quite feeble.

"What?" Mercer asked.

"It's a bloody trap!!!"

34

Operation Flagstaff

UK Security Service (MI5) Headquarters
Thames House
Millbank, London

"What is it?" Hewitt asked. "What did you find?"

"Sir...." The chief analyst paused to breath. "The incident in CERN, whether directly or indirectly, does appear to link with the United States. Intel suggests that Alec Mercer is an alias. The facial recognition that we tried to run on him through the global digital civilian and terrorist archives returned nothing. On paper, the man does not exist; leading us to explore many possible alternatives, including the possibility of him working for any intelligence agency." He forwarded a redacted document from the Brazilian Republican Archives towards the Director General.

"It took us some time but we found this. The Brazilian's do seem to know a lot about this man. "He is the man who they believe killed the dictator Capitán Javier del Mundo back in '15. This document was in their secure archives. It was an assassination fully sanctioned by none other than the CIA." He forwarded another document. "Our analysts were able to separate the inks used to redact the document. This is a transcript of the file, including that which was blacked out."

Hewitt had been listening closely to what his analyst was saying. He pulled out his right drawer taking out a pair of reading spectacles which he wore to study the documents forwarded to him. "Do you know what this means?"

"Yes sir. I believe that this, in light of the recent changes in their policy to share intelligence is indicative of this."

"If you are right then the United States of America has sparked another cold war. As it is their position in the UN Security Council is weakening. As of now, countries are preparing for a terrorist attack, but if the blame for this incident falls on any one country, they will prepare for war. Britain will have to evaluate its international diplomatic policy, especially with the US. I must inform the Home Secretary about this."

"Wait sir, there's more." The chief analyst interrupted.

"We have received declassified intelligence from France listing the different experiments carried out by CERN. There is nothing which remotely indicates that any kind of advanced weapons research was taking place in CERN. This to me makes much more sense. This intel of a bomb also seems to have originated from the US."

"What are they playing at?" Hewitt asked.

"At this point, it is very unclear. We know that Dr. Élénoré Bassét was an employee of CERN but she and about a hundred of other top scientists were also in the employment records of the Brookehaven National Laboratory. It seems the US has played a much larger game here and on whom the blame actually lies is not clear at the moment. Our informant confirmed that they did in fact work in CERN, on an extremely confidential research but as to the nature of the research it is not known. As the only people who knew about it are dead, and whatever records they had in their servers were lost or destroyed in the attack, thereby increasing the seriousness of the issue evenmore. With the world's top scientists and the best research facility, it wouldn't be too much of a stretch if they were actually making a new generation bomb."

"You mean to say they might have made a bomb at CERN?" Hewitt asked.

"Not likely, in my opinion. Though since I cannot be conclusive at this point, I would say that if they did had any type of role in weapons research, it would be in the field of nuclear energy generation. Her entire team had profound expertise in the field of nuclear sciences."

"In any case…" Hewitt exhaled with hollowed eyes. The term Nuclear in context of war was a nightmare for any country; still they go on with it. Hewitt could only wonder if the third world war began, what ashes would remain this time. "I have to inform the Home Secretary. Is that all?"

"Yes sir."

35

Trap

Marvin's Safe house

"It's a trap!!" Marvin yelled with a tinge of urgency and a hint of hopelessness.

"I know", Alec assured, calmly.

"What?!" Marvin replied, baffled.

"Never mind that, I don't expect more than a few minutes", Mercer informed him as he loosely patched the wounds on his body. "Can you move?"

'Uh huh", he dosed as he raised his head to face his friend as it glittered with counterfeit hope which showed in his eyes. He knew the facts; it was time to face reality. His injuries, though not life threatening, had caused too much blood loss already. He'd have a better prospect of survival in a hospital, not there.

"Ugh, come on!" he grunted as he tried to drag Marvin's weak and tattered body back the way he came.

Agh! It hurts.

In any type of injury, even if it is patched and properly sutured up, it hurts more when you try to move it than when you keep it still. A day-to-day experience. But if you're full of *damages,* it hurts like hell if you'd be dragged on the solid ground. Marvin felt the same pain. He'd had enough of pain, of torture. He had lost his determination. The spark in his eyes, for which he got praises from women, had diminished along with his radiating spirit.

"Ugh, Ah! KILLER, please stop! I can't go any further." He gloomed.

"Shut up! We're just there", Mercer lied.

"My injuries are bad. You know it. There's no point. I'll never make it out alive. I'll be nothing but a burden and besides there's no time!"

There was no way that Mercer was going to leave his friend in there to die. The idea simply was out of the question. But he had to be real. He had already known that the things were bad as he descended down the singular elevator shaft, down the safe house, but never could he have guessed the pressing emergency of Marvin's extraneous situation. He could have never known that it was that bad. He did not know that the path was so deep and the way out would be just as long. The thought came in his mind and projected future scenarios in his brain.

There's no time.

"No way!" he recoiled, "You're just delirious from the blood loss. Of course, we'll get out of here...alive...and together or did you already forget what I am capable of?"

He was not going to leave him there. If not for Marvin then for himself; he had lost way too many friends, loved ones. He was definitely not going to lose more. But what could he do?

What do I do?!

He pulled up his friend close to him. *You are gonna be alright. I promise.*

What do I do?

His head frayed here-and-there, spinning everywhere, looking for something...*anything!* There were quite a lot of times in his life where he had been in quite a pickle, where his life depended on his improvisation, but he carved out those situations most beautifully. All was due to his charms, sweet talk and creative mind. But the pressure of losing his friend got to him. His focused eyes scanned the cold dark room as hard as could.

"You're gonna have to leave me, and you know it."

Mercer remained silent.

Marvin voice softened as it slowed down, "You wouldn't believe the dream I just....Listen closely."

Mercer pulled his ear near Marvin's mouth, "It's much bigger than you think...bigger than you...a global conspiracy to subdue...meet this woman, Rebecca Belluccio, she left the agency and now freelances in European countries..." Marvin's chest cried for air desperately. But he was not getting any. His left lung had been nicked. Wheezing and coughing, he tried desperately to convey that what could even be his last message to KILLER. "She's got all that you need to go...home. Take *this* with you", handing over the key to a subway locker, he recognized even in the dark. "There are things...you...need to...know." The painful words became silent. Marvin just lay there motionless.

Knowing that there was nothing else that he could do, he just stared directly into Marvin's eyes "I'm sorry!"

Central Intelligence Agency
Headquarters at Langley, Virginia
Signals Intelligence Division (SID)

No sooner did the Director of Operations leave, than all the monitors displaying the feed from the remote WET operative's started showing static instead of the high definition video.

"What!" Jenifer flustered in panic. She gave a helpless glance at Brian, who she knew had better technical skills than herself.

"I'm on it!" Brian resounded.

The director turned around, as an instinctive stimulus to all the sudden commotion which had aroused the whole room. "What happened?" He demanded.

"Somebody is jamming our signal!" Brian reported.

"Can we atleast communicate with our men?" He asked, patiently, as patient he could be, before he could storm them into oblivion.

"No sir, we can't." Jenifer reported. "But we're working on it!"

"Well...work faster!" Jameson pounded as he exited the floor.

"Jenifer!" Brian called. "You changed the signal encryption from linear to radial! I'll use a multiwave tracker to locate signal bandwidth outside the range of jammer!"

"If it is a jammer—that is!" She gave a satirical pray of hope. "If its full range, then nothing we can do!"

"Let's hope it is not!" Brian prayed back.

After a whole five minutes of meticulous commands and operations, they failed to provide any successful results. Even Chloe had joined their duo. The task given to her was to provide images of the location from the local City Cams which had conquered every nook and cranny of every metropolitan city across the world. Unfortunately, even that gave nothing but static. All the cameras in a one mile radius were completely blacked out, leaving her completely baffled as to how it was even possible. What was present on her screen was evident enough. All their trials useless.

"It's back up!" An analyst replied.

"What? What happened? What did you do?" Brian quested.

"I don't know!" The analyst replied, pounded by the string of questions. "It just happened!"

"Sir.... it's back online!" Jenifer reported through the intercom.

Inside his office, the director after being briefed about the turn of events raised his head up. His eyes, at perfect distance and height from the large CGD screen, were keenly observing the contents which it displayed through his transparent walls of his balcony office, which oversaw the entire floor.

His jaws dropped in shock and excruciatingly terrifying horror at what he was seeing, and the same was the situation for everyone who was present on the floor.

In horror, they saw the display panel which projected an image showing the entire building, crumbing on its knees, violent explosion centering the evident load bearing columns, shattering, squeaking, exploding. The building which they had to surveil.

"What the hell..." They all queried. But no one knew.

What's happening?

36

Tremors

Outside Marvin's Safe house

"Sir, it's done." Hunter reported. This was the first time he was making any type of contact with his ultimate boss—Sir Richard Meyers.

"You are sure?" Meyers articulated.

"Affirmative!" the Commander replied but with a sense of microscopic hesitation in his voice.

"And the drive?" Richard pressed.

"It's en-route to your location." Hunter replied.

"Locate the girl; she's the last piece of the puzzle. Locate her...quietly." Meyers ordered. Much emphasis was placed on every wording.

Finally, some good news.

Richard Meyers leaned back a bit in his ergonomic reclining chair, stretching his hands and interlocking them at the back of his head supporting his cranium, relieved; but not completely. There was still another task at hand.

The arm of his chair had a rectangular screen on his right. It contained many icons and functions which comes very handy from time to time. Expensive gadgets like these were a big liking of his and were also a big hit among many other corporate giants. He pulled down his hand hovering over the screen and pressed the call button which floated about a centimeter in the air above it.

"Abay Bayev."

A green holographic projection had appeared which curved around the edges of the table.

'Dialing' appeared on the virtual screen with the photo id and the familiar dotted circling animation which always comes when working.

A map appeared on the side showing his real-time location, local time and everything. All the existing data got sidelined to the corner and a big blank area took one half of the screen. Its job was to write down and translate the conversations to the default language in case of international calls, a *plug-in* he had installed to reduce the problems while speaking to non-English speaking people.

"Yes Sir."

"Initiate Protocol LIBITO."

"You sure…Sir? The program still has quite a few years to go." Abay stated carefully.

"Yes. I am quite sure!!" Richard pounded.

"I am going to need conformation from Aurora himself." Abay replied shyly.

"How dare you?" Meyers became aggressive.

"Sorry sir. Bosses facilities…bosses rule." Abay replied.

"It's my holding. I can do whatever I want with it." Richard Meyers argued.

"I really am sorry, Sir." Abay apologized as hard as he could. "But it does not work this way. You given up your legal authority the moment you signed the agreement. I need majority consensus and Aurora's okay to do as you ask."

"Never mind…" Meyers realized arguing was pointless. "I'll get it done directly."

Staring across the alley, gazing at the painful remnants of a beautiful building which was now making its way towards the dense and dirty aquatic sub-terrain of the sea beneath, Hunter took a deep thoughtful gulp.

"Sir…I think we should report what just happened!" His specialist urged him.

"That could have been anything! Why do you want to complicate things?" Hunter justified.

Earlier, when Hunter had pressed the button which wirelessly sends a charge to the ignition mechanism, the building was supposed to blow up into tiny smithereens. But it did not. For exactly ten minutes, to the clock, the pack of C4 did not blow. That was ten minutes too much that was unaccounted for.

"Sir..." The specialist pressed harder. "We should send a WET team down there just to be sure! We still think—"

"Well, I don't!" Hunter cut him off. "Let's move out!" He ordered. "It's gonna be a mess out there!"

37

Executive Order

The Oval Office
West Wing
The White House

"Mr. President! There has been another incident overseas." The Secretary of Homeland Security reported.

"What's it this time?" President Wilson inquired inquisitively.

"The Director of Operations SID, Jameson Theroux is on line one. I'll patch it through!" Nolan stated. "Mr. Theroux... you are now speaking to the President. What did you want to report?" The Secretary of DHS questioned.

"My people were conducting an investigation into the security status of the Agency...whether it was compromised or not...after that incident. Their work led us to a man named Henry Bale...currently worked under the alias Marvin Calloway, CIA, who abandoned his operation and went AWOL in Rome. Then we received an electronic whisper..."

"Be brief, Mr. Theroux!" The secretary of the Department of Homeland Security urged. "This is the President you are talking to! Mission specifics are best sent through Agency transcripts!"

"Let the man speak!" The President retorted. "Director... I assure you, you can be frank and lengthy...as long as it is leading somewhere!"

"Thank you Mr. President." Jameson gratified and then continued. "We intercepted a transmission into a rogue mercenary operation. It was a location. Co-ordinates. It took us to Venice, Italy. It was a safehouse belonging to our AWOL agent, Henry Bale. We were hoping to catch a glimpse of his contact when our signal was jammed. When out analysts got the stream back online, we found that the whole building was demolished."

"So..." The President's advisor scoffed. "What was so important that it required the President's personal attention?"

"Because...our agents flagged ILSA soldiers all around the vicinity. But the worst of all, we tagged somebody else." Director Jameson sent a digital image to the President, which opened on the console inside the Oval Office. "His name is Alec Mercer." Jameson explained at the image of a man who was swimming out of the debris of the fallen wreck. Displayed alongside was a photo which was obtained from his redacted file. "Surprisingly, our systems flag him as CIA. A rogue agent who was supposed to be MIA. It seems I do not have enough clearance to read his file." Jameson exhaled. "Now Mr. President, I'm sure you are aware of the CERN incident, and perhaps that this man is the prime suspect. If word leaks out that one of our agents is responsible for that tragedy...it can spark an international incident...it could completely ruin our credibility."

The President was stunned. Director Jameson knew that his bold words were receiving the attention required.

Apart from the fact that he had just been sucker-punched, the President could not make himself believe what he had seen. President Wilson distinctly remembered sending a decorated war hero and trained CIA agent on a very special mission to CERN. He remembered signing the papers which covertly issued the brand new credential of Alec Mercer.

"What do you suggest, Director?" The President asked, keeping up appearance.

"Issue a kill order on him. He is a walking security breach. We need to get rid of him." Jameson urged. "If this fact becomes public, the CIA will stand for nothing...our credibility will be nothing."

"Do as you feel right...you will get all the clearance you need." The President responded. Then he leaned forward and disconnected the phone call.

"Mr. President, I can assure you that the man came with the highest recommendation from the General." The secretary of the DHS said.

"What do you make of all of this?" The President asked.

"Sir, I had a brief talk with him a long time back. He was a believer. He trusted the system with his heart. I know after what he had been through makes him more likely to defect. But trust me on this sir, there is a deeper reason I chose him for this mission.... No matter what happens, he will pull through."

"So what should I do?" The President asked.

"I'll get a team prepped to find and extract him. It is more than obvious that things are different from what they appear to be." The secretary replied. "Then we can find the truth."

38

Contact

5:30 PM
Saturday, 13th June, 2026
Outside Café L'Amour

These were details written in the crushed up piece of paper that Marvin had handed to him. He read it again just to recheck everything again as he walked through the bustling streets dodging cameras and checking for tails if anyone be following.

Café of Love, he chuckled to himself. It was one in the list of many highly overrated things in the world, according to Mercer himself. Europe or States alike, there was not a single city which did not boast a Café L'Amour in its heart. A mystical heavenly place where cupids buoyant with the winds of love and lust joined eager souls ready for union into a loving and caring metamorphic blob. Where men, whether young or old, whether student or teacher, all fall head over heels to the damsel's countless seduction tricks. Every character finds him in such a place, some by choice and some without it. Mercer certainly did not want to be there. But his choice was irrelevant. The place was set. Cards were dealt. And he did not have much time.

After a minutes jog, he reached his destination. It was located at a three-way crossroad. There were bright white chairs outside with matching tables but he could not spot anyone who matched the description, so he walked up to the mud-brown door with square transparent glass panels. He pushed them forward with his strong muscles and walked in with a breeze which hulled through the whole restaurant, as Zeus walking on the clouds.

He could smell the sweet aroma of the freshly baked croissants and pastries as if they were all inviting him, tempting him so that he got lost for a bit in the cakes and melted butter cookies which his mother used to make at home when he came back from the grounds after a long tiring day practicing his slam dunks.

There are many ways in which different unfamiliar spies meet. Subtle hints to tell them that I am the one you are looking for, but in many cases it was quite easy to spot the odd one out by just looking for the signs. The person would be alone. Perhaps, reading newspaper and generally, not talking on the phone. Patient, anticipating, cautious, and extremely alert.

His eyes glanced all over the room until he found the one. She was a tall woman, about Mercer's height, or maybe a bit more. She had a well-toned body which was tanned to perfection and ample breasts and hips which gave a great figure and all the more attractive that most of the men were discretely gazing at her with amazement which she knew but seemed to enjoy it. Her long and luscious hair was sort of a darker blonde shade with strokes of auburn and chestnut underneath to give them a rich contrasting depth. She was wearing a sparkling white sleeveless shirt top which sort of hugged her bosom and the first two buttons unbuttoned revealing just enough part of her chest and some frail purple clothing underneath it, her legs folded on top of each other as women usually do and a big black tinged goggles through which she was reading the paper while sipping her steaming coffee. She seemed to be beauty personified, the goddess Aphrodite herself, and every man young or old had indeed fallen head over heels to her charms.

Mercer had walked right up to her and was about to approach her when she greeted him abruptly.

"Mr. Mercer, I presume." She asked.

"Yes." Mercer replied crudely.

"I'm Rebecca Bellucio, as you must already know." She introduced herself with the charms of the skilled Mentalist that she was.

"Yes...Marvin told me *about* you!" there was a hint of undercurrent sarcasm in his voice.

"What's that supposed to mean?" Rebecca enquired inquisitively.

"You know...agent turned freelancer." Mercer ejaculated.

"I had my reasons." Rebecca justified.

"I'm sure you did." He replied in the same voice. "So...", he extended, *"The Café of Love...*huh...why'd you choose this place?" Mercer asked his longstanding question.

"Two helpless lovers...in over their heads... a perfect cover. In a bit of a romantic mood myself." Rebecca explained. "Nothing sinister."

"Uh huh." Mercer expanded.

"And how do you know Marvin?" Mercer enquired.

"He once did a favor for me." Rebecca informed.

"You'll not tell me what it was, will you?" Mercer smiled.

"No..." Rebecca smiled back.

"You have what I need?"

She had a parcel which she had kept close to her, away from anybody's sight which she picked up, placed it on the table and pushed it towards him. Mercer picked up the yellow colored parcel and was about to open it when the waiter came up to him to take his order.

"Would you like to give your order, sir?" A waitress crept up from behind her, though Alec was well aware of her presence.

"Yes, I'll have a Cappuccino, cold with ice. Extra sweet. Can you get that?" He answered with a smile.

"I'll see what I can do." The waitress replied as she turned her back towards him and marched towards the kitchen to place his order.

"Thanks!" He replied.

Backing his focus to the parcel, he opened up the seal, opened its mouth and glanced at the contents, while Rebecca narrated what gifts she had brought for him.

"There are two passports, for you and the girl." Rebecca iterated. "A few hundred thousand dollars in small unmarked, non-sequential bills, and some global currencies, mainly Mexican. Your name will be Antonio Fernandez and hers will be Katiana, your wife. The plane tickets are for Mexico. From there you'll enter States through the sea. Go over to this location. You'll find a white boat 'Endeavour'. The boat is registered in the States so if the coast guard stops you show them the paper inside. You know how these things are done, don't you?" Rebecca smiled again.

"Of course." Mercer replied with pride.

"All this is a bit generous of you. Too generous. What do you want in return?" He probed.

"Just that the next time you see Marvin...tell him that we're even." She commanded, revealing a bit of her volatile nature.

"Marvin's dead." Mercer stated.

"It's a shame! He was good at what he did." Rebecca stated with admiration.

"So...now that the business is done. Would you like to follow me back to my place?" She suggested leaning forward revealing bit of her inviting cleavage.

"Thanks but pass." Mercer walked away.

39

Déjà Vu

It had been a very long time since he last visited the place.

The building had definitely lost its charms. Even with all the advancements in the fields of science and technology, the rocketing prices of gasoline and diesel made it hard for the common man to afford the most basic essentials of life. A means of transportation. They moved on to the cheaper alternative, a solar powered tram service which began dominating the streets of every metropolitan city in the world, forgetting its once majestic predecessor which was now becoming a diminishing breed.

The bus station in Langley, Virginia was once bustling with people. Being the bedroom community for Washington D.C., many middle-class citizens who worked in Washington lived in Virginia. The historically important State of Virginia also houses the headquarters of the only civilian government agency, which is legally sanctioned by the government to conduct covert operations outside the country. The Central Intelligence Agency, known by its many colloquial terms was now facing a grave problem.

The building had definitely lost its charm. Walking on those familiar paths, he reached an end of the long corridor. Standing at the sole entrance of that corridor, Mercer felt as if he had been hit by a nauseous *Déjà vu* moment. He remembered the time when he used to periodically return to this same place for countless reasons, but never did he have this sense of foreboding on him like he had now. He took out the key, given to him by his closest friend, from his right jacket pocket and held it in front of him, staring at it keenly through his lustrous black eyes. It was a bronze-like, old and rusted small key which was broken at one end.

Why did he want me to come back? He wanted to show me something.... What could it be?

Marvin's last words, still ringing in his ears, were giving him even more confusion and dilemma. He could hear those words so clearly as if Marvin himself was speaking them at that very instant. Leaving him behind was painful, but it was a necessary step, cold and calculated, even though he was not at complete peace with himself for doing that. He had to. He had to be realistic.

Global conspiracy? What the hell is it all about? And to subdue what?

It won't make any sense right now, not until I get to see the big picture. Things that I need to know? It must have been very important....for him to waste his last words on that.

By this time he had already reached at the middle of the corridor. He gazed left and then he turned right, trying to find the locker which had the matching series engraved on it.

Five-nine-two-four...five-nine-two...hah! Here it is.

He scraped off the dust, softly with his palm, which covered the particular locker and all those around it. The shining metal underneath reflected back the fluorescent glow of the singular torchlight which Mercer was emitting. A bronze badge was located in the center in which '5924' was engraved in black. Quickly, he inserted the same key which he had held in his hand and twisted it. The square door creaked and through the void Mercer could spot a few of optical Blue-Ray disks securely stored in the locker. The one on the top was facing him and he quickly noticed that something was written on it.

"This first!" was written in black felt on the white background.

What could it be?

But Mercer didn't know. All he knew was that whatever it was, it was very important. Without wasting an instant, he emptied the contents of the locker into his back pack and strode off, innocent to the upcoming events which were going to change him completely.

40

Moving Target

A Safe house
Langley, Washington

"Hey Mercer...if you're watching this then you know, I'm dead. I need you to understand that at the time the intel reached me it was already too late; the damage was done. I never had the heart to tell you. When Christina died, you were devastated...I guess I was waiting for the right moment. Maybe it was stupid to wait...first you regressed and then when you turned back to civilization, I thought that I can't tell about the burden I was bearing. Every damn time I saw you, the same ran in my mind. It would have torn you apart, and it will be painful even now. I'm sorry my friend, more sorry than you will ever know!" The video ended. Mercer was puzzled.

Not sparing any time, he quickly pressed Eject, causing the disk to come out. He switched the Blue Ray disks with the next one in the series. Another media file popped up. This one was an audio container. He double clicked the icon and the audio started playing. Mercer leaned forward, and with his chin resting with the support of his strong arms, listening attentively what intel was so devastating that his best friend had to keep it secret, even from him for so many years.

"...word about this leaks out, you know the outcome. He's constantly asking questions, digging deeper. Soon enough the red-tape won't be enough to stop him and he'll find our identities. What should we do? Kill him. KILLER is a liability, now more than ever. We can't risk it. We've invested more than seventy trillion dollars in the Jami Project, not counting the money spent in constructing remote facilities and miles of oil pipelines. Mobilize our local assets. Make it look like a robbery gone bad. I'll not accept any more screw-ups, you hear me? Yes, your highness, I'll inform you when it is done."

"Is this what I think it is?" Thought Mercer taking out the disk from his MacBook Pro.

The disk was one of many in the collection which was delivered to Marvin from his contact at ECHELON. Most of which he had heard, but some were new to him. Some which Marvin had ignored earlier due to priority. ECHELON is a multinational multi-government organization, similar to the NSA in the US. But due to its international status, local governments are able to circumvent their country's laws, and still continue operations which were illegal in their countries, like phone tapping citizens, satellite surveillance, and other operations like providing tactical support, encryption, decryption, etc. Their outside status allowed them to complete operations which in the normal course of things would have been denied.

Since tremendously huge amounts of data torrents its way through their systems, it is impossible for ECHELON to monitor all recorded suspicious conversations and transactions. Instead they run a tracking module on their servers, which mechanically listen to the conversations for marked keywords, like Osama, POTUS, Black Stone, and as it does it automatically records the conversation and tags it according to the priority of the keywords used.

In this conversation, the keywords were 'Jami Project', 'KILLER' and 'Aurora', which led the conversation to be flagged and recorded. But they weren't that high up in the list so eventually it was ignored, after all when the conversation was being recorded, ECHELON had bigger problems.

He pulled out the next Blu-ray disk from the collection; all of it was related to Bearing PetroTech. He looked at the cover; it was dated November 16, 2007. He placed it inside the drive and the computer pulled it in. He pressed the play button, causing another recording to play.

"...Sir, I'm afraid, I've got some bad news.... Of course you do, what is it then...the KILLER situation has reached an elevated condition. The assets we had sent to his location were unable to find him at home. He was supposed to be alone that day, according to his online calendar, but he went somewhere, his wife and kids were apparently at the scene. The asset in frenzy, killed them, and to extinguish any evidence, set the apartment on fire.... Is he aware of the agency's connection?... He appears not to be.... Good, then. This would keep his mind off of us; all the same keep a close eye on him. Inform me of any suspicious activity."

By the time he reached the middle of the recording, Mercer had closed his eyes in sorrow. He fully understood the context of that classified conversation. He wanted to cry, to let it all out, but no tears rolled down his chiseled cheeks. It was against his internal nature to cry. His ears were unable to bear hearing the words which were falling on them as they weighed too much. He was full of vain, angry at himself for being who he was angry at the people who did this to him but only one thought was going through his mind.

Only if...only if I were there instead of them...then things could have been different.

Now there was no sorrow, no pain. What was left in him was anger. Anger at himself, but mostly anger at those who killed his family. He swore in vengeance that he would avenge the death of his family and give them the same suffering which he had endured for all these years.

But for that he needed to know who they were; he needed information. Coincidentally, Marvin left him with plenty. It appeared as if Marvin had been collecting all this intel for quite a while. A collation which not only included abstract recordings and phone tapings but maps, grid locations, GIS and GPS coordinates, redacted documents, mission transcripts and lot more, including a name Sir Richard Meyers.

He opened the Safari web browser and googled the name 'Richard Meyers'. He saw another familiar name, the company Bearing Oil & PetroTech and this Meyers was the CEO. He was under many types of investigation, even with criminal charges yet nobody was able to pin him, and under stringent surveillance not only by the FBI but all the military and civil intelligence agencies in the world; the CIA, NSA, ECHELON, the Ml6 and 5, GCHQ, Mossads and many others. Yet he roamed about blatantly mocking all these intelligence agencies.

"He's the one! At the eye of the storm." He thought. "I'll kill him!" he finally said it and he said it out loud.

But he soon felt a presence of somebody else in the room, somebody who was not supposed to be there. Mercer's super trained senses could deduce the entire frame of the immigrant, as if he was standing almost beside the assailant. He had a 9 mm pistol neatly balanced on his lap. He diverted his attention to the rest of the room, behind him, where the assailant would be slowly making his way to pounce on him. The fairly sized room had a very queer design and walls painted deep red textured paint and almost no furniture at all was now brimming with tension. At the moment everything was visible to him. His hands slowly left the keyboard and started reaching towards the same pistol. After grabbing it firmly, his thumb silently turned the safety off and suddenly and briskly he turned back towards the intruder with his gun pointing at him held firmly with both his hands. On the other end of the suppressor, a woman was standing, crying. "How many times do I have to tell you…don't sneak up behind me like that!" He scolded her as he pulled back his gun and turned the safety back on.

"Is it true?" The woman asked him. Her deeper platinum blonde hair was dyed entirely to the deep dark black shade. Just as Alec's lustrous eyes, her hair glistened like the clear summer nights in the equinox.

"What?" Mercer peered, confused.

"That you had a family." Mercer took a deep sigh as he nodded yes.

"And they were killed?" Élénoré countered.

"Killed and then…set on fire. Bodies were charred beyond recognition." Mercer stated. The heartbreaking pain still projected in his eyes.

"I'm terribly sorry…I know what it's like." Élénoré consoled.

"Oh, do you now? Terribly sorry!" He spoke with a sarcastic chuckle. "Everybody is terribly sorry! You being sorry isn't going bring them back! What do you know about death, huh? You're just an anti-social scientist, who has no place to go besides your lab." In a fit of anger, Mercer poured off all his hatred on her.

Éllén was silent. She gave a quick nod and after an awkward moment staring at him turned back and silently started walking towards one of the other rooms.

"Crap!" He said to himself with a huge sigh. "Wait...Éllén wait...where are you going?"

"Thanks for all you did for me...but you don't need to save me anymore." Then just for a second she turned back only her head and as she gazed in his same deep black eyes she said, "Thank you Alec...for everything. I'll miss you if I live long enough...good bye." She waved her right hand at him as she said goodbye.

"No wait...no, you can't step outside the safe house." Hurriedly, he ran towards her, intercepting her and quickly turned to face her, blocking her by standing in the path.

"Step aside Alec...please don't make it any harder than it already is." She tried to flank him from his right but Mercer had much faster reflexes, getting past him was impossible. He then tried to squeeze through the left but to no avail. Then she tried to push him off his path but he was impenetrable like a wall. Seeing that she had no option, she started throwing punches at his chest and as she did she found herself helpless, not because of Mercer though. Even after a minute she was still throwing punches at him but Mercer felt that they were getting much softer and lesser in frequency. Then she tipped her head, resting her face on his chest. Mercer could even hear her crying. She pulled him closer, feeling his heart strongly beating in his chest and the warmth of his body.

"Why couldn't you just step aside, huh?" Her arms spread around his waist, held him tightly, tears rolling down her cheeks.

"I'm sorry." He apologized silently. "I shouldn't have—"

"Shh...shh...it's okay. I understand what it feels like." Élénoré consoled again.

"What is that supposed to mean?" He asked her with a puzzled look on his face.

"When I was just a little girl", Éllén elaborated. "My father Dr. Giuseppe Beauvais...a scientist...a great scientist, um he was working back at CERN...actually on the same project I am. One night I was waiting for him; it was three o' clock in the night." She permitted herself a small smile as she remembered the Saturday nights when her father used to cook gourmet food for the both of them. "He...umm usually worked late. But that night...he never came home that night. All I got was a text. 'Au revoir'...it means—"

"Goodbye..." Mercer cut her off.

"Next thing I know my estranged mother came from Marseille and took me back with her. I still dream about those blinding lights, the ambulances, the police cars, screaming at me. Hearing words like radiation, fallout…but I was too small to understand what any of that meant."

Mercer could not even begin to imagine what it feels like; being on your own in the world…alone. She was surrounded yet she was alone. Orphaned at such a tender age and made to face the world, the brutal world, the dreaded cocktail of mystery and despair. Compared to what Mercer had been through perhaps Élénoré had been through worse.

He took a deep breath, pumping the conditioned air into his lungs and as he exhaled the moist air out of his nostrils he could feel the courage streaming through his veins.

"Éllén…" he exhaled. "There is something you should also know."

"What do you mean?" She looked surprised as she looked up at Mercer's face with her child-like innocence of her petite little façade.

"That night…when your dad died…it was no accident… he…" Mercer paused. "they were murdered."

"What?!" She tried to pull herself away from him but anticipating her reaction he had already grabbed her arms with his strong hands. "Let go of me!" Élénoré screamed with the excruciating pain which riddled her heart.

After applying all her force she was able to break loose off of Mercer's strong grip. Her eyes were red and sore because of all the crying. Frozen in shock, her hands covered her mouth in astonishment.

"How long had you known about my father?" She questioned him with a stern voice.

Mercer nodded his head in denial. "Believe me…I didn't know until you told me yourself that your father was in that accident." He explained.

Her legs were tired from the chase. Her own body was feeling to her much more like dead meat and the foreboding was a burden even still. Her legs were weak and trembling so she came down crashing where she was. Her thin arms instinctively came down and broke her fall. She found herself on her knees. The tear drops which were rolling down her cheeks to her chin collated together and fell down and splattered on the floor like rain drops.

Breathing out she marked, "I guess there's no point in crying over the same broken egg twice."

"Don't lose hope…" He told her as he helped her up. "Keep

anger instead...that's what keeps me going."

"You know who killed my father?" She demanded in a tone Mercer had never heard from her before. It was anger in her voice.

"That I don't know...but you see that guy?" He asked pointing to the picture dominating the holographic screen on his MacBook Pro. Éllén turned back her head and located her target. He was an old aged man, with pale skin and silvery hair. Even in the file photo he had a smirk on his face. To Éllén it was as if his innate imitation was taunting her.

"What do I have to do?" She asked, turning her face back to Mercer. *Mercer smiled.*

41

Sous-Chef

"No, no, no dear...you're butchering it!" Giuseppe shrieked as he rushed into the kitchen. "French cuisine is an art...c'est l'amour."

"I know father..." Élénoré worked hard to control her chuckle. She always felt like laughing when her father described cooking as c'est l'amour or 'it is love'. But she did not like her father's intrusion into the kitchen. Every time Giuseppe interrupted her cooking she felt like she was inept at what she was doing. After all, it was not like she was preparing the complex Beef Wellington or the intricate Béarnaise sauce, rather she was making one of the simplest French dishes known to man, Nutty Pasta and Balsamic Chicken and Fig Brochettes. And yet her father arrives, nothing short of a prince to rescue his damsel in distress, not realizing that the damsel is in fact NOT in distress, let alone in need of rescue.

But then, he was rarely at home to arrive for rescuing, as he was so insanely busy at his work. When she thought of what little time they actually spend together, she stopped minding of her father's innocent intrusion into the kitchen.

"You're cutting against the fibers, honey." Giuseppe tried to explain. "Even chicken needs to be treated properly...needs to be pampered...needs to be cared." As he gently took the knife from Élénoré's hand and placed it into the sink. Then he pulled out a more favorable knife from the set to prepare the chicken for marinating.

"You say that as you drive a knife through its body." Élénoré gave out a teenage laugh, taking a step back to give her father enough space to work in. The brilliant orange overhead fluorescent lights in the kitchen were just perfect for the craftsman to perform his masterpiece. While the sixteen year old fair maiden, in her brazenly colorful full-sleeved winter top and pink short skirt took her time to adore the beauty of the surrounding they lived in. It was just over dusk.

"At least...this is better than what you were doing to this poor succulent soul." Giuseppe laughed heartily.

The evening street lights came to life perfectly on time. Under the sudden illumination, she noticed some movement on the marbled street beneath. At first instant, she believed the apparition to be her boyfriend as her friends never came alone, always in mobs. On another glimpse of that apparition, she realized that it could not be him as the man that came was much taller, was of good athletic built, plus he came wearing the same white lab coat.

Élénoré's velvet soft skirt rustled as she ran towards the glass wall through which she had been observing the road so keenly to get a better view of the person, who in a few seconds would be well inside the house. She turned towards her father and observed something to which she had been oblivious the whole time. Her father was also wearing that same white lab coat, indicative that he would be going to the LHC that evening. Élénoré's heart drooped. She stood there in her thick white woolen socks, her silky flaxen hair flowing down her miniature head, and her petite little face dropped, sulking.

Soon, Uncle Carlisle entered the kitchen through the entrance from the living room. He knew the combinations to almost all the locks in the house, so it was not unnatural that he did not ring the bell instead.

"Ready Giuseppe." Gaulle asked chirpily.

Giuseppe, who had been unaware of his presence or the time, was fairly surprised to see him in the kitchen. Instantly, his eyes panned towards the clock on the oven. "I'm late!" He gasped.

"But I thought we were going to have dinner together..." Élénoré's hurt voice flowed throughout the kitchen. She stood there in her pink skirt and winter top, with a sulking petite little face, like a little hurt pup. She curled up her pink rosy lips in a pout and crossed her arms together as shifted her body weight on her right leg, as a display of her resentment.

"Don't worry dear; I will be home even before you will take the chicken out of the brochette. And one day I'll teach you the real French cuisine." Giuseppe consoled her teenage daughter as he left her in the kitchen. "Au revoir Élénoré." He yelled from the road beneath, where he could see the faint silhouette of her daughter through the semi-translucent one-sided glass. Élénoré placed her hand on the glass and moved it to and fro as she said in a hushed voice. "Au revoir papa."

She then went back to station in the middle of the room. Her father had already prepared the chicken. She emptied the chicken into the bowl containing the Balsamic Vinegar and grounded Herbs, mixed up the contents, covered it with cling foil and placed it in the fridge.

That night she waited up to 2 AM in the night, waiting keenly for her father to return from her work. She was starving from hunger, but she'd rather have dinner with her father beside her on the table. When her body got the best of her mind, she finally gave up waiting for her father. She knew her father might not return the whole night. He had stayed away at work entire nights many times before. When she knew she was at the brink of what her weak body could support, she slowly walked into the kitchen, pulled out the marinated chicken from the fridge, placed the chicken pieces on the skewer and put them inside the rotisserie.

An hour later, she was still waiting keenly for her father to return, but he didn't. She put on her oven mitts to pull out the chicken from the oven. She de-skewered the pieces into a platter, and ate it as she watched some random channel on the television as she sunk into her favorite sofa.

She was woken to her mother's shouts. People had captured her home. She was confused and petrified but she knew then itself that something was terribly wrong.

42

Eye of the Storm

Outside 233 South Wacker Drive, Chicago

The crossroads was buzzing with traffic streaming in from all directions. Pedestrians were rushing to their offices in the area while the tourists were visiting the tallest skyscraper in America; the famous Bearing Tower.

Neatly camouflaged in the crowd, Mercer was also heading towards the tourist entrance to the same building whose silvery shine glimmered under the sun's reflection.

"Welcome to Bearing Tower". The door man in his iconic green and khaki uniform as he gave a quick tip of the hat to Mercer and opened the door. As the door opened, Mercer saw the queues and the people standing there. He glanced at his ChromeX and as the minutes hand struck '12', he sprang into action.

Emerging from the horizon, ripping the sky with its blaring turbine, a light green corporate helicopter with deep streaks of yellow, orange and white pierced through the clouds, making its way towards the tallest building whose majesty defined the skies of Chicago and dominated the skyline.

"Helipad clear for landing." Denise reported on the transceiver.

"Cutting too close there, Denise", the hoarse voice replied. "Boss is just a minute away."

"Hey! It's not my fault that the earlier pilot couldn't move his ass." She replied in a defensive tone.

"Whatever...", the speaker did not care.

Denise noticed that this time the voice felt closer than before. She turned behind her and laid her eyes on the one ugliest looking creature she had ever seen and many others behind him, following him to the helipad.

"What brings you up here on this beautiful day?" the satire remark she made at her boss.

He was just about to counter some smug remark to Denise but luckily for her, his hoarse voice was cut-off by the deafening noise transmitted by the approaching corporate chopper. As it came closer, it came down as a cyclone in its early stages reaching from the clouds to the ground. Their crisp grey office suits were fluttering under the influence of the strong winds radiating from the turbine which did not hinder them from making their way to the chopper, now only about a meter above the ground.

Steve, the ugly looking head of the Surveillance & Security stepped forward, climbing the small flight of stairs, he stepped onto the elevated helipad and as the chopper landed with a jerk, he quickly opened the door to greet his boss.

"Good Morning, Sir Meyers" he said trying to smile as best as he could. "How was the meeting?"

The boss did not response as he exited his luxury class corporate helicopter.

"Next time either land correctly or kiss your job goodbye." He warned the pilot who clumsily exited the chopper with the boss's briefcase and stuff.

"Yes sir...sorry sir." He apologized.

"Sorry is not nearly enough." Richard berated violently.

The peon was just standing there, below the helipad, he grabbed the stuff from the pilot and ran ahead to prepare the office for Sir Meyers.

"Walk with me Steve..." Richard was angry.

The Bearing Tower was an iconic destination for every tourist who made his way to Chicago. It had a history like no other. The Bearing tower to Chicago was like The Empire State Building to New York City.

And like many other skyscrapers of its kind, the tourists were not allowed to visit the floors on which the offices and suites are located. They were instead taken to a special visitor's area with viewing platforms and the Sky-deck. But there were elevators which had access to all the various floors and were located in the restricted areas and one needed to have access.

But issues like these were never a problem for Mercer. He timed his approach to one of those elevators. He pressed the call button. The door opened instantly as it was lodged on the same ground floor. But he waited just for a second as he started his march inside the elevator.

"Wait, Wait...hold the door!" A nerdy looking chap ran towards the same open elevator door.

Mercer pressed his right hand at the sides of the door, preventing the elevator from closing.

The man reached the elevator bank and with a sigh of relief and a deep exhale he said, "Phew... Thanks man." The apparent incumbent greeted.

"Don't mention it." He shrugged. "But which floor are you going to?"

"One-O- Seven. IT Department, Bearing Oil." He replied.

Perfect!

"Sorry man...security asked me to keep this one reserved for the boss, he's on the way. You know how he rolls... with full security detail and everything." Mercer chuckled slow and steady.

"Yeah tell me about it. Sucks though...never mind I'll just get the next one." The IT personnel stepped back.

"Wait!" Mercer called hastily. "Who won the game last night?" Mercer delayed.

"Oh man!" The employee's eyes glimmered. "It was simply awesome! The Red Sox obviously!"

"Pity!" Mercer sighed in his mind. He used to be a hard-core Yankees man by blood, but he did not care. That was another life and he was simply buying for time.

"See ya." The IT guy replied.

"Yeah."

The Roof
Bearing Tower

"About that little security breach that occurred few days ago…how could you let something like that happen?" Meyers scolded.

"I apologize for that, Sir." He apologized sheepishly. "It was a sole incident…won't happen again. Ever."

"You are saying that when you let the FBI in…and kick our front door!" Meyers retorted. "See… I don't mind these petty office politics but I won't stand another one of your…incidents. Understood?" Meyers pointed.

"Yes sir." Steve begged.

The elevator door had closed but it was still on the ground floor. Any moment, anybody can just walk up to it and press the call button. That was something he could not afford at all. But the lift would not move. For that he needed a keycard. Till now he had managed to keep himself away from the security camera's line of view, but now he needed some wiggle room. He tipped the camera above him, if only a little, just to prevent suspicion and then kneeled down. In his left hand, he had a device, something essential for his break-in. He had been flashing it at the IT guy. He must have thought it to be a cell-phone. In fact, it was an RFID receiver. Radio Frequency Identification. The access card transmitted an array of characters and digits which is similar to any password. Only after receiving the correct *password* will the elevator operate. On top of that the key card must have access to the suites of offices of Bearing Oil & PetroTech. The guy worked in IT in the same company so he was just perfect. His receiver was essentially just like the one installed inside the elevator, but it did not just receive the code, it recorded it and had the ability to retransmit it in all commercial frequencies. Just below the panel of buttons was the area where the receiver was installed. 'Swipe your card here' was written. He held the receiver just a few centimeters off the mark but there was no response. The machine was not responding.

He pulled out his ceramic knife and wedged it at the side of the panel, pivoted his knife outwards which ultimately shoved the panel open. He could now see the inside mechanism of elevator panel, but most of it was irrelevant for him. He needed to know the specific range the receiver was set to receive. 'Caution: Tampering with the RFID head will void the insurance cover on the elevator.' His eyes squinted while his index finger ran through each line to read the fine print which included the device specifications. As he found the correct values, he tweaked them in his own gadget and again placed it in front of RFID receiver.

The elevator gave the green light. He pulled out the knife and re-attached the panel back in its place and pressed the button. The elevator rocketed up at full speed.

"Sir, sir…hold up." A man exited his office on the 101st floor at the first glimpse of his boss and slowly sprinted to intercept him.

"What is it, Dylan?" Meyers enquired of one of his more competent employees.

"Minister Rathi is onboard. He has agreed to change the corporate petroleum laws in India but he is demanding fifty million dollars wired to his usual Swiss account. He says that he is taking a big risk doing this…so he deserves it." Steve informed.

"Peanuts…compared to what we will make. Good job." He patted Dylan on his back. "Anything else I should know?"

"Yeah, I was getting to it." He said in a very dull voice. Sir Meyers raised a brow. "Although he is going to change the petroleum laws, he says it is going to take some time. There is some sort of political crisis in India. He can't act until it all boils down."

They were walking on the same L-shaped path which led to Mr. Meyer's office suite. They were just ahead of the elevators on that part of the floor. The lift clinked open. The lobby was very crowded at the moment. As the new arrival stumbled into the group of people. "Excuse me!" He apologized to the people he was bumping into.

"Watch your step." He yelled at the stranger but did not give much attention. His mind was preoccupied with many other things. "Oh…sorry Sir Meyers." the newcomer apologized and moved on.

Sir Meyers turned towards Dylan. "No! That is unacceptable! This deal needs to go down right now, which means he has to change his position. Use everything at your disposal. Whatever the issue is, get it sidetracked, blackmail him if you must, you have enough dirt on him...but get it done! And yes...while you are at it, call the White House. I want all country and state subsidies striped off... not reduced! Pressure their government, I want those subsides...gone!"

They came to a halt in front of the office suit.

"I'll see what I can do, sir." Dylan stated.

"Get it done, Dylan. It's the only option. At the end of all this there might just be a substantial raise with your name on it." He smiled.

"Yes sir. I'll get it done." He replied confidently and strode back, retracing his steps to his own room.

Meyers' cell phone was ringing. He pulled it out of his waist case and pressed the flashing green button.

"Richard Meyers." He greeted the caller as his peon opened the door for him. He reached his secretary's room. Her office was the only connecting passage to his suite. One must traverse through the room before reaching the office of the Chairman.

"Good Morning sir. I've—" She greeted as she rose up but seeing as he was busy on the phone she sat back. Besides, Richard signaled her to sit.

After crossing the guest waiting room, he slid the door to his actual office. But to his surprise, his eyes were blinded by radiating white light. For many seconds, he couldn't see anything but white, blinding, flashing light.

What's happening?

"I hear that you are color blind. I wonder what you're seeing." The caller's voice echoed in his ears.

"Who is this?" He asked in a demanding tone.

Suddenly, the blinding white light vanished. His eyes took some time to adjust to the sudden change in intensity and as it did, he noticed something was off in his office. A stranger was sitting at his ergonomic recliner. His gun trained on Richard's right eye and its laser flashing at it.

"I think you know." The caller smiled.

Channel Seven News

For those of our viewers joining in late, tonight's segment is on bio-fuel. We have us Dr. Harold Kumar, absolute expert on the field…I believe you have also written your dissertation on the topic, right?

Yes I did, Mike. As I was saying, it seems the world is simply load-shedding our requirement to bio-fuel. We all know, load-shedding is only a temporary solution to keep the system running, but eventually it will fail. You know, we had been warned well at hand. Well before any of this. The scientists had foretold this day would come. But we did not listen. Today, our own system is so crazily inflated that the cost of researching alternate source of energy has become almost heavenly. I bet some of the scientists would be turning in their grave saying, "You were warned." As for bio-fuel, there is not nearly enough fertile agricultural land on the planet to meet the demand of the planet. We are simply throwing away another resource crucial to our existence. One day, we might have no food, as there would be no more fertile agricultural land. It seems the more we are turning towards the future, the more we are going towards the past, and I'm talking about Stone Age. No food. No water. No electricity. No energy. In a world like this Mike, I ask you, "What's the point?"

Those are strong arguments we have got, and stronger use of words from Dr. Kumar.

I've just looked at the statistics, Mike. Saw the research. I'm just being realistic. I'm not saying that there's no hope. There's always hope. But then….

43
Control

Bearing Tower

Control Room

"H-Hey…Jimmy! What are *you* doing up here?" the analyst laughed with a vibrant chuckle. He knew that James usually did not prefer spending much time in the Control Room.

"Uhh…you know…" He replied back but even he did not have an answer. It was just that he felt like it, so he came up. He did not know why, but he did. Quickly changing the point, he deviated, "Where's Steve?"

"Well…he went to kiss up the bosses boots for the security breach the other day; not that it ever works." The analyst replied. "Still, you've gotta give him points for trying though."

"Good for me, huh." He chuckled. "How's it going with you? Looking busy over there; need a hand?" He pointed as he walked up to him and sat on the desk on his workstation.

"Nah…you can't help me anyway." He exclaimed.

"What do you mean?" James enquired, puzzled.

"You remember I'd been called up to head a group to re-task the servers…so that they'll not crash during this year's expo." He explained. "The management has gone all out on this one…but the techies are the ones who now have to do the hard work. I mean worldwide broadcasting, social networking, managing transport streams…and making sure that the servers don't crash mid-way."

"Well, don't burn out. I need my go-to guy in surveillance." He smiled. They both smiled.

"So that you get to take all the credit?" He inquired with a raised brow.

"So that our dear head of security can filch all the credit." He replied sarcastically. "But it's not all bad as the bastard is also accountable for all the mishaps…like that breach a couple of days ago."

They both laughed to their hearts content picturing how Steve, their boss, in the bosses office being scolded like a frightened child for not completing his homework. The very image, the thought was bliss in itself.

"Ah! Speaking of the devil." He remarked pointing to the surveillance feed displaying in the console. They could see Steve's frightening face which in his current disposition appeared to be even scarier. It was very unclear as to how he got those hideous scars and wounds. Nobody knew and yet it was a very popular topic of discussion behind his back. "Just look at him…his very sight gives me the shivers. You know, he's one of the reasons that I don't work much over here. What I would have paid to see his sorry face in the CEO's office! Not my luck, I guess."

"I know what you mean." James concurred. "Hey! Who's this guy?"

"Who? Him? I don't know." The analyst replied as he shrugged, not making a big deal out of it. "Must be one of the IT guys, see, he's chatting with Robert."

"No, he's wearing our wire and transceiver; that's security not IT and he's even chatting with him…he sent him off. See!"

James tried to remember if he ever saw him, but he didn't and it did not take him much time to realize that, which was odd as he literally knew everybody in his department.

Something is off over here!

"Pull up the feed from the elevator and video IQ his face; and gimme your phone." The analyst did as he said.

"Call Robert." James pronounced in a crisp and clear voice and the handheld machine did so.

"Hello?" The voice resounded.

"Robert?" Jimmy enquired.

"Yes?" was the curious reply.

"Hi, this is Jimmy, up from surveillance, friend of Dwayne's." James informed.

"Yeah."

"Hey, what's the name of the guy you bumped into at the elevators?" He questioned.

"I don't know." The listener responded. "But -you ought to know! He is in security."

"It's…" James diverted. "What did he talk to you about?" He pressed again.

"He just said that I had to take another elevator 'cause that one was reserved for the big boss. Nothing special. What is this about if you don't mind me asking?"

"Just a wager between me and him; I was checking if he had upheld his end." James lied.

"Oh, okay." Robert replied with an unsatisfied laugh but before he could realize James had already disconnected.

He lied to him!

"Boss came in from his chopper; no point in keeping an elevator in the lobby."

"Yeah…that one is not even the closest one from the helipad. There's no way somebody would be that stupid. Unless…" Dwayne answered back.

This doesn't add up.

"And check this out! He stayed clear off the camera's view." The analyst added.

"That's it! I'm gonna have a little chat with him." Saying that, he turned around to go.

"Wait! He's not over there." Dwayne shouted. "There's a delay in feed to all terminals. I needed the processing power for what I was doing."

"So where he's at?" He enquired quickly.

"Either go to the mainframe or…" Dwayne stretched.

"Or what?" Jimmy urged.

"Or I re-route the processors to their original module." He replied, not realizing that he would regret his words.

"Mainframe is far off." he pondered. "Is there anybody down there?"

"No way to know." Dwayne informed.

"Then I suggest you get cracking." James countered.

"What! No way! After the whole drill it's gonna turn out to be nothing. Do you have any idea how difficult it is?" Dwayne argued. What started as a fun activity did not seem that much fun anymore.

"No…but you do and that's all I need. Now come on." James countered to Dwayne's resentment.

"Okay…but it is going to take some time." Dwayne complied.

"Then hurry!" James leaned behind on the wall.

Office of the CEO and Chairman (Bearing PetroTech)
Bearing Tower

It took him some time but Meyers was finally able to recognize the apparently arrogant figure.

"You've got some nerve, breaking into my office!" He said furiously.

"Please…take a seat." He pointed to the visitors chairs and with a chuckle he continued, "It's your office…after all."

"You'll never get away with this." Richard bellowed. He shouted back, "I'll hunt you down and squash you like the mere insect that you are."

"Only if I let you live…you son of a bitch. Now…please, have a seat." He commanded in a gentle tone but pointing to the seat with his gun. Meyers obliged to the request and sat on the chair. "And no funny business." He added.

"You'll never get away with this!" Meyers repeated.

"Yeah…I got it the first time!" Mercer stated with a smile.

Mercer gazed around admiring the unique architecture of the room which was quite different from all of the building.

"It's quite an office you've got here!" Mercer gazed with admiration.

"Thanks." Meyers gave a sarcastic smile.

"That's a nice secretary you've got there." Mercer questioned him casually.

"You came all the way here just to make small talk?" Meyers laughed.

"You see…the sole reason I accepted the CERN assignment was to find out who killed my family and now that I know that it's you…I'm going to kill you!" Mercer indicated.

'You're gravely misinformed." Meyers articulated.

"Am I now?" Mercer replied with his calming voice.

"It wasn't me; I have nothing to do with the death of your family. I swear." Meyers pressed forward.

"You swear? And you're such a man of your word, right?" Mercer made a satirical remark.

"As a matter of fact, I am." Meyers argued.

"Okay…but you do know who did kill them, don't you?" Mercer spotted 'the tell' he was searching so keenly for.

"I don't know, I swear." Richard pleaded.

"You know that you swear a lot?" Mercer commented as he played with his gun. "Look, I've interrogated, tortured and killed more people than you have followers on Twitter. I know when people are lying; it shows on their faces just as it is showing on yours."

Richard knew that there was no point in arguing with the maniac who had his gun trained at him.

"You are way out of your depth, Mercer...against forces bigger than what you can comprehend."

Mercer didn't say a word, but instead pointed the gun back at him.

"Ugh...alright! If I tell you, will you shoot me?" Meyers articulated.

"That depends..." Mercer smiled.

"The contract on you was issued by Aurora. I promise; I had nothing to do with it, your family was nothing more than collateral damage." Meyers informed, but distorting the fact just enough to paint a cleaner image of himself in front of Mercer.

"Tell me more about this Aurora!" Mercer questioned. His interest increasing speedily.

"Nobody knows who he actually is; just that he is some kind of royalty. When we talk to him, we all greet him as 'your highness'...that's how big he is. I have a feeling that he's a very big public figure. 'Aurora' is just his codename. That's all I know. I sw—promise!"

One of the recordings which Marvin had left for him began playing in his mind. He clearly remembered that the man said the same words, 'your highness'. Now he had a name, Aurora.

"And that's all you know?" Mercer raised his brow.

"Yes, that's all I know!" Richard exclaimed at the top of his voice. He was restless.

"Alright then...." The gun was trained at him. Mercer pulled back the metal jacket, turned off the safety. His right hand arm, instinctively, reached the butt of the gun, firmly gripping it, bracing for impact.

"No, no, wait. I told you everything, I promise." He urged.

"Oh yeah, I believe you." Mercer smiled.

Richard realized that there was no point begging for his life. Instead, he tried to reason with him.

"If you shoot me, the whole security will swarm into my office like anything. Use your brain, think rationally."

"I wouldn't worry about that, your office is completely sound-proof." He laughed. "I checked!" Mercer knew that Richard was bluffing. It was the last card which he could play. All he could do now was embrace his death and die peacefully. Mercer pulled the trigger. Richard saw the brilliant white muzzle flash and heard the bang the gun made; and that was it.

Back at the control room, Dwayne was working harder than ever to bring back the systems online. "Okay Jimmy, all systems operational." Dwayne reported to his colleague in the Control Room of Surveillance & Security.

"It's about time, you know." Jimmy retorted, impatient as he was.

"What do you want me to do?" Dwayne asked.

"First of all, get a usable footage, run it through facial. I want to know exactly who he is!" James commanded.

"Okay." Dwayne replied as he turned back towards the computer, carrying out the given instructions.

After a few seconds later Dwayne remarked, "This guy is good but not that good. I've got one usable frame for facial.

"Finally!" James exclaimed.

The screen changed with Mercer's face dominating the left and thousands of larger flashing in the right.

'No Match Found' blinked at the center of the screen.

"What! That's impossible. He's not in any database in the world. He doesn't exist." Dwayne was baffled. "Shouldn't we inform the security personnel?"

"We can't." James replied in a grim tone. "He'll know that we are coming. Fast forward, I want to see how it plays out and where he is now!"

As the video continued their jaws dropped in shock.

How did this happen?

Oh god!

"I'm going in." James declared as he turned around to address the rest of the people in the Control Room.

"Listen up, people. We have a confirmed security breach on our hands. Subject is White, male, 40's, wearing our security uniform. Last seen in Sir Richard's office, 101st floor. He might have patched into our frequency so maintain radio silence. Dwayne?"

"Yeah?"

"Send Code Red message to every personnel through the ghost server! There are definitely more than one. Rest of you follow me!" He commanded decisively.

Seconds later every person in surveillance got the same text message in their inbox.

"Code Red: Confirmed Security Breach. Subject White, Male, 40's, wearing security uniform. Maintain radio silence. Last Known Location: CEO, Bearing Oil's office." The entire building sprang into action.

44

Zeroing In

Meyers' Office

"You shot me?" Richard Meyers cried in agony as he bled on the pristine white chairs in his office suite.

"Oh relax, it's just a flesh wound, possibly a little grazing to the bone but it'll heal right up." Mercer explained.

"You bloody shot me!" Richard cried.

"Just making a point." Mercer smiled. "You were very smug, lose the attitude."

Richard bit his tongue and cursed him and his head of security with all hatred in his heart as he pressed his palm over the bullet hole in his arm, applying pressure against the blood gushing from the puncture in the skin.

"Now, were you or were you not responsible for the CERN incidents now and in 2014?"

"I um…I…I was." He replied, rattled and delirious.

"I want a name?" he questioned. "Who caused the gamma blast in CERN?"

"There's no point asking. He was starting to know too much. He needed to be eliminated. So I got him killed along with the other scientists in CERN."

"And the people you've sent after me?" Mercer leaned.

"Private security contractors. ILSA. I contracted them to track you and kill you." Richard informed.

"Make them stop and I'll spare your life." Mercer bargained. "Our life for yours." His own life was the least of his concern; it was Élénoré he was worried about.

"Never!" Meyers shouted.

"In that case." Mercer got off Richard's ergonomic arm chair. His gun was already cocked. He traversed around him till he reached Sir Meyers back. "Say your prayers Meyers. It will be your last."

Richard heard the clicking noise of the gun's internal mechanism just behind his cranium. The injury he had got did not pain anymore. He knew that he was going to die but he did not pray as he knew that he was damned and would go only to hell. Instead he closed his eyes and tipped his head, thinking of his cottage in Scotland where he had been longing to go back for a very long time.

•

"If you are going to do it...then make it fast. Please!" He cried. "I don't want to die in fear!"

After a whole minute, he turned his head and to his amazement, there was nobody in there. All alone.

Was it a dream? He questioned but the shooting, throbbing pain was evidence enough that it was real and tangible as it could be.

Suddenly, the majestic doors to his office flung open. It was James who was the first to arrive on the scene. He did not notice the blood drenching from Richard's custom tailored suit, ruining it. He asked but one question.

"Where is he?" James stressed.

Richard, unable to speak, nodded that he did not know.

"Dwayne? I need a location now! Over." He shouted on his cell. Since they suspected that their communications were compromised, Dwayne managed to get a substitute in all the commotion. He remotely configured all the cell-phones of all the security personnel in the building, activating the Push-to-Talk feature in their hand sets. It was similar to their hand sets, and just what they needed.

Turning his attention to his boss while he was waiting for a reply from Dwayne, he noticed that his boss was hurt.

"Oh shit! Don't worry sir, help is on the way", he told him, then in the cell he shouted, "I need medical team in Sir Meyer's office. Stat! Note he has received GSW to his arm and has blood loss."

"James, medical team is en-route." Dwayne responded.

"Call nine-one-one. Inform them that we have an armed suspect who is on the run." James ordered.

"Okay." Dwayne replied.

"Dwayne?" He shouted in an agitated tone. "Where is he?"

"I'm working on it! Do you even know how many cameras are there in the building? He could be anywhere. It takes time. I'll let you know soon enough."

He turned towards Richard. The blood loss was not stopping. "Apply pressure on it." He told him as he was looking at the injured arm. "Sir, there's another thing that you should know. The suspect made contact with you once before near the elevators...and it seemed as if he lifted something from your pockets." He informed.

"What?!" there was pure terror in Richard's eyes. He frisked himself with his other hand hoping that he could find what he was looking for but he did not.

This isn't happening! He thought as he heaved himself up with the one arm and slowly made his way to the table, to his chair. The sudden change in altitude made him feel weak and dizzy and his head started spinning but it did not hinder him to go around the desk. Slowly, he bent down to lay his eyes on yet another horrifying sight.

This can't be happening. He has taken everything. He said as he gazed at the open locker. He lifted his head. Weak and nauseous, the baffled old man raised his hand towards James trying to call out to him.

Wait! Don't call the police. He thought, but James wasn't listening anymore.

"James!" Dwayne's voice echoed through James' cell-phone. "Subject is heading upstairs; west-end staircase. Over!"

"I'm on my way." James shouted. "Tell Hodges to cut him off. Over!"

45

Grande Exodus

103rd floor
Bearing Tower

"Even breath, Mercer." Mercer reminded himself as he sprinted himself up the stairs so that he would not burn out. The one thing which was hoping not to happen happened. A siren started buzzing throughout the whole building, red lights started blinking. He was nearing the tourist floor where he heard the automated warning. "Visitors evacuate the building through the nearest exit." This was an unexpected hitch in his escape.

I guess this is my stop. He noticed the camera recording with the blinking red light which was currently pointed at him; he quickly ran out of its scope. He reached the door, the second one which came in his way. He noticed that there was a black box attached next to it with a red LED light which lined its top.

Crap!

He did not plan for this, but there was nothing he could do. He had the access card for it but they had changed the security codes. He hung to the wall next to the door listening closely to any voice approaching him from any direction. Seconds later, he heard hurried footsteps of an unsuspecting man, rushing towards him from the other side of the door. Mercer realized the man was talking on the wire, but he did not hear anything from the one he had.

They know! But it did not matter.

"Hodges here, approaching the west-end staircase." He stated as he reached the door, he put in his newly made card which was handed to him only seconds after the alarm went off. They wanted to box him inside the building; arm themselves before they strike him. The LED turned green as the door unlocked, telling him that he could walk through. He opened the door, pulled out his card from the security console. As he pushed the door away from him, suddenly the door jerked back, and with full force. It hit him in the head and eventually knocked him unconscious.

This was a floor which Mercer remembered. Back in the day, he came here with his wife and children.

"Dad, wouldn't it be cool if I could jump off from the building and fly. Like Superman." His son shouted in excitement as they were standing on the Sky Deck of the iconic Sears Tower, as it was known back then.

"It would be cool. But don't even think about it; you're not Superman." Mercer explained the tiny little prepubescent child.

The iconic all-glass Sky Deck was both elegant and magnificent in its essence. Armed with features which mesmerized its visitors and left an everlasting impression on their minds, it was a perfect stage to boast one of the biggest architectural feats in the world which paved the way for further advancements in the field. As the ferocious winds continuously lashed against the silvery silhouette, as evident from the Sky Deck, the tower rocked like a cradle, from side to side.

"I know Daddy. We are not that stupid! He needs to go to learn how to fly first. Otherwise, he would get a terrible boo-boo." The tiny daughter reciprocated with her cheerful face.

Mercer could do nothing but smile.

I guess today's my chance to fulfill my son's wish.

There were very less people left on this floor. And those who were waiting near the elevator bank were waiting for one of the elevators to come back. One of them, a tourist, spotted the newcomer to the floor, and his gun. He pulled out his camera phone and started recording the assailant as he began sprinting towards the Sky Deck shooting at the hardened glass when suddenly security personnel in black suits flooded the floor in the dozens.

"On the floor, now!" the security personnel bellowed as he pointed his gun at Mercer.

Mercer heard the order but did not care enough to pay attention. He raised his gun, forward, not backward. Aimed at the glass, and fired. There was no effect on the glass. He then shot all the bullets in the clip, a few went through. But this did not hinder his determination. He cased his pistol and pulled out his Belgium VBR from the bag, aimed at the same door and exhaled, as he completely emptied the cartridge. At the end of the successive thunderous jolts, the glass had more holes on it than Swiss cheese. Still sprinting, trying to quickly cover the distance, before his pursuers caught up to him.

"He's not gonna stop. Cap him in his knees." James instructed his subordinates.

Now only a few paces away, he felt the bullets all around him, he started taking long steps; just as a trained diver does when he is about to make his dive.

Even breath. He thought as he did it, and he did with the magnificent sound of the crashing glass and as he made the dive, there was a 103 floors fall.

West Jackson Boulevard

"Aisha Summers." Aisha announced in her car, to the person at the other end of the call as she drove her Sedan.

"Where are you?" the caller asked in a very singular tone.

By now, Aisha had recognized this particular tone of voice. Something had happened, she did not know about. "Just checking a hunch."

"Uh-huh."

And there was an awkward moment of silence.

"Ugh, if you know something sir, just tell me." She groaned.

"It is your case, Aisha." He stated. "You should be all over it!"

"Just tell me!"

"A nine-one-one call was made from Bearing Tower, not more than a few minutes ago. Apparently, an armed assailant, broke into the executive floors, injured one personnel and stole something, something valuable."

"I'll look into it."

"There's one another thing." Valerie said to her in a different tone. Aisha detected the sarcasm in his voice. "I'm sending you a picture. You'll want to look at it."

She peeped at the dash board, the media player dissolved into a message on the touch-screen. "You have one new message." She read as she pressed it open. There was a picture, a single frame from a building's security feed and a single person in the frame. It was Mercer, and there was a wicked smile on his hazy face.

"I'm just a few blocks away. I'll be there in a minute." She told her boss as she glanced at her newly changed destination. Something caught her attention. It was almost magnificent at a distance while it lasted.

"No, wait. I see him."

"You see him?" Valerie was baffled. "Where are you?"

"He just jumped, from one of the Sky Deck's!"

"What?!"

"Send backup. Seeing who he is, I think I'll need it." She told him as she hung up the phone.

Outside Bearing Tower

The fiber of the parachute was fluttering, the winds, though not strong enough, roared in his ears. He swayed, from left to right whilst his skilled arms carefully piloted him through his descent. Just before reaching the road, he was struck by a similar updraft but this time he was dexterously able to detach himself from the parachute, and as he did, he fell to the ground where he came to a halt after a complete somersault which he did to prevent any bones from breaking.

It is a major factor in injuries sustained from a fall. Not from how high or how fast you fell, but how quickly you stopped upon impact. Increase the duration, and you will decrease your chances of getting killed, or hurt.

It was little things like this, things he was trained to do, which made him quite adept to adapt in such situations.

He stood up to run, and did not take more than one step, he tripped and fell back on the hard concrete floor with a sudden pang gushing throughout his right leg. Again he heaved himself up and as he did, he noticed the fresh blood stain on his jeans in the lower right leg.

Did I break something? He questioned himself. His right hand quickly ran across to investigate the issue. He noticed the hole in the cloth and knew what had just happened. He had been shot, but in the heat of the moment the pain did not register in his brain until now. He tore a piece of fiber and tightly bandaged the wound. The bullet went through and through. It was only a flesh wound and given the circumstances it was not that bad at all. At least, he could run, escape from the dangers lurking over him.

It's only a matter of time. Time which I don't have.

He noticed that people had gathered all around him in a crowd, whispering to each other, curious as to what just happened. One startled woman started dialing 911. A lot was going around there. Mercer certainly started feeling like a celebrity with curious bystanders with their phone cameras trained at Mercer with curious excitement, and perhaps he enjoyed it because as he sprinted to his next destination, there was a smile on his face.

Son, even I wanted to do that. He would have said if he were alive.

46

Executive Order

Central Intelligence Agency
Langley, Washington

"Director Shepherd's office, how may I help you?" a young female voice asked her next incoming caller.

"This is Richard Meyers." Richard announced.

"Oh…yes sir, just a minute." The assistant replied calmly.

"Be quick!" Meyers urged.

"Sir Richard! How can I be of service to you?" The Director greeted, but Richard was in no mood for it.

"It's about time you prove that you were a prudent investment."

"What's this all about?" Shepherd asked in a frantic voice, baffled. "What do you mean?"

"Your man just broke into my office, and stole something from me. I want it back!" Meyers articulated.

"Sir, I can assure you that I have no part in this." Nathaniel informed.

Nathaniel Shepherd was the Director of Operations in United States Central Intelligence Agency's National Clandestine Service's Special Activities Division and a very powerful man.

"I meant CIA in general, not your division. Listen, you said SAD couldn't operate in foreign terrain. Not now! You said! So here's your chance. Find him, kill him. And I'll make it easy for you, he's number one on terror watch list. No one will give the whole issue a second thought." Meyers stated.

"Some guy named…uh Alec Mercer. You're saying he's ours?" Shepherd checked on his computer.

"Not anymore." Richard replied. "Just find him, kill him! I want the data back!"

"But the CIA can never operate in the homeland!" The Director fumbled cowardly.

"Just get it done, for Pete's sake!" Meyers was adamant.

"Okay, I'll get it done." The director assured. The line disconnected.

Back at the 101st floor of Bearing PetroTech, "Sir, it is imperative we find him. If even one copy of the research gets out, our company will get destroyed, our shares will be worthless, and on top of all this we'll be accountable for trillions of dollars in liabilities." His employee informed.

"I know! I know! You don't need to tell me twice but there's nothing we can do, can we?!" Meyers proclaimed.

"Sir, this is insane! Why do more damage? Leave that project and release our deposits into the markets, while they are worth something." The employee was insistent.

"If this project doesn't pull through, we are screwed either way. Let's try not to delay the inevitable." Meyers justified his actions.

"Sir please…." The employee begged.

But Richard signaled that he did not want to hear another word of protest. "Not one word." Richard ordered. "Talk to our friends in Kazakhstan, I had kept some of our reserves aside for times like this. Never thought that I would need it but given the circumstances I think we should release it in the market from the next week. It'll give us some leeway, I hope." Meyers prayed.

Downtown Chicago

"Here, take my place." Éllén stepped back as she courteously offered her place in the queue to the woman behind her.

She was in a very nervous disposition; nervous because Alec was nowhere to be seen. She checked the time, it was 12:10. She was standing in a queue, but tried her best to stay at the back of it. If somebody would join the line behind her, she would give them her spot and join back.

Come on Alec! Where the hell are you?

Alec's directive was still clear in her head.

"If I don't come, you have to assume the worst." Alec had explained to her. "You will have to go. Understand?!"

Éllén was tightlipped and did not say a word.

"Understand?" Alec repeated with force.

"Yes." She regretted saying.

"You will have to go. You hear me? I have arranged everything, your passport, work visa, flight plan. When you land in Brussels, take a cab, and go to this place...over here. See!" Alec pointed firmly over the foreign map. "I have kept aside some money for you. It's all the money you'll ever need. And there is a gun, a pistol. Keep it under the pillow when you sleep, always. This is your apartment...here." He pointed again at a different location on the map.

"—and what about you?" she asked, in a very soft voice masking her pain.

"If I don't make it, and you board that bus, then I should mean to you nothing more than a half-forgotten dream. Nothing more!" he pressed strongly.

Éllén could feel herself take a step back. Everybody dear to her was dead. Even her family in Marseille, her mother had moved on with her new family. "By the time all is said and done, and the matter subsided, you will have the freedom to whatever or be whoever you wish to be. But not Élénoré Bassét. Take this!" Mercer handed her a folded piece of paper. "When your visa expires, talk to him; only him! He will set you up; till then lay low. Okay?"

Éllén was hesitant, but she obliged as she nodded in approval, taking the piece of paper from Mercer's hand.

"Come back to me. I don't want to be alone anymore!" Éllén pleaded.

"I will" He reassured her.

The fact that the bus was running late, gave her a little bit of relief. But it was momentary because at 12:15, a big white Metropolitan bus screeched in front of the bus stop, in one of the most lively streets of Chicago.

Please Alec, don't abandon me again! You promised me!

One by one, people started boarding the bus and slowly, the line started moving forward, but for her the process was taking ages, and her anxiety kept on increasing. She was sweating like a pig, trembling, scared.

"Are you alright, dear?" the woman in front of her asked Éllén like a Good Samaritan.

"I'm fine." Éllén gave a dull reply, trying to keep her outward calm, but inside, there was a hurling storm and a blazing, lashing volcano. Her hands constantly fidgeting with her newly obtained mobile phone with a burner network card. Staring constantly at the two-dimensional clock inside, the thought of calling Alec crossed her mind several times, but she did not. If she tried to contact Mercer through it, it could have been used to ascertain her exact location as the call would be traceable.

One by one, the line shortened, till no one was left except her as she stood in front of the automatic doors.

"Come on! I have a schedule to maintain!" the bus driver shouted at loudly. "It's because of people like you, why the busses get delayed."

If only you knew about my condition! Éllén thought to herself.

She was dumbstruck. She did not move or say one word; just stood there like a stone pillar.

"I'm not gonna wait for you till you make up your mind. Either get onboard, or stay behind! Your choice."

"No, wait! Just a minute." She pleaded. The driver checked the time, "One minute. That's all you get!"

Phew! She took a sigh of relief. *Come on Alec, don't fail me, now!*

"One minute is over, Missy. Either climb onboard or…" The driver snapped. He made it very clear that he is not going to stay.

This is it! I guess.

As she stepped on the pedestal and tightly held the railing which ran on both sides of the door, she turned her head, and gave one last glance behind her. Mercer was still nowhere to be seen. And all this was going to be an obscure dream, half forgotten.

A couple of blocks over, Mercer was sprinting as fast as he could. In suitable conditions, he was a very fast runner, and could give quite a chase. But right now things were against him. He was shot in the leg, of all places and there were many obstacles in his path and add the fact that he was not well versed with the roads. It had changed tremendously since that last time he was here.

He had his cell in his right hand and his pistol in the other and on the cell the Google Maps app was running and Éllén's location had already been fed in it and a path was clearly marked between his current location and that bus stop where Éllén was supposed to be waiting.

I'll never make it!

"Out of the way! Move!" he yelled to the pedestrians and by-standers that were in his way while constantly checking his phone.

A cyclist was chatting with some girl, few paces ahead of him. Then it struck him. As he reached the same cyclist, he pointed his pistol at him, "Back off!" he ordered. And at the same gun point he stole that cycle from him. As Mercer peddled away, the man was still in shock, but the woman quickly started dialing 911 to report the theft. The thought occurred to him that they could track his movements by that but it subsided when he realized that they would have already been tracking him through satellite surveillance.

The signal was red, and the road was crowded with cars and bikes, one way or the other he was able to keep his pace. He checked his watch. It was 6:10.

Why did I tell her to leave? Of course, he knew why he had told her to leave *but...if she boarded that bus, it was all over!*

For once I hope that she did not listen to me!

He was pedaling constantly as he maneuvered in between the cars through the jam-packed streets of Chicago. Whatever happened, he did not stop at all. If there was no place on the road then, he would turn to the foot path as the pedestrians would nearly miss him as they, in a frenzy jump out of his path while others more fortunate would try and stay clear of his way.

Slowly, he started recognizing where he was; when he recognized a huge sky scraper to his right and the entrance to its underground parking-lot. Still pedaling constantly, he switched his lane, and maneuvered towards that same entrance.

The security guard who noticed him, jumped to his toes as he shouted. "Stop! You can't just barge in here like this!"

Mercer pointed his gun at him. The guard backed off. There was a drop barrier in the way. The cycle was multi-gear one but it could not breach it. He slightly slanted the cycle, and still in a leaning position stood on his metal frame, easily balancing himself as the cycle, now completely horizontal, skidded forward. As he neared the guard post he contracted his thigh muscles and took a huge jump, as he overcame the obstacle, and landed back on the cycle which had already slid underneath the barrier and as he stepped on the same pedal, he applied force on it, the cycle stood back upright, Mercer assembled himself back on it and pedaled away.

12:15. I'm almost there!

He traversed the diagonal length of the parking lot, cycling hard, pedaling constantly, and breathing hard, his heart pulsing, beating strongly. He had been on the run for quite a while now. He was tiring, but still didn't stop pedaling. Pumped up full of adrenaline, he exited the building from the other side of the building. As he crossed the multi-lane road, crossing the broad lanes, speeding straight ahead, the device, echoed, "You have reached your destination."

The cycle wheeled to a stop. Frantically, he turned around, looked everywhere; the bus was nowhere to be seen. The time on his cell was 12:17. He was late and she was long gone.

I'm doomed!

His hands ran up to his forehead, rubbing against the skull, trying to ease out the tension, his plan had just fallen apart and he needed something else good enough to call his bluff. Suddenly, he felt a soft tap on his shoulder. "Alec! I'm sorry but I couldn't just leave like that. And when you think about it, my plane doesn't depart for another hour, and I could have taken a cab instead, to the airport."

He was overcome with joy, so much that as he recognized the woman, he held her tightly to his chest and swept her off her feet.

"You're so stupid, you know! Deviating from the plan like this!" he scolded her but did not mean a single word.

"Oh my God! Alec, you're bleeding!" Élénoré exclaimed.

"Oh, it's nothing." He tried not to put much weight into the issue. "Come on. We don't have much time. We've got to run!"

"Why what happened? What did you do?" Éllén asked as she ran along with him, on foot. "Did you do it? Kill him?"

"No…I couldn't. There is a bigger fish in the ocean." Mercer stated. "...that would have not been the right play here."

"What do you mean?" Élénoré quizzed.

"No time for chit-chat. This place is going to be a war zone." Mercer hurried.

"What?! Could you just stop for a minute?" she asked frantically. "Who is following us?"

"Best case scenario? Every federal agency in the state, possibly the country!" He replied grimly.

"Worst case?" Éllén enquired sarcastically.

"We'll talk about that when we cross that bridge." He replied. "Now, come on!" He urged.

Not more than fifteen clicks south-south-west from his current location a Sikorsky MH-60 'Pave Hawk' helicopter violently paved its way towards the given coordinates, hovering through the dark gray skies.

"Listen up, ladies!" The sergeant ordered his squad. "A known terrorist has been identified…get this *causing disruption in the streets of Chicago.*" He told them with a chuckle. "He's armed…and dangerous."

"When is it ever that easy?" One of the soldiers remarked.

"Check your PDA, file photo is attached. He was an agency asset for about twenty-five years. Our mission is to bring him in at…all…costs; Dead or Alive. Minimal Agency exposure; is that clear?"

"Clear!" the same voice echoed through the noise of the twin turbo-shaft engine.

"Just get in…apprehend him…get out. Nothing fancy! Local PD will handle the rest. Get your assess in gear! Weapons hot! We deploy in thirty seconds." He instructed.

There were two rows of soldiers, six of them in each row. They waited keenly for their deployment into the streets of Chicago, with their M16A1 assault rifles held tightly in their arms.

Thirty seconds later, Mercer and Élénoré, both were wheezing, breathing hard as they had been running for quite some while now.

"Will you wait for a minute?" She asked him in desperation. She had stretched more than her limits, and had had enough. Resting her lean arms on her knee caps, she was having trouble breathing. "Who the hell are we running from?"

But Mercer was distracted. He had completely turned back and was facing Élénoré, but he was looking at something in the sky, where he pointed out with his two forefingers. "Them!" He shouted. Éllén turned back. She noticed a lonely, black helicopter, emerging from the left side of the same Bearing Tower from where Mercer had made his escape, hovering in the sky, three and three soldiers clad in black uniform zip-lined from either sides of the airborne vehicle, seconds later another batch of soldiers zip-lined with the others to the ground, only one or two blocks away from them.

"Worst case scenario! You asked." Mercer replied to the long pending question. "Run! They are after me, not you!" he instructed her. "No, wait! Take this with you!" he gave her his gun. "You know what you have to do?"

Éllén nodded yes.

"Good" Mercer nodded back. "Now go! I'll take care of them."

"Operators note that target is not alone. A female is along with him." An analyst's voice crackled in their HF Military transceivers.

"Negative! Our mission specifics do not change. Our target is still the defector. Is that clear?"

"Clear!" A echoing syllable resounded.

"Let's move out!" The sergeant ordered.

"Hoorah!" Each and every one of them shouted at the top of their voice as they exited the military chopper and zip-lined down to the road beneath.

"Subject is entering 207, West Jackson Boulevard."

"Copy That." He replied on the transceiver. "Okay people, our target is armed and dangerous. Do not take him lightly."

"Yes Sergeant." They replied back.

"Now come on! We've got quite a chase on our hands."

47

Chicago Battlefield

Outside Bearing Tower

"Hey back off!" the police officer growled as he made his ground. "Behind the line!"

"Let me go!" a woman hurled herself on him, trying desperately to squeeze in between the commotion through the yellow 'DO NOT CROSS' line. "My daughter is still inside!" the woman yelled with agony.

"Our officers are evacuating the premises. She'll be escorted from the grounds." He explained. "Don't worry, she'll be just fine!" The officer consoled.

"How do you know?" she asked for reassurance. The officer smiled to strengthen her confidence, "I just know." He said in a calm soothing voice, but the truth was that he did not. He did not even know why he was doing the Class-1 evacuation, just that his precinct, closest in the vicinity was ordered to do so. It was after dusk, but some sunlight was still to be seen. A dark blurred out figure emerged from a distance. Seeing it, the woman burst out into tears. As she cried, she wailed, "Oh, my baby!" as she flung out her arms and grasped her child and held her close to her bosom, and went back. Most of the people, workers, tourists, or employees all alike, had been evacuated, but many were still left.

"Hey! Hey! Back off!" The officer kept shouting, berating the crowd, trying all his might to keep them at bay.

Agent Summers approached the same frail yellow barrier, the officer had a lot at his hands but he still was able to fling out his arms in a defensive stance. Summers shrugged as if asking him to relax, as she pulled out her badge, opened it, and allowed him a quick peak at it, which certified her authority apart from her black work suit and her obvious air of confidence. "What seems to be the matter?" She asked not wanting to reveal her cards.

"Class-1 evacuation has been issued for this area. I'm just following orders."

"When? FBI has no knowledge of any such orders."

"You should! You are the ones who sent the Memo."

"Let me have a look at it", Aisha demanded but the officer ignored, trying to put her off. He had much to worry about. People were getting aggressive; the crowd was becoming a mob, which was getting into frenzy. "Now!"

The officer had gone out back, but Summers could still make out where he was. He returned soon enough with a sleek PDA in his hands which he quickly handed out to Summers.

Summers read the first few lines of the digital document. It was as the officer stated. It was an FBI issued document which issued a Class-1 evacuation of Bearing Tower and all the facilities, nearby.

As she motioned forward leaning to cross the yellow barrier, the officer briskly stood as a wall and stopped her catching her off guard.

"What?!" She probed furiously.

"No one is allowed! No exceptions!" the officer specified.

"You've got to be kidding me?" Aisha pierced with anger.

"Sorry miss," he gave a shallow apology. "Just following orders."

"Who's in charge here?" She grilled, still furious. "I demand to see the person in charge over here!"

The officer hesitated, but realized that every passing second, this woman was getting more and more out of control and he had already had his share of annoyance for the day.

Better let the boss handle it. He thought.

So he quickly jogged a couple of paces inward and as he walked up to his boss, he informed him about his encounter with the FBI. "Sir, there is an FBI agent over here who wants to talk to you." Detective Anderson gave him a curious smile as he got up from his chair on which he had been leaning. To him the officer's words told him everything. Detective Anderson exited the camp, from where he had been held up, to check what the hub-bub was all about. And to any detective in police department, FBI is a probing, invasive, frustrating, irritating department. He reached the boundary, and looked around, puzzled. "Where is she?" The officer who was not more than a few paces behind him took the lead as he watched like a sucker, at the same spot where she was standing earlier. He asked the rookie about her location. "Must have slipped in the commotion." The rookie replied.

"Ryan, you just got duped!" the detective replied.

"But sir? She must have gone inside. Our orders were clear!" he argued with his boss.

Summers hid herself on the blind side of the closest building that she could find. And as she was panting hard, gasping for breath, she knew that she could trust no one. She heard the noise of rotor blades, zooming towards her from a distance. The noise increased towards her ever so rapidly, and even before she knew it, she could see the carbon black chopper, closing in at her position, and instantaneously went ahead, hovering over the parking lot, located at the east façade of the Tower. She hid herself from their view trying to gauge what she was batting against. She noticed the military blokes, exiting the chopper, zip-lining to the ground. Their futuristic guns, massive that they were, could scare the hell out of anybody; Aisha was no exception to that. Instantaneously, she realized the exact motive of their arrival. Their fully automatic assault rifles were evidence enough that their mission was to kill Mercer; which was counterproductive to her own operation. She could not let that happen. But she did not know what to do, where he was. The obvious course of action came into her mind; following their track, somehow pull off the impossible feat to save Mercer so that she could use him to meet her own ends.

The obviously evident commanding officer of the squadron, a muscular person with heavy built and wide frame, blonde hair in small military crew cut was talking on his HF transceiver and after the brief inaudible discussion, the whole squadron sprang into action. Summers followed discreetly and tactfully.

Think Aisha! Think! You have to get ahead of them!

I won't last a minute out here in the open! Mercer thought as he saw Éllén's distanced image blur into the obscurity. He needed something of a battlefield or a base camp for home front advantage. His eyes panned right to one of the major buildings around him. The display read: 'One Stop Mart'. He knew that it would be perfect as he ran inside with complete momentum. He had his gun in his hand, he knew it would not be enough but at the moment it was all that he needed. As the door flung open, he charged into the main entrance of the complex. It was not a picture of people loitering about themselves, shopping, spending some time. Instead, some of the remainders had bunkered in that building. It saddened his heart to see other people get in the line of fire, because of him. Most of them, especially the workers were hard working middle-class citizens. It would pain him to see them get hurt. As they noticed the immigrant in their building, their hearts collectively skipped a beat when they noticed the blood still gushing through his right leg and the chrome black, matt finished pistol in his left hand.

They had the same petrified look Mercer had seen countless times in the past. The same scared look of fear. "Out, now!" He ordered them in a harsh frightening expression. Those of them who were frozen in fear he thawed them at gunpoint. Eventually, the whole building was abandoned, deserted, prime for his disposal, and soon enough his battleground.

At the moment there were more satellites and UAV's per grid square in Chicago than they during any past operation and every lens or sonar was trained on Mercer.

But to their disadvantage, he knew that too.

Mercer had been prepping the ground floor of the complex, tailored to his need; ability to flank opponents, complete invisibility, as if hidden in plain sight. The analysts in the remote CIA substation had seen what he was doing, but it did not make any head or tail to them, so much so that one of them remarked, "Is he shopping?" to which the other replied. "Who knows..."

Tired and exhausted, he dragged himself to the Manager's office, his eyes keenly searching for something. He spotted the thin wire casing which ran out from his office close to the floor. He followed it throughout the complex and when it reached its end, it finally turned upwards in the backroom of what appeared to be an employee's break room. The wire opened into a security panel which appeared more and more like a wall safe. He aimed at the lock, and shot it open, the cover lunged itself outward under its own weight, revealing an array of switches on the console. He started flinging whichever switch he felt appropriate, starting by tightly securing all entrances, turning off all the lights in the ground floor, turning off the escalator and most importantly disabling the fire alarm off. There was no switch for that but he knew which wire connected them to the nearest fire department, he just had to hack it off, which he did quite easily with a little help from his ceramic knife. Having done that, he shot about ten rounds at it, making it completely inaccessible to anybody else. Everything was set; he was armed and as ready as he could be. The task ahead was an impossible one, taking on the NCS, even spooks do not joke about things like this and he knew that the odds were against him; even with all his preparations.

"Be advised. Shots fired. Remain on your guard." The analyst warned the troopers, as they made their approach towards the same building, Summers was not far behind.

"Copy that. Approaching…back alley side door. Maintain visual."

"Sir…think we have a breakthrough!" An analyst working in a remote cell located in Manhattan reported to his superiors with an impromptu joy clearly visible on his face. He had a similar job description, similar objectives and a similar assignment. He signaled his boss with pride.

"Finally!" the boss exclaimed as he raised his phone the second he heard the good news.

Mercer dragged his body back, into what appeared to be the main section of the floor, though he could not clearly make out his exact location in the dark. The only light now available, was the moon light which was filtered by various obstructions till it reached him. He was practically running blind, but that was about to change. He sat down in one of the aisles, hiding himself from anybody's vision. He was losing blood as the wound was not clotting as it should, mainly because he was not letting it rest as he should have; but he could not just sit and rest, not in his current situation.

There's only one way! He thought.

He knew if the blood would keep on gushing out like this then, he would be unconscious soon enough and that was not an option. There was only one alternative available. But first he had another task at his hand. He pressed the release button on the butt of his US army issue M9. A work of art in itself. The magazine slid out revealing the only two 9x19 mm bullets left in the chamber. He took one out leaving the other one inside. There was a pool of liquid meandering on the extremely gentle slope of the floor. He aimed at the puddle and fired.

"Shit!" the CIA analyst shouted in frustration. They were tracking his movement inside the building through thermal imagery. Now that Mercer had played his card, they were left baffled. Not many options left for tactical support.

"Be advised, be advised. We have lost visual. I repeat, we have...lost...visual. Target can be anywhere in the building!" He notified the combatants on the scene.

"What?" Sergeant Cooper cried in amazement. "Copy that." He reported in the transceiver.

Looks like we are gonna do it the hard way! He pondered.

A single spark, transformed itself into a raging flame which followed the liquid to the ends of it trail. Anybody who had done a course in pyrotechnics can tell how easy it is to start a fire, or someone trained by Intelligence agencies like CIA for covert operations. Mercer's reason was not to create illumination, but generate heat. More heat than what the thermal imagery can filter, and differentiate Mercer from the rest of the environment. Invisible in plain sight, as it were. Soon it would be dark again. He had used a special mixture, a creation of his own design, which could be created from household supplies. It burnt fast and brightly, and as the reaction reaches completion, diminishes just as instantaneously, dissolving into a solution which is non-combustible.

He opened up the shell of the one bullet in his hand, collecting the gun power in his, war-hardened palms. He carefully placed the powder on his injury, brought forward a white hot splinter placing the flame near the wound, and groaned heavily as he lit it on fire, cauterizing the wound, sealing it permanently. Even as the blaze neared the wound, he could feel the burn. But when the gun powder caught fire, the flesh, the skin burnt, melting, fusing into itself, as if a firework rocket firing over his leg. Something he had seen in the military about a thousand times. After the wound was sealed shut, and there was no more blood loss. He pulled out his MP7A1 sub-machine gun, hung its strap on his back, and attached its suppressor and extendable butt. Just in time too, because no sooner did he attach the suppressor than the alarm system of the complex went off driving away the silence.

The perimeter had been breached.

Downtown Chicago

"Be advised. Shots fired. Remain on your guard." The analyst warned the troopers, as they made their approach towards the same building, Summers was not far behind.

"Okay! Listen up!" Cooper signaled his men to gather around him, south-east to the light sepia-toned building. "Target is armed and dangerous. If you take him lightly, it will definitely be your last mistake; I promise you." He pulled out his PDA from one of the many front pockets on his Kevlar jacket, and pulled out the building schematics which were downloaded to it instantaneously by the analysts providing tactical support from the remote Joint Special Operations Command. "Now, Alpha-Two, Alpha-Three, you're on me. Four, five, six, you'll be Team-two and breach through the main entrance. There!" He was pointing to the main entrance evident west of their current location. "The rest of you six...in teams three...four...five...will be covering each of the three loading docks in pairs. We'll breach the east entrance, first. He'll run the other way. Then you'll breach from your end and cut him off. We'll corner him in the middle, and leave no chance of escape. Are we clear?" He asked, trying to ensure that the immediate action plan was correctly imprinted in everyone's minds. "CLEAR!" was the prompt reply. "Let's, move out!" The teams divided, making their way towards their destination.

"Copy that. Approaching...back alley...side door. Maintain visual." He reported back to the same analyst as he along with Alpha-Two and Alpha-Three, raced their way to the next milestone, suspiring heavily.

They sprinted towards the only single entrance on the east façade of the building, careening close to the rugged wall, irregular with seemingly random light brown pillars and columns. It was a long way down. Cooper was at the big white door. It was going to be the entry point of their divvied squad. Soon enough, he like the others in his team heard a familiar voice echoing in their ears.

"Be advised, be advised. We have lost visual. I repeat, we have...lost...visual. Thermal imagery offline! Target can be anywhere in the building!" The analyst notified the combatants on the scene.

"What?" Sergeant Cooper cried in amazement. "Copy that." He reported in the transceiver. "Report if he tries to escape the building.

Looks like we are gonna have to do it the hard way! He pondered.

"Okay..." he said plainly as he exhaled rapidly. They had reached the door. Alpha-Two was on the lateral side of it, facing him his gun pointed down but his strong arm holding the heavy metal tightly in his grip. Alpha-Three was right behind Cooper, so close that he could hear him breathe. They stood there patient, listening to the voices crackling in their ears. "Team-two in position!"

"Team-three, in position" The group stated.

"Team-four in position; waiting for your go/no-go!"

All the teams were set and in position. Waiting for their sergeant's command.

"Alpha-Three! You're up!" he awkwardly patted him as he over took him, because of all the weapon and armor hung on his body it was not that easy to move. Alpha-Three went ahead, in front of that same door. His job was to place strip charges on it so that when it is detonated the directed concentrated explosion would blow the door to bits, so that they would barge in, surprising the stunned enemy.

Alpha-Three stood before the large bright white door. He took out a small rectangular piece of something, which appeared to be wrapped up in duct tape. As he exhaled, he attached it to the thick wooden door. Kneeling down, he started connecting the wires to the claymore, so that they could detonate it remotely. "Hey! Hurry up!" Cooper shouted. Alpha-Three was taking his time, not messing around with the heavy payload.

More than a thousand miles away, at CIA headquarters in Langley in one of the classified floors underneath the building, the Deputy Director, Special Activities Division was entering one of the most secret rooms in the building. The room from which every CIA sanctioned clandestine operation had been coordinated from, in the wake of the 9/11 incident.

"What's the status?" He pressed for in his usual charismatic voice as he sipped ever so gingerly from his thick ceramic mug of extra sweetened soy milk latte. The room was filled with graduates from top engineering institutions like Harvard and MIT, who were selectively hired by the agency after rigorous background checks. He entered the dim lit room through one of the back entrances. So naturally everybody was facing the opposite side. The only meager flicker of illumination which was there was the stone blue light emitted radiantly by the desktop workstations and the countless screens which hung on the wall ahead of him. One of the men turned back and informed him, "They are about to breach the compound. Joshua is trying to ascertain his current position."

"You don't know where he is?" He asked the specialist. Somebody else stepped forward. "No, sir." The child-like adult crossed the supervisor's path with a confident impulse which faded just as soon as it came. Sheepishly, he tried to explain their condition. "He's set the whole ground floor of the structure on fire. If he comes up even for a second, we can pin-point his exact location, but as long as he stays at that level, he's virtually untraceable."

"Let me complete my sentence..." Carver reiterated. "You don't know where he is, yet you are sending them inside that building?"

"Umm...yeah. There are twelve of them and one of him. He has no chance!" The analyst stated.

I wish that were true!

There were things the analyst did not know, there were things the operatives did not know. They never know.

"Bring up the feed to the big screen. I want to see what's happening."

"Of course." The techie remarked, as he instructed the engineer ahead, "Pull up the video feed to Screen One."

"Video feed up on Screen One." The employee replied.

"Alpha-Three! You're up!" the strong confident words reverberated in the shady room. Deputy Director Carver's gaze widened in exasperation, rooting to find out the outcome of this entire covert operation as he stared at the big screen which dominated the far edge of the room. As the video progressed he could see the first person view of the soldier hauling the camera, from his mounted head cam, reaching the white door apparent even from his angle. The man stopped in front of the huge entrance, stooping, he placed the explosive charge on the door. All heads in the room rose up and turned towards the big screen.

For a minute they observed as the man did what he was ordered to do, preparing the charge, so that they could breach the door. But soon enough they trembled in shock and bewilderment. Carver's hands jolted so abruptly that the hot amalgam of soy milk and exotic Jamaican coffee which was brimming the edges of his clay coffee mug, foamed over the rim, and spilled on the freshly polished floor, burning his fingers in the process.

"Oh my God! Oh my God!" were the frantic words now coming out loud from the many high-definition speakers installed during the room's inception. The sight was terrifying to say the least.

"Man down! I repeat. MAN DOWN!" The team leader Cooper informed on his transceiver to the other teams, and to the people far-off listening in as he jolted towards his fallen partner. The door was booby-trapped, and the explosive, burst straight in the face of Alpha-Three, who was flung ferociously a couple of feet where he lay there on his back, as if the mighty lion had pounced over its target, dragging him to the dining table.

Carver and the others got the wobbly view of the action. They saw it as Alpha-One-Actual was running towards Alpha-Three.

"Copy that. Extraction team en-route." One of the analysts replied in an unnervingly calm voice.

"Buddy! You Okay?" He asked the fallen combatant who was knocked almost unconscious. The Kevlar and the dominating black face mask absorbed most of the blast impact, but his arms and legs were tattered. His cranium fractured where he hit his head in the fall. He was knocked up; not including many injuries which had permeated through the Kevlar, and also the mask. After all, they were only bullet-proof, not blast-proof. Alpha-Three's eyes reeled around. For a moment he was completely thoughtless, but soon enough he came back to his senses, barely. His eyes were blinking almost rapidly, reeling around, trying to assess where he was until his instincts came back to him. Between his military issued boots, he noticed the inferno which blazed though the void, his leader leaning over him, shouting, yet as his ears were ringing, he only heard muffled noises through them.

"What happened?" He tried to relay, but he was stuttering, unable to speak.

"Stay down!" Cooper instructed him. "Help is on the way!"

"Teams! Use shotgun. No explosives—doors are hot!" He ordered the rest of his soldiers as he turned back to his objective. The door had been breached; it was a botched attempt, true. But the job was done. And there was no time to lose. "Teams! Go, go, go!"

His eyes turned towards his sole team mate who was capable of wielding a gun. Nothing was said but all was understood, as he double tapped over his shoulders, they moved through the hole where the door used to be, giving one last agonizing glance to his fallen and moved on.

Slowly and quietly, they moved about, almost tip-toeing on the smooth tiled floor of what used to be the ground floor of a vibrant Mart. It was something like those old-fashioned oven, where one could look at the streaming, glowing bright orange charcoal flame. It was indeed an inferno, and they were right in the middle of it.

"Teams! Positions?" The team leader whispered in a muffled voice.

"Team-Two. Here!" "Team-Three. Here!" There was a demoralizing and intimidating silence, lashing at them. Cooper's throat took down a big gulp as he heaved a deep sigh. "Team-Four?—Report!" he ordered. "Report! Team-Four? Report!—damn it!" he exclaimed in utter frustration.

"Control! Team-Four's down." He himself reported to the analyst.

"Copy that." The analyst replied in the same unnervingly calm, distant and inhumane voice.

But Cooper was full of grief. His people were falling like chess-pieces. They were being executed like a deer hunted mercilessly in the savanna grasslands.

"No they aren't! Their transmitters are still active. Heart rate normal." Another analyst turned on the microphone attached to his work station. *Were they dead, we would have heard something!* He thought to himself. "Their signal is still moving! Right where they are supposed to be!" He transferred the data he had to the main screen. "See!" He expressed with joy, for several reasons.

Carver noticed it with a smile, still licking his burnt fingers, caressing them.

"Alpha-One-Actual. Team-four not down—Not down…must be a transmission slip. They are west-north-west of your current location." The first analyst replied.

"Copy that" Alpha-One-Actual replied back, but his joy was neither evident under the mask wrapped face nor in his deep manly voice. "Team-Two! Move to that location!" he then instructed his soldiers. "Make contact with Team-four and report—and be on your guard. Our target is armed, trained and extremely hostile. Tread lightly. We should be hunting him, instead of him hunting us!"

"Copy that!" The leader of that team reported back.

Now, time to find that bastard!

"He's here somewhere!" Cooper warned his teammate. "Eye's open!"

Some hundred feet apart, the three members of Team-two made their way towards their mark, towards the electronics section, near the CGD screens. They walked at a slightly faster pace, some place between walking and running, but they did that without a whisper. No tapping of the hard leather boots or the rustle of their Kevlar re-enforced carbon black clothing. They were moving in a specific formation, each member of the unit covering each side. Team Leader was in front, the rest of them strafing sideways managed to cover their right and left. Their individual Carbines held high up to their face, at horizontal level, their eyes squinting to see through the red-dot optical scope. Their humungous fists tightly clenched the sandpaper textured grip, holding it as tight as humanly possible.

They were not your average military soldiers. They were the elite, to say the least. The Air force had the 1st Special Forces Operational Detachment-Delta (1st SFOD-D) or Delta Force as they were popularly known. The US Army Special Forces had the 75th Ranger Regiment, the Green Berets. The Navy had the United States Naval Special Warfare Development Group or DEVGRU as they now call themselves. It was the DEVGRU BLUE Detachment in which Alec served before the incident, before being taken up by the CIA. The list goes on. But all their actions if not like an open book were still open to bureaucratic scrutiny and political coverage. Sometimes things need to be done quietly and in times like this only one name comes in mind. The Special Activities Division of the National Clandestine Service. National Clandestine Service being one of the four core divisions of the CIA. This group is more exclusive than any, though everybody, intelligence or military knows and fears them. They are the elites chosen from the elites in DEVGRU or Delta Force.

Their clothes were black so that they could camouflage in the dark, but there is no symbol or sign of the United States Government on their clothes or armor to have Plausible Deniability about US Military Support.

In "SPECIAL OPS: AMERICA'S ELITE FORCES IN 21ST CENTURY COMBAT", THE AUTHOR STATED:

"HIGHLY CLASSIFIED, THE SAD IS REGARDED AS THE PREEMINENT SPECIAL

OPERATIONS UNIT IN THE WORLD. MEMBERS ARE THE ELITE OF THE ELITE; "THE BEST PERIOD." THIS RESULTS FROM THE SOURCES FROM WHICH THE ORGANIZATION RECRUITS ITS MEMBERS: SPECIAL MISSIONS UNITS (SMUS); SUCH AS DELTA FORCE AND NSWDG (UNITED STATES NAVAL SPECIAL WARFARE DEVELOPMENT GROUP)...."

Any clandestine or covert operation ever conducted whether it was foreign like Bay of Pigs Invasion, covertly extracting Dalai Lama to India and Nepal, locating and killing Osama Bin Laden or conducted stateside, it was absolutely done by the Special Operations Group of the Special Activities Division.

"We've reached our destination." The operative remarks.

"Where the hell are they?" The operative covering the left questioned in frenzied restlessness.

"This doesn't make any sense!" the Team leader had his PDA pulled out; he tried to glance it under the bright light of the blazing fire. "It says we're right on top of them." There were two beacons on the screen which indicated Team-four and the other overlapping indicated the other operatives of Team-two. One of them tried to peek down ahead of the Kevlar, "What the hell—?

Special Activities Division
Central Intelligence Agency
Langley, Washington

"Come on! Give me something!" Carver shouted at the guys.

A young female walked up behind his back. "Mr. Carver! I have Secretary of Homeland Security on the line."

Crap!

"If you guys don't get me SOMETHING when I'm back, its back to 'The Farm' for all of you!", he relayed his warning to every person in the room. His secretary was shocked. "Not you!" he replied. "That would be all. Thanks." He showed his gratitude towards her and soon she went on her way.

"Carver speaking!" he declared on the phone.

"This is Harvey Nolan. Secretary of Homeland Security." The deep and extremely bold voice echoed in his ears.

"Yes Sir." He said.

"Mr. President wants to talk to you." He stated.

"Yes, of course." Carver's mind was reeling about in all directions. There was ten seconds of silence and some static.

"Mr. Carver?" The dominating voice resounded in all its majesty.

"Yes, Mr. President." Carver replied.

"I'm seeing the live feed over here, and I must say that I'm not impressed at all. Rogue operator or not, I cannot have a confirmed terrorist roam about the streets of Chicago. Is that clear?" He ordered. "Bring him in. Discreetly. Alive."

"Yes sir. Absolutely sir." He replied, apologetically.

The cell-phone was pressing next to his lips as he stood there for a minute, brainstorming. Then he flooded back to the room with all the heat packed in him.

"Okay!" he announced. "What've you all got?"

"Team-Two is approaching the coordinates." The lead techie replied.

He looked up the screen.

"What the hell—?" the long puzzling fragmented question hollered through the room, which originated from the military operators mouth. Suddenly, much to everyone's surprise, especially Carver's, they heard three distinct sharp pinching muffled noises through the same set of speakers, which resembled more like gun shots. Things had not even registered in Carver's mind when all the five transmission beacons started displaying the one, most dreaded message. All the vitals showed zero. The operatives were down. He knew that they were dead.

❧❧

"What was that?" Cooper asked anxiously, but somewhere in the back of his mind, he along with the rest of his team, already knew what it was.

His voice reverberated in the room.

These soldiers are trained super-humans...and they are just falling like crazy!

"Team-two down!" the analyst remarked.

"What are you all doing?" Carver asked frantically. "Send in back up!"

"Back up is en-route—but 200 clicks away. They'll not reach in time." The tactical analyst reported.

"Okay people. This mission cannot fall apart. They need to stay alive till back up arrives. If he escapes Chicago will make front line news in tomorrow's papers."

Carver was still trying to come up with something. "What we need is…is to draw him out. He's familiar with the area, and has all the advantage, while our people are at a major disadvantage." He was talking to himself, but also bouncing off ideas with the others.

"I don't think he'll give up that advantage." The person standing in front of him replied.

"Yeah, I know!" Carver was getting agitated.

"It's getting dark!" Cooper remarked as he noticed that the flames were diminishing as he stared across the floors of the vast One-Stop mall. "We minimize our signature! Lights off!" He ordered.

"Switch to Thermal Vision!" He instructed his operatives in a gasp of desperation. The team was on the edge.

❧

"What did he say?" Back at Langley, one of the analysts jumped on his toes, as he heard the words coming out of the speakers.

"They're switching to Thermal." His colleague reported.

"They can't do that!" The analyst urged with the utmost importance.

"Why?" was the confused reply.

"The place may be dark, but it was on fire minutes ago. There would be enough infra-red radiation…from everything around them…it'd blind them!!" The urgency in his voice was more than apparent.

The senior analyst didn't take more time arguing with him. Because he had not specialized in tactical equipment. Things like that never happened with him, but it did make some sense. "Negative…I repeat, that's a Negative." Hastily, he tried to convey the warning to operatives on the ground.

But it was too late. Before they were able to heed to the warning, the operatives switched the dial on their ACH helmets to Night Vision pulling down the goggles mounted on top of the helmet in front of their eyes. Cooper was the first to realize his possibly fatal mistake. As the device came to its active position, it hummed into action but to the operatives' extreme surprise; they were all blinded by the intense bright white light.

"Shit!" Cooper shouted as he quickly pulled off the goggles from his face and his eyes. But the damage was done. Cooper opened his eyes, he could not see anything. Stark darkness.

Oh hell! I can't see anything!

Same was the condition for the rest of team. All of them, at the peak of their vulnerability, could not see a single thing. "What to do?"

"I can't see!" somebody shouted rather hysterically on the transceiver.

❧

"Come again?" the analyst requested at the peculiar statement strangely curious as to how things panned out.

"I can't see damnit! Nothing!" the terrified voice of the elite operative struck fear in everybody's hearts. On the ground, the operative was having all the painful difficulties any blind man has to go through. His gun was hanging to the strap around his neck. His hands stretched forward were trying to familiarize with the environment, trying to grasp something and dodging obstacles as he desperately tried to walk slowly, without hitting himself.

"The extreme light must have destroyed the photo sensory receptors in their eyes. They need to find cover. Their sight will come back gradually but the target is still at large." The analyst with biology major and specializing in tactical equipment shared his expertise with the rest of the class.

The senior analyst relayed the dire message, bringing slight relief to the lone operatives.

"What should we do?" The senior analyst shouted out loud, but the question was directed towards the one person whose power superseded all of them, Deputy Director Carver.

But Carver was at a loss of words. "I—I uh…I don't know." He replied back, but so softly that it appeared as if he was whispering. He did not want to admit his incompetence to co-ordinate the operation. In the world of Intelligence, you do not make the same mistake twice, whether you are in the field or behind the desk; especially if a certain operation goes awry. In situations like this, failure is not an option, uncountable lives are at stake, and many are changed forever. Failure is never accepted, and inability to bring out results is never tolerated.

Carver knew this firsthand. His first taste of a major promotion at the CIA was provided to him at the loss of his superior.

"Check the building's schematics. He must have turned off the power. We just have to turn it back on." The Deputy Director answered after the momentous pause.—"And how far is the back up?"

"Reaching 90 clicks mark." The analyst reported as he glanced on his terminal, at another MH-60 chopper which was making its way towards the given co-ordinates.

Again, the same sound riveted on their minds as they heard another suppressed gunshot, which was soon followed by the grunts and noises of what appeared as the sound of choking.

"Don't fight it!" the alien voice resounded as the subject of the sound slowly choked the operative to oblivion. It came through the microphone woven neatly inside the operatives Interceptor Body Armor. What they were hearing were desperate attempts to breathe, under the influence of the powerful hands which were increasingly squeezing the owners wind pipe. Then there was silence.

"Sir! We've lost another." The analyst remarked as they all were occupied by the voice of the soldier, wheezing for a single breathe, gasping for air. "—and another...Sir, Team-Three also down!"

"ETA for back-up?!" Carver demanded.

"Seven minutes."

"Shit! They won't survive that long!" the Deputy stated his biggest fear.

❧

Alpha-One was the first field operative whose sight came back to him, but all the while only one thought was spinning in the whirlpool that his mind was in.

If I just get my hands on that slippery bastard.—Oh the things I'll do to him...before I kill him!

"Sir...the mains terminal is located in a back room. I can't seem to override the controls. It has to be done physically." The tactical analyst reported as he turned away from his terminal in JSOC Center.

"How's he seeing in the dark?" Carver was genuinely baffled as he looked at the video feed of one of the men still alive. Even he was not able make out head or tail of the video. "Give Alpha-One-Actual the location of the back room. Tell him to turn on the power." He commanded as he pulled himself together.

He's using the darkness as cover. We'll take away his only advantage from him!

"Sending current objective…co-ordinates…now." A female voice sounded.

"Alpha-One! Proceed to…."

48

Objectives

Cooper's PDA was buzzing. He observed at the small console attached at the comb of the rifle and the digital display attached to it. He had just received the new objective and decided it would be best if he would do it himself. As the co-ordinates reached his PDA, the pointer on the Carbine buzzed into action as it twirled about aiming at the direction signaled to it.

"Alpha-Two? I'm gonna try to bring up the power." Cooper informed him. "You maintain your ground, till I come back. I'll inform you on the transceiver when I approach you. If anything moves…open fire."

"Copy that." Alpha-Two countered.

Leaving his teammate alone, he slowly and unobtrusively made his way towards the given location. It reminded him much of his training exercise, alone in the dark when the enemy is still at large and could pounce on him at any second from any direction; chills ran down the spine. His heart was throbbing, knocking against the ribs inside his chest but fear was not to be seen on his face.

He crossed the video games and movies aisle, reaching the HI-FI, home theater and CGD screens. There was a comparatively bland white door tucked behind one of the displays. Cooper would have missed in the dark, were it not for the compass which told him otherwise. Slowly and steadily, he quietly turned the knob, opening the door with his left hand, his index finger still trained at the trigger, sensitive to any movement. He opened the door just enough for him to be able to slide through the space and as he slithered into the rather tiny room, the first thing he did was check for signs of enemy presence.

He verified every inch of the room. All he found was chairs and tables and coffee-makers which evidently were unaffected as the fire never reached that room. Then he turned his attention to the LCD panel attached at the edge of the wall left of him. Speedily, his fingers ran meticulously at the console. But the machine did not respond. Cooper turned on the flashlight attached to the gun, to view the problem, and as he did, he noticed the LCD screen was riddled with countless bullet holes. He knew that the controls were bust, destroyed for the obvious purpose.

"The controls are busted!" Cooper snapped into the receiver.

"There must be a small switch of some kind! Press it and it'll switch to analog mode." A voice answered back to him.

Indeed, there was a small button on top of the device and as he pressed it, the whole fragmented screen, lifted on itself and slid upwards revealing the array of plastic circuit breakers and wiring underneath.

Cooper played with many of them, turning them on and off, but still there was no reaction. He noticed that the bullets had managed to pass through the board underneath too. He toggled many switches before he realized that it was nothing but a waste of very crucial time.

He reported back to the Control Room saying, "It's still not working. He has destroyed it completely!"

"That's it! I'm pulling them out!" Carver had finally had it. More than half of the elite operatives had been killed, just like that. "Red Flash them. I want them out, A S A P!!" He articulated.

"I don't think that's an option we have," one of his subordinates tried to explain to him. "Washington has made it very clear. He needs to be taken down. As it is, it looks bad from every angle, especially for the Agency. After all, he is one of our guys. For all we know, every other country would already be trying to poach him. In any case, other agencies must already have gotten involved. If he defects then only God knows what beans he would spill on their table! We need to stop this now!"

"I know…" Carver concurred with a sigh.

"Director Marty has paged me more than fifteen times!" The subordinate continued.

"Decisions taken during live operations are never perfect! You know that!" Carver barked at the man. "It's the best option we currently have! If we don't pull them out, he'll take them out and escape before we even get the chance to set up road-blocks, not that road-blocks have ever caught an operative!—Now...do you have a better plan?—I didn't think so!"

"What do you suggest, then?" the man asked impatiently as he glanced at the screen.

"We pull them out...and then we wait." He replied with a cunning smile.

"Wait...that's your big plan?" The man was sarcastic.

"Look...if he tries to escape we can nail his ass. If he stays we can have the whole battalion on him." Carver reasoned.

"Not very quiet...but since we have no other option..." The subordinate agreed.

"I thought so!" Carver buffed as he turned towards the array of terminals and the analysts working over them but surprisingly there was a short pale guy with glasses who was standing right next to him. His face looked as if he had found some hidden treasure, ecstatic.

As he was panting hard he talked to Carver with a smile, "I think we have a solution to all our problems."

Both of them were confused.

"What are you talking about?" Carver enquired inquisitively.

"Follow Me!" The networks analyst urged.

Speedily, they moved halfway across the room till they found themselves at the side of a lean yet quirky woman, much younger than many people in the room.

"I don't know what Alpha-One did, but it seems I now have total control over the buildings electrical systems." The woman exclaimed.

"So you can..." Carver enquired.

"Yeah! I can light up that building like a Christmas tree!" The perky analyst chirped. "Sorry!" Realising her tone to be inappropriate.

Carver ignored her statement but urged her to do what was necessary.

"It's going to take some time." She informed.

"Hurry!" Carver pressed.

Cooper heard some of his people talk on the radio.

They are losing it

But the question was whether he was too. There was an armed

and dangerous rogue CIA-operative who had done something grave enough to make himself an enemy of the State. And he was in the same building and the same floor. He had already killed seven of his operatives and gave life-threatening injuries to one of his closest friends, who was still fighting for his life. It was hard not to be intimidated.

Seeing that there was nothing he could do in that empty void of a room, Cooper decided to join his men in the field outside. There was a real chance that he would go out of the building in a body bag and add an additional silver star in the Memorial Wall, but it was a chance he was willing to take for his people, to avenge the cold deaths of his men.

The world had moved on, nations had moved on. Even post Cold War, no one felt more strongly for their country than any operative whether he was from the NCS or SIS. They would do anything for their country without asking a single question. Working in Intelligence, not asking questions comes with the job description. It's not hard to imagine how Mercer would feel when he realized that he was being used. What he did not realize was that being used also came with the territory.

Alpha-One took a long and deep breath as he quietly rotated the door-knob and with his other hand grasped the grip of his Carbine. Slowly and quietly, he strolled on his toes through the different sections of the displays, making his way towards Alpha-Two. As he was just about to reach the Blue-Ray and Games aisle, he intimated Alpha-Two that he was approaching him. "Alpha-Two, I'm coming back!" he whispered softly but the high quality microphone encased in his tactical mask picked up every little vibration.

"Copy that! I see you!" Alpha-Two heaved a sigh.

"Alpha-Two!! Alpha-Two!!! I'm locked in the employee room! That's the target!" Cooper's voice stormed into his ears. "That's not me! Shoot him!!!" The familiar voice pleaded hastily.

"What! No wait! I'm Cooper! Your brot—!"

Alpha-Two's Carbine was cocked; his index finger was ready at the trigger. Without giving it a second thought, he tightly clenched the trigger and aimlessly targeted the shadowy creature he saw ahead. The automatic assault rifle burst open, and with thunder and lightning emptied all the bullets in the magazine. What was left were the cartridge shells lying all around him.

For a whole minute the only source of light in the room was that sole Carbine which lit up the whole floor. Were he on the other side of the muzzle, perhaps under the reflection he could see who he had just killed.

"Oh no! What have I done!" Alpha-Two was traumatized. The last words he heard, your brot…your brother. He ran up to the oozing corpse quickly covering the huge distance. There was just one thing on his mind and just one wish. *Please be the target!* He neared the body and as he reached it and recognized the frame in the dark all he wanted to do was cry, but tears would not come. His hands dropped the gun which fell until the strap took hold of it. He fell on his knees. In the darkness, the blood coming out of the lifeless body looked black, mirroring the black uniform they wore and also his current disposition. He was about to check for signs of life, but he noticed something. His head turned up, and even before his brain could register what it was and before hands could reach for the gun, he fell. All he saw was the single strand of muzzle flash before there was eternal darkness all around.

49

Oh My God

"Oh my God!" the senior analyst cried.

"Will anybody please tell me what just happened?!" He questioned with the sternest look on his face.

"We think our systems have been hacked!" one of them shouted as he bounced about the room in total frenzy. It was chaos. "Atleast our communications channels!"

"Switching to back-up channels." A voice declared. "Changing Encryption Protocols."

"Network Debug running." Another announced.

The analysts were working furiously over the situation.

"Sir…you have a call from Homeland Security!" Carver's assistant came back.

"Yeah…I'm busy right now!!" He pressed harder.

"He says it's urgent." The assistant pressed forward.

"Tell him…if the President has a solution to the problem then I'm all ears but until then…." He pushed her off.

They heard the sound of the firing machine gun."Sir… Alpha-One-Actual is down."

"What!?" Carver remarked.

Carver was still next to the perky woman, who was still trying to get the lights turned on.

"Run vocal stress-print analysis on that voice...I want to know who that was!"

"The voice belongs to umm…Alpha-One." The woman replied in a grim tone.

"What!?" Carver was shocked even more.

"Alpha-Two is also down."

"Sir…Mr. Nolan insists that it is urgent!" the secretary came back. Carver gave her a serious look.

"He's very busy. He can't take your call." The secretary informed the caller. "Yeah, I can do that." Carver heard her speak.

It did not take long for him to realize that they had been played.

"Sir…what I'm about to do is pretty illegal." The lady network security analyst informed Carver. "You don't got any problem, right?"

The Deputy Director of the SAD had but one priority. "Just do it!"

"Alrighty then…" She turned back towards the computer. Different consoles and windows were buzzing through her screen.

"Sir…we've located the source of the security breach!" the senior analyst pronounced. There were just two green beacons flashing on the screen, which belonged to the members of the last surviving team. But now, there was a third blue beacon which was fleeing away from the location where Alpha-One and Alpha-Two were.

Finally! Time to nail that bastard!

"It doesn't matter whether it is a trap or not. As the light comes up, he'll lose more than his advantage. All it takes is one bullet!" He instructed his men to proceed with the operation, then turning towards the young female analyst, "It all depends on you now!" he acknowledged. The woman was really starting to feel the pressure.

I can do this!

50

Wasted

Mercer kneeled over the two inanimate bodies and rustled through the Body Interceptor Armor both of them were wearing, searching for the transmitter chips hidden in the layers of the Kevlar.

One by one, as he found them, his strong fingers broke them into two.

Then he stood up. There was a similar transmitter in his own hands. He was standing at the end of what used to be a very long games rack but perpendicular to his sight there was an even longer corridor which seemed almost end-less in the queer darkness and was crisscrossed with analogous aisles and passages. He turned back and threw his own transmitter far into the darkness. As it fell on the ground, it made a sharp metallic clank and then smoothly slid on the polished floor and then waited; waiting in the dark, like a fisherman patiently waits for the fishes to take the bait. After all, he was counting on them to take the bait.

A lot of things were running through his own mind. Killing all these men, it was an unnecessary waste of life. But it was either their lives or his. A lot depended on him, even the fate of all the people in the world, as it were.

Does it justify my actions!

He was confused, still his path was clear. It was like a friend of his in the British Security Services used to say, "When it comes down to it, they are your enemy. That's what they are: Your Enemy. Nothing else. You just have one momentary lapse in judgment, and you are dead."

His friend's words were still ringing in his mind.

They are my enemy, nothing else!

But does it make everything alright? The difference between right and wrong is much clearer in the battlefield. In Intelligence, it is just gray and murky.

They are my enemy, nothing else!

He reminded himself. *Justification has no place right now.* He realized.

All the while, he had been staring in the blank. But now, there was movement. It was dark but his eyes had become accustomed to it. His training was very different from anything the operatives in SOG had been through. They work in teams but he worked alone. Always had been working alone for a very long time.

I've used up all my rounds! Hope I can pull this off!

By the faint sound of tapping made by the military boots, Mercer could deduce they were two operatives. As he calculated, he knew that the two were the last of the operatives sent to kill or apprehend him; most likely they came with a kill order.

Mercer slowly made his way towards them. He walked without making a slight creek. Partially kneeling, but moving swiftly at the same time, he was getting closer and closer to his enemies.

Just steps away from them, he could see them as clearly as he could see his own hands as they reached back, pulling out the huge ceramic knife wedged between his jeans. In attack formation, he was ready to strike. But lights turned up. The whole store lit up. The lights mounted on the ceiling brightened up the place but the floor and all the displays was charred black from the fire which was once blazing ferociously. For a second he was taken aback, unlike the men in front of him who evidently were yearning for this to happen. He did not know because he ditched the transmitter he had as a bluff, but it now seemed that the SOG had a pair of aces up its sleeve. He was baffled as to how they were able to bring up the light, but it was on; and there was no time. Unfortunately, he was a bit too far.

It took them less than a second to get tuned to the bright light and as they did they tried to assess their surroundings. The first thing which jumped out at Alpha-Eight was his target, Alec Mercer as he threw himself at him. He motioned his gun to shoot at him, but Mercer knocked it off course. Alpha-Nine was a few paces ahead. He was checking their forward surroundings but as he heard the commotion, he knew what he had to do. They were not afraid anymore; instead they were fuming in anger. Promptly, he turned back and his gun pre-cocked and his fingers ready to fire.

Having his gun knocked off, Alpha-Eight did not have the chance to strike back. His palm tightened into a fist and hurled into a confident jab into Mercer's lower abdomen. But Mercer was too swift for his rigid body. Blocking the jab, he countered with a strong punch which was rendered ineffective against the thick body armor. He tossed the knife in his hands so much that he caught it by the hilt, only upside-down which he stabbed into Alpha-Eight's thigh. Alpha-Eight yelled in pain. As Alpha-Nine turned back, he noticed his friend held captive by his target.

Mercer knew that the situation was quite serious. There had been incidents cited where Task Force members had shot through their own friends to execute the target and this situation was no different. Instantaneously, Alpha-Nine raised his Carbine to shoot the target. His partner may die or not, either way Mercer was going to die. There was a side-arm holstered in Alpha-Eight's uniform, tucked underneath the armor. Mercer knew exactly where it was. Before Alpha-Nine could pull the trigger, Mercer drew his captive's sidearm and shot multiple rounds at the operative in front of him. Alpha-Nine was stunned by the bullet impact but unhurt from the 9 mm cartridge as his Kevlar armor absorbed a crucial portion of the force; he was stunned nonetheless. As he recovered from the impact, he noticed Alpha-Eight, head-first flying towards him, knocking him off the ground.

❧

"Carver?" A late incomer entered the room. His voice was stern and his stride commanded respect.

"Yes sir?" Carver replied feebly.

Could it possibly get any worse!

"Are you so big that you can ignore the calls from White House?" The incomer, the Director of the National Clandestine Services asked sarcastically.

Carver was mum. "No…sir." He replied feebly, desperately biting his tongue.

"Pull out your men!" Director Shepherd commanded.

"What!" Carver reported. "A second team of operatives is en-route!"

"Call them back!" Shepherd ordered.

"Director?" Carver replied, baffled.

"You heard me! Pull them out!" Shepherd restated violently with anger which shook the entire hall.

"But sir?!" Carver tried to argue.

"The orders have come from the highest place possible! Don't think—just act!" Director Shepherd decreed.

"Yes sir." He agreed despondently as he relayed the orders to his people.

❧

Mercer knew he had a small window of opportunity to escape. It was possible that a secondary wet works team was already en-route. He could not get caught. His plan depended on him staying alive, for now.

As he pushed the side-door open, he walked out silently. All his faculties focused on not getting noticed by the people around him, especially the local police force. He dropped the VBR and assault rifle inside the building. All he had now was his favorite Beretta 92FS pistol concealed nicely, tucked in the crevices of his denim jeans.

Mercer could clearly hear the shouts and sirens from far away, but the area was as clear as a ghost-town. Nobody to be found.

He would have kept walking, were it not for the sound of the cocking of a gun which registered on his mind. Instinctively, he turned back, pulled out his gun, and aimed steadily at the intruder's face.

"Drop it, Mercer!" The woman screamed authoritatively. She shifted her stance as she let one hand let go of the gun and to get her badge from the inside jacket pocket. She pulled out her badge and showed it to Mercer, all the while, keeping a steady gun aimed at him. "Special Agent Aisha Summers." She announced.

"You know me?" Mercer asked.

"You are a tough man to find!" Aisha chuckled. "You are under arrest!"

"There are twelve SOGs in that building who failed to do just that!" Mercer explained pointing to the One-Stop Mart. "Are you sure you want to do this?" Mercer asked slyly.

Aisha knew she was out of tactics. She would never be able to survive him single-handedly, let alone overcome him, not without backup.

"I am working undercover. Richard Meyers? Name ring a bell?" Aisha explained. "I just wanna make my case, bring that scumbag to justice. Tell me your side, that's all I want!"

"You want me to come in?" Mercer smiled. "You know I cannot do that!"

"Look around. It's not like you can escape!" She tried to explain. "The police has cordoned off the whole area. FBI, DHS, SWAT. You just cannot escape!"

"Tell you what...you help me escape and I'll hand you Meyers in gift wrap." Mercer tried to persuade Aisha. "I'm the best lead you have!"

"You expect me to let you go?" Aisha asked.

"With or without your help, I'm gonna try. But if they catch me, you will never see me, we both know that! You can kiss your case goodbye!" Mercer leaned.

"Okay fine!" Aisha yelled after a momentous pause.

Minutes later, Mercer found himself in a small service lane. He noticed few police troopers maintaining their posts at their distance. He had been following Aisha's instructions to the word and he had to admit that having information from a local did help him a long way.

The officers had their attention to other rather important things while Mercer turned towards his. A lot of time had passed since he had last seen Éllén. She must have travelled quite the distance by now. Mercer tried to deduce where she could have been.

Mercer's eyes rolled on a nice black BMW sedan, almost a block away. He ran up to the vehicle. Shot a few rounds at the boot cover behind. As the lock gave up the hydraulic system automatically pulled up the cover revealing the contents inside the boot. Mercer was looking for a particular item; a tire iron, which he found easily without much effort. His hand reached inside and pulled the tire iron out, walked around the car and reached the driver's seat, tightly holding it by the longer side; he smashed it ferociously into the window. The translucent glass came crashing down as the siren gave a deafening screech. He threw the tire iron on the passenger seat. Then grabbing the upper rims of the broken window sill, he jumped into the seat. Taking the same tire iron, he wedged its end into the ignition key hole, and twisting it with a huge grunt, popped the ignition wires out of plastic concealment. He took two ignition leads from the bunch of multi-colored wires and joined the copper mesh inside together. Although many research and advancements have emerged in the automobile sector, making boosting cars a dwindling profession in the thieving line, yet if one is not afraid of cops and is eventually going to dump the car anyway a simple tire iron has proved countless times that it was more than just a simple tool.

The car came to life. The engine was revving vehemently. The GPS and navigation systems came online. After a quick glimpse at the digital map, he turned his attention towards the road. He popped the car straight into second gear and floored the accelerator as the car bulleted through the empty road heading straight into the crowd.

51

Grand Theft Auto

The bulky vehicle briskly screeched to a stop with black tar skid marks which ran through half a mile behind it. Mercer felt his body weight pulling himself towards the dashboard till the seatbelt pulled him back, hitting his head against the soft seat covers like a dog on a leash. His eyes rolled around checking for markers to reassure him of his current location. He had reached his destination. The door of the sedan was broken. He had to get out the same way he broke in, through the window.

Hunching forward, he did not waste a second's time in unlocking the seatbelt as he turned around and awkwardly, he grasped the window sill tightly with both hands, and with a slight grunt heaved himself out of the hole above the door where the tinted glass used to be, and thumped heavily on the concrete pavement. His hands were empty; he left the tire-iron inside the car, most of his weapons were used up and empty, the bullet wound on his leg was all closed-up. His mind, preoccupied as it was, did not register the pain. He looked up, at the far end of the extremely straight road. It was night and the moon was shy, but the roads were riddled with all sorts of different lights. In the distance, he could clearly see the lean figure staring back at him with an unnerving smile and a settled disposition. Slowly but firmly, he made his way towards the same individual as she leaned on the street lamp. She had a smile on her face, a smile which was imprinted on Mercer's mind along with her jet black hair, same as Mercer's.

Élénoré's sight was not as accustomed to the dark as Mercer's but under the bright reflections of the Freon Street lights she could faintly make out that the person staring at her was none other than her only friend.

She had been leaning against the brick wall for quite some time now. Mercer's commands were clear and decisive. "Run!" Earlier he had painted quite a picture for Éllén about how the streets of Chicago were going to be a war-zone, but she did not see anything. As the lactic acid began accumulating in her thigh muscles, she began feeling the sharp pang and fatigue as exhaustion dawned over her; she knew she could run no more and heavily she came to a halt as she gasped for air, panting and breathing heavily as she rested her body. She looked back. Many cars and pedestrians were going up and down about the road but not one of them appeared hostile.

All this running for nothing! What a waste!

She did not know whether to laugh or cry at her own misery. Alone in an alien city, alien state, alien country, scorning destiny who left her there, stranded. But Mercer's orders echoed at the back of her head. "He might seem a bit too paranoid but he knows what he's doing." She announced, reassuring herself.

Now, as the sudden screeching noise fell on her ears, her attention was captivated towards the same road on which she had 'marathoned' some time ago. She saw the car come to a halt, she noticed the chiseled figure, and 'spiderman' his way out of the window, she noticed as the figure stared at her with a newfound smile on his face. He was covered in black soot, and was barely recognizable, were it not for his well-shaped physique, and distinctive demeanor.

For a brief moment, she just stood there as her happy smile instantaneously covered her face. She was thinking something, but awestruck and completely amazed, she forgot what she was doing. Alec was walking towards her. She also started making her way slowly towards him.

An earsplitting crash echoed behind her. The deafening sound was similar to the one she had heard earlier but it was certainly louder and intense and much closer. She stopped for a second, looking back over her right shoulder, noticed an array of scary looking blokes careening towards her.

Her brows rose up. It was definitely a genuine surprise for her but her non-chalant smile did not fade, it stayed still even as she realized the reason for their arrival. Her head turned back to Alec. She noticed him sprinting at speed far beyond his superhuman capacity, jetting towards her, vehemently. She shook her head at him, as if saying no to Mercer, telling him to stop, with the same unnerving smile on her face.

❧

Mercer wanted to do something. But he was too far off. Passerbys on the road were scarce and those who were gave a big squeal of terror as they noticed the men almost identical to each other. Each of them had the same bland uniform, each carrying a standard-issue Magpul PDR, and each of them striding with the same military precision flanking her from each sides of the pavement. Seeing her signal him, he stopped and stood there as he saw them take her, right in the middle of the street, and threw her back in the passenger seat of a black almost mammoth looking Chevrolet Tahoe, after which the car screeched out, vanishing under the veil that was night.

Mercer just stood there, frozen. His mind was clear and one dialogue was playing in his mind.

"You'll protect me, won't you?" He heard Éllén's similar nasal but crisp and clear voice in her head.

"I won't let anything happen to you! I promise!" Mercer reassured her with his similar charismatic but trustable way, with a slight soothing stroke on her lean arms.

I promise! I won't let anything happen to you!

But there was nothing that he could do, not now. As the car and its bright red tail light blurred into obscurity, he turned back and strolled off but the chase was not over yet. There was a long way to go.

52

Venicia Flashback

Marvin's Safehouse
Venice, Italy

"Sorry." Mercer grunted as he stared strangely at Marvin's eyes. His soul was not lost, yet.

Marvin found it unable to speak. He struggled hard, raising his left eyebrow as if asking why. "For what?" Marvin finally asked.

"For this..." Alec replied.

Suddenly, Marvin felt a sharp sting on his cranium. The pain, white hot, spread radially throughout his head.

"Sorry." Mercer apologized again.

Marvin lay there unconscious. Alec relieved him of his pain by the only other way he could think of. He knocked him out by a blow on his head.

He let his eyes gazed up and around the cold and dark room. Streaks of blue rays, filtered through the sea water above it, swayed on the walls and on the floor. As the surface of the water above to swayed and whirled, the patterns in the room followed. The view was almost peaceful.

With one eye trained on his watch, Mercer hurriedly gazed around looking for something, something which could pull him out of his current situation.

He had a lot going on his mind. The key, Marvin's words, *and things I don't know?* On top of that the issue of making out—alive. It tends to create a blockage in the brain's functioning, negated any actual thinking, like an infinite loop.

Seeing the tranquil scene of the dancing light rays, Mercer's anxiety level decreased a bit, reducing the bottleneck jamming in his brain.

"I don't have enough time to drag his ass all the way out of the building, and I can't leave him out here. They must be waiting for me up there!" He raised his watch, glancing at the distinct titanium arms of his chronographer.

Not much time!

Suddenly, an idea hit him.

Many a times, he had seen the words, ARMORY written clearly on top of one of the doors.

Armory!

Briskly, his body sprang into action, as he jetted towards the same hollow door, leaving Marvin's body behind.

Seconds later, his confident visage emerged out from there with a collection of metallic black circular disks in one hand and a rectangular object with bright red buttons in the other. Galloping about the same room in which Marvin's body was resting; he first reached one of the same Plexiglas walls, from where the light rays were streaming inside the room, and slammed the disk on it, which glued itself to the polymerized hydrocarbon, then adjusted carefully the dial present on it. Then he dashed back, and repeated the process on the opposing wall but approximately in the same position.

Having done that, he ran back towards Marvin, where he knelt down beside his body and with his arm raised, and his sleeve pulled up just enough to reveal his watch, he gazed on the electronic timer, racing down to zero.

About time! Fifteen, fourteen, thirteen....

He began timing himself along with his stopwatch. Then he turned his attention towards the rectangular electronic device he had in his hands, adjusted the dial on it, and grabbed Marvin by the torn-and-tattered shirt on him.

Three, two....

The floor started shaking, many miscellaneous articles lying here and there, all began rolling about. A distant blast could be heard from where Mercer was kneeling, the after-shock could be felt on his skin. Mercer could pin-point the exact origin of the blast from his own experience, though experience was not needed. The blast took place just above him, many floors above.

Timing is everything!

The noise above was still roaring hard.

One.

Silently as his eyes fixated on the Plexiglas wall, Alec gently squeezed the red button on the device he had clenched tightly in his palms. The whole room lit up with a bright orange flame, distinctive of a plastic charge. With the blast, water began surging rapidly through the crack formed in the same wall, taking the place of the metallic disk on the glass. With immense force, the water started lashing on Mercer, gushing through the crevices. The water, extruding through that fissure, soon began pushing them towards the other wall with massive force.

Mercer had trouble holding his ground. But he had to. His plan depended on it. Everything depended on it. Other alternatives were to get crushed by the doing of his enemies or get blown up by his own doing. Neither seemed lucrative enough to accept.

Timing is everything!

Crashing down, just a couple floors above him, the entire debris and rubble from that abandoned safe house, was tearing all the floors one at a time. He keenly observed the hole the earlier explosion had caused. He adjusting himself along with Marvin's body, he looked back, gazing at the metallic black circular disk he had attached to the Plexiglas wall. It was a directional C-4 charge, generally used for breaching doors in line of active combat. But Mercer had to improvise.

It's getting too close for comfort!

Mercer thought as he realized that the water was pushing him too close inside the blast radius of the plastic explosive. Knowing that there was no time to waste, grabbing Marvin with one hand, and the remote detonator in the other, he somehow managed to switch the dial to another frequency, corresponding to the second charge, and again as he ducked over his body taking cover in the water already flooding in the room, he squeezed the singular red button on the detonator.

A loud thud jolted the whole area. Mercer could feel its impact right down to his bone, transmitting to him through the water. Then, as if he was caught in a current, Alec, along with Marvin, found himself flowing through the torrent, as they exited through the mighty hole in the wall, they escaped, only by a matter of seconds, from being crushed under the weight of an entire building which came down crashing through the safe house and completely obliterated it in its underwater grave. While he was still flowing in the drift, Mercer couldn't move his body. All he did was what he could do, and that was grabbing Marvin tightly. He needed to reach the surface—for oxygen. Marvin's condition was already critical; he couldn't be stressed as the chances of his survival were decreasing every instant.

As he found himself out of the clutch of the current, he began paddling desperately, to reach the surface. Heaving with all his might, he paddled as hard as he could at what appeared to be the surface of the sea. An opening for that life supporting air. Indeed, it was crucial for Marvin's sustenance.

With great momentum, and after a great deal of strenuous paddling, the too singular images of Alec and Marvin emerged from the watery horizon. Behind them the building was crumbling onto itself like a pitiful sand castle constructed only a wee-bit too close to the sea.

The place was getting hot. Soon, local authorities and media sharks would be swarming the whole area. Mercer knew he had to make himself air, in which he could vanish. But it was not easy. And there was the matter of Marvin; he required medical attention immediately. Marvin had a weak pulse, which would not stay forever.

There's no time to waste!

53

Captured

The shiny black Tahoe rolled synonymously through the streets of Chicago. All the different lights in the city whether they were shiny or dim or bright, all of them reflected off of the same black hunky SUV. There was nothing differentiating it from the rest of the mechanical crowd dominating the roads. But it was different from the inside. Éllén regained consciousness with the sound of the car's tires rubbing to a halt and then continued its almost rhythmic motion.

When she was thrown in the car, the sudden jerk and recoil knocked her unconscious. Now, she was waking up and just for a second there she had almost forgotten everything, everything she would want to forget, and then the latest events, the tragedies of her life dawned on her. Her eyes were still closed, as she did not open them purposely; keeping her senses agile, trying to deduce anything she could use to her benefits. The first thing she realized after that, much like remembered, was the distinct embassy license plates which she glimpsed at, as she was being dragged murderously into that vehicle. All embassy vehicles have diplomatic immunity. No officer would dare to do so much as ask the driver to halt and she knew that. She knew the men she was riding with, that they were trained professionals who in all likelihood had killed people before. She was in a car with professional killers who are not afraid to pull the trigger. As she lay on the soft, gray carpeted floor of the vehicle, she could clearly hear the sound of the rolling wheels or the shifting transmission and thought to herself, "There is nothing I can do over here. Why can we not be civil about all this?"

She heaved over her lean hands, rose up and sat on the cushioned seat right behind her, almost in an elegant fashion with her thin smooth legs crossed over each other and both of her arms resting on top of them and looked straight into the driver's rear-view mirror with a pouty look in her face.

"'ey boss, look who's waking up!" the driver remarked. Éllén looked around. She was sitting in the middle row. There were two armed personnel in front of her and three in the back. The window panes were heavily tinted, jet black. Though all of them were wearing shades and it was extremely dark, she could clearly understand the anger directed towards her.

The mercenary in the front row passenger seat stowed back and gazed at Élénoré as he took of his jet black glasses, which camouflaged with the environment and the shiny black SUV. The battle scars of his face and body were eminent.

"You are a slippery little fish, aren't you?" He smiled at his conquest. "You know, I've been tracking you and your bastard friend for long time now. I was there that night. I had the misfortune of being assigned to a different job, otherwise... I would have killed him and most certainly killed you." He told her calmly but ended with a smile, an unnerving laugh.

As a blow to his ego, Éllén just smiled back and with a sharp exhale she told him. "Keep dreaming...he would have just killed you, as he did to all your friends. Did you see them?" She questioned. "Did you see those charred bodies? I saw them alright...many were blown to ashes, many beyond recognition and many burnt to a crisp." She taunted him. Hunter's face dropped as he remembered those sights. But there was no sign of guilt or sorrow or pain. Just his ego was hurt and that was what he could not bear. "And they were all burnt....and they will still burn in hell!" She paused for a moment. She could not believe that she could speak so coldly about death, but there was anger in her too. Her friends were killed and she was angry indeed. "And I watched their dead bodies...standing over them!"

"You know, people used to say I was...I am clinically insane. A psychopath. A degenerate. I was a serial killer, a mass murderer. I even killed many women in the city on these very streets. Until I worked my problems...and used my...skills as a profession." The foreign accent was not very distinguishable to her but it was very apparent. "I served in many countries...served five tours in Iraq, China, and Kuwait. And now I work paramilitary. I kill to work!" Hunter also came to a pause and then he said with his index finger pointing at her. "Now you listen to me...I'm gonna find that slimy son of a bitch and then I'm gonna torture him till he begs at my feet to kill him...and then I will...kill him."

Éllén was silent, frozen.

"It seems a frog got stuck in your throat...I thought as much." He gave a satirical remark with a smile. "Nothing to say anymore?" He asked with a raised brow and a wide smile. Éllén was mum.

"You have reached your destination." A hollow female voice echoed through the GPS on the dashboard.

Éllén leaned towards her left and peaked outside the car. It was night and the dark tint of the window made everything dark and hazy and unclear but she was able to make out the distinct frame of the building which they were now entering. The car meandered left till it reached a security check post with many serious men staring at the vehicle. They began their scrutinous security protocol that was initiated for security lockdown. As the car reached near the security booth, the window rolled down and the driver boasted a paper at him. The guard keenly scanned the whole document and then with a precise salute, he went back and raised the barrier in their path. He came back to the driver and returning the piece of paper to the driver replied. "You're good to go."

The driver gave a quick nod and pressed on the accelerator. The car quickly made its way into the vast underground complex where again it came to a stop.

"Out! NOW!" he shouted at her, as he violently slammed the SUV's door and made his way towards Éllénoré's door. In a very awkward fashion she tried and unlocked the door with her hands cuffed in the front, and then she dragged herself out of the vehicle. Standing upright, she noticed the leader now standing right in front of her. With piercing glare he removed the cuffs from her hands.

"Don't give me a reason to shoot you!" he said. As the handcuffs were removed, she quickly brought her arms in front of her, started rubbing her wrists with her hands. They had been bruised terribly in her unfruitful attempt to get out of them.

"Behave!" he warned her as he pushed her to move on. Slowly and steadily, they moved towards the elevators.

"Where are you taking me?" Éllén asked the man. In the bright fluorescent lights in the parking lot, she could now clearly see each aspect of her captors in detail. The boss, Hunter, was wearing normal clothes, possibly a mud green T-shirt and trousers but his black chest and body armor prevailed over the rest. The rest of them in the back were in similar attire and had a military air about them.

"You don't need to know!" Hunter barked at her. "And don't even think about running! Your pathetic attempts are useless. I'll gun you down like the bitch you are, you hear me?"

"Yes!" She replied in a whispering frightened and pained voice.

"Good!" Hunter replied back in a satisfied tone.

They reached in front of a group of elevators in the underground parking complex. Éllén, being in front, pressed the call button. The elevator doors opened and both of them stepped inside turned around and the doors closed. Hunter swiped his access cards and pressed the floor number and the lift shot upwards.

54

Revelation

The patient couldn't help but feel some previous trauma which he had undergone. The ample number of stitches on his body was proof of that. But he was unable to remember what it was. He was in a helpless state. With enough anti-psychotics in body to put an elephant to sleep, he was pulling all his senses to not fall asleep and crash down. The night was upon him. The street lights came to life. Dragging himself through the pain, he could almost feel for sure that there was somewhere he had to be. But alas, he did not have the slightest idea.

The pain began to grow up on him. The blood gushing through his body was like a pounding hammer striking at his sutures from the inside and as his blood pressure rose, he was all but certain that his body would be torn from inside. He tried to calm himself but instead he fell down, crashing like a stumped up tree. Groaning with pain, he rolled over to lie on his back.

"Where am I supposed to be?" He asked himself. "What am I to do?"

The collection of CGD television panels on the window of the electronics store hummed to life. The patient was lying just outside it. He could almost see the various hazy shapes from the ultra-clear television panel, but he could hear just fine.

"Bearing Expo 2026!" A voice emerged from the CGD screen. An advertisement. "Just one month to go!"

"Bearing? Bearing Oil!" The patient began wondering. "Richard Meyers! Élénoré! SORCE! Mercer!" He began connecting the dots.

A phone began ringing. The patient was unaffected by its irritating noise. He was much too engaged with the constant string of thoughts which were streaming through his mind.

"Pick up the phone, damn it!" The caller swore out loud.

The patient did not even realize that it was his phone that was ringing. Suddenly, he emerged from his saintly trance. He began checking his jacket pockets for the source of that musical noise. The jacket pocket which he had picked up from his ward in the hospital.

Feebly, as he picked up the phone, he said. "Who is this?"

"Marvin!" Alec rejoiced. "They have her! And the data! They have everything!" He informed him grimly.

"What do I do?" Marvin asked.

"Meet me in Washington!" Mercer instructed. "You know the location."

"Okay." The line disconnected.

55

Mission Accomplished

The elevator doors opened with its familiar clinking tune and as it did both of them quickly stepped out of the cuboid steel box, into the clear and pristine corridors and hallways which made the floor they were standing on a giant maze. Even Hunter felt a little bit lost in the almost vacant suite.

To their avail, a man was waiting for them to escort them to their destination but he also seemed a bit distressed about something. Clearing his throat he came up to them and said, "You've finally found her!" He cried in amazement, masking his tension.

"Yes." Hunter replied back with impatience.

"Boss is preoccupied at the moment. We will have to wait for...."

"I don't do waiting!" Hunter made it clear that he would not have any delay. "This stupid mission has already cost me too much!" He impressed on their attendant. "Now! You are going to take me to him! Clear?" He said with a serious face.

"Clear...I guess", the attendant replied in a slightly confused voice. "This way please." The attendant pointed the direction as he led the way. The three-membered group made its way to the boss's office. Two of them were going to see him for the first time. Hunter was new to leadership after the CERN incident. He was the new Leader of his team. His word was their command. But it also meant he had to answer directly to his superiors. His neck was in the line and he proved his worth by tracking Élénoré and bringing her to them. Éllén looked around what appeared to be an office. It was empty. No paper-pushers to be seen. All of them were security personnel. Every person carried a piece. Most of them were identical, with similar uniforms, and radio transmitters, and ear-pieces attached with a coiled wire connecting to the radio transceivers. Weapons in their holsters. Many carrying automatic weapons in their hands stood at equal distances, their stances were up to military precision. The atmosphere was thick with tension and seriousness. Éllén felt as if she was being taken to a high class security prison facility. It made Éllén scared, scared for her life but soon the fury and rage overcame her and she was not afraid anymore. In a cool fashion, she made her way, walking in between the attendant and Hunter, towards the office of this fabled boss. As she walked, all eyes stared at her and she felt each of those multitude of eyes piercing at her. She tried hard to mask her worry and replace it with anger. After all, the people who had captured her had much to do with everything that had happened to her, all her life.

They had taken just one left and after some walking they were reaching a genuinely massive mahogany door, heavily guarded. Five armed guards on either sides of the ginormous door and many more in the surrounding area. The big door stood at a crossroads of two corridors and the intersecting area was no doubt the most heavily guarded stretch in the whole building.

Just as they neared the heavily guarded no-entry, restricted zone, the massive door lunged open, and for a slight moment revealed the single person occupying the huge office suite, but everybody including Élénoré's sight was drawn to the young female, with long and luscious blonde hair, wearing black coat and trousers over a white shirt, stomping out with her high heels, walking on the same path on which they were walking earlier on. The woman noticed all three of them, who were different from every other person around them. Quickly, she noticed their body language, she noticed the lean woman, with shiny jet black hair, her eyes staring the floor, and there was anger and sadness in them. Sandwiched between the two men, the man in the behind was clearly ex-military. She noticed the clear face of the woman in between them. As she did, her eyebrows rose up in bewilderment. She recognized the petite but mature face from one of her files, in the MERCER file. But she was not sure who this woman was or what she was doing here. What the connection was. But it was enough to give her a new lead. She noticed the concealed weapon, and knew exactly what was happening. Hurriedly, she turned her head in front of her, as she quickly made her way to the elevators.

The attendant stopped near the gate, another person took over as he went back. His work was done.

"Excellent work!" the man applauded. "Boss is extremely happy with your work. Your fees as per contract, for the completion of your mission, has been transferred to your account and all the members of your team. Only one thing remains...."

"Right." Hunter remarked, satisfied. "It'll be done." He replied in his usual inhumane voice.

"Get it done and you will be paid well!" The person said. "There is one more thing –a side mission for your team—Very easy, big payout. Do you accept?"

"Yes."

"Here...mission details, transport, everything is in this." He gave Hunter a small drive. "Support package has been dropped at O'Hare International Airport. You know what to do?"

"Of Course!"

"Good!" The man smiled. "We'll take her." Hunter walked back leaving the poor innocent woman in the custody of the man. With all the armed men surrounding her, the thought of escape shriveled inside her mind.

"Come on!" the man urged as he pushed open the big majestic door revealing the single man inside the vast room. Slowly, she ambled her way inside. The door closed behind her.

The room was bright magnesium white, not many accessories in it, a single white desk, matching colors, the wall on the right was made entirely of glass panes, the night life of the city outside was clear. It was as if peeping outside of an airplane as it descends in the night, with all the city's lights glowing brightly like arrangements of orange dots.

"Please take a seat." The man occupying the sole white ergonomic chair on the opposite side of the table asked her as he motioned his right hand, pointing at the seats on the other side.

Éllén obliged to the request and sat down quietly.

She noticed the blood soaked chair next to hers, blood stains on the arm rest, on the floor and then the blood on her host's right arm. Soon, she recognized the old wrinkled, sagging face of the host whose men had held her captive and then her expression changed completely. There was anger in her eyes. It did not take any time for her to realize exactly where she was.

"Yeah...your boyfriend shot me!" Richard Meyers grunted. "But even he couldn't kill me! And now...nobody can!" He tried to laugh at her but the intermitting pain did not allow him to do so. "Oh...how rude of me! My name is Sir Richard Meyers, the CEO of Bearing PetroTech." He introduced himself with an air of pride. But for Élénoré, he needed no introduction, she knew enough to hate him deeply.

Élénoré was silent.

"Do you know why you have been brought here, to me?" Richard asked her quickly, not wasting any more time as he leaned forward, resting his wounded injured arm on his pristine white desk. Éllén shrugged her shoulders as if saying, "I don't know and I couldn't care less!"

"You remember Sasha, don't you? Sasha Zubrensky?" He questioned her with a keen eye.

Meyers had hit a soft spot. Sasha's face came back to her mind. Sasha used to be her best friend. Many people who did not know them personally, thought them to be twin sisters, with same looks, same light shade of blonde hair, same sharp nose and highlighted features of a female Caucasian woman. Apart from being almost identical, they had similar tastes in many things except in clothes and boyfriend. Sasha had even spent hours teaching Russian to Élénoré, shared breakfast, lunch, dinner together, and spent much of their time with each other. They were practically sisters and Élénoré used to confide every little secret with her. Now she knew that her, so-called 'best' friend was the mole in the organization, a sleeper agent. Sasha was dead, killed, by none other than Alec himself in a desperate attempt to escape from their own deaths, which they did by just a hair's length.

She nodded her head saying yes. Tears almost emerged from her eyes but stopped.

"Her body was found in the debris." Richard informed her with a deep sigh. "Her job was not to just infiltrate your research team, she was the lead researcher in my own pet project, and she was working on her own fusion source which was supposed to yield almost complete perpetual source of energy—supposed to...but couldn't...due to her untimely death."

Élénoré was not surprised. Any scientist in the field of particlė physics would definitely want to grab his hands on the research data. Such research is bad for any MNC in energy and crude oil sector. Corporate Espionage was already a big viable threat to the research group. No company would want the research to come out in the market. It could dissolve the private energy sector. A zillion dollar market, ready to dominate. The only sorrow was that the mole turned out to be her best friend.

"I don't get it!" Éllén remarked in astonishment. "If the research gets public, your company will get destroyed. You'll have to be completely...."

"There's a catch, see. Do you want to know how I am where I am? I don't just defeat my opponents, I crush them completely. Now, there are twelve major petroleum companies still operating in the world, which I have not bought yet. And that pain in the ass Chinese petroleum company, bloody communists! The bloody State owns it! Countless times I've tried to take over it, but who can outbid an entire country. The free energy would give us the chance to make an early transition into the global fusion energy market. ITER project has reached its deuterium-tritium operation phase. Still has twelve years left for its slated completion. That's more than a decade. It's a lot of time to make money. After all, there's not much oil left in this hollow planet. It's a market ready to dominate, with no other player at play."

Éllén realized what Richard was hinting at. "You mean?"

"Yes...the production would cost us peanuts...facilities, reactors, employees. I already have all that! If we sell the energy below competitive prices, CPNC will never stand a chance! We will dominate the world."

"You say as if we are in this together!" Éllén remarked. "Do you really think I'm going to help you rob from public? Never. Project SORCE was successful! I'll tell everybody, I'll go public!" Élénoré coerced on Richard.

"No. You won't!"

"I won't be so sure about that!" Élénoré retorted.

"I've read your file. You have family in Marseille, right?—mother, stepfather, two cousins. You do care about them, don't you?" Richard struck a wrong note.

"You wouldn't dare!" Éllén was furious.

"Why won't I? Right now everybody in their lives...their maids, their teachers, their mailman, milkman...everyone works for me...and each of them, a professional killer. You wouldn't want anything to happen to Amanda, won't you? How long has it been since you last saw them? Huh? You know where they are? Amanda is doing a course in fashion designing. Jeremy, a computer engineer. He's here—in Chicago. In this very building. He thought he caught a big break, getting a high-profile job in a multinational company. You wouldn't want him to get laid off—or get killed? Would you?" Richard blackmailed her. Richard continued with deep intent.

Élénoré was silent. "You cold hearted bastard! Je vaistetuer!"

Richard motioned his left hand towards his phone. "You were saying?"

"I'll do it. Whatever you say, I'll do it."

"Good. Now, your friend took original research documents, but we made copies. Your work hinges on the verge of science fiction, it seems. Many of our scientists couldn't even replicate the process; replicate those ions and what not. I want you to get me the same results. You have five months to complete her work. In five months, there is a big annual Expo in which we will announce the new energy source."

"Okay." Éllén replied plainly.

"You have five months. Only five months. Failure is not expected."

"You'll have your energy source. Then you will leave me, my family, and Alec! Deal?"

"Whatever." Richard remarked. "—Only if you pull through!"

Élénoré nodded her head.

"Now…" Richard pressed a button concealed under his bright white desk. The door behind her whirled open and familiar face approaching her. "Kevin will see you out." He told her pointing the way behind her.

"Madam?" Kevin greeted her, "If you would just follow me? Welcome to Bearing PetroTech. We have everything arranged for your comfortable stay with us." He welcomed her as she briskly rose up from her seat and slowly followed Kevin outside room.

Oh Alec, where the hell are you?!

56

Game Plan

A Safehouse
Industrial District
Washington DC

"Are you crazy?!" A recovering Marvin revolted. Now, his condition was comparatively more stable, but his mental anxiety rocketing sky high. "Your plan is suicide!"

"Can you just do your bit?" Alec stressed impatiently.

"I can easily do mine provided your girlfriend does hers." Marvin argued. "And there's the reason for my concern. It's not that I doubt your capabilities, it's just that there's too much uncertainty! Everything needs to be done just perfectly…and we all know how these missions tend to deviate from track. Every mistake could be fatal. These aren't boating accidents, remember?" Marvin pointed to one of the many surgical stitches on his body.

Alec let out a deep sigh. Somewhere in his mind, he felt guilty for the pain Marvin had to bear.

"I can see only one way how all this will end. At least think of her!" Marvin stressed.

"I am! Damn it!!" Mercer recoiled with force. "I am!"

It's better this way! He knew. *It's better for everybody!*

"If you wanna die, I can't stop you…but I hope you understand what you are throwing away!"

"I do!" Mercer explained. "But sometimes…sacrifices have to be made. Sometimes if you stand for something, you got to fall for it! …some day you will understand!"

For Marvin, Alec's speech was a big pile of crap, but it did seem that he had given much thought on the matter and was not taking things lightly. His plan might be crazy, but Mercer was not. A considerable amount of planning must have gone in its preparation to care it to perfection. And he knew that there was no arguing with him.

"So…can you do it?" Mercer asked the question again. He knew what he was asking of him.

"I thought after all these years you'd be tired of asking such questions! Of course I can do it! Even if nobody can't, I can, provided you gave her the right equipment! Besides, don't worry about me. I'm worried about her. And about you." Marvin said.

"Now remember! When their event goes live, Élénoré will plug-in your virus into their remote access mainframe terminals, which would be located somewhere near the area. Then you do what you do best. Remember, they have their own transmission towers, their own relay stations, high bandwidth, high frequency, high security, their own satellite uplink, all multi-encrypted. I hope you can pull through!" Mercer remarked.

"I hope you do too!" Marvin replied, there was a hint of cynicism in his voice.

Me too!

57

Safe Haven

Villa de l' Bassét
Marseille
Bouches-du-Rhone
Provence-Alpes-Cote d'Azur

The majestic iron red villa which stood tall in the posh residential quarter of Marseille. The moderately cool misty winds of the port city of Marseille provided adequate cooling to the unchecked garden which had begun to run wildly about the villa. The swimming pool in front of the house, filled with the clear and serene blue water had been uninhabited for quite some years now. Only two of the four bedrooms were now occupied, one by Amanda who was studying a course in fashion and designing and the other by her mother, Dorothée.

"Mama!" Amanda's cheery voice resounded in the majestic old home. "Où êtes-vous?"

Dorothée woke up from her half sleep from her bed where she lay alone. It had been some time since her second husband passed away. Doctors told her the disease was of a class of non-Hodgkins Lymphoma, Cutaneous T-cell lymphoma. For her, it was all the same. Another person close to her, left her.

She was not of a cynical mind; she was one who would try to see the best in life. But life did not like that. It was pain enough for her that her own daughter chose her work obsessed first husband over her, then her second husband died of a disease she had never heard of, then her son left for America for a high profile job. Countless times does she calls him and advises him to be safe. A fear had grasped her heart. She could not lose anyone anymore.

"Mama!" Amanda yelled, unable to find her mother in the eerily silent house. "Where are you?"

"I'm coming, dear..." Dorothée answered back. Her mind pulled back to the painful reality, but glad to hear her daughter's joyful voice.

Gracefully, she climbed down the flight of stairs to the lower floor of the house, where she could see that Amanda had already sat down on the dining table, eating the food prepared for her by the maid. "How was the day, honey?" She asked like always. Amanda looked just like her older sister when she used to be of her age; young and vibrant. She had the same blonde hair which she had bundled up neatly in a fashionable knot. Her clothes were a product of her own creativity; she wore a pink and white stripped top along with an excessively adorned short denim skirt. Her eyes were like two crystal clear pools of blue which simply boosted her youthful beauty causing anyone to lay eyes on her thinking her to be extremely cute and adorable.

"Fine." Amanda gave a dull reply. "Hey, you will not believe who called me today!" Her cheery voice came back. The maid came back from the kitchen, pouring fresh grape juice from the jug she had brought on the serving tray. Wearing the traditional black dress with a sparkling white apron in front, she had an extremely fair complexion with shoulder length jet black hair which went straight as silk behind her back. The grapes picked earlier in the morning from a sizable château they owned in the North. The ceramic crockery cluttered as the maid clumsily brought the juice to the dining table.

"Careful Isabella!" Dorothée yelled at the immigrant maid. "Who?" She asked turning her mind towards Amanda.

"Élénoré!" Amanda said.

"When?" Dorothée became excited. It had been years since she had heard from her daughter. All she heard were the news of her actions, spread around, like the Nobel price she received and the incident of bombing in CERN in which she later became a suspect. It was a matter which had been cleared some time back, branding Élénoré a survivor of a terrible mishap. Dorothée remembered how she had lost her night's sleep unaware of Élénoré's safety.

"In the morning..." Amanda replied. "She just asked me if we were all right...and then she just hung up! I could not tell her that Jeremy also got a job in Bearing PetroTech...but she seemed to be in a hurry!"

"Hmm...."

The kitchen was situated in the back side of the villa. It was like any other French kitchen with an attached kitchen garden, brimming with the aroma of fresh herbs and spices.

"Did you receive any word?" Isabella asked as she cleaned the barrel of her gun.

"Yes."

"And..." She asked impatiently.

"Our objectives remain.... Follow the mother and daughter for the time being. They are not to be harmed."

"Understood." Isabella gave out a deep sigh as she securely placed her gun among other things in a secure hidden cabinet in the kitchen.

58

Gotcha

"Sir! We've got him!" a young analyst exclaimed as he jolted into the room of his superior. Torres's heart rose up. It was good news. Extremely good. He knew exactly who he was talking about. It was Mercer who was the burning topic of their current discussion. For months, they had been conducting a strenuous manhunt. Searching every part of the planet, grid-by-grid, but Mercer was nowhere to be found. Thousands of man-hours wasted on searching him, every country, every city, and every metropolis. All that data, all the evidence, the research, the data, he had everything but what was he doing with it? He took it and just went off the grid. And all the while Mercer was running interference, providing false trails, booking flights from Chicago to every city in the world, London, Melbourne, Hawaii, New Delhi, phone records, credit card transactions. It was hard to differentiate, what was real and what was fake.

"Where?" he countered just as quickly.

"Here!" The analyst replied back. The amazement was clear in his eyes.

"What?" He asked him quickly, skipping his breath. Torres quickly jumped from his black leather chair, and followed the analyst to the work room.

"I couldn't believe it either, but he is!" The analyst was firm, confident.

"Brian... are you telling me that the world's biggest terrorist threat is still in America and neither US Government nor we could track him for months?!" Both of them briskly made their way through the slightly crowded corridors. There was a rare hurriedness and commotion about everybody on the floor.

"It seems so!" The analyst uttered.

The corridor opened into a giant room with bright navy blue walls and fluorescent white light panels. Many employees sitting on their workstations but staring at him.

"Mr. Torres!" another analyst came up to Torres. "He was smart. But we have him now!"

"You're sure?" Torres was skeptical. He had heard the same words all too many times. "This better be good! What've you got?" Torres asked impatiently as they reached one vacant workstation which he knew belonged to Brian.

"This!" Brian remarked as he quickly pressed a couple of keyboard buttons on his computer and immediately screens start flooding the wall-size huge CGD screen placed accurately in the end of the room. Brian's workstation situated just right, was the best place for Torres to check the progress of all his employees on the big screen.

"This is a partial profile picked up by one of the street cams located in downtown Manhattan." Torres's eyes widened as he tried hard to make sense of the hazy out-of-focus image displayed brightly on the CGD. The picture which dominated a major part of the room's wall had a bluish hue to it which indicated it was captured during evening. It was but a singular frame taken from a street cam, aiming its lens at an alley behind some shop which was a victim of gangs tagging its walls and dealing drugs in the same alley. In the background, there was a stout man, with long radiant blonde hair, wearing black sunglasses, talking on his cellphone, clad in a thick winter coat and boots as he appeared to walk to the pavement. He had turned his back towards the camera, but due to whatever reason, he had turned back, staring at something or most likely someone down the same pavement. His face was highlighted by a yellow square around it which was blown up and displayed prominently on the remaining part of the wall, with the following text along with it. "Possibility of Match: 47%", written in bright bold yellow color.

"47% match!" The second analyst exclaimed with joy.

"I don't know—it's pretty slim." Torres did not raise his expectation so that he would not have to be sorry later. "I'd be much more happier if that said ninety-seven percent. It feels like another goose chase."

"No, no, no wait, look!" Brian responded quickly as he pressed yet another button and then another. The picture frame rewound itself like a video and after the second click started playing itself. Indeed it was a video. "He has every markers of a spook. See, he's wearing sunglasses in the night!"

"So?!" Torres demanded. "Could be anything."

"No it can't! We have analyzed it many times before bringing it to you!" Jeremy, the second analyst was adamant. "This man has worked the cameras all the way. Not one street cam could get a single usable frame—besides this one of course; and that too obviously by mistake. Do you know the possibility for that to happen in US? It's impossible! I'm telling you this man is a pro!"

"—And the obvious getup! How many blonde males do you know who keep long hair like him! Sir, please! I'm telling you, this is him! I can feel it!" The analyst pressed.

There was a moment of stressed silence in the room. Torres was silent as he keenly watched the whole video, waiting for the video to end. The video was a computerized compilation of various street cam footages following the subject as he walked through the pavements of downtown Manhattan.

"See, he tilted his head just before entering this camera's view." Brian remarked.

"—And here! This was the only camera in his path where he couldn't possibly weasel his way without being recognized by the system…and there just outside its view he entered this shop and exited from the backdoor exit!"

"Okay! I've seen enough!" Torres remarked, his mood still unclear. "Where does this end?"

"Luckily we tracked him to the fifth floor of an abandoned building in the commercial district, next to this sewage water treatment facility. We've already put the building under satellite surveillance from GCF-3F and GEOSAT, and thermal and sonic surveillance. Our friends at ECHELON are running point on electronic surveillance and phone tapping. All calls made further on, will be routed through our servers instead." Brian explained. He was extremely confidant and had already acted on the information he had. There was only one thing left to do. "We're just waiting for your orders."

"Where's he right now?" Torres asked the next obvious question.

"He's holding up in there; hasn't come out! It's most likely a safe house."

Torres was quite pondering.

"Sir?!" Jeremy pressed. "He has the experience and knowledge to trick satellites and cameras and would easily spot a tail if we put one on him. We need to act now! Catch him on his blind side!"

"Hmm…okay I'm convinced. If this is him then we can't lose him! Dispatch the teams, flash them that location. Tell Hunter to run point on this. Make sure he understands that failure is not an option. Give him fifty men if we have to; it appears a dozen men weren't enough to pin him. Where is he by the way?" Torres enquired.

"He's arriving from France in one hour at J.F.K. International." An incumbent reported.

"Perfect. Our men will be ready in an hour. They can pick him at the airport, and we will be mission ready in two. Brain, you'll be providing Tac-Support. If it is him, he has to die tonight, during rush hour. In the meantime, keep the building under strict surveillance; circle three UAVs over the building, our company satellite should be currently orbiting over Milan; tell Ruth to reposition it over Manhattan, it has better surveillance capabilities, train it over that safe house— not even a bird should escape without our knowledge. Get local assets to cordon off the whole block in case he makes his move. And secondary teams ready to sweep the building for any and all data found over there. That is crucial!"

"Yes sir!" Jeremy replied promptly.

"—And...keep me in the loop." Torres extended.

"Off course." Jeremy replied.

"—And...inform Kevin at Bearing PetroTech, he's our liaison to the company."

"Will do, boss." He nodded.

59

Ground Zero

The isle of Manhattan was brimming with vibrant street life with working women powerwalking in the parks, hotdog vendors selling their hot stuff on the streets, roads dominated with the new electric trams and overhead metros. The sight was not as it once used to be. The cars and buses were now a rare sight. And the only buses were the Metropolitan Buses running on the new age fuel.

But all this was soon about to change.

The building on 709 Lorimer Street, between Frost and Richardson once used to house a colorful candy store and apartments on its upper floors in its time, but now after all these years, the closed down and abandoned building's exterior walls were riddled with black and green moss, the paint wrinkled on itself under the scorching summer sun, the color faded, the windows broken and the iron railings rusted. Located in a very aloof region of the downtown area of Lower Manhattan, its fate was very unclear. This part of the city was extremely quiet save for the usual prostitutes and drug dealings. A block from that once-iconic building, ten black utility vans inaudibly came to a stop. Its doors opened as quickly as it came to a stop with two rows of ten paramilitary soldiers exiting from each van. As they exited from their vehicles, each clad in heavy military-issue body armor with their standard Incendiary Carbines and M14A1's held tightly in their palms, their motion swift, fluid, their weapons cocked. Hunter, the leader of his small army, knew the gravity of their situation, the things at stake. Their enemy was highly skilled and highly trained; he had killed more than a dozen men since his arrival in the States, and even more before that. Highly dangerous.

With precise hand movements, he ordered his men to swiftly make their way towards the same abandoned candy shop. This was a moment Hunter was waiting for. It would be his first encounter with Mercer.

"Target is on third floor." Brian's clear voice relayed the necessary information to the men on the ground.

"Copy that." Hunter responded.

From gutter to pavement to the broken tarmac, the men dashed inaudibly towards the same building, managing to stay outside the view of any unwanted bystanders or their target himself. Soon, they were waiting on the blind side of the building next to their destination. Hunter, leading his men with leadership, courage and revenge, hugged himself to the corner of that adjacent building, glaring through the dark with widened eyes. He raised his arm in a fist, signaling his men to stop and pulled out a pair of binoculars with one of his front vest pockets, placing it in front of his face; he focused his keen eyes at the same building. "Switching to thermal." He said out loud. He noticed many human figures inside that building. Many were prostitutes, drug addicts and other kinds of loafers a place like this usually attracts, but only one soul on the third floor. The multi-colored image through the thermal scope had pigments from light blue to bright white and all in between them and in it the red-orange figure of the man was almost so clear that Hunter could exactly figure out what he was doing. The image of his target showed him in a seated position leaning in front of some kind of heat emitting device which resembled much to a laptop.

As the leader he began instructing his men, giving them their separate objective; they were already separated into groups, now he instructed one group to cover the elevators, in case the target tries to escape, covering all the escapes. With military precision and clear inaudible hand movements, he ordered different groups of his men, to move out quietly and take up their positions. After all of them had gone, he along with the last remaining team, his team, which contained many top-notch ex-soldiers and Para-militarists, elite in their own sense, were left behind. They were the selected team to make direct contact with the subject, the entry team.

"Kill the cameras!" Hunter ordered the analyst providing him with tactical support.

"Copy." Brian, the lead systems analyst and Internet Protocol Manager at ILSA, responded back on the transceiver the next second. "Cameras are looped, you're clear to proceed."

But Hunter was cautious. His target was extremely smart, skillful and resourceful. His previous boss was overconfident and did not live to tell the tale. He pulled out yet another device from his vest pocket and holding his massive weapon firmly in his right hand; he took the phone-like device with his left hand and turned it on. As the device hummed into action, it started scanning the area like a hi-tech probe for hidden traps and ambush in place.

"No LIDARS, no sensors, lasers, no wireless cameras or surveillance equipment." Hunter talked to himself as he read the emerging text off the screen, "We're good to go!" He announced on his walkie-talkie.

"Response Code Niner—three…two… one…. Go-go-go!" a voice called out. The operation had started.

No sooner than they heard the words Go-go-go, than everybody in the vicinity who was in that uniform jolted into action. Different teams slowly made their approach towards the same building, with Hunter's men in the lead. Other teams had different objectives. Some were responsible for collecting all the incriminating evidence the target could have against their company or its primary client, while some were responsible to extract innocent bystanders non-coercively to a more safe area, without compromising the integrity of the whole operation.

With even breaths, pacing steadily and softly, Hunter and his teams, first to make contact with the building, quietly entered the half-broken and constantly deteriorating wooden door with tinted and cracked glass panels and they did so with extreme dexterity and finesse. Hunter noticed the old-fashioned elevators sporting itself in the right, but they were not going to use it. Elevators are kill-zones, the worst point of entry possible and Hunter knew that, hence the stairs. He waved his left hand in a precise manner, with his forefinger and middle finger stretched outwards, aiming at the same pair of elevators, signaling the secondary teams to cover the elevators.

"Perimeter secure!" A voice came out of the radio and echoed in Hunter's ears.

"Right." Hunter remarked. Everything was set and happening without a hitch.

Time to take on that bastard!

He signaled his primary teams to follow him to the stairs up to the third floor. There was only one stair case in the building. Rest of the exits was covered by his men. Nobody could leave the building.

Hunter, leading his pack, ran up the flight of stairs but he did so with extreme caution. His eyes looking at all places, at all times, not putting his guard down even for a second. They were scanning the area, searching keenly for any type of trap like a tripwire attached to a frag-grenade, a garden variety IED or something more sophisticated. Either way, his trained mind was determined, and they were not going to fall for anything. Every step they took was deliberate and decisive, with hands gripping their heavy weapons at chest level, clenching them tightly with their palms, their eyes following the muzzle of the gun everywhere it went, their index finger held at a mere inch from the trigger, ready to open fire instantly at the enemy.

Floor by floor, they slowly made their way to the third floor. They were unobtrusive and hard to detect. Quietly, Hunter inspected the door which would lead them to the third floor corridor, and finding it to be safe and unhampered, he opened it ever so lightly that even they did not hear a creak from that rusty old door.

Now the door was wide open. Inside the third floor corridor, the hit squad was pouring in heavily. Hunter performed the same routine he did when he was about to approach the building. They were too close to their target. Much was at risk. They did not want to tip off their target. Maybe he installed cameras in the corridor leading to his door, or perhaps he already had an escape route pre-planned. The device scanned the whole floor and found nothing which could be transmitting any type of data throughout the floor.

"Location on target?" Hunter questioned his tactical support.

"Fifth door to your right." Brian responded quickly.

"Any change in his status?" Hunter asked him again, curious about his situation.

This does not feel right! He let us walk in so easily. No resistance at all!

"Nothing. He is sitting in front of his computer." Brian replied, relaying to him what he saw on his screen.

Suddenly, everything was too conspicuous for him. The place had absolutely no markers of a safe house which felt very contradicting to what he was told earlier on in his mission briefing. A safe house would be in a very public place, the crowd could be used as cover. It has various exit points, and someplace where it is easy to create a diversion but this building was a bottleneck, and with the sewage treatment plant and other abandoned buildings, each connected to each other by humungous walls which were impossible to climb. Every safe house has fortifications of some kind, concrete walls, thick steel and titanium doors, separate and inaccessible air-ducts, cameras, sensors and what not. But he did not see anything. Hunter knew that there were no fortifications because the density of the walls of that room and other room were the same; otherwise it would have messed up the data collected from the thermal vision. In his gut, he knew that something was off.

"You're sure?" Hunter probed.

"Yeah I'm sure. He's there, he's sitting." Brian answered back.

"It doesn't seem right!" Hunter exclaimed, spelling out his concerns.

"The intel is actionable, it's—" Brian replied, or tried to before he was interrupted by his superior.

"Listen Hunter, our client's requests were very specific. That man dead. Now your job is to kill—not ask questions. Understand?" Torres chided him.

"Yes sir." Hunter softly replied.

"Floor is clean." He whispered to his team members as he noticed the message displayed on the device in his left palm as he signaled his men to amble slowly and silently and cautiously towards that same fifth door to their right.

It was dark, and quiet. In such a metropolitan set-up there weren't even any owls or crickets to break the ice. The stillness itself felt hostile, but such personal feelings were irrelevant. They moved quietly and steadily. The faint rustling of their military uniforms was masked by the flapping of pigeons from its nest above.

Soon, they were outside that ominous wooden gate, with the number '305' painted in the center. Hunter leaned to the wall on the right side of the door. There were men behind him and men across the door. All of them waiting keenly for Hunter's command. It was a portentous moment. Everything destined to happen from that point on, hanged solely on how things would pan out in the next few seconds.

Hunter heaved a long deep breathe, mustering his courage, recalibrating his perception under the effect of the adrenaline pumping heavily through his body. Now, he was sure, confident. Ready to pull the trigger. He had to extract his revenge after all.

He took a glimpse at his partner, leaning across the door. It was clear in his eyes that he was eager to kill.

I've selected my team wisely! He thought. All of them, just like Hunter, maybe lagging a bit in experience, but as a team they performed with clock-like precision.

He lifted his arm, making a three, with his fingers, as he said in a very hushed voice which echoed clearly in his squads transceivers, "Three! Two! One!" Now!" He shouted.

Elsewhere, one of his team members remotely launched a flash grenade. As it lobbied into the room, breaking the window, it came down crashing in the middle of the room, rolling over there for a bit, when the cap burst open the violent reaction that took place inside it gave out a blinding white streak of light which covered the whole room.

On the other side of the door, Hunter and his team waited patiently for that familiar crashing noise. In the meantime, his partner was securely placing the block charge on the door wall and he did that with extreme dexterity. When that was done, he went back and assumed his position opposite to Hunter and waited with the cylindrical matt-black remote detonator held tightly in his fist with his thumb trained on the red button on the cover. Seconds later, they heard the crash, and the thumping and the radial bang and they knew that they were up. Instantaneously, the man with the remote detonator squeezed the switch with all his might, as his face and body instinctively shied away from the door, just for a second, protecting themselves. Hunter did the same, and so did the rest of the guys.

With another burst of bright white light, the door blew up unto smithereens, with wood shards radiating everywhere. Without wasting a second, Hunter and his team came charging through that hole in the wall, their automatic rifles cocked and their fingers trained on the trigger. They carried themselves with such momentum, and with their dreadful weapons, and clothes and armor any weak person would faint.

They found Mercer, sitting on a rag-tag sofa seat, parching over a sleek looking metallic brown colored laptop. The stun grenade had dulled his senses, in a frantic and desperate attempt to save himself he tried to shake off the effect of the blast. His eyes were ringing, his sight blinded, he truly was at the intruders' mercy. As some of his vision quickly came back to him, he noticed the paramilitary soldiers who were dominating a major portion of his living room, shouting viciously at him but under the effect of his ringing ears he couldn't hear a thing.

"Mercer! Down on the ground! Now!" Hunter shouted repeatedly. "Don't play with me, Mercer!"

Deaf that he was, he quickly tried to gauge where he had left his gun, instead of following the orders that were given to him. He found it at the edge of a table only a few steps from him. Thinking that he could grasp it in time, he quickly bent forward trying to reach it as fast as he could.

Seeing that Mercer was not following what he had ordered, he decided to kill him. As it is, he was under no obligation to save him. In fact, his mission itself was to terminate him. But things didn't seem right, and he wanted to find out the reason why. And as his employer had so eloquently put, "Your job is to kill—not ask questions!" As he remembered. The mess which might erupt afterwards was not his concern.

"You're too late!" Hunter could hear his target mumble. "You can't catch me!"

"No... we just have to kill you." Hunter replied with a smile.

He squeezed the trigger, aiming the rifle directly at Mercer's chest. Instantaneously, all the men behind him opened fire with each rifle trained at the one man. For a minute, the room lit up like the fourth of July, till the magazines in the rifles were exhausted and empty bullet shells scattered on the floor.

Alec had lunged himself towards that desk on which he had placed his weapon but as the voluminous shower of bullets struck him, the sheer velocity and inertia of those tiny pellets changed his course. Despite his best attempts, he could not reach his weapon; instead his body was pushed behind as blood started spurting from his chest, his mouth foaming with blood. As the bullets went through him, they struck the wall behind him, and even tearing that apart. There was a big window behind him, now as those fiery arrows completely destroyed it, and left another big rectangular hole on that wall. Mercer's leg stumbled onto something, as he was being pushed back by the constant and combined forces of the bullets. As he tripped, unable to regain his balance and completely destroyed physically and perhaps mentally, his body fell back under the burden of its own weight and fell through the window behind him. Seconds later, they heard a distinct crash from outside the building, right where Mercer's body would have fallen.

"I'd say that was a confirmed kill, don't you think?" He chuckled with one of his comrades.

"Yea…nobody can survive that fall! Not even him!" His comrade replied back. The thick atmosphere filled with smoke and tension slowly began to dissipate.

"It's done." He reported into his transceiver, with a sense of pride and control.

"Copy that! Sending in secondary sweep teams!" Brian informed Hunter.

"Area secure." Somebody in the background declared as he finished his preliminary sweep of the apartment.

"Good job." The foreign accented voice of Torres greeted him merrily.

A self-admiring smile crept up on Hunter's face as he puffed his lungs full with the damp and misty air around him. He had now completely proved himself capable of pulling out any feat. All that was asked of him, he accomplished to perfection. Since his ascension to that cheesy layer, he had successfully tracked and captured Élénoré Bassét, the French atomic research scientist who used to work at CERN, successfully terminated her accomplice, the man who went by the alias Alec Mercer, who had countless times to be a worthy opponent, who had single-handedly annihilated the whole attack team sent to kill the scientists and clone and destroy the data at the SLHC Underground facilities at CERN, and who bested the most elite group of soldiers who came to exist on this planet, which he also pulled off single-handedly. And now, he is dead. The long-standing trouble which kept prodding himself at Bearing Oil was finally dead. All thanks to Hunter and his men for pulling off something like that.

With another big inhale and exhale, he started reviewing the whole room, trying to assess their current situation. Not much time had passed since Mercer's body fell out of the third floor window. Even if he managed to stay alive, the three-storey fall would definitely end him for sure.

"Search for his body!" He ordered on the transceiver which was meant for somebody in the secondary sweep team. "There might have been some evidence on his person!" He said.

"Yes sir!" One of the men responded.

Luckily for them possibly, all the evidence they needed was right there, out in the open. The files and documents, stolen from Richard Meyer's office safe, were all there along with the stolen DataCourier and some other miscellaneous items. The most prominent item in the room was that metallic-brown colored laptop placed neatly in the middle of the desk with its screen open and something already running on the screen.

Just as Hunter eyes went on that laptop, something peculiar happened. The screen changed into a very old fashioned DOS-like black screen with numbers displayed boldly in red. On further inspection, he read the line which was present above the numbers. "SELF DESTRUCTING IN PROGRESS" it read.

The numbers beneath it was a timer, a countdown. Clearly, there was something so sensitive on that computer, so critical that Mercer had set it to self-destruct the moment he dies.

Without wasting a second, he called it in his transceiver. "Send over somebody from the Tech-Lab! There's a laptop over here which is self-destructing itself!" He shouted on the tiny microphone which was jutting out of his helmet.

"How much time?" Brian inquired of Hunter the same moment he heard the words.

Hunter widened his carbon black eyes gazing at the thin LED screen. "One minute." He answered back, in a cautious tone. "There isn't much time!"

"You will have to hack it!" Brian retorted. There wasn't much time. Extreme conditions call for extreme actions. "I'll take you through it!"

"No wait!" Hunter responded. "I can take out its battery; it can't purge its hard disks if it doesn't have any power supply, right?"

"Oh yes! Right!" Brian agreed with him, permitting himself a slight chuckle.

Why didn't I think of that before?!

Hunter picked up the delicate looking instrument with both his strong palms. There was a brown slider next to the microSD slot with a battery icon painted in contrasting colors just above it. As he gently slid that sliding button, the thin block of battery fell out from underneath the laptop and as it did the screen turned off and the machine stopped humming.

"Phew!" he exclaimed with a deep-seated sigh. Twenty seconds in, he had just pulled off another miraculous feat. "It has stopped!" He informed the analyst on the other side of the transceiver. "Tell the techies to bag it and tag it." He told one of his men, as he motioned to give the laptop to him. Just as it touched the soldier's hands, the internal fan began vibrating again in full motion as the laptop sprang to life.

"Huh!" He exclaimed in a baffled tone of voice. "What the hell?!"

"What's happening? Come in!" Brian questioned with a concerned voice. "Report!"

The screen turned back on; now displaying the message 00:00:39. For a second the message did not change but when it did, it began counting down towards Zero; but the numbers began flashing faster than the speed of light.

"No! No, no, no! NO!" He shouted as he hurriedly pressed all the buttons on the keyboard. "Shit!" He gave out a huge grunt of despair. Cinders of smoke started blowing out from the fan vent on its base. All the lights and symbols shut off. He knew the device had been purged of all its information. The data inside it was lost. "Maybe, tech-lab can recover something off it." He said as he handed the laptop to the person standing in front of him.

Despite this, Hunter's pride remained unhindered. His mission was finished the moment his target was killed, and the evidence against Bearing PetroTech which was stolen from their headquarters was recovered; which they did. With Mercer dead, he had nothing to do, so he walked away; after all he was a busy man and he had to christen his arrival to his home city.

The cynical smile on his face was unsettling. Evil.

60

Curtain Raiser

A chrome-black Mercedes-Benz CLS C217 350, fourth generation in its series, was elegantly strolling down the streets of Chicago. For the first time, the driver deviated heavily from his normal routine and was now making its final pit stop. It was approximately six in the evening. The car stopped in front of a huge decorative gate. The driver frantically ran out towards the back passenger door, and hurriedly opened the door, giving a gentle nod, to the esteemed passenger. "Ma'am."

Élénoré slowly exited from the beautiful executive class sedan. Only one thought was storming in her mind.

How did I end up here? What did I do?

All those years she lived on by upholding her rules, her virtues. Now she was throwing them down the drain, by helping the same men who murdered her father in cold blood.

"Finally, there will be peace!" Éllén held on to that blissful feeling in her heart, even though she knew.... She knew her probable fate. After the announcement and her speech, her work would be done. Officially, and unofficially. Now she was nothing more than a liability. "At least they are alive! That's all that matters!"

Five months had passed since that night, that starry night when she had laid her eyes on Alec for the last time. Almost six months since all her problems began. And seven and a half years since she had first started working on this jinxed project, when she had at last found the research notes which her father had hidden so skillfully. And about two decades since her father had died.

But none of that mattered now. She had a big task at hand. A task so important, she was told would decide the course of events crucial in Élénoré's and everybody's lives. She was waiting desperately to talk to Alec, to feel his chiseled body, his scent; to feel his warm secure safe hands around her, consoling her. But most of all, she had something that she needed to tell him, so big that it would probably blow his mind, and change their relationship with each other.

She was feeling sick which added to the pressure and stress already piling up on her. It was definitely a big day. But she was having many days like these.

Oh Alec! It's been five months! You said you would not let anything happen to me! You would save me, rescue me!

Thoughts were buzzing in her mind. All she hoped that after the evening ends, Richard would let her leave so that she could be with Alec, forever. Never, she had been so madly in love with someone, so deeply agonized by his absence. Whatever she was feeling, even she wouldn't be able to explain. She would only keep gazing into the middle distance, absent-minded, lost, and fantasizing about the time when she and Alec would be with each other. Whenever she would see rain drizzling outside, or a rainbow peeking out through the concrete structures around the complex where she developed the SORCE Fusion Reactor, she would raise her hand in the sky, collecting the tiny water droplets in her tiny palms, her heart uplifting, happy, cheerful, and exultant. Her heart yearning for one man. Her apartment at CERN was secretly packed and shipped to the new research facility with everything as it was where it was. Now, she didn't spend her time alone, crying as she sipped her favorite wine and watched her childhood videos, of her along with her father. Instead, she consumed all her time and effort to the completing of the perpetual fusion reactor, so that she could leave, and finally have that one thing which her heart was longing for. She knew that in the end of it all, she would either be where her heart belonged or she would be dead, but in either scenario her sorrows would end permanently.

"Ma'am." Kevin greeted her with a slight tip of his head. Élénoré greeted him back, but her mind was somewhere else.

"Everything is set! You are scheduled for the six fifty time slot, after our PR agent addresses the press." He informed her. "You are prepared, I presume? Millions of people will be watching the live broadcast! We've tapped into every form of communication. Press, media, social network are just the start!" There was a hint of joy and pride in his words. After all, it was ILSA which was organizing the whole event. And being a liaison to the company, he was coordinating it all.

"Yea…I'm not very good with people." Éllén told him shyly. "Is there any way somebody else could do it instead of me?"

"Oh no! That's impossible! It's always the lead researcher who announces about the launch of any new product! Anything else is out of the question!" Kevin was adamant. "It's the last thing you will need to do! That's it, I can personally guaranty about that!"

"Okay…" She said in a hesitating tone, unsure of her words.

"I'll manage."

"That would be great!" Kevin returned to his normal tone of voice as he bid her adieu.

Élénoré was alone once again. And again she began strolling absent mindedly. The crowd around her didn't affect her and neither did the fact that she might not live to see the radiant sun the next day.

Slowly, she reached an entrance which was guarded by three of the most hefty men. The one in the middle raised his hand, signaling her to stop. Élénoré did not give much attention to it. She instinctively raised her ID badge, telling him that she was authorized to go inside.

"Oh sorry ma'am!" he hurriedly apologized to her as he stepped out of her way. Élénoré began walking in her non-chalant fashion, not taking much notice of whatever happened around her.

She walked and walked and continued walking till one of the spot boys spotted her, ran up to her and began babbling about something. Then he pointed to a direction and told her to follow him. Élénoré gave him a slight nod as if saying yes, and began following him mindlessly. Her body was reacting only to the external stimuli but her mind was somewhere else. Lost.

She followed the spot boy to a room, which not coincidentally was also packed with people and completely buzzing with energy. The room was painted with a dark shade of orange texture paint. There were chairs arranged in a single row in front of mirrors fitted with bright incandescent bulbs on its borders. And men and women all alike sitting in front of them, some of them applying makeup and stuff or rehearsing their dialogues or speeches. But this also managed to escape from Élénoré's mind. As directed she sat on one of the vacant seats, and the makeup artists began dressing her up for her speech, applying foundations, mascara, eyeliners, lipstick, powders and what not. When it was all done, her body itself rose up and started moving, walking out towards the other door in that room.

Again, as she stepped outside, the place was crowded even still. There were people from camera crew, taking their equipment to positions, various spot boys, technicians working on their gear, Internet Protocol Managers for web broadcasts, experts working on live video broadcasts, people from PR deciding about their media strategies and a whole bunch of different other. All the while Élénoré kept on walking.

"Excuse me!" Somebody apologized as he bumped into Élénoré, trying to squeeze in the gap between her and somebody else.

The unexpected contact brought her back to her senses. She looked up, baffled as to where the hell she was. Her head and mind started spinning around. Her purpose suddenly came to her; she still had one piece of work left to do, more important than anything she had ever done. Much was risking on her lean shoulders.

After a whole minute of looking around, she finally spotted her target and then walked towards it decisively. But as she neared the metal sheet plated door of a thin box-like rectangular room made of white colored wooden panels, with grey metallic borders, her legs began trembling under the pressure of the assignment on her. But she had to do it, there was no other way.

Taking a big gulp, she collated her courage together as she pushed the metallic panel attached horizontally in the middle of the door, which was needed to be pushed in order to open it. The door opened with an ear-aching screech and Élénoré popped her head inside. Nobody was in there save for the wide assortment of computers and machinery which dominated the whole room. Seeing the room to be empty, she took her chances and sneaked inside knowing very well that there was a very small window of opportunity. Everything needed to be executed with military-like precision. The stakes were too high for things to go wrong.

She tiptoed across the polished floor, making her way towards the computers. The equipment was divided among the two sides of the room. The front had the computers, the wires which provided the direct feed from the numerous cameras outside and on the stage, the controls for various lights, curtains, fog blower, sound systems and other relatively mundane things while the back portion contained the servers, which were the backbone in managing the whole operation. She quickly moved towards the computers, her eyes scanning each computer and everything around it as she walked from one terminal to another, searching for one thing. Unable to find what she needed from there, she turned back towards the servers behind her. The rectangular black boxes, stacked on top of one another with blinking green and red lights provided them with many gigabytes of processing power necessary for running the whole operation. After much inspection, she finally found what she needed on the blind side of those same boxes.

In hurried excitement, she quickly pulled off the high heels she was wearing, and held it high as she twisted the sole revealing yet another device from its false heel. It was an extremely tiny thumb drive. She had to conceal the drive, because no one other than the trusted employees at ILSA has the access to bring in any kind of electronic device. Her plan was not very elaborate, but it was not like she was breaking into the CIA or the NSA. Sometimes, the simpler, the better.

As she stared at that curious device for a moment, her brain reeled back to the time when she was with Alec, alone, in Rio de Jeneiro, now more than six months ago where they maintained a low profile in that dinky motel room, and where he had shown her the same Sony MicroPD.

"You see this?" Alec had asked her.

"Yeah…it's a thumb drive. So?" Élénoré was curious.

"One day, I will give it to you, and tell you to keep it safe. You might have to keep it with you for months if you have to—But you have to keep it safe at any cost! At any cost!" He repeated. "And after that you will have to do something for me."

"What?!" Élénoré demanded.

"You will have to get caught!" Alec told her in a grave tone, extremely serious.

"Okay." Élénoré replied in a cool, decisive and determined voice. She had lost too much, suffered too much. Now it was her time to extract her revenge, and she would go to the ends of the worlds to get it. Besides, she knew that if he asked for anything it had a deeper purpose. She knew whatever he did was preplanned and a giant web where people would knowingly or unknowingly be his pawns and his endgame would always be unclear until he sucker punches his opponent in the face.

"And?" Élénoré pressed further.

"I'll tell you that later." He told her with his usual smile.

"Whatever you say!" She replied in her also similar non-chalant fashion, but inside she was serious.

Then her mind reeled five months back, when they were running through the streets of Chicago, when both of them gazed inside the eyes of that demonic Sikorsky MH-60 aircraft personnel carrier.

"Run! They are after me, not you!" he instructed her. "No, wait! Take this with you!" he gave her his gun but with that he also placed that microPD in her slender hands. "You know what you have to do?"

Éllén nodded yes.

"Good." Mercer nodded back. "Now go! I'll take care of them."

And after a thoughtful pause, "I will come back for you!"

Those were the last words that he ever spoke to her. The last time she laid her eyes on him, when he had sprinted across three blocks in downtown Chicago, fearing that the security services did not arrest her, because if they did she would be lost to him in the government red tape, and all his plans would fall apart. Luckily, Élénoré was captured by the right people and his plan was on course.

The drive was very small, not even one-fourth of an inch in length, and a shiny black body with a yellow stripe at its end. She hurriedly took out the even smaller cover and wedged the drive into the socket on the side of the mainframe-server.

Behind her the dark screen of a cold monitor came to life. It started displaying messages, on its screen.

'New Removable Drive detected'

'Installing Device Driver and Software'

'Sony-MicroPD is ready to use'

'Scanning device for viruses'

'No threats detected'

Just as the last popup display vanished, a set of black command screens appeared. With data flashing through like crazy, executing thousands of lines of codes per second, the technical gibberish kept on scrolling through the screen. When it was finally over, there was a moment of silence and nothing changed when all of a second, the whole screen turned navy blue, with a grayish white horizontal bar near the bottom. Slowly, the bar started filling up as one-line sentences began displaying in the middle of the screen.

'Extracting...'

'Recompiling....'

'Loading...'

"You are not authorized to be in here!" A stern voice demanded at Élénoré who was still staring at the mainframe, baffled as she thought nothing was happening.

Confused as to what she would do now that somebody was onto her, she turned around with the same baffled look on her face. The first thing she saw was that active monitor screen to which the man had turned his back. The bar in the bottom was filling up, but slowly. Slowly, the intruder began shifting his body weight which inadvertently signaled Élénoré that he was just about to turn towards the monitors. The moment he would, he would realize everything and all would be lost. She had to do or say something, fast. "Uhh...I was looking for you!" She retorted.

The man raised his eyebrows staring inquisitively at the woman.

"Why would that be?" He asked in a demanding voice with a subtle hint of pride in his voice. The obvious question came at her. But she was unprepared, unlike Alec or any conman or a psychic trying to manipulate. She did not have their improvisation skills.

"There is something I have to ask from you!" She answered in a hesitant tone, but actually she was only trying to delay him.

"What might that be?" He asked. His brows went higher still.

The bar had filled up mid-way. But there was much left still.

After a second, she replied saying, "I'm scheduled to speak today's at event—but I'm not very good with people...." She explained. "If I go blank in front of billions of people, I don't want to look like a fool on international TV."

"I get what you mean." He nodded with her. "Although nothing will happen, I'm sure of it, yet if it does happen, I'll take care of it!"

On the screen behind him, the bar had just crossed the seventy five percent mark.

'Running Exploit...' displayed on the screen.

"But you can't be here right now! You have to go!" He demanded as he again began turning towards the monitors behind him.

"No! Wait!" Éllén shouted out loud but regretted it just as soon the words came out of her mouth. "Well...there's one more thing!"

"What is it?" The operator-in-charge focused his attention back at her, curious.

"You must be good with computers." She exclaimed with her eyes gazing all around the room, hinting towards the various electronic devices and gadgets present in the room.

"Well...yeah!" He laughed as the answer was so very obvious.

"My laptop seems to be broken!" She explains. "Can you do anything about it?" She asked hesitantly as her face shied away from him.

"In a jiffy!" The computer science graduate boasted with pride.

"Great! Let me give you my number!" She raised her bracelet, revealing an inch-by-inch square shaped pendant. The thin bracelet was made up of gold, with the white pendant which had some black design printed on it.

The operator finally knew what was going on, or he thought that he did. By then it was obvious that she was hitting on him. A blind person would see that. He quickly pulled out his cell phone, turned on the bar code scanner and placed it in front of the bracelet so that it would be inside the camera's view. Seconds later, her number was decrypted on his phone with all her details inside it.

"I'll call as soon I'll get the chance!" He replied with a smile, but again began turning back. Élénoré knew she had played her last card. Geeks always fantasize about being with a beautiful woman, and somewhere inside she knew that she was beautiful and pretty.

Think, Élle think!

He had almost turned half-way when, her hands instinctively reached forward and grabbed his hands, pulling him closer. With one eye trained on the screen, stretching her odds to the limit, her eyes pierced the screen. "I'll be waiting!" She told him in a flirty voice.

The computer operator's heartbeat began racing at the mere touch of her soft, smooth hands.

"Me too!" He replied back and shied away, turning back completely. The computers were as he had left; nothing out of the ordinary. He turned back towards Élénoré but she was nowhere to be seen. She had vanished into thin air.

❧

"Are you ready?!!" The anchor addressed the crowd with a rejuvenating zeal.

"Ready!" came back the response.

"I didn't hear you", the anchor replied. "I said, are you ready?!!"

"Ready!!" This time the response came louder reverberating through the whole acoustic auditorium.

"All right then, let's get this party on!!" He shouted through his microphone.

That dialogue was a cue to the jockey to put on some music to uplift the people's moods. He put a track from Linkin Park's Meteora. After three minutes, as the song was finishing, the anchor came back on the stage and said, "Today, at the Bearing PetroTech Expo 2026, we come here bearing gifts. But before we get on to that and I tell you what the gifts actually are, let me tell you something about our company, Bearing PetoTech and what it does for you, right?... Okay!"

The screen above him, turned on, and just as it did, everybody present there, including the public, the shareholders, the media, the journalists, and the management, everybody, received a text message on their cell-phones.

'THEY LIE' were two words written in capitals in the message. The curious message began widespread murmurs and rumors all across the crowd.

Soon words started appearing in white on the black background.

"Bearing PetroTech, then known as Bearing Oil was established in 1953 in Britain.

At the time, its sole function was refining of crude oil and manufacture of bearing oils, brake oils, engine oils and other motor lubricants.

Now, the company toils hard conducting geographical surveys searching for Crude Oil pockets which are still untapped by us, refines it, and produces all varieties of fuels, lubricants, etc. known to man."

Another text came to their cell-phones which said, 'WATCH THE SCREEN, YOU WILL KNOW'.

"Our company has extracted 756,000 billion gallons of petroleum till date, refined 1,200,000 billion gallons of petroleum and manufactured different petroleum related products from it.

Seven months ago, we found another petroleum reserve deep in the Atlantic Ocean, which provided for countries all across the world, it helped in keeping the markets worldwide aloof from a fourth recession. That's how; Bearing PetroTech touches the lives of millions of people across the world, either directly or indirectly."

There was a brief moment, when the video stopped playing.

Back in the IT department at Bearing Tower, a systems analyst spotted some suspicious activity happening in their mainframe servers.

"Sir!" the Internet Protocol Manager shouted out to his boss. "Our systems detect a network intrusion into our server.

"Nothing we didn't expect. Every low life with a computer must be thinking that they can rain on our parade." Kevin replied calmly.

"The odd thing though is that breach appears to be coming from inside our company firewall!"

"What?! That's impossible!" Kevin exclaimed. His mood changed drastically. "Try to assess the point of origin. Isolate it, and contain it! I don't want anything to disrupt our event! Understand?" He realized that he might be dealing with a very serious threat.

"Yes sir." The analyst replied as he quickly went back to his work, trying to contain the crisis.

After a minute, the analyst called for Kevin once again, who was not very far from him. This time the terror could be felt from his voice. "I've been locked out from my terminal!"

"Come again!" His boss heard the words clearly, but still couldn't believe what he had just heard.

"I'm locked out of my terminal!" The analyst repeated.

"Oh my God!" he screamed. "This is really happening!"

"Everybody!" He spoke out loudly so that everybody on the floor could hear him. "We have an active threat to our mainframe. Our systems are being hacked! I want everybody to work on this, only. Nothing else! From now on, preventing this attack is our only priority!"

Kevin's phone began ringing. He pulled it out of his pocket, and read out the name of the incoming caller. 'Sir Richard Meyers' was written on his iPhone 10GS.

"Sir?" he wished the caller as he stepped away into a corridor.

"What is the meaning of this?!" Richard berated him in a furious tone of voice.

"What?" Kevin was baffled.

"The video presentation in the event! It is revealing all our secrets! Do something! Stop the show, right now! Or we will be ruined completely!"

"Yes sir!" he answered sheepishly. The phone line disconnected.

"Sir! You need to see this!" Robert shouted.

Kevin came back to the control room. His eyes panned towards the array of huge CGD screens mounted on the wall. Big words were displaying on the screen in bright orange text, with one huge word on each screen.

YOU CAN'T MESS WITH THE KOBI
The words were horrifying to say the least. They began causing widespread commotion throughout the room. The analysts began murmuring amongst each other. For the first time someone was able to hack into the military grade firewall and security systems which Bearing PetroTech had installed.

As Kevin's eyes went towards Richard who was still calling for him, he saw the terminals in front of which he was standing. The same message was being displayed on all the screens in the room.

"You Can't Mess With the Kobi! What the -?" He was baffled. "This is a nightmare!" Kevin told himself.

"Sir!? If I access the mainframe, I might be able to isolate the virus, from causing more damage." Robert told him.

"Then what are you doing here! Hurry up! Fast!" Kevin bellowed.

Back at the Expo, things were not going out as planned. The audience gazed at the screen with a feeling of anguish and disgust.

"That's how; Bearing PetroTech touches the lives of millions of people across the world, either directly or indirectly—Only if that were true!

All you have heard are lies; secrets inside of secrets inside of secrets! Truth is they have been pulling out their petroleum from the markets, creating a virtual drought, inducing the prices to rise; telling you they did you a favor."

After that the text stopped. Instead a video live stream began playing out. In the center, Mercer's face was in the middle.

"My name is…uh classified. I was an ex-covert operative; I worked for the United States Central Intelligence Agency. I'm going to tell you about the highest level of corruption, that has led the general population to poverty." Mercer said to the crowd. His words reverberating all across the world, through the Internet and the media.

Élénoré was ecstatic. Her heart pumping fiercely from the second she saw him from where she stood near the crowd.

Inside Langley, CIA Headquarters, the recent turn of events had caused an unexpected uproar all across the building.

"Director Jameson speaking." Theroux spoke into the receiver of his phone. "Yes, I'm on my way!" He declared as he made his way towards his office.

As he pushed the door, and stepped inside, he addressed the room saying, "Talk to me, what have we got!"

"Sir, we've got a situation!" Pamela told him as soon as he entered the room, as she walked him along the floor. "It's Mercer!"

"He has resurfaced in Chicago; you've got to check this out!" She told him as they walked up to her terminal. "This is the live feed of a video transmitting from inside Bearing Tower! And at this rate it will break the record of most watched video on the internet. Facial Recognition has tagged him in the video to our servers!"

"The research team's main objective was to develop a source of renewable energy which could provide free, cheap and clean energy which could provide for the whole world." Mercer explained

"Can we stop it? We cannot let a delusional spy ruin the credibility of our Agency!"

"No sir, we can't stop it!" She replied in a sad voice. "I've already tried. They are server-jumping!"

"Server-what?!" He exclaimed, ignorant of all the technical jargon.

"Server-jumping. Basically, they have setup different servers through proxy. The video broadcast keeps on jumping from one server to another. By the time, we are able to shut down one server, they have already moved to another. It is happening so fast I didn't think it was even possible! There's is no way we can overtake the process because there's no way we can predict the next server."

"So we can't stop it?!" Jameson cried out loud.

"We can…but we will have to shut down the Internet!"

"Years later, when the project was re-initiated in twenty-nineteen, headed by Dr. Élénoré Bassét. After seven years they had finally developed a more efficient process—ninety seven percent efficient. It could provide twenty-four hour energy for every household in the world, be it Africa, or India."

"Shutting down Internet is out of the question!" Jameson told Pamela in a decisive voice. "It would crumble our markets and destroy any chances of economic recovery!"

"Then…we can't do anything but watch!" Pamela replied in a dejected tone.

Inside the IT department in Bearing Tower, Kevin was frustrated beyond his normal capacity. Meyers had just called him thrice on his cell phone. He had told him to call his lawyers. Richard and the upper management had already fled the premises; he had already booked a flight to South Africa.

"Where's the original broadcast we had prepared for the show?!" Kevin demanded from all the workers present in the room.

"We don't know sir. It is transmitting from the tower, but somehow, it is not reaching the satellite." Somebody replied. "Now, we can't even try to do anything! All the systems in the building are offline! They have shut down the whole building!"

"—Corruption to the highest level…lobbyist in every government agency…moles inside the CIA, NSA, ECHELON, even the White House. They have knowingly killed more than seven hundred people, and caused thousands of deaths in Third World countries in Africa." Mercer was still speaking.

"Dammit! Can't you just shut it off! Pull the plug or something!" He shouted.

"We can't! The virus has uploaded itself onto our company satellite! Now, there's no way to stop it!" Robert explained. "We're running blind!"

On one single screen the live feed was being displayed like a soccer match. All the eyes in the room pointing towards it.

"—in China was to destroy a government building giving shelter to a HVT, High Value Target. We were told to bomb the building; and we did just as ordered. Later, we realized, bombing that building destroyed the underground oil pipelines underneath the building! Our actions set back China's oil supply by fifteen years. The oil spill caused in China in 2007 was also a CIA sponsored mission. Today, each and every member of that team is either missing in action or killed in action."

Only one thought was going through Kevin's mind. *I had him killed! How is he even breathing!*

Inside the FBI building in Chicago, Summers was walking quickly towards her boss's room. With two brisk taps on the door, she rushed inside, not even waiting for a response.

"Check this out!" Aisha announced as she reached for Valerie's computer. She opened the Safari web browser and typed the link of the same BP broadcast.

"I was not supposed to live; somebody going by the codename Aurora had sent professional hit men to kill me! Only they killed my wife and my beautiful kids instead! Their bodies were burnt beyond recognition." The Mercer's voice resounded in the room.

"What is this?" Valerie was confused, unable to gauge the context of the dialogues.

Aisha had something in her hands. A big pile of files and documents. She threw them on Valerie's desk.

Valerie put on his reading glasses as he slowly began turning the pages of the documents and after a brief moment he said, "Is this for real?!"

"I bet these are admissible in court, right?" Aisha put up a rhetorical question to her boss in a joyous tone.

"How did you get this?" Valerie questioned.

"A favor from a friend." Aisha replied back.

"I'm calling Judge Emerson, to issue a warrant against Richard Meyers, Bearing PetroTech, ILSA, all their bank accounts and everybody whose name is on this list!"

"You go ahead and arrest that bastard!" He gave her the permission to do what she had wanted to do for months.

But there was an issue. "Meyers has fled the scene from the Expo. The crowd over there has turned into a mob. Local Precincts have been called in to control the situation. I think he will try to flee the country—

I've informed the TSA and also put him on the no-fly list, but he is a man of means, I fear that sooner or later he will escape to some non-extradition country!"

"Don't worry! I had put thousands of man-hours on tailing this guy. Finally, all that efforts seems to have provided some result." He told her with a smile. "Here! My man checked in with me minutes ago. He is in his penthouse! He really is planning to flee the country!"

"I won't let that happen!" Aisha told him in a determined voice.

Back at the Expo, Élénoré along with all the public and the police were keenly gazing at the giant screen above the stage, only she was happy, while the rest of them felt that they had been wronged and used. So many scams had already taken place, the mortgage scam, insurance scams. It seemed that they couldn't trust one word that these companies say.

"I have sent all the research data to all the nuclear research and testing facilities around the world, CERN, Brookehaven National Laboratory, are just some of them. Hopefully, soon everybody will now have 24 hour supply of electricity, hot water, energy for vehicles and they will be able to live their lives once again just like they used to!" With these words, Mercer finished his expose on Bearing PetroTech, sparking a violent chain of events which had already begun speeding all across the world.

After the speech, he picked up a bottle and began drinking from it as he glanced at his ChomeX watch for the time, and then pressed a button on the computer on which he was working, but the video feed did not close. Mercer's chiseled face still dominated the screen.

Through the body language, it was amply clear that he was waiting for someone. Seconds later something happened. It was the sound of a metallic cylinder rolling on the metal floor, then the blast of a flash bang. The next second, there was a cracking sound of the wooden door which could be seen at the corner of the screen. Huge blokes, in black armored vests and heavy automatic weapons streamed through the room. Élénoré noticed their leader in the very instant; it was the same person who had captured her months ago, Hunter.

Mercer was noticeably shaken up and as he came out of the effect of the flash grenade, he reached for his gun, his Berreta 92FS. Seeing Mercer reach for his gun, the operatives opened fire at him. The muzzle flash was so bright that on half of the screen only the color white could be seen. Just as Éllén saw that, her eyes closed in shock, and her jaws dropped, her palms reached up to cover her mouth; tears were rolling down her gentle cheeks. On the other hand, Mercer was being pounded by the bullets, so badly that he tripped on the chair behind him, and fell through the hole in the window behind him which was already shattered into pieces.

Now, even Élénoré's heart was broken. It had skipped a beat as she came down crashing on the floor. The video continued as Hunter joked among his collogues after killing the only love of her life, as he inspected the video, as he tried to stop the self-destruction of the laptop. When the laptop finally died, the video also ended.

❑❑❑

Epilogue

"Sir Meyers!" A strong female voice hollered from behind. Her very voice reflected a sense of pride and boast. Richard Meyers' elegant visage panned back as he hurriedly made his not-so-daring escape from the clutches of the government at the international terminal of the O'Hare International Airport. With utter shock he witnessed fear after a long time when he saw FBI Special Agent Aisha Summers as she reached him with a battalion of officers behind her.

"Richard Meyers! You are under arrest for murder in the 2nd degree, conspiracy against the Government of the United States, insider trading, stock parking, and a dozen more charges!"

"You can't arrest me! Do you have the slightest idea of who I am and what I am capable of?" Richard debated with the miniscule of pride in him even if he seemed like a sore loser.

"This time...I do." Summers stated. "Richard Meyers. You have the right to remain silent. Anything you say or do can and will be held against you in a court of law. You have the right to speak to an attorney. If you cannot afford an attorney, one will be appointed for you." She informed him as she cuffed Richard as tightly as she could. Pleased with her success, she waved at a state police officer and signaled him to escort the criminal into the police unit.

"Watch your head, Meyers." The officer warned him as they enter the police patrol car.

"This is your last chance special agent!" Meyers played.

"See you in court." Aisha scoffed.

The array of police cars drove away from the international terminal of the O' Hare International Airport, till Aisha found herself alone on the portico. She sat down on the moist concrete pavement and pulled out a cigarette from her purse. As she lit, the nicotine wrapped bundle of paper, and took a deep whiff of the intoxicating smoke, she began pondering on how far she had reached. The arrest of Sir Richard Meyers was magnificent boon for her sparkling career. Things could not have been any better.

From the distant turnpike, a couple of state police patrol cars rushed towards the international terminal of the airport and came to a screeching stop inches in front of Agent Summers.

"Special Agent Summers!" The passenger of the dominating car shouted as he exited the shining chrome painted car. "I'm Staff Sergeant Gilroy. I was told you needed backup in apprehending a criminal."

"Come again!" Aisha replied baffled with the smoke hitting her face. "I don't follow you!"

"We're your backup! To arrest a Richard Meyers." Gilroy articulated clearly. "We started more than an hour ago but we were stuck because a faulty signal caused a mile long jam! We came as fast as we could."

"I don't understand! I handed him to the state police ten minutes ago!" Aisha stated in confusion.

"What?!"

"Call dispatch! We have a high value criminal on the run! Alert Border Patrol, the TSA, the fucking Coast Guard! The suspect is a man with means and influence! We need to stop him! And check your men! This is the list of officers who came with me!" Aisha handed over a typed transcript to Gilroy. "They had perfect credentials! The FBI vetted them before they came with me! I want each and every one of those bastards!"

Her cellphone began strumming. Valerie was displayed in bold text.

"Yes sir." She greeted. But before she could tell him anything, Valerie's tensed voice flurried.

"What's happening?" He questioned. "Our systems are flagging Richard Meyers all over the globe! Where is he?" Valerie pounded.

For a minute, she stood on the pavement, frozen, lost. Her mind disconnected from her surroundings, trying to gauge what had happened. She began to realize slowly. Richard Meyers was escaping. The masterminds behind it were creating a diversion, a smokescreen, to mask Meyers's movements when he would actually try to flee the country.

Slowly as she came back to reality, her mouth opened to respond to her bosses continuous enquiries. "Sir..." Aisha paused to breathe. "He's gone!"

❑❑❑

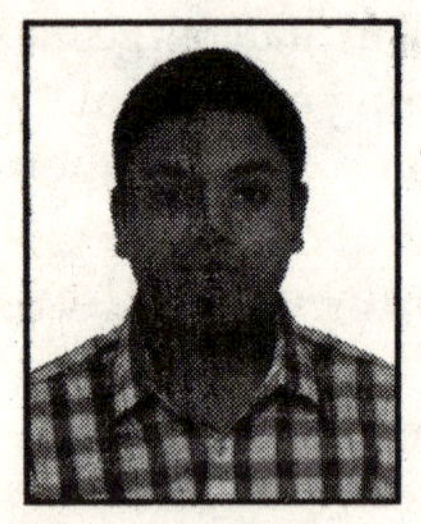

Jaideep Bhoosreddy is one of the youngest novelists in the Indian sub-continent, who likes writing novels and short stories of various genres. His first novel **'Dead Underground'** is a spy fiction thriller. He is an avid reader and enthusiastic explorer. He travelled across many parts of the world and draws his experiences from abroad for the Alec Mercer series.

His profound interest in the military intelligence, world politics and his scientific knowledge and bureaucratic exposure from his family background provides well-rounded, deeply researched novels for his readers. His non-linear writing style captures the readers with surprises and intrigues whilst maintaining a gripping suspense in them.

He currently lives in New Delhi with his parents and a younger brother and enjoys long distance runs and swimming. He enjoys communicating with his readers and shares his interests with them and can be reached by the links below.

Join the conversation

f /JaideepBhoosreddy

/jaideepKiller

g /jaideep_bhoosreddy

t jaideepbhoosreddy.tumblr.com